Elizabeth Heiter likes  heroines, chilling villa... little romance. Her rese... of serial killers, throug... the FBI Academy's shoo... ...um graduated from the University of Michigan with a degree in English literature. She's a member of International Thriller Writers and Romance Writers of America. Visit Elizabeth at www.elizabethheiter.com

Ever since **Lisa Childs** read her first romance novel (a Mills & Boon story, of course) at age eleven, all she wanted was to be a romance writer. With over seventy novels published with Mills & Boon, Lisa is living her dream. She is an award-winning, bestselling romance author. She loves to hear from readers, who can contact her on Facebook or through her website, www.lisachilds.com

Also by Elizabeth Heiter

K-9 Defence
Alaska Mountain Rescue
K-9 Cold Case
Bodyguard with a Badge
Police Protector
Secret Agent Surrender
Disarming Detective
Seduced by the Sniper
SWAT Secret Admirer

Also by Lisa Childs

His Christmas Assignment
Bodyguard Daddy
Bodyguard's Baby Surprise
Beauty and the Bodyguard
Nanny Bodyguard
Single Mum's Bodyguard
In the Bodyguard's Arms
Colton 911: Unlikely Alibi
Colton Christmas Conspiracy

Discover more at millsandboon.co.uk

K-9 HIDEOUT

ELIZABETH HEITER

CLOSE QUARTERS WITH THE BODYGUARD

LISA CHILDS

MILLS & BOON

All rights reserved including the right of reproduction in whole or in part in any form. This edition is published by arrangement with Harlequin Books S.A.

This is a work of fiction. Names, characters, places, locations and incidents are purely fictional and bear no relationship to any real life individuals, living or dead, or to any actual places, business establishments, locations, events or incidents. Any resemblance is entirely coincidental.

This book is sold subject to the condition that it shall not, by way of trade or otherwise, be lent, resold, hired out or otherwise circulated without the prior consent of the publisher in any form of binding or cover other than that in which it is published and without a similar condition including this condition being imposed on the subsequent purchaser.

® and ™ are trademarks owned and used by the trademark owner and/or its licensee. Trademarks marked with ® are registered with the United Kingdom Patent Office and/or the Office for Harmonisation in the Internal Market and in other countries.

First Published in Great Britain 2021
by Mills & Boon, an imprint of HarperCollins*Publishers* Ltd
1 London Bridge Street, London, SE1 9GF

www.harpercollins.co.uk

HarperCollins*Publishers*
1st Floor, Watermarque Building,
Ringsend Road, Dublin 4, Ireland

K-9 Hideout © 2021 Elizabeth Heiter
Close Quarters with the Bodyguard © 2021 Lisa Childs

ISBN: 978-0-263-28342-6

0621

MIX
Paper from
responsible sources
FSC™ C007454

This book is produced from independently certified FSC™ paper to ensure responsible forest management.

For more information visit: www.harpercollins.co.uk/green

Printed and bound in Spain
by CPI, Barcelona

K-9 HIDEOUT

ELIZABETH HEITER

I love writing strong heroines. This book is dedicated to a few of the strong women in my life: my mom, my aunt Andy, my sisters Kathryn and Caroline, and my sister-in-law, Lamia.

Chapter One

Desparre, Alaska, was so far off the grid, it wasn't even listed on most maps. But after two years of running and hiding, Desparre made Sabrina Jones feel safe again.

She didn't know quite when it had happened, but slowly, the ever-present anxiety in her chest had eased. The need to relentlessly scan her surroundings every morning when she woke, every time she left the house, had faded, too. She didn't remember exactly when the nightmares had stopped, but it had been over a month since she'd jerked upright in the middle of the night, sweating and certain someone was about to kill her like they'd killed Dylan.

Sabrina walked to the back of the tiny cabin she'd rented six months ago, one more hiding place in a series of endless, out-of-the-way spots. Except this one felt different.

Opening the sliding-glass door, she stepped outside onto the raised deck and immediately shivered. Even in July, Desparre rarely reached above seventy degrees. In the mornings, it was closer to fifty. But it didn't matter. Not when she could stand here and listen to the birds chirping in the distance and breathe in the crisp, fresh air so different from the exhaust-filled city air she'd inhaled most of her life.

The thick woods behind her cabin seemed to stretch forever, and the isolation had given her the kind of peace none of the other small towns she'd found over the years could match. No one lived within a mile of her in any direction. The unpaved driveway leading up to the cabin was long, the cabin itself well hidden in the woods unless you knew it was there. It was several miles from downtown, and she heard cars passing by periodically, but she rarely saw them.

Here, finally, it felt like she was really alone, no possibility of anyone watching her from a distance, plotting and planning.

After a year and a half of living in run-down motels and fearing each morning as much as she feared putting her head on her pillow at night, she'd desperately needed a change. She hadn't expected to end up here. She'd driven north for days, finally stopping because heavy snowfall had made traveling farther impossible. And for the past six months, she'd stayed. There was something magical about Desparre.

It was far from the kind of place anyone who'd known her as a sun-loving city girl would have expected her to end up. Far from anywhere she would have expected to ever call home.

But damn, did she love it. If she had to spend the rest of her life in solitude, this was where she wanted to do it.

Tipping her head back, she closed her eyes and let the crisp, cool Alaskan air refresh her. With a smile, she pulled out her phone to check the time. Although she had nowhere to be, she wanted to run into town early, then get back to do some work.

As soon as she saw the date on her phone display, her smile dropped under the force of her shock. Today marked exactly two years since she'd left New York City. Two years since she'd left behind everything and everyone she knew. Two years of missed birthdays and holidays. Two years of not being able to talk to her mother or her brother, not being able to see her friends.

A familiar ache welled up, one that only Alaska had been able to keep somewhat at bay.

When she'd said goodbye to New York, she'd expected—hoped—to be home long before now. The police couldn't guarantee they could protect her, but they were hunting for her stalker. She'd believed it was only a matter of time. But with her in hiding, new leads had probably dried up fast.

An image of her mom and her brother back in New York City looking at the calendar together popped into her mind. Her mom would be frowning, a tightness to her jaw that Sabrina had seen in her childhood. Her brother would try to comfort her, try to hide his own anxiety. But they would both be wondering where Sabrina was, wondering if she was okay. Wondering if she was still alive.

She tried to suppress the instant mix of anger and sadness. She'd explained to her family what the PI she'd hired had told her: disappearing was the only way to ensure her safety—and theirs. She wouldn't be able to contact them, and she couldn't tell them where she was going.

They'd fought her on it, but it hadn't mattered. She wasn't going to let anyone else die because of her.

Tucking her phone back into the pocket of her pajama pants, Sabrina stared into the woods, hoping to regain the peace she'd felt only moments ago. But tears pricked her eyes, and today even the woods couldn't ease the tension between her shoulders.

Six months was longer than she'd stayed in one location since she'd gone into hiding. Three months ago, she'd actually started venturing out for more than just essentials. This tiny little town had given her back something she hadn't felt in a long time. Something she hadn't felt since that very first contact from her stalker.

Despite all the solitude, she felt less alone than she had in almost two years.

She'd actually made friends here. Sure, they didn't know

her real last name, and in her normal life, she would have called this level of familiarity simple acquaintances. But with two years of loneliness, two years of running whenever she saw a shadow out of place, it felt like real progress. It almost felt like a real life again.

Guilt surged at the very idea that she could just move on with her life, in any small way. Now, the three months of memories she'd built with Dylan felt so distant, so short. She'd been naive to invite him into her life with a stalker following her, leaving her his twisted version of love notes. It wasn't that she hadn't been taking the threat seriously; it was just that she'd thought the threat was only against her.

But on a brilliantly bright Saturday afternoon when she'd gone to meet Dylan's family for the first time at their lake house, Dylan had been late. She'd been annoyed until police had shown up to tell his family why.

He had died simply because he'd dated her. It was something she'd carried with her ever since.

Before Dylan was killed, police had been taking the letters seriously, but compared to the other crimes they were investigating, it was low priority. When Dylan had been shot inside his own home and then the letter arrived, telling her not to be sad because Dylan had been standing in the way of her true happiness, the police response had been much more intense.

A month later, though, they'd been at her door, their discouraged, too-serious expressions telling her everything she needed to know. With fingerprints and some DNA left behind at the scene of the crime, they were sure they'd get Dylan's killer eventually. But he wasn't in the system, so they couldn't match the forensic evidence to a name. In the meantime, he'd continued to contact her, somehow slipping past the cameras police had installed, and once, slipping a note into her purse on her way home from work.

Dylan's murder showed that her stalker was escalating,

police had told her. She was in real danger, quite possibly his next target. They were committed to keeping her safe, committed to stopping the person who'd killed the man she had only just begun to call her boyfriend.

But they couldn't provide twenty-four-hour protection. And she hadn't been willing to risk anyone else she loved.

Sighing, Sabrina stepped back inside, all the healing powers of the Alaskan wilderness no longer working. The PI who'd helped her create a fake name and then disappear had set up a system, a place for her to check safely for updates. The investigator would post a specific message on her website if the stalker was ever caught.

In two years, there had been no updates. But no one else had been hurt because of her, either. If she had to spend the rest of her life running, at least she'd finally found somewhere she could imagine having even a fraction of the life she'd left behind.

If the years in between had taught her anything, it was that living like this could break your will, break your heart if you let it. Her stalker had taken the life she'd built, but he wasn't going to steal all of her happiness.

"Buck up, Sabrina," she told herself, then squared her shoulders to face the day. By the time she'd gotten dressed and was headed for the door, ready to run into town for some groceries, she felt almost normal. She was even smiling at the thought of trading small talk with the owner, Talise, who'd lived in Alaska all of her seventy years and always had good stories.

Then she opened the door, and the whole world spun in front of her. All the oxygen seemed to disappear as she gripped the doorframe to keep herself upright.

There was a single white card on her doorstep. On it, the same angled, spidery font she'd come to dread back in New York. The same bright red ink that reminded her of blood even more since Dylan's death.

The message was simple, exactly what she would have expected if she hadn't started to believe she'd finally out-run her stalker.

I've missed you.

Chapter Two

Her first instinct was to run. As far as she could, as fast as she could. Just like she'd done countless times over the past two years.

Instead, she put on latex gloves and picked up the card carefully by the corner, even though she knew it was wiped clean. Her stalker had left prints and a small amount of DNA at the scene of Dylan's murder but never on her notes. She sealed it in a plastic bag and then ran to her truck, almost tripping as she glanced around for any sign of him—a man she'd never seen but who'd somehow tracked her almost four thousand miles.

Then she was driving, white-knuckled, eyes dangerously focused on her rearview mirror, toward downtown Desparre. The roads were unpaved, and the rough winters didn't do them any favors. The rusted old truck she'd gotten at a steal when she'd crossed into Alaska six months ago jolted her with every uneven patch of road. Her head started to throb from her clenched jaw, shooting pain up the side of her head with each bump. But she couldn't seem to unclench it.

No one was behind her.

Of course, she'd been assuming that for six months. And yet, somehow, her stalker had found her.

Tears of frustration welled up, and she blinked away the

moisture, refusing to give him more power over her than he already had. If he could find her here—a place that felt like the end of the earth—was anywhere truly safe? Was running the wrong move?

It was time to find out.

As she steered her truck down the incline onto Main Street, right into the center of what passed as a downtown in Desparre, she ignored the cheerful laughter coming from the little park. A few months ago, a bomb had gone off in that park, shattering her illusion that Desparre was one of the most peaceful places she'd ever lived.

But people here were resilient, and they'd rebuilt the gazebo that had been destroyed. The scorched earth was now covered with green grass and blue irises, and the metal butterfly benches she'd admired when she'd first driven into town but had been blown to bits in the blast had been replaced with new ones. Residents who thrived through dangerously cold winters, who knew how to avoid the avalanches that could slide off the side of the mountain, had flocked back to the park as if the bombing had never happened.

She needed some of that Desparre resilience right now.

Parking the truck, Sabrina took a deep breath and glanced around the small downtown, looking for anyone who seemed unusually fixated on her.

The downtown was tiny, with a post office, clothing store, bar, drugstore, grocery store and church lining the unpaved street. To someone who'd grown up in the big city, it looked like one of those fake towns where tourists came to see reenactments of miners showing off their pans of gold.

None of the people walking around, soaking in the sun as if it were ninety degrees instead of fifty-five, showed any interest in her. From three months of coming into town, she recognized many of them as longtime residents.

That was the thing about Desparre. It wasn't New York City. It was much bigger in terms of land size, but population density was minuscule in comparison. Yes, people came here to hide, many of them running from their own tragedies or threats. Some even running from the law. But most of them had lived here a long time. Most of them knew each other. They might wholeheartedly embrace a *Live and let live* attitude where they allowed everyone to keep their secrets—something she'd greatly appreciated when she arrived—but they still recognized the outsiders.

Maybe, just maybe, they could do what the New York City cops had been unable to accomplish. Identify her stalker and end her nightmare for good.

Glancing around one last time, Sabrina strode up to the other building located downtown, the police station.

Nerves churned in her stomach as she pulled open the door, wondering if she was being watched even now. Wondering if involving the police again would make her stalker more violent.

The front of the station was a small area mostly taken up by a desk where a young officer sat. His reddish-blond hair looked vaguely familiar, and she remembered he was the officer who'd been hurt in the bomb blast. Maybe he was still healing and had pulled desk duty in the meantime.

He looked up when she walked in, his expression a mix of boredom and friendliness. "Can I help you?"

"Y-yes," she stuttered, trying not to lose her nerve. "I-I'm being stalked." She held up the bagged note as he stood, his brow furrowed.

Then the door opened behind her, and a white-and-black dog bounded toward her.

"Sitka, sit."

The commanding voice, underlain with humor, made Sabrina's gaze jump from the dog up to the man coming in behind her. Nerves immediately followed.

Officer Tate Emory. She'd seen him around town over the past six months and been immediately drawn to him. She'd even talked to him a few times. Back in her old life, the six-foot-tall man in the police uniform with the angular cheekbones and the dark, serious eyes would have had her flirting hard. Here, she'd stammered her way through their brief conversations, her gaze mostly on the floor, hoping she'd be unmemorable.

That was what her stalker had reduced her to. Hoping no one noticed her. Hoping she could slip through life silently, until what? He finally caught up to her and killed her and no one even knew to look for her body?

Shaking off the morose thought, Sabrina glanced at the dog she'd never seen before, who had followed instructions to sit—right at her feet.

Tate shook his head at the dog. "She's still a puppy. She finished her K-9 training, but sometimes she needs to be reminded about her manners."

At the words, Sitka glanced back at her owner and wagged her tail.

Tate's smile at his dog faded as his gaze locked on the paper Sabrina was still holding up. Then, his attention was entirely focused on her. "Is someone harassing you?"

She nodded, then blurted, "Stalking. For two years." She almost succeeded in keeping her voice steady as she added, "He's found me again."

Tate walked past her, using a key card to open the door marked *Police Only*.

"I've got this, Nate," he told the other officer.

Then he looked at her again, his gaze projecting confidence. "Come on back with me, Sabrina. Let's talk through what's going on, okay? We take care of each other here. We'll take care of you, too."

As she followed him, Sitka sticking close to her side, something fluttered in her chest, something that felt suspiciously like hope.

THIS WAS *NOT* how he'd hoped to strike up a conversation with Sabrina Jones.

Tate Emory had seen her around town for the past half year, usually on the outskirts of Desparre. But to his frustration, it was always when he was in uniform, on the job. He'd struck up a few short-lived conversations with her, but he kept hoping to run into her when he was off duty. He'd wanted to get to know her a little more, maybe even ask her out.

Right now, though, seeing the fear in her green eyes, he just wanted to help. Holding open the door to the back of the station, he ushered her through.

His newly certified K-9 police dog, Sitka, followed. She was seventy-five pounds of Alaskan Malamute, a funny mix of puppy energy and police-dog intensity. He'd been petitioning the department—and his previous chief—for a K-9 practically since the day he'd joined the force five and a half years ago. The last thing Chief Hernandez had done before leaving Desparre was grant approval.

Now, after two months of training, his shelter-dog adoptee was a full-fledged police dog. He smiled down at her as she stayed in Sabrina's footsteps like the woman's protection detail.

"This way," he told Sabrina, leading her through the mostly empty bullpen toward the glass-encased office at the back where the chief worked.

When he knocked on the door, the new police chief, Brice Griffith, called out, "Come on in."

Chief Griffith was seven years older than Tate's thirty-

one, with fourteen years of experience in police work back
in Vancouver. He'd made the jump to Alaska with his young
daughter in tow when the town's old chief had decided to
follow her new boyfriend to Anchorage and return to detective work.

So far, Chief Griffith seemed like a fair boss. He was
personable enough, though like most of the people in this
town, he'd definitely come to Desparre to outrun something.

Not that Tate could throw stones. If the chief knew Tate's
true history, he'd probably be fired on the spot.

"What's up?" Chief Griffith asked, standing as Sabrina
followed Tate into the room.

"This is Sabrina Jones," Tate said, noting the surprise
on her face that he remembered her full name. "She's being
targeted by a stalker."

The chief frowned. "Take a seat," he told Sabrina, then
added to Tate, "Close the door."

Tate did as he was told, then sat in the chair next to Sabrina. Sitka settled in the space between them, her ears
perked as she glanced from Sabrina to Tate.

"This was left on my doorstep today," Sabrina said,
handing the note to the chief.

The chief read it, then stared at Sabrina. "This isn't the
first time you've been contacted by this person, I take it?"

"No. He followed me from New York." She took a shaky,
visible breath. "I've been running for two years. I thought
I'd lost him here."

Two years? Tate stared at her, wondering how he hadn't
realized sooner she was trying to escape a threat.

He should have. Every time he'd spoken to her, she'd directed most of her responses to her feet. He'd thought she
was shy, maybe even nervous because the attraction he felt
for her was reciprocated. But the truth was that she'd been
afraid of anyone taking too great an interest in her.

Had he gotten so comfortable here that he'd forgotten what it had been like in the beginning? Gotten to accept this life so much that he'd completely let his old one go?

The idea made an old ache start up in his chest.

Even though his previous chief had known his history, had helped him come on board with his faked background and fake last name, he'd spent a long time thinking he'd made a mistake. That staying in police work would be a way for the people who'd tried to kill him once to find him again.

He should have recognized that same fear in Sabrina, should have found a way to help her sooner. Some police officer he was.

Chief Griffith's eyes narrowed at him like he could see Tate's internal struggle, like he suspected Tate wasn't quite who he said he was. Then his attention was fully on Sabrina. "Tell us about this stalker."

She shifted forward in her seat, her hands gripping the arms of her chair as her wavy, blond hair fell over her shoulder, obscuring part of her face. "It started two and a half years ago. I began getting notes on my doorstep." She nodded in the direction of the note the chief had placed on his desk. "They all looked like that, with the red text and the creepy messages. The first one just said *I've been watching you*. They were always short, usually things like *One day, we'll be together* or *You must know how much I love you.*"

She shuddered a little, glancing at Tate and then back at the chief. "The first one spooked me, and my friends convinced me to call the police. Initially, they took my report but didn't seem that interested. But when this guy kept writing, they said they could officially call it a stalking case. Still, it didn't feel like much was happening until—"

Her head tilted toward her lap, her hair falling over her face even more until Tate couldn't see her expression at all. "I started dating someone."

Dread sank to his gut, suspecting where this was going before she continued. "Three months later, he was shot in his home. Then my stalker left me a note saying *Don't be sad. He was just in our way.*"

"That's when you ran," the chief said, sympathy in his voice and an expression on his face that told Tate he was familiar with that kind of pain.

The expression was gone too fast for Tate to figure out what it meant. Next to him, Sabrina swiped at her face quickly, like she hoped no one would notice.

Her head lifted again, and she squared her shoulders, nodding. "Yes. I hired a PI to help me disappear. I spent a year and a half running from one tiny town to the next, trying to stay below the radar. I never got another note, but sometimes I'd just start feeling…jumpy. So, I'd go somewhere else, get a different car, leave anything unimportant behind. Then I arrived here."

A smile trembled on her lips. "I've been in Desparre for six months. I've felt more normal than I had in a long time. I thought… I really thought I'd finally escaped. Then I got this letter. I considered running, but…" Her knuckles whitened around the edges of the chair, her jaw clenching. She turned toward Tate, pleading and hope in her gaze. "I want this to end."

The new chief had been here for a few months. Most of that time, Tate had been doing K-9 training with Sitka. But he'd still felt constantly on edge, worrying Chief Griffith would notice something off in his doctored personnel file and realize Tate wasn't who he said he was. He'd feared that the life he'd built for himself here could be destroyed at any moment. He'd worried about a threat to his life, too, but he was a trained police officer. He was armed and relatively dangerous if provoked.

What must it feel like to be a civilian with no training?

What must it feel like to be completely alone, being chased by a threat that hadn't even been fully identified?

Not waiting for the chief's assessment, Tate said, "Desparre isn't New York. We have resources we can put on this."

He kept his gaze fully on Sabrina, wanting her to see in his expression how committed he was to helping her, but from the corner of his eye he could see the chief's raised eyebrows. Still, Chief Griffith didn't contradict him.

The fear in Sabrina's eyes started to shift, turning into tentative hope.

"We're going to find this guy," Tate promised. "It's time to stop running and let us make a stand for you. We're going to get you your life back."

Chapter Three

Sabrina Jones had chosen a good place to hide.

Desparre was a big town in terms of geography. It stretched from wooded patches with houses hidden among the trees through small commercial areas and across half a mountain. Besides the tiny downtown, they had other, more out-of-the-way spots to get supplies if you really wanted to stay unseen.

Tate had grown up on the other side of Alaska, in a coastal town that was much bigger and busier than Desparre but still boasted that wide-open-spaces Alaskan charm. But he'd lived in Boston for so many years that when he'd moved to Desparre, the expansive spaces without people had felt as foreign as the big city had initially seemed.

Still, he'd never hidden away in the woods or up in the mountains, like so many people did who came here running from something. He'd been confident in the backstory that had been created for him, confident that Alaska was too far for anyone to even think about searching for him. But the threat against him was one of revenge, not an obsessed wannabe-lover.

The fact that Sabrina's stalker hadn't given up after two years, hadn't found someone else to fixate on, was worrisome. His department back in Boston had handled a couple of stalker cases. They'd tried but been unable to keep either of those stalkers locked up, and he'd felt frustrated for the targets who'd continued to live in fear.

Tate frowned as he opened the back of his modified police SUV for Sitka to jump in. The department didn't have the money for a true K-9 vehicle; they'd barely been able to cover his and Sitka's K-9 training.

But all he'd really needed was the official approval. He'd been happy to shell out the money for Sitka's special stab- and bulletproof vest, happy to pay out of pocket for her vet bills and food. She was his partner, but she was also his pet. Every night after their shift was over, she came home with him. If all went as planned, eight years from now, she'd retire and just be his dog.

His puppy's tail wagged as she leaped into the vehicle. She knew it meant they were going to work.

He glanced back at her as he climbed into the driver's seat. "How about we practice your tracking today?"

Her tail thumped harder, and she gave an enthusiastic *woof!*

Grinning, Tate put his SUV in gear. But his smile faded fast as he thought about the message Sabrina had found. Being such a small town, they used the state's forensic lab for big, complicated jobs, but all of the local officers knew how to do basic work, like dusting for fingerprints. The note left on Sabrina's doorstep had none.

Maybe her stalker had left something else behind, like his scent.

Heading out of downtown, Tate turned onto one of the dirt roads that passed as a highway around here. Sabrina's address wasn't in the most remote part of Desparre, but she'd definitely picked a spot where people weren't likely to know she lived there unless she told them. Or unless someone spotted her elsewhere and followed her home.

Once they did that, the location was much less appeal-

ing. It was too far for neighbors to hear a cry for help, too
secluded for anyone else to see a threat.

Gripping the wheel tighter, Tate wondered if they were
doing enough. Based on what Sabrina had said about the
investigation back home, there wasn't much to go on there,
especially since NYPD had determined it was someone on
the very outskirts of her life. Still, she'd been cagey with
the details, flat out refusing to give them her boyfriend's
name or the names of the investigating detectives back in
New York. She'd asked them not to contact the police department there, insisting that her family's safety would be
compromised if they learned where she was.

She'd looked so panicked that they'd finally agreed. The
fact was that if the NYPD had gone two and a half years
without being able to identify her stalker, even after he
became a murderer, the leads in New York were slim. For
now, it made more sense to concentrate on new arrivals to
Desparre, people who might have tracked Sabrina here.
After Sabrina had left the station looking a lot more confident and hopeful than when she'd walked in, he and the
chief had finished mapping out a plan to keep her safe.
They'd already given her an emergency-alert button that
connected directly to the station. They had scheduled police
drive-bys of her house multiple times a day, with scattered
times to prevent her stalker from seeing a pattern. Sabrina
was supposed to call them if she had the slightest concern,
wanted a police escort somewhere or just wanted someone
to do a walk-through of her home.

Hopefully, they'd spot the guy before he could get close
again. But Tate and the chief had agreed they needed to get
more proactive rather than just hoping her stalker made a
mistake.

So today, he and Sitka would get a chance to test out
their training.

As he pulled into Sabrina's long dirt driveway, Tate

glanced around. There wasn't much to see besides trees. Someone passing by on the street wouldn't spot the cabin without binoculars or very keen eyesight. To drop the note on the doorstep, her stalker had probably left his vehicle on the road and crept through the trees. Otherwise, Sabrina could have seen him coming.

When Tate put the SUV in Park, the curtain moved on the front window, and Sabrina's face appeared in the crack. He hopped out of his vehicle and waved at her, then let Sitka out, too.

Sabrina stepped outside, scanning the woods before her gaze settled on him.

"Sitka and I are going to try a little tracking work," he told her.

She looked surprised, probably having expected he was doing a check-in. Her gaze went to Sitka, whose tail wagged at the attention.

"She's a tracker dog?"

"Actually, she's a dual-purpose dog." He rubbed her head, the thick coat perfect for Alaska, even if Malamutes weren't usually used as police dogs. "She specializes in both patrol and tracking."

"Patrol?" Sabrina smiled, humor in her eyes that had been missing every other time they'd spoken. "Does she write speeding tickets with those big paws?"

Tate smiled back at her, wishing he'd realized something was wrong one of the dozens of times he'd chatted her up around town and reached out to her sooner. "Close. She's my partner. So, if I need to chase someone down, she can help me. Or she can clear a building or provide security. She's trained to bark and detain, too. That's pretty much exactly what it sounds like. She finds someone and keeps them from running so I can come in and cuff them."

"Can I pet her, or is that off-limits when she's on duty?"

"Go ahead." Although he didn't let civilians pet Sitka

while she was actively tracking or doing a specific patrol task, she was great with people. Letting the people in Desparre pet her also made them comfortable having her on the force, something which was brand-new for the town.

She was off leash now because they weren't downtown, but at the chief's request, Tate had been using a leash in town while people got used to her. He hoped she'd bring good press and pave the way for expanding their K-9 team in the future.

Sabrina smiled at Sitka as she rubbed the dog's ears.

Sitka's head tilted up like she was enjoying the attention, and her tail thumped.

When he'd gone to the shelter, he'd been hoping to find a young German Shepherd or Malinois, both typical breeds for police work. But as soon as the little Alaskan Malamute had seen him, she'd dropped her chest to the ground, backside still in the air, tail wagging, and barked. She'd wanted to play. And he'd been totally charmed.

The shelter hadn't known anything about her background, other than that she was obviously a Malamute and not afraid of people. She'd been found alongside a highway, way too thin but anxious to please.

Although he'd been approved to become a K-9 officer back in Boston before the attempt on his life, he'd never actually gotten a dog or gone through training. He'd done research on traits that made good police dogs, but ultimately he'd known that whether or not Sitka would make a good partner would only be determined once they started training.

Still, his mind had been made up the moment she'd demanded his attention. He had to take her home.

After some initial hurdles with her energy level and distractibility, she'd received high scores in all of her certifications. But now was the real test.

She'd only been patrolling with him for a few weeks,

not enough time in a place as low in crime as Desparre to really test out her skills. And so far, there'd been no reason for her to do any tracking in real conditions.

Tate could happily stand around half the day, chatting with Sabrina while she pet Sitka, but he was on duty. "You can watch from inside if you want. We're just going to see if Sitka picks anything up here."

The smile that had stayed on her face the whole time she pet Sitka faded, replaced by wariness at the reminder of her stalker. "Okay. Thank you."

Tate watched her walk inside, heard the loud *click* of the dead bolt turning and then said to Sitka, "Let's see where this guy came from."

Most likely, they wouldn't get much. But knowing which side of the street the stalker had parked on might indicate whether he'd come from the direction of town or somewhere more secluded. Tate was betting on the latter, betting that her stalker had chosen an out-of-the-way cabin, too.

Directing Sitka onto Sabrina's porch, he told his dog, "Scent, Sitka!"

She sniffed the air briefly, then her nose went to the ground, and she barked at Sabrina's door.

"Another one. Scent again," he told her, knowing she'd just alerted on Sabrina, since the woman had been on the porch most recently. Hopefully, the stalker's scent was still here, too.

If it was, Sitka should be able to find and follow it. Compared to the paltry five million scent receptors in the noses of humans, dogs had two hundred and twenty-five million.

Sitka's nose went back in the air, then down to the ground, sniffing around for a minute. Then she walked off the porch, nose still down. She headed straight into the woods off the side of Sabrina's porch like he'd expected. But instead of bounding toward the street, she ran around the side of the house.

Had the stalker crept around Sabrina's home, maybe peered in her windows? The idea made his fists clench, but it shouldn't have surprised him.

Instead of circling the cabin, Sitka raced into the woods, away from Sabrina's house.

Frowning, Tate ran after Sitka. He glanced back once, saw the big sliding-glass door at the back of the cabin, Sabrina's face peering out at them.

Then he was hurrying after Sitka again. She was definitely tracking a scent. Her nose came up a few times, as she slowed and sniffed the air, before dropping down again.

As they moved away, the woods got more dense. It wasn't long before he glanced back, and even knowing where the cabin was, he couldn't see it.

He couldn't imagine a stalker finding a random road somewhere else alongside these woods and then trekking through the trees for miles to leave a note on Sabrina's doorstep. But Sitka seemed certain, her tail wagging as she ran, because K-9s were trained to think of their police tasks like games. She kept a pace that was hard to match.

Then a noise up ahead put Tate on instant alert. A rustling, like someone was there. Had the stalker stuck around this long?

His hand dropped to the grip of his gun in his duty belt even as he continued to scan the woods ahead of Sitka.

She'd slowed, the fur on her back rising. The fact that she hadn't shifted slightly and raced toward the noise meant it wasn't the same person who'd left the scent she was tracking.

Tate swore as a shape materialized from behind the tree. A black, furry shape, a solid twenty pounds lighter than Sitka, followed by another.

His pulse spiked, and he tried to keep the panic out of his voice as he called, "Sitka, come! Back up, girl."

She backed toward him, her movements slow and controlled, like she was backing away from a suspect so he could take over.

Only this time, she was backing away from a pair of baby bears. The question was, where was the mom?

Then there was more rustling, and Tate saw her. A cinnamon-colored black bear lumbering after her cubs. Her head swiveled in his direction, then Sitka's, as her babies continued to run perpendicular to his dog.

"Sitka, slow, girl," Tate said softly, hoping the bear wouldn't see either of them as a threat. The bear might have weighed about the same as he did and was probably only a foot shorter if she stood, but he was no match for her strength-to-weight ratio. And his pistol was no match for a furious mom protecting her cubs.

Sitka's movements became even slower, but she kept backing toward him, showing no fear even as the bear got up on her hind legs, still watching them.

Then the bear dropped back down, and Tate held his breath, wishing he'd brought the bear horn he kept in the back of his vehicle. He reached for his pepper spray with one hand and got ready to shout and try to seem as large as possible if she rushed them.

He let the breath out slowly as she followed her cubs instead, but his pulse didn't return to normal until she was out of sight and Sitka had backed up against him.

"Good girl," he whispered, stroking her head as her tail wagged.

She looked up at him, then back in the direction she'd been tracking, ready to keep working.

But Tate didn't want to risk running into the bear again. They usually weren't dangerous if you were smart, but he didn't want to startle a mom with cubs. He had no idea how far these woods went before they led to a road. "We'll look at some maps instead," he told Sitka.

Her talents were unproven in the real world, and Tate

knew his boss would question whether the stalker had actually trekked so far through the woods, not giving himself easy access to a getaway vehicle if Sabrina or someone else had spotted him. But Tate trusted Sitka.

He glanced around, seeing nothing but woods in all directions. If Sabrina's stalker was confident enough to sneak up on her house through a mile or more of woods, he was more skilled than a typical city boy. Or maybe he hadn't just recently found Sabrina. Maybe he'd been right behind her all along and only today decided to make himself known.

But if he'd been in Alaska for six months like Sabrina, what had changed to make him announce himself? And what did that mean for Sabrina's safety?

Chapter Four

"He came through the woods."

Sabrina stared at Tate, a sick feeling in her stomach. "Through the woods?" Had her stalker seen her in the mornings when she stood outside on her deck, enjoying nature, sometimes in her pajamas? How close had he gotten without her ever suspecting anyone was there?

She resisted the urge to reach up and touch the alert button that was hanging on a thin chain around her neck. There was comfort in knowing Tate and the rest of the Desparre PD were on the other side of it.

"Yeah, I know it's strange," Tate said, misinterpreting her surprise. "I'm not sure where he came from, because we ran into a bear."

"A *bear*?" She glanced from him to Sitka, relieved that they both looked fine, then realized she'd basically been parroting his words since he'd returned to the house after trying to track her stalker.

Flushing, she stepped back a little and did something she hadn't done in two years. "You want to come in?"

The words felt foreign on her lips, and she realized just how much had been stolen from her. Even the little things, like feeling comfortable enough to trust anyone in her home, had become a thing of her past.

Not anymore. She stared at Tate, watching a debate play on his face. He was on duty. But he wanted to come inside.

She hadn't been imagining that the attraction she'd felt in the brief moments they'd spoken over the past six months was reciprocated. A zing of excitement darted through her, lodging in her chest and quickening her breathing.

"Can you tell me more about the tracking?" she asked, hoping it would make his decision easier if it was connected to his work.

"Sure." He wiped his boots on the mat, and Sabrina held in a smile.

She wouldn't have cared if he'd brought in all the mud in the forest. Despite the nerves suddenly dancing in her stomach, this was the most normal she'd felt in a long time.

"Come on inside, Sitka," she told his dog, and the Alaskan Malamute glanced at her owner.

When Tate nodded, Sitka bounded inside, danced a circle in the tiny entryway and then sat.

Laughing, Sabrina asked, "How come I've never met Sitka before?"

Tate stepped inside, closing the door behind him and throwing the dead bolt for her.

The loud sound made her jerk, her nerves doubling at having a man she'd admired from afar for six months crowding her entryway. He was tall and lean, but whether it was the six inches of height he had on her, the fact that there was obvious power in his frame despite his lack of bulky muscle or just his nearness, the space suddenly felt much smaller.

"I only got Sitka a few months ago," Tate answered, either not noticing or pretending not to see her discomfort. "The two of us have mostly been down in Fairbanks for the past two months getting our training."

No wonder she'd seen him so infrequently lately, even

though she'd gone to town more often, hoping to run into him.

"What was that like?" she asked, tilting her head back so she could see his face better.

"A lot of work." He grinned, and the expression softened the sharp lines of his face, made him seem even more approachable.

It eased her nerves but only increased her awareness of how little space was between them.

For six months, every time she'd seen this man, she'd wished she dared risk asking him out. Now he was in her home.

Taking a step back, she gestured for him to follow, then headed into her combined kitchen and living area. The big sliding-glass door, nestled between two equally large windows, showcased a gorgeous view into the forest. This had always been her favorite spot in the house. But now, as she peered into the dense woods, she wondered if the solitude that had always made her feel so safe and alone had just been camouflage. She wondered how often someone else had been staring back at her unseen.

"He's not out there now," Tate said.

When she glanced at him, there was sympathy on his face, and anger, too, like he was as upset about the invasion of her privacy as she was. "If he was, Sitka would have found him?"

At the mention of her name, the dog hurried over to stand between her and Tate, tail wagging.

Tate reached out and stroked Sitka's head. "Yes. The guy trekked a long way to get here."

"I wish *he'd* run into the bear," Sabrina muttered, earning a brief laugh from Tate. Then, she awkwardly gestured to the couch facing the view. "Have a seat. Do you want something to drink or—"

"No, I'm fine." Tate settled on one side of the couch,

giving her plenty of space. Sitka followed, lying beside the sofa.

Sabrina sat on the opposite end of the couch, twisting slightly to face him. He looked at ease in her home, and she wondered if being a police officer brought that level of calm confidence or it was just his natural personality.

She was the opposite, usually filled with a jittery energy, a need to be active or creative. Sitting still had always been a challenge. As she stared at him, he watched her quietly, and she wondered if he could tell that she wanted to jump right back up and move. She wondered if he could tell just how much nervous excitement filled her at his nearness.

"How does it work, the tracking?" she blurted, partly because she was curious and partly to fill the silence.

"Whenever you move, you leave a scent behind. So, on your porch, Sitka actually scented on you first. She followed the scent to your front door." He laughed, then continued. "Then she found the second scent, presumably the stalker. She sniffs the air to locate a scent and then puts her nose to the ground. Dogs can track scents for long distances, through water, through all kinds of weather conditions. It's pretty amazing, actually."

Sabrina looked at the Alaskan Malamute, who had enough of a gangly puppy look that she couldn't have yet been quite full-grown. "Very impressive."

As if she knew she'd just been complimented, Sitka's tail wagged.

"Did you grow up with dogs? Is that why you wanted to be a K-9 officer?"

"I *didn't* grow up with dogs, which is probably why I wanted to be one," Tate said, leaning back against her couch, shifting to more fully face her.

Suddenly, despite his uniform, despite the reason he was here, it felt more like a first date than an update on the investigation. Not just that, but it felt like a *good* first date, the kind that would ultimately lead to a second date.

"I always wanted a dog. When I saw Sitka in the shelter, she was just so—" he grinned at her, his expression full of affection "—energetic and goofy."

Her tail wagged again, and he added, "She was also smart and eager to please, which helped her in training."

Then Tate's expression got more serious. "What about you? Did you have a dog? Who's waiting for you back home?"

"I didn't have any pets, mostly because I lived in a fifth-floor walk-up in New York City. But I guess it was a good thing, since running with a pet would have been harder and might have been a way to track me. I'm close to my mom and brother, though. They're both back in New York. I haven't dared to contact either one, and I miss them every day. The PI who helped me said it was safer to cut all contact on my end unless there was an emergency."

Tate frowned slightly, sympathy on his face, but instead of turning it into a discussion about her stalker like she'd feared he might, he said, "I haven't seen my family in a while, either. I can imagine how much you must miss yours."

She nodded, trying not to dwell on the memory of the last time she'd seen them both, when they'd fought her so hard on her decision to go into hiding. Now, after all the sacrifices she'd made, her stalker was still right behind her.

Shaking off the frustration, she focused on the fact that she had Tate here. After two years of trying to keep everyone at a certain distance, she deserved at least one normal conversation. One semi-*truthful* conversation. She hadn't told him her real last name to protect her family's safety, but this was the closest she'd felt to normal in more than two years. She could actually be herself and not have to watch every word, worrying she might accidentally let something slip about who she really was, why she was here.

And talking to Tate was easy, comfortable. Despite her hyperawareness of him, she'd gladly just sit and chat with him all day.

"Have you always lived in Desparre?"

He looked surprised by the conversation turn. "No. But my mom's family is part Tlingit, and they've been in Alaska forever. My dad's family has a long-running charter business, so they've been here a long time, too. My parents divorced when I was young, and I was an only child, so I was shuttled back and forth a lot. We lived in a bigger town than this, but it was still small enough to run into one parent while I was with the other. They get along okay now, but in those early years, not so much."

"Where in Alaska did you grow up? I got here and pretty much headed straight north until I was snowed in. But I've heard some parts of Alaska actually get a real summer." She grinned, because the locals always seemed silently amused by anyone who wasn't native to Desparre and was bundled up when the locals were wearing shorts.

"I…" Tate frowned, shook his head slightly. "My family is from here originally, but I actually grew up in the Midwest. I moved to Desparre five and a half years ago."

She stared at him, wondering why his words were suddenly so stiff, his gaze averted like he wasn't giving her the full story. But why would he lie about where he'd grown up?

She'd probably just become unpracticed at getting-to-know-you conversations. But if she was truly going to stop running, if the Desparre PD was going to help her make a stand here, then maybe all the things she thought she'd never have again were actually possible. That meant she needed to figure out how to talk to a man like Tate Emory again.

After what had happened to Dylan, she'd vowed never to date again, never to put anyone else in danger. But now, staring at Tate, seeing how dedicated he was to helping her, seeing her interest reflected back in his gaze, everything seemed possible again.

WHAT HAD HE been thinking?

Tate had managed to spend five and a half years without telling anyone—not even his old partner, Peter—the real details of his past. Half an hour with Sabrina at her house yesterday, and the words had just come out of his mouth, without him even realizing his mistake until she'd asked which Alaskan city he'd lived in as a child.

Hopefully, his awkward attempt at correcting his mistake hadn't been an obvious lie.

Tate had spent most of his morning patrol going over the conversation in his mind, trying to figure out if he'd just blown his own cover. He didn't think so. Despite having been on the run for two years, Sabrina seemed to take his word at face value. It made him feel worse about needing to lie to her.

No wonder he hadn't entered into many deep friendships, let alone any relationships, since he'd come here. It wasn't in his nature to lie to people.

He missed having someone who knew the truth about him. Even though he and Chief Hernandez had rarely talked about his real past, knowing that someone here was aware of his secret had made him feel less alone.

It had also given him a stronger sense of security. Chief Keara Hernandez had let him go through the police academy as if he really was a rookie, then brought him onto the force. She could face legal repercussions if the truth ever came out, but she'd done it as a favor to an old family friend who worked for Witness Protection. That family friend also knew Tate's family. The man had agreed to help him hide outside official channels. That favor had allowed Tate to return to a career he loved, let him return to a state he loved.

Yes, he was more than a thousand miles from his childhood home, from his family. But the beauty he'd taken for granted as a kid made him feel closer to them now, even if he couldn't see them. It made him feel one step closer to who he really was.

Chief Griffith had no idea he wasn't actually Tate Emory, security guard from the Midwest who'd moved to Desparre for a change of pace and a chance to fulfill a lifelong dream of becoming an officer. Tate had no idea what the new chief would do if he found out.

As he parked his SUV outside the police station, ready to spend some time in downtown after a morning patrolling the outskirts, Tate vowed not to be so careless again. He wasn't sure what about Sabrina Jones made him so unguarded, but he needed to be especially vigilant around her. Just because she was being honest about her past didn't mean he could do the same.

As if thinking about her had made her appear, Tate spotted Sabrina walking out of the grocery store. She had one small bag in her hand and was glancing around anxiously.

"Come on, Sitka." He hopped out of the vehicle and put on her leash. "Let's go say hello."

Woof!

His dog's enthusiastic reply caught Sabrina's attention. As soon as she met his gaze, her shoulders relaxed, and she smiled. It was a real smile, not the nervous, hesitant kind she'd given him over the past few months. A smile born of the belief that she knew him, that she could trust him.

It made guilt bubble up, and Tate tried to suppress it. She might not really know him, but she *could* trust him.

He headed toward her, and she met him halfway, immediately bending to pet Sitka. "How has your day been?" She peered up at him from where she'd crouched down. "Did Sitka help you write a lot of speeding tickets today?"

He grinned back at her. "Nah. She was in a good mood. She just handed out warnings."

Woof! Sitka's tail thumped, and she glanced back and forth between them, as if she knew she was the subject of conversation.

"What about you? How are you doing?"

When Sabrina stood again, she was smiling, too, looking far less worried than when he'd spotted her. "I'm just trying to live my life like normal." She shrugged. "Well, as normal as it gets these days." She lowered her voice, glancing around again, even though the closest person was across the street. "I don't suppose you've made any progress at figuring out who's doing this?"

Tate shook his head, expecting disappointment, but she didn't seem surprised. After two years of running, her expectations were probably pretty low. "Just keep being careful. The chief and I talked through strategy yesterday after you left the station. I know you're worried about us contacting New York, but we'd like to dig into your history to see if fresh eyes make anything pop."

She immediately tensed. "My cousin's wife works at the station. You contact them and she'll find out and it will get back to my mom and my brother. Then they'll come here. And after what happened before..."

Tate held up his hands, understanding her fear for her family. "Okay. Most likely, we'll find him by looking at people here. So, if anything seems unusual or anyone gives you a weird feeling, let us know. There's nothing too small for us to check out."

She gave him another smile, but this one was shaky. "Thanks."

"Why don't you drop your groceries in your car and walk with me and Sitka? We were going to the park, to let some more people meet her."

"Okay."

There was happiness in her voice, and as he walked with her to her rusted old truck, he tried not to let it ignite a similar thrill in him. She was a citizen who needed his help. Yes, he'd been considering asking her out for months—something he hadn't done any of since he'd gone into hiding himself—but things had changed. He couldn't be distracted by her, not when he needed to be thinking about her safety.

Still, he couldn't keep his gaze from lingering on the way the sunshine created golden highlights in her hair, the way it emphasized the smoothness of her ivory skin. Couldn't keep his mind from traveling down an imaginary road where she wasn't living in fear and he didn't have to keep his real identity a secret.

She dropped off the groceries, and then they headed toward the park, Sitka tugging slightly on the leash and giving him glances as if to ask *Why am I wearing this?* In that moment, it felt like he was off duty. It felt like he was just enjoying the company of a woman he liked and a dog who'd given him family here.

From across the street, Yura Begay gave him a nod. The gruff former Marine and lifelong Alaskan resident owned a check-cashing place on the outskirts of Desparre. He was known to be rude, but ever since Tate had gotten Sitka, he'd been warming up. Tate hoped it was a sign of how the rest of the town would respond.

It was the middle of the day, and the sun felt fantastic after the brutal winter, but it had been raining half an hour ago, so there were only a handful of people besides Yura downtown. Still, there were a group of kids in the park, parents chatting on the benches nearby. Hopefully it would give Sitka a chance to charm some more people and Sabrina a chance to relax. One thing he could be relatively confident in: if her stalker had tracked her across the country over the past two years, he was pretty unlikely to be chasing her with a wife and kid in tow.

The closer they got to the park, the slower Sabrina's steps became.

"Do you know anyone here?" Maybe he could introduce her to some of them while he was introducing them to Sitka.

She shrugged. "Some. I've been trying to talk to people more, but it feels insincere when all the typical questions you ask someone you've just met are things I have to lie about."

The same guilt filled him, the desire to share his secret with her, to trust someone enough to be truly honest. But it was a selfish wish, one that could put her in danger. So, he kept quiet and just continued walking.

As they reached the park, Sitka whined, tugging on her leash like she wanted to cross the street.

Tate frowned, pulling her back as he glanced around, trying to figure out what had caught her attention. He didn't see anything. Then again, despite two months of intense training, Sitka was still a year-old puppy. And walking with Sabrina probably felt more like off duty to Sitka, as well.

"Come on, Sitka. You'll like talking to the kids."

She glanced at him, whined and tugged once more, then gave in.

As he stepped onto the grass, a shout from the far side of the park commanded his attention.

"He's going to fall! Help! Help!"

The group of parents who'd been talking and laughing near the benches jumped up as one and raced toward the gazebo, where a boy of about seven had somehow managed to get on the roof. Now he was dangling off it.

"Stay here," he told Sitka. Because she'd been acting unusual, he looped her leash quickly around the edge of the bench, knotting it to keep her in place.

Then he raced toward the gazebo, passing the group of parents just as the kid's grip slipped and he slid farther, hanging only by fingertips now.

Pushing his strides as hard as he could, Tate suddenly

felt like he was back in Boston, chasing a suspect down a city street. But the speed he had now, after two months of chasing Sitka around practice obstacles and trails, made his Boston days seem slow.

He reached the gazebo just as the boy lost his grip with a pained cry.

Skidding to a stop underneath him, Tate braced himself as he threw his arms out.

The boy landed awkwardly, smacking Tate in the face and sliding half out of his grasp. But Tate broke his fall and was able to set him on his feet without injury.

"Thank you, thank you, thank you," said a man who had to be the boy's father.

The boy had been fairly calm but burst into tears as his dad scooped him up.

Tate's heart rate slowed as the other parents reached them, clapping him on the back and hugging their own kids even as they admonished them not to climb the gazebo.

He smiled and accepted the accolades. He was turning back toward Sabrina and Sitka when Sabrina's shocked scream burst through the relieved voices. Sitka's panicked yelp followed.

A big green truck was rolling backward and at a slight angle down Main Street, rapidly picking up speed. It was headed right for Sitka.

His dog was straining against her leash, but he'd tethered her too well to the bench.

Tate started running again, pushing himself as hard as he could, but he was too far away. He'd never be able to get back to her in time, let alone unhook her.

Dread, guilt and anger slammed through him like a punch to the chest, then doubled as Sabrina raced in front of the truck to help his dog. He was about to lose them both. And there was nothing he could do to stop it.

Chapter Five

Panic intensified as Tate ran faster, his frantic strides still not good enough. The truck was speeding up, the incline working against him.

Sabrina dropped into an awkward squat and worked at the leash, struggling with it as Sitka whined and pulled, probably yanking the knot even tighter.

The truck hit the grass, no difference in height from the unpaved street to slow it, and Tate's whole body jerked in response, not wanting to see Sabrina get hit. Not wanting to see Sitka get hit.

Then suddenly Sabrina shifted, unhooking the leash from Sitka's collar instead.

Sitka scampered backward, away from the oncoming vehicle.

Sabrina twisted, throwing herself to the side. She landed hard on the grass as the truck zoomed past, plowing into the bench.

The metal bench crumpled under the truck's bumper, screeching enough to raise goose bumps on Tate's arms. As the bench collapsed and split, the truck kept going, then got snagged on the twisted pieces of metal. The truck made a sputtering sound, and then the engine cut out.

"You okay?" Tate panted as he slid to a stop beside Sabrina, his gaze searching for Sitka, too.

Behind him came the gasps and shouts of worry from the group of parents and kids, but Tate ignored them as he dropped to his knees next to Sabrina.

She rolled over and pushed up on her elbows, her arms shaking. There were grass stains streaking the front of her T-shirt and dirt on her face. "Did Sitka get out of the way?"

Woof!

His dog came running around the back of the truck. She didn't stop until she'd bumped him, knocking him off his knees and onto his butt.

"I'm sorry about the leash," he told her, burying his head in her fur for a moment, relief relaxing the tightness in his chest as he saw that she hadn't been hurt.

Then he lifted his gaze to the truck, stalled and silent. When he'd seen it moving toward Sitka, it had appeared empty. As if someone had forgotten to put on their parking brake. But was it really that simple?

Dread built up again. The truck hadn't been aimed at Sabrina. But it had been close enough to her. Could her stalker have sent it down the street?

From what he knew about stalkers, it seemed unlikely. After two years of chasing her, why would he try to kill her in such an impersonal way? Usually, when stalkers got violent, they did it up close, with a gun or a knife.

Still, he swept his gaze over the area where the truck had come from. No one was there.

Pushing himself to his feet, Tate scanned the rest of the park. All he saw were the parents and kids, looking horrified.

Sitka pivoted away from him, moving to Sabrina, and gave her a sloppy kiss across the side of her face.

Sabrina laughed, petting her. "You're welcome."

Tate held out a hand for Sabrina. "Are you okay? Do you want to have a doctor look at you?"

She put her hand in his. It was a little shaky, but there was a power in her grip as she helped him pull her up.

"No doctor. I'm fine, just a little freaked out." She glanced up Main Street, where the truck had come from. "What happened? Do you think this was an accident? Or…"

Reluctantly, Tate let go of her hand as the rest of the people in the park surrounded them.

"What happened?" The dad of the kid who'd fallen from the gazebo put a hand on Sabrina's shoulder, looking worried as he clutched the boy with his other hand.

A woman bouncing a crying baby leaned closer to Sabrina, too. "Are you okay?"

"Look at the bench!" someone else exclaimed.

"Who would be so careless?"

The cacophony of voices faded into the background as Tate stepped closer to the vehicle and peered through the window. The truck was set right between Reverse and Park, the key fob in the center console. A freak accident? He'd seen it before with these old trucks, where the owner thought it was in Park, but it was actually partway to Reverse. When he glanced up Main Street, he saw no one. No panicked owner racing for the park, horrified and ashamed. But maybe they'd walked away and the truck hadn't rolled backward immediately?

Still, he couldn't take any chances, especially not when Sabrina had been nearby, when they knew her stalker was here. He stepped farther away from the crowd and pulled out his radio. Speaking quietly, he said, "A truck just plowed into a bench in the park. No one was inside the vehicle, but Sabrina Jones almost got hit." Stepping behind the truck, he read off the license-plate number, dreading the potential news that it was a rental, maybe something that would come back to a fake name.

There was surprise in Officer Nate Dreymond's voice as he replied a minute later. "That vehicle belongs to Talise Poitra."

The seventy-year-old owner of the grocery store. She'd been injured pretty severely in the bombing, even been briefly in a coma. Maybe she wasn't back to a hundred percent yet.

Tate relaxed slightly as he glanced at Sabrina, who was hunched inward as she nodded and assured the townspeople that she wasn't hurt. Beside her, Sitka's tail was wagging as everyone took turns petting her.

"I'll walk over to the store and talk to her," Nate said. "I'll radio you once I have an update."

"Thanks." Tucking the radio back into his duty belt, Tate slipped through the crowd up to Sabrina and Sitka. "Why don't you come with me to the station, where you can clean up, and we'll take a statement?"

She nodded, looking grateful for the excuse to move away from the crowd.

"What happened?" Maria Peterson asked, clutching her three-year-old daughter tightly. A few months ago, when the park had been bombed, her husband had been injured.

"Probably just an accident," Tate said. "But we're going to investigate and make sure. Did anyone notice someone by the truck before it started moving?"

The group shook their heads and shrugged, glancing at each other, but Tate wasn't surprised. They'd all been too focused on the kid on the gazebo roof.

If this *hadn't been* an accident, someone had waited for the perfect moment.

Tate led Sabrina back toward the police station. His gaze swept the area as they walked, looking for anyone who seemed out of place, who seemed too interested in Sabrina. But besides a blonde woman facing away from him as she took pictures of the stalled truck and ruined bench, all he saw was Yura Begay.

The ex-Marine called out, "Everyone all right?"

"Yeah. Just a runaway truck," Tate replied.

"You think that's all it was?" Sabrina asked.

When he glanced at her, she was biting down on her lip, her brows furrowed. Guilt was all over her face as she ran her hand down Sitka's back.

"I hope so. But no matter what, this isn't your fault. I'm the one who tied Sitka to the bench."

"Hey, Tate?" Nate's voice crackled over the radio. "I've got an update."

"Go," Tate replied, glancing at Sabrina.

"Talise said she had her keys in her purse and that she'd put the parking brake on. She parked up past the park because she wanted the exercise. Said she's still trying to get back up to speed after the bombing."

"Is she sure about the keys?" Tate asked. "Because there was a key fob in the truck."

"I asked her to check. When she went to grab her purse from behind the counter to show me, it was open and her fob was missing. She thinks someone grabbed it sometime in the past hour."

Tate felt his jaw tensing as Sabrina went pale. But was Talise right about someone taking her keys? Or had she just forgotten them in her truck? "She have any idea who?"

"No. There are no cameras in her store. She says she was in the back for a while, dealing with inventory. Normally, she brings her purse with her back there, but this time she forgot. She said the bell over the door rang a few times, but she figured people would call out if they needed her to ring them up. No one did, and it was empty when she came back up front. She said it could have been anyone. But obviously if she's right, this person knew which vehicle belonged to Talise."

"Thanks," Tate said.

"It was my stalker." Sabrina's voice was barely above a whisper. "He was trying to kill Sitka."

HER STALKER HADN'T been trying to kill her. Not this time.

No, Sabrina felt it in her gut. If he wanted to kill her, he'd do it up close, and she'd know exactly who he was before she died. He hadn't been after her today.

It was worse than that. He'd been trying to kill Sitka. Maybe because he'd seen Sitka trying to track him from her house. Or maybe because she'd been walking with Tate, because the stalker had seen her invite Tate into her home yesterday.

She hadn't even kissed Tate. She hadn't gone on a real date with him. But somehow, her stalker had known she wanted to.

He was punishing her for it by sending a message:

I'm watching. I can get to you—or someone you care about—anytime I want. Just like Dylan.

Shivering as she yanked the curtains closed on her back windows, shutting out the view of the sun sinking below the trees, Sabrina tried to stay calm. It had been hours since one of the officers had driven her home, then done a walk-through of her house before leaving.

Police still weren't sure if the truck backing up had been a targeted attack or just a freak accident. Still, they'd promised to investigate under the assumption that her stalker could have been involved. They might have been uncertain, but she wasn't. Her stalker was here, he'd made contact, and now he was back to threatening anyone who dared to enter her life.

She hadn't heard any updates. Despite the short amount of time she'd known Tate, she knew if they'd found anything, he would have told her.

She should have run the moment she'd spotted the new note on her doorstep. It didn't matter that her stalker kept finding her. She'd let herself become too invested in her life here, too invested in the life she *could* have. And she'd let herself forget how high the stakes were.

Sabrina glanced around the little cabin. It was barely eight hundred square feet, but it was cozy and the rent shockingly cheap.

Here, for the first time since she'd left New York City and her growing career in fashion design, she was doing something she loved again. No more waitressing jobs in dingy diners. No more constantly scanning the customers, searching for a face that was vaguely familiar, that might belong to a man who wouldn't leave her alone. No more endless tension between her shoulder blades, always on high alert for harassment or an attack from someone who knew she didn't want to attract attention, who knew she probably wouldn't risk going to the police.

In Desparre, she'd dared to start designing jewelry. It was what she'd always wanted to do, but back in the city, general accessories, like belts, scarves and sunglasses, were as close as she'd come. Here, she'd used an e-commerce site, made up a name with no connection to her and given it a shot. The first sale had been thrilling. As it continued to grow, she'd started to believe this could be her future.

Would she be able to do it somewhere else so easily? With Alaska's history of gold rushes, big and small, getting the raw materials had been easier than she'd expected. The cabin's tiny second bedroom had been perfect to set up a small workspace. And the view out her back windows was endlessly inspiring.

The sharp set of raps on her door made Sabrina jump. Her hand darted immediately to the alert button around her neck, but she didn't press it. Would her stalker really knock?

He'd knocked at Dylan's house.

Or at least that's what police assumed, that Dylan had opened the door to his killer, because there'd been no sign of forced entry.

The thought refused to go away as she moved slowly toward the door, heart thumping way too fast. But Dylan hadn't had any reason to suspect the person at his door was a threat. She'd mentioned the stalker, but she hadn't gone into details. She hadn't told him to be careful. Even knowing there'd been no reason for her to think he'd be in danger, the same guilt rushed forward, stinging her eyes with old tears.

Blinking them clear, she glanced around for a weapon. Making a quick detour into the kitchen, she grabbed the cast-iron pan the owner had left behind. She hefted it to shoulder height as she approached the door. It was solid and thick, tough to open even when it wasn't locked tight with a dead bolt, and especially now when her hands still shook.

Leaning in, she peered through the peephole.

It was a woman. A blonde with perfectly smoothed hair and a lot of makeup by Desparre standards, but not far from what Sabrina was used to in New York City at a club or at the design studio.

Sabrina had no idea who she was, but she lowered the pan as she leaned back. It seemed unlikely that her stalker was a woman, and equally unlikely he'd be able to convince one to help him. As the heavy pan came down, it banged the door, and she cringed.

"Hello?" the woman called when Sabrina didn't open the door.

She frowned, wondering what the woman wanted. Not that it really mattered. She wasn't about to open up for anyone right now.

When another minute went by and Sabrina continued to ignore the raps at the door, the woman called out, "My name is Ariel Clemson. I'm a reporter for the *Desparre Daily*."

There was a long pause, as if she thought that would be enticement enough, then she added, "I saw what happened at the park earlier, and I'm hoping to do a story about it." Another pause, then a hint of frustration underneath her hopeful pitch. "You know, *Local Woman Bravely Rescues Police K-9?*"

Sabrina's heart gave a small kick of anxiety. The idea of any exposure, even in the small-town newspaper, was a bad idea. There was no telling how it might get shared or who might ultimately see it. Yes, her stalker had found her, but her family hadn't. With her stalker nearby, she didn't want them to have any idea where she was.

"If you change your mind, give me a call," Ariel said through the door, and then a business card slid underneath.

Sabrina stayed quiet, still pretending not to be home, even though the reporter clearly knew she was, until the car backed out of her driveway.

Then she turned back into the cabin that had started to feel like a real home. She took one last look at the closed shades obscuring the view she loved, and headed into her bedroom to start packing.

Chapter Six

Was there anywhere on earth that her stalker couldn't track her?

Sabrina had been so careful when she'd come here, leaving her last hideout in Washington in the middle of the night when there'd been almost no one on the roads. She'd kept a close eye on her rearview mirror for hours, not stopping until she was well into Canada. There was no way he'd been behind her. Was there?

If he hadn't physically followed her, how had he found her here? She'd stopped all contact with friends and family, not even daring to send them letters from the road in case he was watching their mailboxes, waiting to intercept them. She'd stopped shopping at any of the places she used to love, even online. She'd quit her favorite exercise program that let her join in virtual sessions. She'd stopped working in fashion design, only recently making the jump to jewelry—still design, but a different field. She'd stopped using her social-media accounts entirely.

When the PI had first suggested she leave town, when she'd detailed the extent of the changes she wanted Sabrina to make to her life, giving up hobbies and activities that could be a way to locate her, it had all sounded excessive. It had all seemed unnecessary. Now she wondered if she'd missed something, some small piece of her former life that had given her stalker a way to locate her.

She had no idea what it was. But if he'd found her all the way in no-stoplights-in-downtown, snow-you-in-until-spring Desparre, was there anywhere she'd be safe?

Hefting a bag full of her jewelry supplies, Sabrina peered through the peephole at her truck, ready in the drive. Last night, after she'd made the decision to leave, she'd packed everything and then stared, frustrated and tense, out into the darkness. She'd been afraid to go outside. Afraid her stalker was waiting in the woods, ready to ambush her.

This was worse than any of the other tiny towns she'd stopped in over the past two years. All the other times she'd run, she'd done it because she'd gotten jumpy, started seeing every shadow as a possible threat. But she'd never received a note until Desparre.

She'd gotten too comfortable here. She'd actually started to believe she could have some semblance of a life.

Now she was back to where she'd been two years ago. Scared and alone.

It didn't matter. All that mattered was her life, and the lives of the people she cared about. It was what the PI had drilled into her when she'd told Sabrina all the things she'd have to give up if she wanted to stay safe. Back then, even knowing how real the threat was, she'd burst into tears more than once in the days leading up to her planned disappearance, hoping the police would pull out a miracle and catch him.

After all this time, she thought she'd become more hardened. But at least now that she'd made the decision to leave, she knew she could do it.

She could go back to jumping from one town to the next, one state to the next. She could go back to the tedious waitressing jobs, the sleazy hotels. She could go back to being totally alone.

Pushing an image of Tate from her mind, Sabrina willed away the fear and the frustration as she yanked open the door and scanned the area. Then she hurried to her truck, pepper spray clutched in her free hand. She dropped the bag inside, scanned the woods and hurried back to the cabin.

She hadn't run with so many belongings since she'd first slipped out of New York, in the middle of the night. Back then, she'd done it with the help of the investigator, who'd made sure she wasn't followed.

In the time since then, she'd purged more and more of the things she'd once thought she couldn't live without. Small pieces of her past that had started to feel like too much baggage or that she could get a little money for in a pawnshop.

Was it even worth bringing her jewelry supplies? Probably not, since she doubted she'd be able to continue finding the things she needed to keep up her small online business. But maybe she could sell the last of it along the way. The past few years had shown her how expensive it could get to stay invisible.

Any reputable place wanted multiple forms of ID and a credit check to rent to you. Sabrina had a fake ID and the PI had made a fake credit history to go with it. But the woman had warned her that it was always safer not to rely on it. If someone dug deep enough, they'd figure out it wasn't real. Then she'd be in legal trouble herself.

Using her real ID or her real name meant someone could run a real credit check on her. She had no idea what resources her stalker had, but if he'd managed to get a hold of her social security number, he could track her from a simple credit check. She wasn't willing to take that risk, either.

So, she'd stuck to cheap motels that didn't care who she was. She'd stuck to sleazy employers who were happy to pay her cash under the table as long as they could pay her below minimum wage.

Only in Desparre had she dared to rent. She'd stopped

in the grocery store downtown, and Talise had immediately noticed a scared, exhausted outsider and tried to help. She'd introduced her to the only other person buying groceries at 8 p.m., an elderly man who was going to stay with his daughter in southern Alaska, probably indefinitely. He wasn't ready to give up his cabin, but he was willing to rent it cheaply. If she was willing to pay for each new month several weeks in advance, he wasn't interested in anything more than her word.

She'd felt guilty for taking him up on it, even knowing she'd never leave him in the lurch. Now she wrote his name on an envelope and stuffed enough for next month's rent in it, hoping he wasn't relying on the income. Eventually, Tate would figure out she'd gone, and word would get to Talise, who'd pass it on to the owner.

Lifting onto her shoulder her second and final bag, one filled with her clothes and a framed picture of her mom and brother, Sabrina glanced around the cabin one last time. Then she set the emergency button the police had given her on the table in the front hall. There was a lot she'd miss about Desparre, but she couldn't stay.

It was one thing to risk her own life to put an end to her running, to regain an existence beyond simple survival. She wouldn't risk Tate's.

She liked him, probably too much for the short time she'd known him. Yes, he was an armed police officer, but her stalker had already proven how dangerous he could be. No one had seen him slipping into Talise's truck on the street, shifting it partway to Reverse and then disappearing into the woods. What if, next time, he stood in those woods and used the gun he'd taken into Dylan's home? What if he aimed it at Tate and the officer never saw the threat coming?

She refused to be responsible for anyone else's death.

It was time to go.

TATE JERKED UPRIGHT in bed, slick with sweat, his heart pounding as though he was still trapped in his nightmare.

It had plagued him all night, waking him on and off and making him sleep later than usual. As he'd thrashed around in bed, he'd kept Sitka up, too. Periodically, she'd stood up in her dog bed in the corner and whined.

He'd reassure her, try to shake off the memories, then feel himself being sucked right back into the same nightmare of that fateful morning run five and a half years ago. He'd been jogging, pushing his body hard as his mind went over and over the payoff he'd witnessed, as he stressed over the upcoming arrests. Or at least those he'd assumed would be arrested. Not just a crime lord, but also three fellow cops. Officers he'd respected, officers he'd worked with, officers who'd once come to his aid.

Then the past and present had blended. In his dream, Sabrina had jogged up next to him, distracted him with her shy smile and the far-off look in her eyes. When the gunfire had started, he'd raced off the path and into the woods, trying to make himself a difficult target, just as he'd done back then. Knowing he was probably going to die, the same certainty he'd felt back in Boston. But in his nightmare, he'd been pulling a confused and terrified Sabrina with him, and instead of a group of cops trying to corner them, her stalker had stepped out of the woods in front of them.

He'd been huge, just a dark shadow among the trees, except for a wide, evil smile. Tate had lunged for Sabrina, trying to flatten her to the ground, but before he could reach her, he'd woken.

Over and over throughout the night, the same nightmare had plagued him.

Was it a premonition? The subconscious knowledge that he couldn't fully protect her?

Stalkers and abusers were some of the hardest threats

to eliminate. The law got murky, precedent not always favoring the victims, and that personality type—a man so obsessed with controlling a woman that he couldn't let go—was often willing to give up his whole life just to hurt her.

The chance that it was just driver error that had sent the vehicle racing down the street yesterday was strong. There'd been no prints besides Talise's in the car, no cameras on the street to confirm if someone else had gotten inside. So even if Tate could figure out who the stalker was, even if he *had* been responsible, Tate couldn't prove the guy had done anything with the truck.

Whether or not he'd set the vehicle in motion, Sabrina's stalker was here. He was watching her. Was Tate risking Sabrina's life even more by convincing her to stay?

The worry gnawed at him as he kicked off his covers, then stepped out of his shorts and into the shower. The heat and steam relaxed him in a way that nothing else except a good hard run could do. Five minutes later, dressed in civilian clothes since it was his day off, Tate opened the back door for Sitka.

His small house was located on the outskirts of downtown. He'd dared to buy the home, to set down roots here, because the family friend who'd created his fake name and backstory worked for Witness Protection. He hadn't created Tate's pseudonym officially. But if anyone knew how to do it right, it was a man who'd spent two decades doing it professionally.

In the years since Tate had returned to Alaska, he'd struggled with bouts of frustration and depression, especially from not being able to see his family. He could only contact them periodically, through a complicated system that would protect his safety and theirs. He'd left behind all the friends he'd made in Boston, with no notice to anyone that he was leaving. And he'd had to start over in the

Desparre PD, going through the police academy a second time, pretending to be a true rookie.

But he'd taken for granted that he was safe here in Desparre.

Sure, he'd become even more cautious, but he'd been a police officer for two years in Boston, patrolling the streets during the late-night shift. Boston's crime rate was a lot higher than Desparre's. So being safety-conscious was already a way of life. His ability to be attuned to danger was probably what had saved his life five years ago.

He'd had his moments of paranoia and fear since then, but nothing like the constant terror chasing Sabrina. She was convinced yesterday's attack had been meant for Sitka, a warning that her stalker could get to her anytime, that she shouldn't let anyone close to her.

Tate's hands fisted at how well her stalker had succeeded. He'd forced Sabrina to leave everyone she loved behind, to stay all alone for two long years. From the way she'd reacted when people had tried to talk to her in the park, he could see that she hadn't let anyone truly get close to her since leaving.

It was a common tactic of scum like domestic abusers, so why not stalkers, too? Make the target of their obsession feel vulnerable and completely alone. Make them feel that if they dared to try and get help, things would only get worse. And not just for the target but for anyone she reached out to for help or companionship.

Sabrina was going to run again.

It hit him with a certainty that stole the breath from his lungs. "Sitka," he wheezed.

His dog came running across the yard, nudging him with her nose like she knew something was wrong.

"Come on," he said, hurrying back through the house and out the front door to his truck.

She raced beside him, her head pivoted slightly toward

him like she was worried. She knew this wasn't a typical work mission.

"We need to stop Sabrina from running," he told her as he opened the door for her and she hopped into the truck, then leaped over to the passenger side.

His heart thundered as he silently berated himself for not recognizing what his subconscious had been trying to tell him all night. Was he already too late?

He took the roads fast, jaw clenched and his breathing too rapid, like he was headed to a distress call knowing before he arrived that all he'd be able to do was clean up the mess. If she'd already left, he had no idea how to even begin to search for her.

Based on what she'd told him about leaving New York, she'd done everything right. How the hell was her stalker still tracking her?

After what had almost happened to Sitka, she was unlikely to reach out to police again for help. She'd just keep hoping to outrun her stalker, to simply survive. But if he could track her here, how would she ever lose him? Eventually, a stalker this obsessed wouldn't be content with simply watching and leaving notes. Eventually, he'd try to make her his own. And when that inevitably failed, he'd kill her.

A sharp pain sliced through Tate's chest, and he hit the gas harder, making Sitka give a sharp bark as she hunkered low on the seat.

"Sorry, Sitka." She was used to fast driving in the police SUV, but that was better designed for her than the front seat of his truck.

He raced up the dirt road leading to Sabrina's house, and then his heart gave a little kick when he spotted taillights in her drive. Sabrina? Or someone else?

He didn't slow until he'd swung into the driveway, effectively blocking whoever was in that vehicle from escaping. Then, he hit the brakes hard, apologizing to Sitka as she yelped and righted herself again.

The brake lights on the old truck in the drive flashed and then stayed lit for a long moment, until the car turned off and Sabrina stepped out.

She crossed her arms over her chest, glancing repeatedly at the woods as she approached. When he rolled down the window, she demanded, "What are you doing?"

"What are *you* doing?" he shot back. "We agreed that the Desparre PD would help you, Sabrina. No more running. So why are you sneaking away without even a goodbye?"

As the angry words burst from his mouth, he realized how much the idea hurt. They barely knew each other, but he'd felt an instant connection. He admired her strength and determination, the way she was willing to make sacrifices to keep the people she loved safe. He liked the way her eyes lit up when she gave him a real smile, the silly jokes she made about Sitka patrolling. He liked *her* and the idea of her not being in Desparre just felt wrong.

She frowned back at him, then her gaze darted briefly to Sitka, before returning to his. "It's one thing for me to make a stand and try to put an end to what's happening to me. I've lived with this threat for a long time, and I'm willing to take that risk to get my life back. And believe me, I want the help. But this is my fight. And now it seems like he's targeted Sitka. I'm not going to let anyone else get hurt because of me."

"We're trained for this," he insisted, trying to push his personal feelings to the background. "This threat is never going to just go away. We have to stop it."

She seemed to pale at his words, but her jaw clamped down, and she shook her head again.

Turning off his engine, he stepped out beside her. Before he could shut the door, Sitka was out, too, sitting next to Sabrina and looking up at her as if to say *I'm off duty. Pet me, please.*

A ghost of a smile flitted across Sabrina's face as she complied.

"Sabrina."

When she met his gaze again, fear and determination there, he said, "You don't want to spend your life running from this threat. I'm not going to let you do that. We're going to eliminate it."

He tried to infuse his words with certainty. It was his duty to protect her, to help her feel safe again, so she could finally regain her life fully, something he'd probably never have himself.

He couldn't stop himself from reaching out and taking her hand in his, couldn't help himself from wanting to step a little closer, to wrap his arms around her.

Duty was only part of it, he realized. He was falling for Sabrina Jones...if that was even her real name. He didn't want to lose her.

She stared up at him, warring emotions on her face, until finally she nodded. "Okay, I'll stay. Just promise me that you're all going to be careful. If this guy turns his focus on you and Sitka and you can't find him, I want you to be honest with me. I want you to tell me, so I can make my own decision about whether to stay or go."

He nodded, not breaking eye contact. "I promise."

But he knew it wasn't a promise he could keep. This wasn't a fight he was letting her take on alone anymore.

One way or another, they were going to end this here.

Chapter Seven

"Are you sure about this?" Sabrina asked as she let him into her cabin.

In response, he picked up the emergency button she'd left on the front-hall table and slipped it over her head.

She tried not to visibly react as his hands skimmed her neck, lifting her hair out of the way so the thin chain could lie underneath. But even after he removed his hands, his touch lingered, making her neck tingle.

The scent of sandalwood—his aftershave maybe—drifted toward her, intoxicating. This close, she saw how purely deep brown his eyes were, no variation to distract from the intensity of his gaze. Her breath caught, and the tingling in her neck spread down her arms and across her back.

His gaze lingered on hers, and the desire she felt was reflected back at her, beneath a layer of anxiety and concern. The corners of his lips tipped up slightly, making her want to step forward, lean into him and see what happened.

Then Sitka stepped between them, tail wagging, and broke the spell.

Sabrina laughed, releasing some of the tension both from the situation and her proximity to Tate. She leaned down and pet Sitka, giving her pulse a chance to calm.

Then she straightened and asked, "If you're sure this

is the right move, how do we find him? And are you sure you should even be here right now?" Her gaze dropped to Sitka, then rose to Tate. "I'm pretty sure he targeted Sitka because he saw you here."

Because he thinks you could be important to me, Sabrina didn't add. *The problem is, he could be right.*

A pair of vertical grooves appeared between Tate's eyebrows, marring his perfectly smooth skin. He nodded slowly. "I still think this could have been a badly timed accident. But if it wasn't, then yeah, that makes sense. Anyone who might be an ally to you, anyone who might be a friend, he sees as a threat. Competition."

Competition. Sabrina couldn't help her indignant snort, but it quickly turned into a familiar angry frustration. She'd spent two years as the object of some man's unrequited obsession, and he thought it was his right to destroy everything in her life so he could have her for himself.

"I know," Tate said softly, as if he could read her mind. "It's unfair."

Unfair was too simple a word for this. It was more than just unfair that she'd been forced to give up seeing her family and friends again, possibly for the rest of her life. That she had to take low-key jobs so she could stay below the radar. That she never felt truly safe, all because some man she might never have even spoken to thought his right to want her was greater than her right to live the life she wanted.

"Tell me," Tate said softly, compassion in his eyes. "Tell me what you're thinking."

"I just…" She sighed, looked away. She'd grown up with a strong single mom who'd worked hard to raise her and her younger brother. A mom who'd never sugarcoated the dangers women faced in the world or the inequities. Still, she'd always felt loved, supported, protected, *safe*.

Until her stalker had shown up. He was someone she

might have smiled at once politely. Someone she might have had a brief conversation with at a kiosk or never spoken to at all. Someone who lived in the shadows because he was too much of a coward to tell her who he really was.

She didn't realize she'd clenched her hands into tight fists until Tate's hands were over hers, loosening them. Shifting her gaze back to him, she pulled her hands free and missed the contact immediately. "Police in New York said my stalker probably wasn't anyone identifiable in my life. They think he was somewhere on the outskirts, that I might not even recognize him at all when—if—they finally figured out who it was. But *he* has some kind of fantasy where he's essential in my life, and *I* have to live with that."

Breathing through the tears that wanted to rush forward, Sabrina said bitterly, "I can't even use my real name."

"Your name isn't Sabrina?" Tate asked softly, not sounding particularly surprised.

"It is Sabrina." The way he said her name made her suddenly glad she'd only changed her last name. She'd done it because the PI thought keeping the same first name would be easier to remember and respond to. Over the years, she'd had moments where it had felt like the only thing left in her life that was still *her*. "But it's not Jones."

His eyes narrowed slightly, and she could see him debating whether to ask what her real last name was.

"Don't," she told him. "It's better if you don't know."

He continued to stare back at her, like he might argue, until Sitka stood, spun in a quick circle and barked.

Sabrina laughed, and a grin broke out on Tate's face. "You're right, Sitka," he told her. "Maybe we should go sit down."

Realizing she'd kept him standing in the entryway a long time, Sabrina felt her cheeks heat. She turned into the house, leading him toward the living room where they'd sat before. Even though she was all packed up to disappear, the house looked mostly the same.

Seeing how small an impact she'd had on the space in the six months she'd lived here was slightly depressing, but it was less depressing than the series of dingy hotels she'd called home before this.

Glancing around as he chose the same side of the couch he'd sat on before, Tate asked, "You want me to help you bring your stuff back in?"

Shaking her head, Sabrina sank onto the other side of the couch. Her gaze was immediately drawn into the woods. But the view that had inspired so much of her creativity now made her shiver. Was her stalker outside right this moment, seeing that his attack hadn't scared away Tate and Sitka? Was he already planning a new way to permanently remove them from her life?

Anxiety bubbled up, the certainty that she'd made a mistake letting Tate block her in. "I—"

"Don't," Tate said.

Woof! Sitka contributed, either picking up on Tate's tone or stating her own agreement. She pushed her way between Tate and the coffee table and sat in the space between them, her brown eyes intent on Sabrina.

"I feel selfish staying," she admitted softly.

"That's ridiculous." He shifted on the couch, one knee up so he was facing her. "I'm a police officer. Believe me, I've faced worse threats."

He said it like he was speaking about something specific. Sabrina couldn't help the shiver that went through her, imagining him in danger. But in law enforcement, it was part of the job.

When he'd first promised to help her get free of this threat, she'd immediately seen all the possibilities open up in her life again—possibilities like asking him on a date. But she was wrung out from two years of impending danger. How would she handle being in a relationship with a man who went to work each day anticipating danger?

"Running forever isn't the worst thing," Sabrina told him. Having police show up at Dylan's family's lake house, hearing the news that he'd been shot inside his home and then getting the note a few days later? That was the worst thing.

"No," he agreed. "But that's not your fate, Sabrina. So let's talk through some things, see if we can figure out how he found you here."

She couldn't stop herself from glancing out the window again, into the vast woods. She didn't think she'd ever see them the same way again.

"You said you haven't spoken to your family in two years, so I assume you've had no contact with anyone else, either, right? Not even this PI who helped you disappear?"

She shook her head. "No. I check her website every once in a while, to see if the New York police caught my stalker. She's supposed to leave a coded message there if it happens. In the first few months, I checked it a lot. Now I look once every month or two." Was there some way to look at her site and see where people accessed it from? "You don't think he's somehow tracking me from that, do you?"

"No. What about jobs, hobbies?"

Sabrina sighed, shook her head. "The PI I hired was good. And expensive. She worked with a skip tracer to help me disappear. What it boiled down to was basically that I needed to change everything about my life to stay safe."

Something flickered in his eyes at her words, something more than sympathy.

"Back in New York, I was a fashion designer. Accessories," she added, when he looked surprised. "Here, I've been selling jewelry I make over an e-commerce site. It's the closest I've come to normal, but it's a pretty different field."

"What did you do in all the places you lived in between?"

"Waitressing. I picked cheap diners or places near highways that were open all night and catered to truckers. Places that didn't want an employment check or actual ID."

His lips tightened into an angry line. "Places where they could pay you under the table in cash, which means they didn't bother giving you a living wage."

"Yeah," she agreed. "But I could manage on the money." Anxiety twisted in her belly, remembering what had made that year and a half before Desparre so unbearable. "It was the other threats."

The anger on Tate's face shifted into a deeper fury. "From the people working at these places? Because they saw you as part of a vulnerable population, someone with no real ID who wouldn't dare go to the police about anything illegal?"

"Sometimes," she agreed, because at almost every place she'd worked, dodging someone's hands as she served food had started to feel normal. "Sometimes it was the customers, because these places weren't exactly in the safest areas. And I'd take any shift I could get, which usually meant nights."

Her mouth suddenly went dry, thinking of all those nights rushing to her crappy car after a shift, usually in a parking lot where they didn't care about safety lighting. More than once, she'd used pepper spray on a customer who'd tried to corner her, even one who'd tried to drag her into his long-haul truck.

That had been one of the scariest moments of her life, second only to the moment she'd realized Dylan's death was because of her. She'd been exhausted after a long shift and fitting the key in the twenty-year-old junker she'd been driving in Iowa when goose bumps had erupted across her neck. She'd already had her pepper spray out because she'd learned the hard way that she needed it. As she'd spun around, lifting that spray, fear had exploded. The guy was huge, well over six feet and at least twice her weight. It might not have all been muscle, but it didn't matter. She'd barely started to depress the trigger on her pepper spray before he swatted the canister away like he was swatting a fly.

She'd choked on the fumes, but he'd just coughed and slapped a hand over her mouth, as if there was anyone around to hear her scream or care if they had. His other arm had yanked her flush against him, shoving her face into his sweat-stained T-shirt. It had been hard to breathe as he'd dragged her, ignoring the fists she'd slammed into his arms and the one solid kick she'd gotten to his knee, like he barely felt them.

He'd loosened his grip slightly to open the door of his truck, and she'd wrenched herself away, simultaneously flinging a desperate punch. She'd gotten lucky as he'd twisted back toward her and her punch had landed right on his prominent Adam's apple. He'd gagged and she'd run.

She'd gotten in her car and raced out of that town, out of Iowa. She'd never had such a close call again, but it had been a tough reminder: her stalker wasn't the only threat out there.

"I've been careful," she told Tate, trying to shake off the remnants of that memory. "He shouldn't have been able to track me here. I've changed cars. I've lived in eight different states before coming to Alaska."

Frustration bubbled up, stronger than it had been in a long time, because she'd actually started to hope again. "So how the hell did he find me here?"

TATE RAN UP the hill outside Desparre's downtown at a punishing pace, let the steady rhythm of his pounding feet calm his fury.

Sabrina had almost left. If he'd been seconds later, she'd have been gone, and he wouldn't have been able to find her.

The idea hurt a lot more than it should have and Tate

tried not to focus on why. Because right now, his feelings for her didn't matter. Only her safety did.

Gritting his teeth, he pushed himself harder, his chest heaving as he finally crested the hill. He was alone, having dropped Sitka off at home after they'd left Sabrina's cabin. Sitka liked to run with him, but when he was in this kind of mood, he never brought her along. There was no reason to punish her for his bad mood.

Bending over, Tate rested his palms on his knees as his heart rate slowed. Then he straightened and peered over the edge of the hill. If downtown Desparre was sleepy, the outskirts were damn near comatose. There were lots of places to get lost in nature. A boon for locals who knew the area and the safety precautions. Not so great for unprepared tourists looking for adventure. Or for a cop who'd been ambushed on a quiet trail.

These days, though, he didn't constantly scan his surroundings on his run. The impulse was still there, but he tried to resist. It was a slippery slope from appropriate caution to paranoia.

When Sabrina had shared some of her experience, he'd wanted to open up about his own. He'd wanted to tell her he knew exactly what it was like to have someone come after you. Sure, the reasons and methods were different. The outcome, too. But the terror of that moment in the park would never fully go away. The nightmare he'd had last night was rare, but the fear was always in the back of his mind.

One of the officers who'd tried to kill him was in prison. The moron had actually used his police-issued weapon to shoot Tate, so when the bullet had been dug out of Tate's arm, that had cinched Officer Jim Bellows's fate. But the other two had gotten off. Not enough evidence, the jury had ruled. Not enough evidence that they'd participated in the payoff, and not enough evidence that they'd participated in the attempt on Tate's life.

Tate had only seen Jim in the park. But Jim wasn't the only officer there, Tate was sure. Jim must have brought his two closest friends on the force, Paul Martin and Kevin Fricker. Tate had seen all three take the payoff, but financial forensics had only found a large deposit to Jim Bellows.

It was no surprise that the other two had used throwaway weapons or that they'd hidden the money better. Jim had always been a liability, constantly on the verge of an Internal Affairs investigation for one reason or another. Usually his inability to curb his drinking, since he'd shown up intoxicated at work a few times.

Kevin and Paul were smarter, more cautious. It had turned out they were just as crooked.

Still, Kevin and Paul had managed to stay on the force, at least for a time. But Tate's accusations had stained their reputations, as well as his own. The rest of the officers hadn't known who to believe, or who to trust. Eventually, Kevin and Paul had left—and so had Tate.

The court had decided Kevin and Paul hadn't been involved. The feds decided they weren't an ongoing threat. But Tate knew otherwise. The last thing Kevin had whispered as he'd walked past Tate on his final day at the police station had been "Jim was my best friend, and you destroyed his life. Watch your back. One day, we might just destroy yours."

Tate hadn't bothered to tell the FBI about the threat. The case had been closed. And a vague threat wasn't enough to reopen anything.

Instead, he'd contacted an old family friend and asked what it would take to disappear. Until that moment, he'd expected to stay in Boston. Even though the other officers hadn't gone to jail, the fact that he'd accused them would make them immediate suspects if any harm came to him. But the look in Kevin's eyes had told Tate he wasn't the only one in danger.

Now, staring down into the town he'd grown to love so much, the town that sometimes made him wonder why he'd ever left Alaska in the first place, Tate wished he'd seen it coming. Some of the signs were there, but until he'd stumbled onto the three cops taking a payoff, he never would have guessed it was happening.

Before the incident, Jim Bellows had seemed like a time bomb. Kevin and Paul had seemed more even-keeled, more professional. They were partners and had actually come to Tate's aid on a dangerous call once. Still, he'd always seen something volatile in them, something vague that made him intuitively understand why they'd befriended Jim.

One of the lieutenants used to call Paul *Napoleon* because he made up for being five foot six by lifting weights until he resembled a tank. The officer had always loved to intimidate with his size. Kevin, who looked a solid decade younger than his thirty-nine years, used the fact that he *wasn't* particularly intimidating—even at six foot four—to get close to someone. Then he'd bring the hurt.

Both tactics were fine, in the appropriate situation. But Tate preferred to stick to tactics that didn't have an undercurrent of bullying.

He hadn't destroyed their careers fully. Both had gone on to other departments in other cities. But he doubted he'd happened to catch them taking their first payoff. What he probably *had* destroyed was their illegal-income source. And that day, Tate had known they'd never forgive him for that. Or for putting Jim behind bars.

So, when his family friend had said he could do unofficially for Tate what he'd done for years for federal witnesses—only to a lesser degree, giving Tate some contact with his family—he'd jumped on it. Better to start over than to constantly live in fear. Especially if that fear was for more than just himself.

In the years since, he'd kept tabs on Kevin and Paul, expecting one day their illegal activities would catch up to them. But they were both still police officers, both still a potential threat. He'd finally accepted that this was his life now and allowed himself to embrace it.

He would probably never go home again. But he was going to make sure that wasn't Sabrina's fate.

paying

Chapter Eight

Someone was staring at her.

Sabrina's breathing became shallow as the certainty washed over her. She glanced around the little downtown, trying to be subtle but feeling obvious as her gaze lingered on any man she didn't recognize as a longtime Desparre resident.

Maybe she just sensed the police watching her.

Tate had told her that the police wanted her to act normal, try to get out and engage with people. She was supposed to notify them whenever she went anywhere, so they could watch from a distance. They figured that's what her stalker was doing, so they would look for anyone paying her too much attention.

As she glanced around, Officer Lorenzo Riera nodded briefly at her. It evened out her breathing, made her shoulders relax from where they'd crept up her neck. If she couldn't have Tate watching over her—she knew he was off duty today—having the serious veteran officer keep watch was a close second.

Walking from where she'd parked near the grocery store toward the park felt strange today. She'd done this walk many times, but somehow, even after doing it just once with Tate and Sitka, it felt unnatural not to have them at her side.

Every step felt stiff, and the swing of her arms that was

meant to look casual seemed awkward. No matter how many times she told herself not to make it obvious she was watching for someone, she couldn't stop herself from scanning the area.

A tall man with dark hair and a terrible mustache stood up the hill, near a vehicle that was parked close to where Talise's truck had been yesterday. He met her gaze and gave her a brief nod the same way Officer Riera had done. But this man wasn't a cop.

She didn't know him. The way he immediately averted his gaze after that nod made her shoulders tense up again. Was the bad mustache a disguise? She didn't recognize him from around town, but then again, she didn't know everyone.

Her gaze went back to the officer, to see if he'd noticed, but his expression was even. He didn't even seem to be paying attention to her as he meandered across the street, stopping to chat with people along the way.

She tried to will Officer Riera to look her way as the mustached man got into a light-colored sedan, but the officer still wasn't watching. So, she picked up her pace, hoping to get a license-plate number. As the vehicle pulled onto the street quickly enough to make the tires squeal, she saw that the plate was caked over with mud.

Frustrated, she glanced back at the officer again.

This time, he looked in her general direction, his gaze sweeping over and past her. As he continued walking, he shook his head.

Did that mean he knew the man? Was she being paranoid? Seeing every man as a threat now?

She reached for her phone to text the officer, to make sure he'd seen what she had.

"Sabrina!"

She jumped at the sound of her name, almost dropping her phone as her hand jerked automatically toward her purse, where she still kept a canister of pepper spray.

When her gaze swung toward the park, she saw Lora Perkins and Adam Lassiter waving. Lora was frowning, like she knew something was wrong, and Adam seemed like he was faking enthusiasm at seeing her.

After Talise, they were some of the people she knew best in Desparre. So, she tucked her phone away and pasted on a smile she could feel quivering as she walked toward them.

"Are you okay?" Lora asked, putting a hand on her arm when she reached them. "We heard about the truck almost hitting you yesterday."

Sabrina nodded. "Yeah. The police think it was a freak accident." It was what they'd said to tell anyone who asked about it, just in case her stalker had been responsible. They wanted him to feel like he'd gotten away with it, so he'd be more confident continuing to follow her. Talise had been asked to play along, pretend she couldn't believe she'd forgotten to engage her parking brake. Police hadn't given her specifics on why, just that they thought the ploy would help draw out the person responsible.

Lora's frown deepened, the perfectly smooth, pale skin on her forehead furrowing as if she could tell Sabrina was lying.

Lora was only a few years older than Sabrina, but from the moment they'd met, she'd mothered Sabrina. She'd even commented on it once, laughingly telling Sabrina she knew she was doing it, but that she couldn't help it. She'd grown up in the mountains of Desparre, with drug-addicted parents and three younger siblings who needed to be fed and cared for. They were all adults now, all successful and married and living far away from the town where they'd grown up. While Lora claimed she couldn't bring herself to have kids and spend the rest of her life the way she'd spent her childhood—looking after others—she couldn't seem to stop herself from doing it with everyone she met.

"Are you sure?" Adam asked.

Sabrina's gaze shifted to him. He, too, was a few years older than her. He was newer to Desparre than she was and knew even fewer people. He probably never would have spoken to her or anyone else if Lora hadn't pressured him to do it. Once you befriended Lora, it was hard to say no to her good-natured attempts to help.

He didn't seem particularly suspicious of her lie, but it was hard to tell beneath the look of despair and grief that was always on his face. His wife had died a few months earlier, and he'd left behind their home on the other side of Alaska for some peace and quiet here.

She shrugged, trying to sound flippant. "Yeah, what else would it be? It was scary, but trust me, Talise will never forget to put her parking brake on again!"

Adam nodded, his gaze drifting to the other side of the park, where a group of kids were playing. But Lora still looked suspicious.

Sabrina averted her gaze, and her attention caught on a man standing by the park gazebo. He was lowering his phone like he'd had it up to take a picture, and his gaze locked on hers, lingering for a moment before he turned and walked out of the park.

Her breath caught. Something about his build and his walk was familiar. From seeing him around town? Or from back in New York?

"Sabrina." Lora squeezed her arm. "Are you sure you're okay? You seem really spooked."

Ripping her gaze away and hoping Officer Riera was paying attention, Sabrina tried for a smile. Because it shook way too much to be believable, she admitted, "I guess yesterday scared me more than I realized. I keep thinking a car is going to come at me out of nowhere."

She tried for a laugh and was amazed when it came out self-deprecating but real. "I think I'm going to head home and relax for a while."

"That's probably a good idea," Lora said.

"Let us know if you need anything," Adam added.

The look on his face—like he'd finally lifted out of his own grief enough to see something around him was wrong—told her this wasn't working at all.

She needed to get it together. Because the best way to find her stalker was to give him a chance to watch her. And give the police a chance to spot him doing it.

The way things were going, she was more likely to alert him to the fact that police were watching. And if he knew that, would he leave? And leave her in a perpetual state of limbo?

Or would he make one last bold move and kill *her* this time?

TATE STARED AT the picture of Dylan Westwood on his computer screen. This was Sabrina's old boyfriend. It had to be.

Leaning back in his chair in the second bedroom he used as a home office, Tate studied the man Sabrina had been dating two years ago. He'd woken early to do some digging into Sabrina's life, but he only had another hour and a half until he needed to be at work.

The photo someone had chosen to accompany Dylan's obituary showed him grinning, amusement clear in his dark blue eyes. According to the obit, the twenty-eight-year-old marketing associate at a record label had been survived by both parents and four younger siblings.

Tate had found the obituary from cross-referencing an article about Dylan's murder from New York two years ago. He'd found *that* article by searching for information about a murder in that time frame that mentioned a stalker. Dylan had been shot in his own home and the story said police believed his girlfriend's stalker had murdered him. They were asking anyone who had information to come forward.

Sabrina Jones's real name was Sabrina Reilly.

Tate tried the name out on his lips. Something about it matched her more than Jones. But Jones was a smart choice for going on the run, since it was one of the most popular last names in the US. If she ever ran into trouble with her fake ID, it might have been easily explained away as a mix-up with some other Sabrina Jones.

Pulling up a couple of social-media sites, Tate typed in *Sabrina Reilly* and searched through the possible matches. He found her on the third site. Her account was set to private, but there were certain things he could still see, including her profile picture, which told him he'd found the right Sabrina. In the picture, her head was thrown back, and she was laughing. Her hair was shorter, still with those natural waves. Her dress was more trendy, less practical than what she wore in Alaska. But mostly, she looked the same—minus the haunted look in her eyes.

Scrolling through the posts that weren't hidden from view, including pictures she'd been tagged in—all from over two years ago—Tate searched for anything or anyone that seemed out of place. But all of the comments seemed to be from friends, and even meticulously cross-checking each of the people who'd liked her photos didn't reveal anything that stood out as odd.

So, he went deeper, checking each of the friends in those photos, until he found a few who had their profiles set to public. He dug into their older pictures, too, looking for anywhere Sabrina was not tagged or in the background, searching for anyone who commented or liked too many of them. Still nothing.

With a frustrated sigh, he kept going, finding other people with the last name Reilly, until he came across one who had to be her older brother. Conor Reilly. He was a stockbroker with a long-term girlfriend and a love of baseball. Two years ago, his posts had suddenly become public. On some of his early posts, there were multiple comments asking about his sister, all of which he'd ignored.

Tate dug into each of the people who'd asked about her, but none seemed likely to be her stalker. They all seemed far too embedded in the Reillys' lives. And Tate agreed with the New York police: the person stalking Sabrina had to be on the outskirts of her life. If he was too close to her, she would have noticed that he paid her too much attention or that he acted extra awkward, nervous, angry or overly emotional around her.

Leaning back in his chair, Tate frowned at the screen. He felt a hint of guilt at digging into Sabrina's personal life without her permission, but if this led to a promising lead, it would be worth it. He'd learned early as a cop that people put way more of themselves online than they realized. And a lot more of it was discoverable by strangers than they probably wanted.

The missing piece he needed might still be here, somewhere, tangled in a web of loose social connections. He'd keep picking at it when he could, but for now, it confirmed what the Desparre PD had decided from the outset: the key to finding Sabrina's stalker would be tracking him here. Not trying to dig him out of her past.

Woof!

Startled, Tate glanced over and realized Sitka was standing in the doorway. "What is it, Sitka?"

She took a step forward and barked again.

Tate frowned at her, knowing she wanted his attention but not sure why. He glanced at his watch, realizing that he'd lost track of time while he'd been searching. He needed to hurry and get ready for work. Jumping to his feet, he said, "Thanks, Sitka." Then he heard the sound of a car engine starting up.

She hadn't been trying to tell him they were running late for work. She'd been alerting him that someone was here.

Hurrying down the stairs, Tate peered through his peephole out to his drive. The area around his house was partly obscured by woods, but he didn't see anyone. The car was gone. Except... He squinted at his front stoop, where something had been left.

Sabrina's stalker had obviously identified him and Sitka as allies of Sabrina. Even if he'd figured out where Tate lived, would he dare to come here?

Thinking of the description of Dylan's death from one of the articles about the unsolved murder, Tate ran upstairs, where he kept his gun locked up. Less than a minute later, he was back downstairs, phrases from the article floating through his brain.

...shot in his own home...house ransacked...only suspect is an unidentified person stalking his girlfriend.

Compared to the fingerprint-free notes the stalker left Sabrina, Dylan's murder seemed uncontrolled, full of rage.

"Sitka, move over here," Tate instructed, pointing back toward his kitchen, away from the front door.

She followed his instructions, backing quickly into the kitchen. But she was looking at him like she didn't understand. They weren't working; they were at home. Home was safe and fun.

He didn't think anyone was out there, but he didn't want to take any chances if the stalker had left some kind of explosive device or wanted to lure him closer.

Peering through the door once more, Tate tried to identify the object, but it was right up against the door, mostly out of view. Instead of opening his front door, he told Sitka, "Stay," then ran around to his attached garage at the side and slipped out that way. He didn't see anyone skulking near his house, but then, he'd heard a vehicle drive away.

So most likely, the person had dropped something at the door, then run.

Locking the door leading out of his garage behind him so no one could slip inside while he was investigating, Tate did one more sweep of the area. Then, gun raised, he crept toward the front of his house. He forced his breathing to stay deep and even, the way he would on a run. Years as a police officer helped prevent his senses from dimming into a dangerous tunnel as he scanned his surroundings. Not having a partner at his side made him extra aware of every twig breaking beneath his feet, telegraphing exactly where he was and where he was going.

When he reached the front of his house, he blew out a surprised breath. The item leaning against his front door was a newspaper. Still not putting his weapon away, he moved closer, studying it carefully as he approached. It wasn't a copy of some New York paper like he might have expected if Sabrina's stalker wanted to send him a message, but the *Desparre Daily*.

As he reached the porch, he was sure it wasn't rigged. There was just a sticky note on it that read, *Thought you'd enjoy this!* It was signed by Ariel Clemson, a local reporter he'd helped out once.

Tucking his gun into the waistband of his pajama pants, Tate picked it up and unrolled it. His heart gave a hard thump as he read the headline: *Woman Rescues Police K-9 from Runaway Truck.*

He swore as he stared at the picture underneath the headline. The photo was grainy, taken from way down the street at an awkward angle, but there was Sabrina frantically trying to free Sitka as the truck barreled toward them. And in the background there was Tate racing to help.

Dread sank from his chest, settling low in his gut. The *Desparre Daily* was a tiny local paper, with such low distribution that they were constantly in danger of folding. But they had an online presence.

Were the officers who wanted revenge on him actively searching for him the way he'd been searching for Sabrina's stalker? Would they find this photo and consequently find him?

He flashed back to the warning from his friend who handled Witness Protection relocations: "If we think someone has been exposed, we don't wait and hope. We get them out and start over somewhere else. New name, new backstory and no contact with their last life. I recommend you follow the same protocol."

The dread he felt expanded outward. After promising Sabrina that he'd help her get her life back, would he have to desert her to save his own life?

Chapter Nine

As he came back inside his house, Tate was swearing enough to make Sitka stare up at him with concern.

He dropped to his knees in front of her and rested his head on top of hers. Although he'd adopted her and covered her everyday costs, the Desparre PD had paid thousands of dollars for their K-9 training. If he had to leave, they'd probably expect to keep her.

"What am I going to do, Sitka?" he asked softly.

She whined in response, then gave him a sloppy kiss across his chin.

The idea of leaving her behind made his chest tighten painfully. But if he took her with him, would the Desparre PD search for them? Since the safest option would be to leave without any notice or explanation, they probably would. He'd be a lot easier to track with an Alaskan Malamute at his side. Plus, if he was in danger, bringing her along would put her in danger, too.

She might be better off staying here, being placed with another officer. But Tate wasn't sure if anyone else at the station would want to become a K-9 handler. Even if they did, he doubted the station could afford more training. That meant Sitka might be paired with someone who didn't know what they were doing, who inadvertently put her in danger anyway.

He swore again, the anxiety in his gut and chest expanding as his head started to throb. Maybe he'd been a fool to get so comfortable here, to make connections that he'd ultimately have to leave. Maybe Sabrina had the right idea, trying not to get close to anyone.

Squeezing his eyes shut, Tate continued resting his head on Sitka's until she let out another whine. Knowing he was worrying her, Tate lifted his head and stroked her fur until it helped relax him enough to think clearly.

Maybe his old police chief would have an idea. Although he and Keara Hernandez had rarely talked about his past, there had been comfort in knowing he *could* go to her if the burden of his past started to impact his present.

He grabbed his cell phone off the kitchen table, then cringed as he glanced at the time while he made the call. He'd have to hurry if he wanted to be on time for work. But should he even go?

When Keara answered, Tate replied, "Hi, Keara." He cringed at the anxiety in his voice.

"What's going on?"

Trust his old police chief to get right to the point. She'd always been that way, and he was happy to see that trading in her job as police chief in tiny Desparre for a detective job in Anchorage hadn't changed her.

"I think I might have been exposed." He told her about the article.

There was a slight pause, then she asked, "How clear are you in this picture? How much detail does it give about you?"

"I'm in the background. The image is a little blurry, but my face is recognizable. And I'm named in the article—by my fake name, of course. The focus is on Sabrina and how she rescued Sitka. It's a feel-good kind of story."

"Sitka? Really? That's what you named your pup?" Keara demanded to know.

"Yeah."

"Well, I was about to say that the risk was minuscule, but that just increased it a little."

"Because someone searching for the name Tate Donnoly—" his real name "—might think to search with Sitka, Alaska," Tate realized.

"Exactly," Keara affirmed.

He'd chosen the dog's name because it had felt like a way to hold on to some small piece of his past, the place where he'd spent his childhood. It had felt like an inside joke no one knew but him. Now it just seemed reckless.

"Did your old colleagues know you grew up there?"

"I didn't talk to those guys much. But it probably wouldn't be hard to figure out if they asked around."

Keara sighed. "It's still probably a low risk level. I'm sure these guys know you disappeared. How likely would it be for you to get another job as a police officer under an assumed name? But if you want to feel totally safe…"

"I know. But I have a life here."

"I'm sorry I'm not there to help," Keara said.

Tate smiled. "I'm not. I can tell you're enjoying being a detective again. Plus, being in Anchorage must be better than a long-distance relationship." Her boyfriend, Jax, was a Victim Specialist for the FBI in Anchorage.

"Well, there's that," Keara said, and the tone of her voice told him what was coming before she announced, "We got engaged last weekend."

"Congratulations, Keara. That's great." He tried to sound enthusiastic, because he *was* happy for her. If anyone deserved it, it was his old chief, who'd come to Alaska to escape memories of her husband's murder. But he couldn't help the tinge of jealousy that came with it. Would he ever be in a place where he'd feel safe enough to let someone in his life that way?

"Look," Keara said, her voice back to serious. "It's pretty

unlikely those officers would dig this article up. But there's
no guarantee. If it was me, I'd be cautiously patient. But,
Tate, you need to get ready to run. I can try to help you.
Jax isn't an investigator, but maybe he can talk to his colleagues at the FBI, help you disappear."

"No," Tate said. Right now, he was using a name ille-
gally. He was acting as a police officer under a false name,
too, and if it ever came out that Keara had known it, he
wouldn't be the only one facing legal action. "If I need to
disappear again, I'll do it alone."

There was another pause, and Tate knew that even
though Keara would risk her own life to help him, she had
to be relieved he wouldn't ask her to do it. "Keep me informed, if you can."

"I will."

"And, Tate? Watch your back, okay?"

"Yeah," he agreed, saying goodbye. He hoped it wasn't
the last time he'd talk to her.

He hoped this newspaper article wasn't the beginning
of the end of his time as Tate Emory.

SABRINA STARED AT the headline of the *Desparre Daily* that
Adam Lassiter handed her when she ran into him later that
afternoon at the grocery store, dread clenching her chest.

"You're a hero," Adam said, looking surprised that she
wasn't excited. "You rescued a K-9."

She offered a wan smile, then glanced at the article. It
was written by Ariel Clemson, the woman who'd shown
up on her doorstep the other day. Apparently, she'd decided
she didn't need Sabrina's input to tell the story.

As she stared at the slightly blurry photo, she remembered a woman standing off in the distance that day, snapping pictures after Sabrina had jumped out of the way of
the truck. At the time, she'd thought the woman had simply

been a gawker. She'd turned her head, hoping the images wouldn't be plastered on social media.

Looking at Adam, she asked, "How many people get this paper?"

He shrugged, reminding her that he hadn't lived here all that long. "I have no idea. I doubt very many. I mean, I came to Desparre because I figured I was more likely to run into a moose than another person most days." He flushed, then added, "Not that I mind talking to you. I just—"

"I understand," Sabrina said softly. She hadn't shared with anyone that she'd come here after losing a boyfriend to violence, but she'd been tempted to share a sanitized version with Adam because he was clearly so lost since his wife's death a few months earlier.

"Yeah." Adam looked away, probably thinking she was just trying to be supportive. "Well, anyway, I thought you might want the paper. I already bought it." He hefted his bags of groceries, then nodded goodbye.

After he was gone, Sabrina read the article more closely. It was heavy on drama, a firsthand report of watching the vehicle slide out of control. It detailed Sabrina's "heroic" determination to free the town's new police K-9, a dog Ariel described as "a town treasure."

Sabrina's amusement faded as she got to the section that described the incident as "suspicious," saying police were investigating the possibility that it had been targeted. Ariel hadn't mentioned *who* police thought the attack had targeted, however.

"Sabrina!"

Her head jerked up at the sound of her name, and she tried to smile as Lora hurried toward her.

"I see you read the paper!"

"Yeah." Sabrina folded it into her purse to look at more closely later. "How many people see this paper?"

Lora laughed, a rich, hearty sound that sounded like it

belonged to a much bigger woman than the barely five-foot-tall Lora. "I never took you for a fame hound! Sorry to say, not very many. I think our population is *maybe* five hundred. And that's including all the recluses up the mountain who avoid everyone and I doubt are keeping up with local news. But it is online."

Online. Of course it was. Sabrina gritted her teeth to keep from swearing.

"What's wrong? You don't like the fame?" Realization washed over Lora's face, and she lowered her voice. "You're running from something, aren't you, honey? I should have realized. So many of the people in this town are."

She put a hand on Sabrina's upper arm and squeezed lightly. "Don't worry. The *Desparre Daily* website is poorly run. It goes down at least once a month, and you'd really have to search hard to find it. Besides, I'm guessing *Sabrina Jones* isn't your real name?"

Sabrina shrugged, not wanting to lie to one of the few people she'd dared to call a friend since going on the run. But she wasn't about to tell her the truth, either.

Lora squeezed her arm again. "This is a pretty remote spot. Someone would have to be *really* determined to track you down here."

Sabrina mustered up another smile, and this one must have been more convincing, because Lora smiled.

Patting her arm once more, she said, "Try not to worry. No one's going to use that tiny little article to track you down."

Sabrina hoped it was true. Because her stalker might have already found her, but he wasn't the only one she wanted to stay hidden from.

Her family loved her. They hadn't wanted her to go. She'd bet a lot of money that both Conor and her mom searched for her still. And she didn't want them to find her, didn't want them to be in any danger like Dylan. If they did, it would defeat most of the purpose of her leaving.

Glancing up as a young officer whose name she couldn't remember entered the grocery store and gave her a subtle nod, Sabrina hoped the Desparre PD found her stalker soon. Because no matter how small the risk of exposure was with this article, she wasn't willing to take chances with her family's safety.

It was definitely time to figure out a contingency plan.

Chapter Ten

A day after her picture had shown up in the paper, people were still yelling out, "Great job!" and "Thanks for saving our K-9!" when she walked around. But the newspaper's online site had been down most of the day, and she hoped it would stay that way. Hoped the only people who'd ever hear about her supposed heroics were Desparre locals.

She'd acted on instinct that day in the park, and she'd do it again. But she could do without the attention.

Stepping out of her old truck, she couldn't help but glance around for the man who'd put her in the paper. Whoever he was, he wasn't obviously staring. Hopefully today they'd identify him.

She walked into the police station and Officer Nate Dreymond rose from the front desk and opened the door to let her into the area marked *Police Only.*

"Good luck," he told her.

"Thanks," she said as she walked through and immediately spotted Tate and Sitka.

Tate smiled at her, a soft smile that somehow managed to be perfectly professional but still completely directed at her.

It made her pulse pick up, and her feet followed suit. When she reached his side across the open-concept space a minute later, he asked, "What's it like being a local hero?"

But something in his eyes told her the newspaper article bothered him as much as it did her.

"You saw that?"

Woof! Sitka contributed.

The dog's tail thumped the floor when Sabrina looked at her, and Sabrina grinned and pet her.

"The reporter left a copy on my doorstep. I forgot that she lived near me. I helped her when she thought someone was sneaking around her house last year and mentioned that I lived close in case she was in trouble. Apparently, she remembered."

Sabrina felt a brief, ridiculous spurt of jealousy that she pushed aside. "So you think we can find this guy today?" She heard the hopeful note in her voice and realized that it felt different than it had in a long time.

The fact that the stalker hadn't left her a note or tried anything else since he'd sent that truck speeding toward them three days ago made her wonder if he'd noticed that police were always around and he'd fled. For once, she prayed he hadn't, prayed he'd stick around long enough to get caught.

"I'm ready to look at those pictures."

Tate had called her that morning, letting her know the officers who'd been watching over her the past couple of days while she walked around town had managed to get pictures of men who might be paying too much attention. She'd been shocked; she hadn't noticed any of the officers taking pictures. But then she'd felt a surge of hope. Maybe she'd recognize someone. Maybe this two-year-long nightmare would actually have an end.

"Let's do it, then," Tate said, leading her into a conference room with a long table where the chief of police was waiting.

Sitka followed, too, pushing past her to stand next to Tate at the far end of the table.

The police chief stood. "How are you feeling, Sabrina?"
She gave a smile. "Hopeful."

Chief Griffith smiled back at her. "Me, too. My officers
got a lot of pictures." At the look she must have given him,
he laughed and said, "Don't worry. We didn't notice tons of
people watching you. But someone skilled who has practice
stalking gets good at blending in, at appearing like he's *not*
watching you. We took pictures of anyone around you."

"Oh." She heard the surprise in her voice. Police in New
York had tried hard to locate and catch her stalker. She
knew they had. But this was a whole different level.

The same hope sparked again, a little stronger this time,
as she took a seat where the chief indicated. On the table
in front of her was a folder.

"Take a look at the pictures in there," Chief Griffith
said. "We printed them out and blew them up to make it
easier. Take as much time as you want. You don't need to
be certain. If you think you recognize anyone from New
York or if you've seen anyone in places you wouldn't expect—near your house or around you more than once—let
us know. It might just be that we're a small town, but we'd
rather check it out. Even if you're just getting a weird vibe
from someone, point him out. Okay?"

She nodded, opening the folder as Tate sat next to her
and Sitka pushed her way between the chairs to sit beside
her, too.

Sabrina smiled at her and paused to pet the sweet dog.
"Thanks, Sitka," she whispered. It might have been her
imagination, but it felt like the dog knew she was nervous
and was trying to support her.

Then she started flipping through the photos. She
stopped periodically to study some more closely, but she
didn't remember any of the people in them hanging around
her in Desparre. And she definitely didn't remember any
of them from New York.

She paused on an image from two days ago, when she'd been heading toward the park. One of the photos had captured the man she'd seen standing beside a car parked right near where Talise's had been before it came racing toward Sitka. Even in the photo, the way he was looking toward her made her shiver. Just like it had when she'd first seen it, his mustache seemed out of place on his face, as if it was some kind of disguise. She pointed at him and looked over at Tate, then Chief Griffith.

Tate shook his head. "That's Shawn. I don't remember his last name, but he lives one town over, in Luna, and has for at least four years. He comes into Desparre pretty regularly. He's kind of antisocial, but there's no way he was stalking you in New York two years ago."

Her shoulders dropped. Was this all for nothing?

She flipped to the next photo, and her anxiety sparked again as she looked past herself, Lora and Adam talking, to a guy in the background watching them from near the gazebo. "What about this guy? I thought he might have taken a picture of me that day."

Tate frowned at the photo, leaning closer and giving her a whiff of the same sandalwood scent she'd noticed the day he'd come to her house to stop her from leaving Desparre. It was a scent she'd started to associate entirely with him, a scent that made her want to breathe more deeply.

"I don't know this guy." He looked behind him. "Chief?"

Sabrina passed the picture over and then watched as the police chief studied it carefully and finally shook his head. "No. And it does look like he might be trying to hide. I'll check with the other officers and see if anyone else recognizes him."

Was this him? Hope started to build again, with whiplash intensity, and Sabrina met Tate's gaze, knowing that hope was reflected in her eyes.

As he gazed back at her, the rest of the room, the chief,

the pictures all seemed to fade into the background. All she could focus on was Tate, on the sharp angles of his face and the fullness of his lips. On the way his dark hair swept over his forehead and the hypnotizing deep brown of his eyes. Her breathing went shallow as a familiar spark ignited inside her, one she'd been feeling more and more often when she was around him. The way his gaze seemed to intensify on her said he felt it, too.

But if the man in the picture *was* her stalker and they could finally end this threat, she'd be leaving. Trying to begin a long-distance relationship all the way from New York while she was trying to reintegrate into her old life wasn't practical, even if Tate was interested. If they finally found her stalker, she'd never get the chance to see if her growing interest in Tate could have become something.

"DOES ANYONE RECOGNIZE this man?" Tate asked, holding up the photo Sabrina had identified earlier. She'd gone home, and Tate had felt a sudden pull to go with her, to stay beside her, but he had hours of work left today.

The few other officers inside the police station stopped their work and came to look.

Veteran officer Charlie Quinn, a gruff guy who looked a lot older than his forty-two years, squinted at it for a long moment, then finally shook his head. "He looks vaguely familiar, but I don't know him. If he's a local, he must not come around town much."

It was a problem they'd run into before in investigations. Desparre was a small town in terms of population, but large when it came to acreage. So, while locals tended to recognize each other, if someone wanted to hide, they definitely could. In fact, one of Tate's earliest cases on the Desparre PD had involved a couple of kidnappers who'd hidden out in the mountains for years without anyone realizing.

Charlie's partner, Max Becker, pushed his way through. "Let me see."

Max was a few years older than Tate and had been on the force a few years longer. He was brash and seemed to think there was no space in a professional setting for friendships, but he got the job done.

He stared at the picture for less time than Charlie had, then shook his head, too. "Nah, I don't know him."

"Nate?" Tate called into the front of the station.

The youngest officer on the force, who'd recently turned twenty, hurried into the bullpen.

"You recognize this guy?" Tate asked hopefully. Nate might have been relatively new to the force, but he'd lived in Desparre all his life.

Nate's lips pursed as he leaned close to the photo, making Max snicker. "Try not to go cross-eyed."

Ignoring him, Nate hedged. "Maybe. He does look a little familiar, but I don't think he's local." Straightening, he asked, "You think this is Sabrina's stalker?"

"Maybe. Any idea when you might have first seen him?"

Nate frowned, creating lines across his pale, freckled forehead. "Not that long ago, actually. Maybe a month or two?"

"You ready to go?" Lorenzo Riera called to Nate as he came into the bullpen.

"Give me a few minutes," Nate said. "I need to find Sam to cover the front desk." He left the bullpen as Lorenzo strode quickly toward Tate.

"What are you all looking at?"

Tate showed Lorenzo the photo and pointed to the guy in the background, skulking near the gazebo. "You know him?"

"This guy?" Lorenzo snorted. "Yeah."

Tate's interest perked at the derision in Lorenzo's voice. "How? Who is he?"

"I don't know his name. But about a month and a half ago, I was at the park with my two youngest kids. You know

Julie Waterman? Paul and Frannie's oldest? She's about to start her first year of college, I think."

Tate nodded. The Watermans had moved to Desparre long before he'd arrived, looking for a different lifestyle than they'd had back in Tulsa.

"Well, like most of the locals, she knows I'm a cop. She came over and told me this guy was creeping her out. Said he'd been watching her all afternoon."

Tate frowned. Was that why Sabrina hadn't gotten a note until recently? Because her stalker had been busy fixating on someone else for a while? It seemed odd that he'd track her all the way to Alaska and then get distracted, but maybe a month and a half ago, he'd known Sabrina was in Desparre but hadn't located her yet. Or maybe he was the kind of creep who always harassed women.

"So I went over to talk to him," Lorenzo continued. "I wasn't on duty, but I let him know I was a cop, tried to get his info. He acted like he didn't have ID on him and gave me a name I looked up later, but it was fake. Claimed he wasn't following anyone, but he was definitely aggravated. He left the park, but a few days later, I spotted him in his truck. I followed him just to see what he was up to, and he headed into the mountain. I lost him there, but I suspect he lives up that way."

"We need to find this guy, see how long he's been in town," Tate said. "See if he's ever lived in New York."

"You really think he's Sabrina's stalker?"

"Maybe. You see him watching Sabrina in this picture. She thinks he took a picture of her, too."

Lorenzo nodded, squinting at the picture again. "Could be he's just a garden-variety jerk and he comes to the park to stare at the women."

"Maybe," Tate agreed. "But he's the best lead we've got right now."

Tate was always careful not to get too excited about leads

that could be coincidence because they could blind you to other options. But something about the way the guy was looking at Sabrina made all of Tate's protective instincts flare to life. His gut was telling him this was the guy.

Now they just needed to find him.

"Hey, Tate!" Nate said, rushing back into the room, wearing a big grin. "Guess what?"

Lorenzo smiled at his rookie partner, obviously amused at his enthusiasm.

"What?" Tate asked, a bad feeling forming that he couldn't explain.

"You and Sitka are famous."

The bad feeling turned into dread. "Why?"

Nate's brow furrowed. "What, you don't want to be famous? You're the only one. Anyway, the local story that Ariel Clemson wrote got picked up by national news!"

From what seemed like far away, Tate heard Lorenzo asking, "You okay, man?"

He couldn't seem to get it together enough to answer. Not only his first name but a picture of him was splashed across the national news.

He needed to drive home, take off his uniform and leave town now.

As the thought formed, his cell phone rang. He glanced at the screen. Keara.

No doubt she'd seen the story, too. There shouldn't be any hesitation now. He needed to go.

But he loved the life he'd built in Desparre. And even though the other officers were committed to Sabrina, he'd made her a promise. Besides, against all his instincts, he'd started to fall for her.

Tucking the phone back into his pocket and ignoring what he knew would be Keara's advice to run, Tate prayed the wrong people wouldn't see the story.

Because he needed to stay long enough to help Sabrina.

Chapter Eleven

It had been two days since the small heartwarming story Ariel Clemson had penned for the *Desparre Daily* had gone national. Two days without anyone showing up and trying to kill Tate. Two days without him receiving any death threats.

Maybe he'd gotten lucky.

The day after the story was picked up nationally, it was bumped out of the spotlight by a multistate manhunt for a group of escaped convicts. That story was still hogging the media's attention, enough so that Ariel approached him as he and Sitka walked downtown.

She had a pout firmly in place as she said, "I thought that story was going to be my big break."

"You'll get there," he assured her. He tried to appear sympathetic, though all he felt was relief that the story had been buried. Ariel didn't seem to notice that his concern was fake. She also didn't seem to notice that he couldn't stop his gaze from wandering away from her to study everyone around them. To see if he recognized someone from his past.

She shrugged and muttered, "I hope so," and then finally headed off, leaving him and Sitka alone.

With her gone, Tate gave in to his desire to scan his surroundings again. The woods up ahead, where Sabrina's stalker might have disappeared after sending Talise's car racing toward Sitka, in particular kept grabbing his attention. Probably because of the way he'd been ambushed on a trail near the woods back in Boston.

Escaping that attempt on his life had been a result of his quick thinking and quick action. But it had also been partly luck. He couldn't help but wonder when his luck was going to run out.

In the news picture he was in the background, he reminded himself. Sabrina and Sitka had been the focus. Plus, the story didn't have his real last name. Even if Kevin and Paul were searching for him, how likely was it that they'd have set up alerts for just his first name? And he doubted they regularly read feel-good stories.

Still, as his cell phone rang yet again, it amped up Tate's anxiety even more. He felt guilty about not returning Keara's calls, but he didn't want to pick up while he was on patrol.

Sitka tilted her head, watching him as she strode alongside him. Her steady attention told him she knew something was wrong.

"It will all work out," he told her, hoping he was right. Every time he thought about leaving Desparre, the same no-win choice kept haunting him: Did he bring Sitka or did he leave her behind?

As if she could read his thoughts, she whined, high-pitched and sustained, until he pet her.

"I'm just trying to do the best thing for you," he said softly. Stroking her fur calmed his heart rate and seemed to relax her, too.

Ever since the incident with Talise's truck, he'd stopped using a leash with her in town. She didn't need one anyway, and if any locals had been wary of her before, Ariel's story seemed to have given them all a soft spot for their new police K-9.

Straightening, he headed for the park. He was hoping his luck would hold and he'd see the guy who Sabrina had identified in the photo, since it seemed he liked to hang out there. So far, police hadn't been able to positively identify him. Even quietly asking longtime locals hadn't yielded any results beyond "He looks familiar" or "He might live up the mountain" or "I think he moved here in the past couple of months."

When Tate reached the park, a group of kids ran over from the swings and started petting Sitka. His dog promptly sat, wagged her tail and tipped her head back, tongue lolling.

Tate held in a smile and resisted the urge to explain to the kids that he and Sitka were on duty. His dog was wearing her thick collar that identified her as a police K-9, but she wasn't wearing the dark vest that immediately screamed *Dog at Work.*

"How old is she?" one of the kids asked.

"Sitka is a year old," he told them. "She's an Alaskan Malamute. Did you know that this kind of dog got its start as an arctic sled dog?"

"Oh, cool," one of the other kids said.

"And feel her fur," he advised as Sitka's tail thumped harder, making the youngest of the kids laugh. "It's a double coat, and it's actually waterproof."

From the benches, several of their parents watched with amusement as Tate shared details about how Sitka worked as a police K-9.

"She can even find people who get lost," Tate continued, "by tracking them with her nose. It—"

Movement at the edge of his line of vision caught his attention, and Tate did a double take as he spotted the man from the picture, back behind the gazebo. When his gaze met Tate's, he slid his phone into his pocket and ran toward the street.

"Sitka, come on!" Tate called, as he pivoted and raced after the man.

Behind him, he could hear the parents calling their kids to get them out of Sitka's way.

Tate didn't wait for Sitka to break free of the kids. He just gritted his teeth and ran onto the street, determined not to let the guy escape.

Instead of taking a sharp turn into the woods as Tate had expected, the guy ran down a perpendicular street.

"Police!" Tate yelled after him. "Stop!"

The guy glanced back, giving Tate a better look at a scowling, scared expression and a lot more muscle than had been evident in the photo. Since that picture had been taken, the guy had grown a short beard, as if he knew someone was looking for him.

Instead of heeding the directive, he ran even faster, and Tate swore at the speed such a muscle-bound guy should have had trouble achieving.

Yanking his radio off his duty belt, Tate panted, "I spotted the guy from the photo. He just took off on foot down Fleming Street. I'm in pursuit."

"Backup is on the way," Officer Sam Jennings returned immediately.

Behind him, the familiar sound of Sitka's footsteps were gaining, but Tate didn't slow to wait for her.

Ahead of him, the guy made a quick turn around the corner onto a street that housed nothing but a big, deserted warehouse. It was an eyesore in Desparre's otherwise nicely kept downtown, and it seemed like a strange spot to try and hide. Unless maybe he'd left a vehicle this way?

Tate pushed himself harder, pivoting onto the street fast.

He realized his mistake before he'd finished rounding the blind corner. But it was already too late.

The guy had stopped, hidden up against the massive

warehouse. He stepped forward just as Tate turned into view, lifted a huge, tattooed arm and clotheslined Tate.

Tate's feet went out from under him, and then he slammed into the dirt and pebbled ground. The impact stole his breath, and his vision went black.

Chapter Twelve

Tate fought his way out of the darkness, blinking his vision clear only to see the guy's massive fist heading toward his face.

Swallowing back nausea, Tate tried to roll out of the way.

Before he could, Sitka flew around the corner and leaped on the guy at a speed that dropped him to the ground.

As he flailed, yelled and swung those fists at Sitka's unprotected back, she bit down on his arm and shook her head.

He screamed louder and curled inward, then his feet rose like he was readying to kick her.

Shoving himself to a partly raised position, Tate pivoted and then knelt on top of the guy's legs, trapping them in place. "Let go, Sitka!" When Sitka dropped the guy's arm, Tate fought to flip him to his stomach.

The guy bucked and yanked an arm free, raising it to take a swing.

Then Sitka stepped closer and let out a deep growl.

The guy froze, panic in his suddenly wide eyes, and Tate didn't waste any time. He yanked the guy over until his face was pressed against the dirt road and wrenched his arms up behind him. As Tate snapped on the cuffs, he asked, "Sitka, you okay?"

Woof!

It was part of her training to take down a suspect this

way, but until now, she'd only done it in practice. At the training facility, the trainers, wearing protective gear, had shaken their arms and lifted her off the ground, teaching her to hang on through anything. They made loud noises next to her ears, lightly hit her back, and still she'd held tight.

Even though Tate had been proud of her, he'd hated seeing her get yanked around. Today had been worse. But judging by the tail wagging as she stood beside him, alert and ready to jump in again, she really was okay.

As his adrenaline calmed, Tate heard pounding feet heading toward them. "Back here!" he called.

"You good?" Officer Riera yelled back.

"All good!"

Lorenzo and Nate rounded the corner. The veteran was breathing hard as he leaned over and asked the guy, "You have anything on you that can stick me? Any needles or a knife?"

The guy on the ground forced his head to the side so he could look up at the five-foot-six Latino with muscles that rivaled his. He scowled, then shook his head.

"Rook?" Lorenzo used the nickname for the partner who hadn't been a true rookie in several months, since he'd marked a year on the force. "You want to check him?"

Lorenzo helped Tate pull the guy to his feet, and they watched as Nate patted him down. A minute later, he handed Tate a wallet and a cell phone.

Scowling at the guy who might have gotten his weapon if Sitka hadn't leaped in at the right moment, Tate opened the wallet and pulled out a driver's license. "Mario McKeever." His scowl deepened as he saw the state. "From New York."

"Let's get him processed," Lorenzo suggested, taking the guy by the crook of the arm as if he worried Tate would start an interrogation out in the street.

This was Sabrina's stalker. A good four inches shorter than Tate's six feet, with flexing biceps that suggested he spent a lot of time at the gym, he wore a snarl that made him look even more intimidating. His face wasn't all that memorable, with small features partly hidden by a thick layer of scruff. Still, now that Tate had a better view than the grainy picture they'd taken in the park, he knew for sure. He didn't recognize Mario from the social-media images he'd been poring over. How far on the outskirts of Sabrina's life had he been?

As Lorenzo and Tate led the suspect around the corner and toward the police station, with Nate and Sitka trailing slightly behind, Tate tried to keep his mouth shut. It was something he was good at; more than once, his old chief had asked him to stand in the room or help out with an interrogation of a challenging suspect because Tate wouldn't lose his cool.

But right now, thinking of the fear on Sabrina's face as she'd been trying to slip away at dawn, he couldn't help himself. "Why can't you just *leave her alone*?"

"Tate," Lorenzo warned.

Tate took a deep breath, then clamped his jaw shut.

Mario looked back and forth between them, then snapped, "I don't know what you're talking about, man. I ran because you and your attack dog started chasing me for no reason. You let me go now and I won't sue you. Look at my arm!"

He tried to pull it forward, but between the cuffs and Lorenzo's grip, he couldn't. He didn't need to move it for Tate to see the damage. Mario's forearm was bleeding, the bite wounds obvious.

Instead of telling him that Sitka wouldn't have knocked him down if he hadn't been a threat, Tate followed protocol this time and didn't engage. He managed to keep his silence all the way back to the station, where the new police chief was waiting.

"Let's get him fingerprinted," Chief Griffith said.

Mario jerked back so quickly that Tate and the chief shared a look as Lorenzo yanked him forward again. The guy had a record.

"I need a doctor," Mario insisted, his eyes wide as he kept trying to pull away from Lorenzo.

"No problem," the chief said calmly. "We're going to get you some first aid right now, and then we'll take you to the hospital."

Tate ground his teeth together, trying to hold in his frustration. It was protocol. And with the guy in custody, Sabrina was out of danger. But he wanted more answers now—like how Mario had managed to track her all the way from New York.

The guy relaxed as another officer came in, snapped on a pair of gloves and wrapped up the wound. Then the chief took Mario's arm, pulling him farther into the station.

"What are you doing?" Mario demanded. "I've got rights! I want to see a doctor."

"And we're taking you to one," the chief replied. "But first we're going to have to get your prints."

Mario planted his feet, and his muscles bulged as he resisted the chief's tugs.

Showing a lot more calm than Tate felt, the chief just smiled and nodded at Officer Max Becker, who grinned and came over with the portable fingerprint system, pressing the suspect's thumb against it before he knew what was happening.

"Hey!" Mario yelled, yanking his hand away.

"Got it," Max said, backing away from Mario's swinging arms.

Mario's snarl returned, and every officer in the front of the station tensed at once, ready to react to an attack.

His gaze swept them, then he seemed to realize he was outmanned, and his head fell forward. The chief pulled him toward processing.

"Mario McKeever," Max announced. "We've got two stalking charges within the past decade. Resulted in a short stint in jail and a couple of restraining orders. And—" Max snorted as he looked back at Mario "—the reason he ran. He's wanted in a sexual-assault case back in New York."

"From when?" Tate asked.

"Four months ago."

"And then he came here," Tate said. "Lucky coincidence, or did he already know Sabrina was here?"

Mario twisted in the chief's grip. "I don't know a Sabrina. And I ran because I was framed."

He continued to protest as the chief frowned and called to Lorenzo. "Can you and Nate manage the hospital transport?"

"Sure," Lorenzo said, and the chief turned to Tate.

"Step outside with me."

As soon as they were out the door, Tate insisted, "I can go along. I'll be careful what I ask."

"Tate, it's not him," the chief said.

"What do you mean?"

"This isn't Sabrina's stalker."

"Come on," Tate insisted. "He was taking pictures of her. He's got a history of stalking. And he's from New York!"

"Coincidences, but not proof. This guy has a known stalking problem, and Sabrina isn't the only woman here he's taken pictures of." Before Tate could continue arguing, the chief said, "He's in the national database. He's wanted in New York. That means he would have popped for police in the murder of Dylan Westwood. But he didn't."

Tate swore under his breath. The chief was right. It was someone else's prints that had shown up in Sabrina's boyfriend's house. Someone without a record.

Was he wrong? Was Mario just a general creep and not specifically the creep harassing Sabrina?

What about the New York connection? He must have

come here within the past few months—and then Sabrina's stalker had suddenly restarted contact. Was it all coincidence?

"Maybe Mario hired someone to make the hit on Westwood. Or maybe the murder wasn't actually committed by her stalker," Tate said. "Maybe he just capitalized on it, sent that note to Sabrina to make her think he had more power than he actually did."

The chief nodded slowly. "Yeah, both of those things are possible. We'll question Mario thoroughly. In the meantime, you and Sitka should take the rest of the day. Fill out your incident report and then head home. Take a break and get your head clear. We'll update you."

Tate shook his head, shocked that the chief thought he wasn't fit to be working. "Chief—"

"You're too invested. And while I'm not worried about you crossing a line, I also know Lorenzo and Nate can get the job done. I'll be watching the interrogation, too. But you were knocked to the ground today, and technically, you need to get checked out. I'll trust you to handle that. But I don't want you back on duty for twenty-four hours. Rest, have a doctor look at you, and I'll update you. Okay?"

Frowning, Tate nodded. It *was* protocol, especially since the world had gone black on him when he hit the ground. The chief didn't know that, but he was being cautious.

Even though Tate wanted to be the one questioning Mario, the closest hospital was one town over. That meant going up and down a mountain, an hour each way. And that didn't include time spent being checked out by a doctor.

That was time Tate could use to return to Sabrina's social media, see if he could find Mario McKeever somewhere on the platforms.

"Okay," he agreed.

The chief's eyes narrowed slightly at his ready agreement, but he didn't say anything as Tate opened the door to the station and called Sitka.

She came bounding out, and he led her to his personal vehicle. As he opened the door for her, she looked up at him questioningly, as if to ask *Why aren't we staying at work?*

"We have some things to do at home," he told her, as Lorenzo and Nate exited the police station and pulled Mario toward their police vehicle.

The criminal's eyes met his briefly, and then he scowled and looked away.

If this guy was Sabrina's stalker, Tate vowed to find the connection before Mario was back at the station for his interrogation.

But two hours later, as Tate checked the time yet again and Sitka whined at his feet, he had nothing. He'd been following every thread he could find from Sabrina's social media, through her brother, through friends and even friends of friends. He'd blown images up threefold, staring into the background, searching for Mario's unremarkable face or his nasty sneer.

How much time did he have left before Lorenzo and Nate brought Mario back to the station for questioning? Finding a link between Mario and Sabrina that they could show the suspect early in the process was likely to be far more effective than if they did it later, after he'd lawyered up and some of the initial shock of being caught had faded.

Rubbing a hand over his head, which was throbbing from two hours of staring at his computer screen and the bump to the back of his head earlier, Tate clicked back to one of Sabrina's friends who posted the most publicly available pictures. She and Sabrina didn't appear to be especially close, but he'd found Sabrina in the background of several of her older pictures. Maybe he needed to go back even further. Maybe Mario had fixated on her long before he'd started writing to her.

He opened a photo from three years ago on the woman's feed and found Sabrina, laughing in the background. The lighting was crap, the surroundings some dimly lit bar. She was surrounded by a couple of people he recognized from hours of looking through feeds as work colleagues. Beyond that were more people who seemed to be part of the same crowd.

His shoulders dropped. It had seemed like a real long shot, but he was still disappointed that none of them were Mario McKeever.

Then his pulse shot up, and he leaned in close to the screen as a familiar face in the background caught his attention.

Beside him, Sitka got to her feet, whining as she caught his mood.

"No way," he muttered, blowing the picture up. It got grainier as the size increased, but he wasn't wrong. The guy standing two rows behind Sabrina—maybe part of the group, maybe not—had his gaze solidly fixed on her.

It wasn't Mario McKeever. It was worse.

It was a man Sabrina trusted, one of the few people in Desparre she seemed to consider a friend. It was a man who'd been in the forefront of the photo in the park with Mario. He'd been talking to Sabrina, completely overlooked as a threat because he'd supposedly moved here after his wife had died.

It was Adam Lassiter.

Chapter Thirteen

"Adam." Sabrina heard the surprise in her own voice as she opened the door to her cabin.

Her friend was standing on the front stoop slightly hunched forward, hands shoved in his pockets. "Hey, Sabrina. I'm sorry to stop by unannounced, but I…" He blew out a breath, then gave a self-conscious smile. "I just needed a friend, and since you lived kind of nearby…"

Sabrina glanced around at the vast expanse of woods surrounding her cabin, the enclosure that had felt like a protective barrier when she'd first arrived. Now it felt like a place for a stalker to hide. Even standing in her open doorway felt too exposed.

She hadn't invited anyone except Tate and Sitka inside in two long years. Adam might be her friend, but the idea of letting anyone too close still made anxiety knot her stomach.

"I should have called," Adam said, stepping back. "It's just—I didn't have your number. But Lora told me where you lived, and I was passing near here, so I thought maybe… I'm sorry."

Her gaze snapped back up to him. They didn't really have the sort of friendship where you just showed up unannounced. She wasn't even sure how Lora had known where she lived to be able to tell him, but it didn't really surprise her that she knew it. Lora seemed to know everything about everyone.

As her attention refocused on Adam instead of the vast expanses where someone could be hiding behind him, she realized he looked worse than usual. There were deep circles under his eyes, as if he hadn't been sleeping. A downward tilt to his mouth as if he'd been frowning all day.

"I'm sorry," she told Adam, trying to shake off her unease. She almost hadn't opened the door, even after seeing through the peephole that it was just him. "It's been a tough week."

"For me, too." His words were soft as his gaze lifted from the ground back up to her. "Today would have been my wife's birthday." He took another step backward, shaking his head, his back and shoulders sloped inward. "I was going to go for a walk, clear my head. And then I realized I didn't want to be all alone. But it's an imposition. I'm sorry. I—"

"No," Sabrina cut him off as guilt bubbled up that she'd made him feel like he couldn't reach out to her.

In the few months she'd tried to venture out more, Adam and Lora had made her feel like she could have friends here. Even if she couldn't tell them the truth about who she was, she'd always thought Adam had sensed she'd also experienced a recent loss. It was in the way his gaze sometimes cut to her when he mentioned his grief, as if he expected her to share her own loss.

She never had. She'd been tempted once or twice to talk about it, to be vague enough that she wouldn't get tripped up on her real past. But something had always stopped her, a voice in the back of her head that sounded like the PI saying not to take any risks she might regret. Not to give in to the desire for connection at the expense of safety.

So right now, instead of inviting him inside, she grabbed her keys off the table in her entryway and stepped outside.

Her fingers fluttered briefly up to the emergency button hidden underneath her T-shirt as she locked the door behind her. Then she mustered up a smile and said, "Lead the way."

An answering smile trembled on his face, but it didn't quite reach his eyes. "Thanks."

He walked down her drive, out to the dirt road. Then, instead of heading toward town, he moved in the other direction, where the woods started slowly thinning out as the road tilted upward. "There's a great view about a mile from here. A good place to clear your head," he said, keeping a brisk pace.

He was about four inches taller than her and Sabrina had to increase her pace to keep up with his long strides. She struggled with the appropriate thing to say, but words evaded her. She had no idea how his wife had passed, but she was pretty sure he was only a few years older than her, in his early to midthirties. Young to have lost a spouse.

He was probably here because he thought she knew that same kind of grief. But although the horror of Dylan's death would probably always be with her, it was different. They'd only been dating for three months before he was murdered. It had been the beginning of something, but where it would lead she'd never know. She couldn't begin to guess the grief he was experiencing.

He kept hurrying along, slightly ahead of her, and unease pricked as he moved off the road and onto a path with a steeper incline. Her thoughts went immediately to the bear and cubs Tate and Sitka had run into behind her house.

"Adam?" she huffed. She'd been in good shape back in New York, often choosing a long walk instead of public transportation. But since going into hiding, she'd been afraid to go running alone. She always felt safer behind the locked door of a vehicle or a hotel room.

He glanced back at her, slowing slightly. "Sorry. I hike a lot."

"No, it's not that. There are bears in the woods."

He laughed, although it sounded a little forced. "Nah. I've come this way plenty of times. We'll be fine. Trust me, the view will be worth it. You wouldn't think so, but there's a big drop-off this way. It's an amazing place to look out onto the valley below. You just can't get too close to the edge." He laughed again, a little chortle that sounded like he was trying too hard to be cheerful for her sake. "And anyway, I have bear spray." He patted the pocket of his cargo pants as he kept moving up the path.

Sabrina hesitated, glancing back down the empty road, then into the forest. The trees were thinner here than by her house, but that didn't mean it wasn't a great place for bears to wander.

Up ahead, Adam was still pressing forward, not realizing she wasn't right behind him. Since they'd left her house, he hadn't said a word about his wife. Maybe he'd just needed silent, understanding company. Or maybe he wanted to wait until they reached this peaceful view he'd mentioned. But something about the way he'd shown up and then just plowed forward was making discomfort creep in.

Was she being paranoid? Adam was her friend. One of her only friends.

But she'd learned a long time ago that her stalker wasn't the only threat. That sometimes, danger came in the guise of a friend. Like the coworker who'd walked her out to her car, joking about women sticking together, then nodded at someone hiding in the shadows. That guy had rushed for her, only charging the other way when one of the cooks happened to pop open the back door for a smoke. She'd left that place behind like so many others, but she thought she'd carried the lesson with her.

Sabrina's hand reached for the alert button without conscious intent.

Then, Adam glanced back and called, "Come on!"

At some point, she had to be able to trust her own judgment again. At some point, her life couldn't be all about fear.

She lowered her hand, hurrying to catch up.

Yes, her stalker was here. But so was Tate, who'd dedicated himself to helping her, who represented a possibility even greater. So were Adam and Lora, people who'd befriended her despite how closed off she was. Who'd given her a chance when they could have walked away. Maybe she needed to do the same.

The path Adam had chosen was thin, not enough room for them to walk side by side even if she could keep up with his pace. The edges of wispy pine trees brushed her arms as she alternated between walking and a semijog. Her breath came in uneven puffs that reminded her how long it had been since she'd felt comfortable going anywhere. The reminder made anger knot in her chest, but it also made the view that appeared as they crested the hill more spectacular.

Adam was right. It was like the forest suddenly dropped away. Way down below was a green valley, spotted with trees. In the middle, she could see a group of animals.

Stepping up beside him at the edge, she glanced briefly his way, feeling a smile break free. An image of his expression, strangely pensive, flickered in the edge of her vision as she moved a little closer to the edge, straining to see. "Moose?"

"Yeah."

His voice was closer than she'd expected, and as she twisted toward him in surprise, she felt something shove against her back, right under her shoulder blade.

Her arms jolted up, a desperate attempt at regaining her balance as her stomach dropped and the valley below seemed to reach up toward her.

Then Adam's arm clamped around her biceps, and he yanked her backward.

Breathing hard, Sabrina stared at him, then glanced behind her. Had she imagined a push? Had something fallen from a tree?

Her arm twitched under his grasp, fear squirming in her belly.

Letting go, Adam stepped slightly away. "Sorry. Did I scare you? You looked like you were slipping. I didn't mean to grab you so hard. I thought you were going to fall."

"No, that's—" The spot beneath her shoulder blade prickled with the feel of that phantom force. Had she imagined it? Had she just slipped?

She glanced down at the loose pebbles where she'd been standing, then back up at Adam.

There was something different in his eyes, hurt that she'd misinterpreted his help. Before she could say anything, he took another step backward.

"Maybe we should head back," he suggested. He didn't wait for her to answer, just moved away from her, down the path.

With one last glance around, Sabrina hurried after him.

Chapter Fourteen

"Sabrina, damn it, call me back!"

Tate hung up the phone and grabbed his keys. "Come on, Sitka."

She leaped to her feet, tail wagging as she chased him down the stairs and out to the truck.

His mood was decidedly less jolly, a dread in his gut that no amount of telling himself he was overreacting would calm. He'd called Sabrina three times in a row before leaving a voice mail. He had no idea how close she kept her cell phone. Maybe she was in the shower, perfectly fine but unable to hear the ringing. Or maybe she was in town, chatting away with Talise in the grocery store, her phone tucked in her pocket, ringing unheard underneath Talise's nonstop stories.

"Let's just check," he muttered, opening the door for Sitka, then hopping up into the cab beside her. Then they were taking a route that had become familiar over the past week, out to Sabrina's cabin.

As he drove, his gaze swept the narrow road, bracketed by beautiful old trees, seeing it all in a new way. Sabrina's cabin was too isolated. Even with an alert button connecting her directly to the police, he'd seen firsthand what the vast distances out here could mean when responding to an emergency call.

He clenched the wheel tighter, pressing down on the gas as Sitka hunched low in the passenger seat. He should have insisted that Sabrina move into town and stay at the hotel until they'd found her stalker. Better yet, he should have offered her his pullout couch and convinced his colleagues to trade off shifts at his house watching her.

It was impractical. Impossible to sustain. But right now, knowing that Adam Lassiter had once lived in New York City, had once been photographed staring at Sabrina from afar, made panic and guilt tense his entire body.

They'd known he was close. They'd known he was escalating.

But they'd never suspected it was someone Sabrina trusted, someone she called a friend. What if they'd miscalculated how much time they had to stop him before Sabrina paid the price?

Sitka whined, catching his anxiety, and Tate gave her a quick pet meant to reassure. She just whined again, softer, as she hunched lower on the seat.

When he finally pulled up to the cabin, he released a deep, relieved breath. Sabrina's car was in the drive. She was home. Even though he'd gotten the impression she'd never let anyone inside besides him, he was happy not to see any other vehicle in the drive.

Parking behind her, he stepped out, then turned back to whistle for Sitka.

She was already leaping out of the truck and bounding toward the front door.

Tate slammed the truck door and hurried after her. Then he knocked on Sabrina's door loudly, calling out, "Sabrina? It's Tate. Are you home? I need to talk to you."

There was no answer.

Unease settled in his chest, and his hand dropped automatically to where he normally kept his duty belt and his weapon. But he'd run out of the house so quickly, he hadn't even thought about snapping it back on.

Stepping off the porch, he followed the same path along the side of her house that Sitka had taken when she'd tracked a scent. Instead of moving into the woods, he crept along the edge of Sabrina's house.

Sitka kept pace with him. Her nose nudged his leg hard every few steps, like she was demanding an answer about what they were doing.

"We're looking for Sabrina," he told her softly. If someone was inside with her, preventing her from answering, they'd know Tate was here. But he didn't want to advertise his location.

He was probably being paranoid, and she was simply wearing headphones or had a dead battery in her cell phone. But he couldn't take any chances.

Knowing how safety-conscious she was, he didn't expect to find an open window, but he hoped to at least find one that would give him a view inside. The curtains were all down, but on the far side of the cabin, he discovered one of the windows was old. It would be easy to pop the lock.

If she was inside dancing around the cabin with music blasting in a pair of headphones, he'd apologize profusely and replace the window. If not… Gritting his teeth, Tate wrenched the window upward and sideways at the same time, and it slipped free of the old locking mechanism.

Pushing it open, he moved the curtain aside and peered into a bathroom. "Stay," he told Sitka as he hauled himself inside. If he needed her, she could leap through that window easily.

He landed awkwardly on the other side, with a lot more noise than he'd hoped to make. Pushing himself to a partially upright position, he peered around the corner. Seeing no one, he eased into the connected bedroom.

It looked like the rest of the cabin, with functional, comfortable furniture. There wasn't a lot of Sabrina's personality on display, except for a pile of colorful drawings pinned to the wall above the dresser and pictures of her mom and brother on the side table.

Moving forward, he did a slow and careful check of the second bedroom, then moved into the open kitchen and living area. She wasn't here.

Confusion turned quickly into dread as he saw her phone on the kitchen table. Tapping the button to check that it wasn't dead, he saw notifications of all his missed calls, but nothing else evident without unlocking it.

Why was her car here if she wasn't? He couldn't imagine her walking into town, but where else would she go? Still, if she was in trouble, why was there no sign of a struggle and no alert from her emergency button?

Grabbing Sabrina's sweatshirt from where it lay draped over the couch, Tate hurried to the front door and let himself outside. Sitka was standing beside him before he'd closed the door behind him. "Time to track," he told her.

Her tail wagged as he held out Sabrina's shirt and let her sniff it. Then her nose dropped to the ground, and she pivoted toward the driveway.

Tate felt a hint of relief as she led him down the drive instead of into the woods, but it faded just as fast. Where had she gone? And had she gone alone?

When Sitka turned right instead of left at the end of the drive, heading away from downtown instead of toward it, his anxiety increased. Then his dog let out a happy bark and started running.

Tate's gaze jolted to the right, where Sabrina was emerging from the woods far down the road. Stifling a curse of equal parts frustration and relief, Tate ran after Sitka.

"Sitka," Sabrina exclaimed, jogging until she met his dog in the middle of the road. She knelt in front of Sitka, wrapping her arms around the dog's neck in a brief hug that told Tate something had spooked her.

Tate skidded to a stop beside them, scanning the woods as his heart thudded too fast and anger knotted in his chest at how overemotional he'd gotten. He'd been so worried that he'd left his weapon behind. Now how much of a barrier would he be against a threat?

"What's going on?" He wrapped his arm around Sabrina's upper arm, pulling her upright.

She flinched, pulling her arm free and rubbing it.

His gaze met hers, even more troubled because he hadn't grabbed her *that* hard. "What are you doing wandering around the woods alone? I've been calling you."

"I—I'm sorry. I went for a walk with Adam and—"

"Adam?" His pulse skyrocketed as he scanned the woods again. He didn't see the man anywhere. Had Sabrina managed to escape from him? Or had they gotten lucky and Adam had just been trying to see how close he could get to Sabrina?

Or was Tate wrong entirely, and it was merely a bizarre coincidence? He'd learned in past cases that you couldn't get too focused on one suspect at the expense of others. Mario McKeever might not have killed Sabrina's boyfriend himself, but that didn't mean he hadn't hired someone to do it. It didn't mean he hadn't been stalking her and simply taken advantage of someone else's crime to scare her.

Sabrina crossed her arms over her chest, and she glanced around the woods, shivering. "What's going on?"

Obviously sensing her distress, Sitka leaned against her. His dog didn't always recognize her own size, and she must have leaned hard, because Sabrina stumbled slightly before dropping her arms and absently petting Sitka.

"Where is Adam now?"

Sabrina shook her head, gesturing vaguely behind her. "I don't know. I wanted to come back, and he said he wanted to keep walking. He turned back into the woods when we got close to the road, and I kept going."

Tate lowered his voice. "So he could be nearby?" Not waiting for Sabrina's answer, he put his hand on her back, ushering her forward. "Let's go to your place. Now."

"Tate, what—"

"*Now*, Sabrina."

She started to run, and Tate gave Sitka a nod. His dog raced up beside her, and Tate followed slightly behind, his gaze pivoting all around, even though he knew most likely if Adam was still around, he was behind them.

His heart didn't stop racing until they were back in Sabrina's house and he'd checked all the rooms again, locked the door and braced the wooden handle of her mop in the bathroom window. Then he called the station and gave them an update, requesting backup and an extra weapon.

After hanging up, he met Sabrina in the living room. She stood in the center of the room, anxiety on her face as she stroked Sitka's head.

"What's happening?" she whispered.

"What did Adam say when he showed up?" Tate demanded. "You took his car out to the woods? Where did he leave it?"

"I…" She frowned, shook her head. "He said it would have been his wife's birthday. She died a few months ago. He wanted company. He said there was a great view out in the woods, and he was right. It was beautiful. We went for a walk. He—"

"You went for a walk? What about his vehicle?"

"I—I don't know. I guess I didn't think about it when he showed up, but I didn't see a vehicle. Maybe he walked here? He said he lived nearby. Or…" She frowned again. "Maybe he said he happened to be nearby. He said Lora told him where I lived, and he just didn't want to be alone today."

"And then what?" Tate asked, knowing his rapid-fire questions without answers were making her more nervous. But none of this made much sense. If Adam had gotten Sabrina alone, why hadn't he made a move to grab her? If his goal was to harm her, why not now? Or maybe he'd come to Alaska, realized he could start over as her friend and woo her long-term, with her never being the wiser that he'd once stalked her and killed her boyfriend.

"Then I followed him up that road awhile, and into the woods. He took me to this beautiful drop-off and…" Her lips twisted, her forehead creasing with confusion. "I'm not sure what happened. I thought someone pushed me, but then Adam grabbed me and kept me from falling. I looked down, and there were a lot of loose rocks, so maybe I just slipped? Or something fell from a tree?"

"Or Adam pushed you, then saved you," Tate said grimly.

"Why would he do that?" Sabrina demanded, crossing her arms over her chest again. She seemed to fold inward, visibly shrinking as Sitka whined, glancing back and forth between them.

"I found him in a picture with you that one of your co-workers took back in New York. I think he might be your stalker."

"But—" fear mingled with the confusion on Sabrina's face "—he's new to Desparre, and he's always lived in Alaska. His wife died a few months ago. He—"

"How do you know that's true?" Tate asked.

"I… I guess I don't. But Lora told me a lot of it. She introduced me. She's known Adam longer than I have. She's the one who told him where I lived."

"Okay." Tate nodded. "You have Lora's number?"

"Yeah." Sabrina spun and grabbed her phone off the kitchen table. She paused, her gaze darting back to him, probably as she noticed all his missed calls. Then she tapped her phone and handed it to him.

She had Lora's number pulled up. He hit Send and waited only briefly before Lora answered cheerfully, "Sabrina! How are you?"

"This is Officer Tate Emory. I—"

"Oh, no! Is Sabrina okay?"

"Yes. I'm sorry, Lora. She's fine. Look, I need to ask you some things in confidence, okay?" When she hesitantly agreed, he asked, "How long have you known Adam Lassiter?"

"Adam?" There was surprise in her voice. "Um, I guess about three months, since he moved here."

"Where did he move from? Did you know his late wife? Or have you seen pictures of her?"

"He lived in Fairbanks most of his life. He said his wife died about a month before he moved to Desparre. He wanted to get away from the constant reminders of her. I'm sorry, but what's going on? Why do you want to know about Adam?"

"What did he say when he asked for Sabrina's address?"

"He never asked me for Sabrina's address. I don't even know where she lives."

A curse lodged in Tate's throat as his own phone rang. "Lora, I'll get back to you, okay? But keep this conversation between us. And one more thing. Do you know where Adam lives?"

"Kind of. If you take the main road out of town north for a while, he's in the woods. A little cabin. I don't know the exact location."

The dread building in his gut amplified. "Thanks, Lora."

"Why did she tell him my address?" Sabrina asked as Tate hung up her phone and answered his own.

"She didn't," Tate told her. "But Adam lives somewhere out this way." Lifting his phone to his ear, Tate said, "Emory. What's going on?"

"We're coming up on Sabrina's place," Charlie Quinn answered. "You'll hear us in two minutes."

"Thanks. We also need to get someone on finding Adam's address. According to one of Sabrina's friends, he lives out this way somewhere."

"Yeah, that's my other update," Charlie said, his tone telling Tate before he finished speaking that it wasn't good news. "We can't find any information on an Adam Lassiter who fits his description. Not in Desparre and, as far as Max could tell with a quick search, not in Alaska."

Tate's gaze darted to Sabrina, who was watching him wide-eyed and wary. "It's not his real name."

"Probably not," Charlie agreed. "And without his real name…"

Charlie didn't continue, but he didn't have to. If Adam got any hint that police were here, if he'd been watching from the woods as Tate ran up to Sabrina, Adam might hide.

Without a real name, how would they be able to track him?

Chapter Fifteen

Two hours later, Sabrina sat at Tate's desk in the bullpen of the Desparre police station. Blown up to two hundred percent on the computer screen in front of her was a picture taken by a coworker back in New York almost three years ago. A good three months before she'd received the first letter from her stalker.

In the picture, she was smiling and laughing. She wanted to reach out and touch the screen, try to recapture that level of happiness. There was no cloud of fear hanging over her then, no paranoia. Three years wasn't that long ago, and yet, that feeling seemed so out of reach now.

Behind her, maybe loosely a part of the group she was with, maybe not, was someone who sure looked like Adam Lassiter. The picture was grainy enough that she couldn't be positive. If it was really Adam, he'd lost about fifty pounds, replacing it with lean muscle. He'd also cut his hair close to the scalp, making it seem lighter than it did in the photo. He even dressed differently now, in a lot of cargo pants and T-shirts, rather than the striped button-down from the photo.

Maybe it was just wishful thinking to believe it might not be the same person. She'd talked to Adam, laughed with Adam. She'd walked blithely into the woods with him alone. She'd almost invited him into her house.

All her earlier feelings of determination to move forward, to trust her own judgment again and stop jumping at shadows, fell away. What was left was a sadness that seemed to hollow her out.

Tate's hand closed over her forearm, and when she glanced at him, there was sympathy in his gaze.

She eased her arm away and turned to face him. The other officers were occupied on their computers trying to dig up more information about Adam, yet she kept her voice soft, so much so that he leaned closer. Ever since they'd gotten to the station, she'd been holding in her question about how he'd found Adam in an old picture. There was only one way she could imagine. "How did you figure out my last name?"

Guilt crossed over his face, quickly enough that she wasn't sure if she'd imagined it. "I looked for information on a murder in New York City from two years ago where news stories mentioned a stalker."

She nodded and turned back to the computer, saying nothing. The most basic information about why she was running, and it had given away more details about herself than she'd wanted to share.

"I'm sorry," he said, maneuvering so he was in her line of sight, as Sitka whined at her side.

She didn't respond to either of them, just continued to stare at the image. How had she been so wrong? "Do you think Adam was trying to push me off that cliff? Then he changed his mind and grabbed me?"

"I doubt it," Tate said, but his tone told her what he thought was worse.

Reluctantly, she refocused her gaze on him.

"I think both were intentional from the start. He gave you a push *so* he could save you. Create a sense of obligation, make you feel grateful to him. More trusting."

She snorted, not quite meeting Tate's gaze. "It didn't

work. I thought I'd offended him, which I figured was why he wanted to keep going on his own."

Tate nodded. "Maybe that's what happened. His plan backfired, and he decided to continue playing the long game."

Her hands tightened into fists, and she knew her anger wasn't all about Adam. Yes, Tate digging into her background had probably found her stalker. But he'd still betrayed her trust. "It's not a game. It's my *life*."

Tate took hold of the arms of her chair and turned her to face him. He knelt in front of her, and Sitka scooted over, forcing her head onto his knee, her puppy eyes staring up at Sabrina.

The expression on Sitka's face threatened to soften her. Before Tate could speak, she said, "I understand why you dug up information on me. It worked, so I guess I have no right to be mad. But—"

"You have every right to be mad," Tate said. "I should have told you. You've given up so many pieces of your identity to try to feel safe, and I broke your trust. That's another way to make you feel unsafe, and I'm sorry."

Lifting her gaze to his, she saw sincerity, even regret, in his eyes. How had he known exactly what she was feeling? He spoke as if he really did understand. But it was more than that. She'd chosen to trust him in a way she hadn't trusted anyone else in a long time. And he'd still gone behind her back.

She'd been by herself for two years. But she'd never felt more alone than she did right now.

Tate cringed, as if he could read her thoughts. Then he fit his hand around hers and whispered, "I really am sorry, Sabrina. You're… I care about you. All I want to do is help you."

She glanced from his hand, which felt so comforting on hers, even though he was part of the reason she hurt right now. She wished they were anywhere but at the police station, with his chief watching across the room. Pulling her hand free, she scooted her chair slightly backward, away from him.

Sitka let out another low whine, and Sabrina forced a lightness to her voice she didn't feel. "It's okay, Sitka." She pet the dog until her tail thumped, then told Tate, "I forgive you. Let's figure out..."

She trailed off as the image of Adam caught the corner of her eye. Seeing it from this angle sparked a memory, brought the image she hadn't really remembered into focus. She'd been out for a coworker's birthday, at a bar that was too loud. The bar had been stuffy, the night too hot, the drinks flowing too freely. After a few hours, she'd started to feel more comfortable, have more fun.

The woman in the forefront of the picture with her—Jessamyn, who'd later become a good friend—had sensed her discomfort, grabbed her arm and taken her around the bar, introducing her to everyone, even people Jessamyn didn't know. And a group of guys who were friends of one of Jessamyn's friends.

"I think I remember him," she breathed, as more of the evening solidified in her mind.

Each of the guys had given their names, and some of them had provided other random information about themselves, like their job or hobbies. Her gaze had floated over each of them quickly. She remembered laughing through most of the introductions, partly because she'd been a little tipsy and partly because she'd been having fun.

She hadn't spoken to Adam again that night, that much she was sure. After being introduced to the group, she'd set down her beer and gotten onto the dance floor with Jessamyn. She hadn't left it until a few hours later, when she'd hopped into a cab and gone home.

"What do you remember?" Tate asked, making her refocus on him.

She let out an ironic laugh. "Periphery of my life is no joke. The most conversation we had was a quick introduction. I told him my name, he said his, and I was off to the dance floor. I never saw him again."

"Are you sure?"

"Pretty sure."

Tate nodded. "I don't suppose you remember his name?"

"You really don't think it's Adam Lassiter?"

"Well, we haven't found any property in his name, nor have we found any Adam Lassiter that matches his description. So, I'm thinking it's not his real name."

"I don't remember. All those guys were a blur, just a quick hello and on to the next person. It was a party. I was new to my job and made friends with coworkers that night. That's mostly what I remember."

"It's okay," Tate told her. "We'll dig it up."

"Tate."

Sabrina looked up, and Tate stood as the chief reached his desk.

"Chief. What is it?"

Chief Griffith nodded at her. "Sabrina." Then he looked at them both as he said, "I spoke to your friend Lora. We asked her to call Adam, but he's not answering."

"He should show up in town eventually, though, right?" Sabrina asked. Or had he been close behind her when she'd trekked back toward the road and discovered Tate and Sitka waiting for her? Had he realized his identity was blown and already disappeared?

The way the chief's lips tightened made dread settle in her stomach even before he replied. "When you were giving me a rundown of what happened with Adam in the woods, Officer Emory here was drawing a map for two of our other officers. He detailed exactly where Sitka went through the woods when she was tracking from your house last week."

"Did they find anything?"

The chief glanced at Tate again, and something unspoken seemed to pass between them, something that made Tate's expression tighten, too. "We found a cabin. It's old, and the bank foreclosed on it last year when the guy who owned it passed away. It's been sitting empty ever since, at least as far as anyone knew."

"Adam was squatting there?" Tate asked, fury on his face. "Where is this place?"

The chief nodded. "We think so. We found evidence that someone has been there recently, including some clothes, food and pinholes in the wall like something had been posted there. It looks like it was cleared out in a hurry."

Tate swore as the chief fixed his attention entirely on her.

Sabrina stiffened as he continued. "This cabin would take a while to get to on the road from your place, but if you go directly through the woods, it's about a mile away, a straight shot. You probably never even knew anyone was back there."

The dread intensified, a familiar feeling from her early days of running, constantly feeling like her stalker was right behind her. She thought it had just been paranoia, but had he been there all along?

SIX DAYS AFTER Adam had cleared out of the cabin behind hers, there was no sign of him.

Sabrina had spent the time alternating between extreme emotions. One day, she'd be certain a police officer would knock on the door to the hotel room where they'd stuck her and announce that it was all over and she could go home to the family she hadn't dared to contact in two years. The next day, she'd be sure this would continue forever and she'd be forced to make a new impossible choice: go back to running and assume Adam was right behind her in every new town or stay here and wait for the police to run out of resources to waste on her. Wait for him to come after her.

Most likely the story Adam had told about living in Alaska all his life, about having recently lost a wife, were all lies to make her feel comfortable letting him get close. It had been brilliant. Especially befriending Lora before he'd ever approached her. Getting the story secondhand that he was a widower mourning the too-recent loss of his wife had immediately ruled him out in her mind as her stalker.

The fact that he'd appeared in a picture with her in New York suggested he'd actually lived there, at least for some amount of time. If he'd grown up in the city like her, there had to be only so long he could hide out in the treacherous Alaskan wilderness before the locals tracked him down.

But they hadn't found him yet.

Meanwhile, she was going stir-crazy in the ridiculously opulent room in Desparre's only hotel, the luxury Royal Desparre. When she'd nervously asked about the cost, Tate had said it was being taken care of and insisted it was safer than being in the middle of nowhere. She still had her alert button and the owners—who doubled as management— knew to call the police if they spotted Adam. Tate checked in several times a day, usually by phone, but he and Sitka also stopped by every night.

Still, she spent most of her days alone. Since she couldn't contact anyone and there were only so many hours she could spend making jewelry, especially with her creativity having taken a dive, she was bored. Having too many hours to think was making her more anxious.

So, when there was a knock on her door, she was up and reaching for the lock before her mind caught up and she checked the peephole. A grin burst free, and a familiar anticipation settled in her stomach when she saw Tate standing on the other side, looking serious in his uniform but holding a pizza box.

He didn't usually finish up at the station and make his way over to her hotel until almost eight, so she'd gotten used to waiting for dinner. They'd never made plans to eat together each night, but he kept showing up until it felt like a standing date. Only the fact that he wore his uniform and always updated her on their progress reminded her each day that it wasn't really a date. Reminded her that nothing she felt for Tate could be permanent.

She still hadn't fully forgiven him for digging into her past without her permission, for not telling her when he'd learned her real name and searched her brother's social media. But he'd done it to help her. And it had worked. The more time she spent with him, the less she wanted to think about the mistakes in the past. The more she wanted to entertain a future that somehow had him in it.

It wasn't meant to be. But she could pretend.

Flinging open the door, she asked, "How did you know I needed some pizza?"

Woof! Sitka walked forward, butting Sabrina hard enough with her nose to knock her back a step.

As Tate reminded his dog to relax, Sabrina laughed and leaned down to pet her. "I think she wants pizza, too."

Woof!

Grinning, Tate followed his dog into the room, closing and locking the door behind him like always.

Sabrina couldn't help the flutter of nerves that erupted in her stomach. They seemed to be increasing in intensity each evening she spent with him. Since updates on the case only took so long—especially since there'd been nothing to report on Adam, and the guy they'd arrested last week still wasn't talking—their conversations had been getting more personal.

He'd already dug through her life on his own, so she'd

decided she might as well tell him the truth about everything. The decision had been freeing.

And, she had to admit as he set the pizza box on the table by the window, the man looked good in his dark blue police uniform. She'd been attracted to him from the start, admired the thick dark brows that added even more intensity to his angular face and fixated on the full lips that drew her attention. But she'd always found that she grew more physically attracted to a man when she was emotionally attracted to him, too. Every day she spent with Tate, that attraction increased.

He turned back toward her, and from the way he went still, she knew her feelings were broadcasted across her face.

Ducking her head on the pretext of petting Sitka, Sabrina cursed her pale skin, which felt like it was on fire.

When she finally had her blush under control, she lifted her head again and found that Tate had crossed the room without her hearing him.

With Sitka sitting between them, he stood in front of her, his gaze locked on hers, a matching desire in his deep brown eyes.

She swayed forward, leaning over Sitka, without even consciously planning to do it.

He leaned toward her, captured her hands in his, and the touch sent sparks over her skin and up her arms.

Her lips tingled in anticipation, and as she moistened them with her tongue, his gaze darted there.

His voice sounded slightly strangled as he told her, "I have news."

News? Her brain struggled to focus on anything other than the heat in his eyes and the closeness of his lips. "About the investigation?"

"Yeah."

She stared at him, trying to decide what to pursue, until he finally gave her a half grin and leaned slightly away.

He kept hold of her hands, though, his fingers stroking lightly against her knuckles a distraction. "Mario McKeever still isn't talking. But we've been able to confirm his whereabouts two years ago. He's from New York, but he hasn't lived there in almost four years. And when you were getting notes, he was living in South Carolina and having regular run-ins with the law. No arrests, but the local police definitely knew his name."

"Okay," she said, her brain still processing everything more slowly. But she didn't want to pull her hands away, break the connection he'd initiated. "We were already pretty sure it was Adam, so that's not much news, right?"

"No. But I thought you'd want to know." He paused again, and she could see the fight in his eyes as his gaze drifted back to her lips. "There is one other thing. Since it's been almost a week with no sign of Adam, Chief Griffith suggested a plan to lure him back into the open. Stop waiting on his timetable and take back some control."

"Okay." Now, this was an idea Sabrina could get behind. She was tempted to lick her lips again, just to see if it would break Tate's concentration, but she resisted as his gaze lifted back to hers.

"Adam's MO has been to go after anyone who might be a source of support, right? I mean, he came after me and Sitka after presumably seeing me stop by your house. And of course, there's Dylan."

Sabrina nodded, the memory of the police showing up at Dylan's family's lake house with the news of his death erasing all desire. "Yes."

"So, the chief thinks we should use that to our advantage. Get him angry enough to come after someone again."

Sabrina frowned at him. "Who? How? I don't want to

put anyone at risk. I don't really have any friends here except Lora and—"

"You have me," Tate said, his tone firm. "We're going to make sure Adam takes the bait so we can take him down. The chief doesn't want it to look like I'm a friend, a source of support. He wants us to publicly play out a romance and get Adam to take his shot."

Chapter Sixteen

Tate held Sabrina's hand loosely in his own as he walked in downtown Desparre. Her long delicate fingers, slightly calloused from making jewelry, felt so right in his. There was a smile on his face he didn't need to fake or force, but it didn't mean he'd lost sight of the dangers.

The bench straight ahead, still crumpled and destroyed from the truck Sabrina's stalker might have sent after Sitka, was a stark reminder. So were the woods beyond that, which looked too much like the forest in Boston he'd darted into to escape his fellow officers' gunfire.

The desire to constantly swivel his head, keep an eye on his surroundings, was hard to ignore. But Tate trusted the Desparre officers he'd worked with for the past five and a half years. This wasn't Boston. Besides, both he and Sabrina wore bulletproof vests beneath their lightweight jackets.

He was a little overheated walking in the sunshine. Or maybe it was just from his proximity to Sabrina.

Except for the weight of that vest and the knowledge that his colleagues were hiding nearby and watching his every move, everything about this felt right. A natural progression of the attraction he'd felt from the moment he'd met Sabrina. Getting to know her more over the past week had only intensified those feelings.

He glanced at her, taking in things he'd noticed the first time he'd seen her: the way the sun cast a golden sheen over her wavy hair, the natural elegance of her face, the depths of her green eyes. But also seeing new things now that she'd truly let him in: the way her lips tightened at the corners when she was stressed. The flush that rose easily to her cheeks when she was flustered or embarrassed. The way her gaze was always moving, taking everything in and strategizing. For someone who made a living in creative arts, she was analytical enough to run through police strategy with him. And successfully evade a stalker for two years on her own.

A swell of pride filled him, even though he had no right to it. Without conscious intent, he squeezed her hand, and she looked his way.

Her smile was equal parts shy uncertainty and knowing amusement. But it was probably hard to miss the effect she had on him. Even his chief had picked up on it, used it as the basis to suggest this pretense.

"Sabrina!" From one of the intact benches near the park, Lora had spotted them. She came running and Tate took a deep breath.

They were about to discover if their ruse was working.

He hadn't been thrilled about telling Lora their suspicions about Adam, but after his call to her, it had seemed like the best approach. She'd promised to keep it to herself and although she was often in everyone's business, she was trustworthy. Still, he and the chief had agreed it was best not to give her any more detail than they had to, including the truth about his and Sabrina's supposed relationship.

Lora slowed slightly as she approached, her gaze dropping speculatively to Sabrina's and Tate's linked hands before she threw her arms around Sabrina's neck.

Sabrina was knocked back a step by the force of it,

and Tate dropped her hand. While she was distracted, he glanced around.

Nothing seemed out of the ordinary. Just another day in downtown Desparre. There were more people out than usual because of the brilliant sunshine, but not so many that Adam would be able to hide in a crowd.

Then again, he knew his fellow officers were close, and he didn't see them. The sliver of anxiety he'd felt since they stepped outside grew, and he wished for Sitka's comforting presence. His K-9 partner was back at his house, since Tate was pretending to be off work. He'd initially argued to bring her, but the chief had overruled him, saying he didn't want to provide a reason for a group of kids to surround Sitka and distract them.

"I'm so sorry," Lora exclaimed, squeezing Sabrina's hand and looking upset. "I had no idea… I believed Adam when he said he'd grown up in Alaska. He knew so much about the state. And his wife—"

"Don't worry," Sabrina interrupted, her smile almost reaching her eyes. "We're not completely sure it was him, but whoever it was, the police seem to have scared him off. And the upside of it all…"

She took Tate's hand again, and he stepped closer, returning the soft smile she gave him.

"I met Tate," she concluded, an upward lilt to her voice that made the whole thing sound even more real.

He wished it was.

He'd shared things with Sabrina he hadn't shared with anyone in a long time. Pieces of his life that he'd been purposely evasive about with colleagues, even those people he called his friends. But after a week of dinners in her hotel room, there'd been only so long they could discuss the investigation, only so many awkward attempts at chitchat before she'd dived in with real questions. He'd looked into parts of her life without her consent, so he figured he owed her some truths, too, even if he couldn't give her all the details.

She was the only person here who knew how badly he missed talking to his parents, their respective partners, and even his mom's boyfriend's kids, who were younger than him and he hadn't grown up with but were all nice. She didn't understand his vague excuses for not having seen them in over five years, but the rest of it had been true. She understood because she missed her family, too.

Their connection went deeper than their shared experience—especially since she didn't even know they shared one. As he watched her smile and tell Lora the story about how they'd started dating, he wished he'd asked Sabrina out the first time he'd met her. Their relationship still would have had an expiration date, but at least it would have been real.

The ache that filled him at that moment must have shown on his face, because Lora shifted her attention to him. As he attempted a smile to cover up whatever she'd seen, she let out a surprised laugh.

"You know, the first time Sabrina admitted she thought you were cute, I told her to go for it. But I thought you were too much of a loner to ever get involved."

Her assessment of him stung a bit, but it was hard to focus on that part. He grinned at Sabrina, couldn't help himself from nudging her the way he might if he was actually dating her. "You thought I was cute, huh?"

She flushed an even deeper red, but instead of mumbling something vague like he'd expected, she countered, "Yep. But it was Sitka who pushed you over the edge and got you a date."

A surprised laugh escaped. "Figures. Everyone always tells me she's the better-looking one in the partnership."

Lora laughed at that, then gave Sabrina another hug. "I should let you two enjoy your date." She glanced from Sabrina to him and back again. "I'm happy for you, Sabrina. You deserve this." Then she leaned in and hugged Tate. "I think you do, too, Tate."

As she walked away, Tate glanced at Sabrina again. She was smiling at him, amusement and something that looked like longing on her face.

The longer he stared into her eyes, the more the amusement dropped away until she swayed slightly forward.

He felt himself lean toward her instinctively and then forced himself to straighten, squeeze her hand and tug her forward again. He made his voice overly cheerful, overly loud. "Want to walk around the park?"

It was a reminder to himself as much as her that most of the Desparre police department was watching them right now. As much as he wanted to kiss her, he didn't want to do it in front of an audience. And he didn't want to do it when it wasn't real.

At least if Adam was watching, he should have no doubt that they were a couple.

Sabrina blinked a few times, the desire there fading away until she gave him a tentative smile. "Sure."

As they continued down the street, regret welled up. Regret that he hadn't given in to the moment and kissed her. Regret that he couldn't tell her the full truth about who he was. But even more than that, regret that their time was limited.

Because once they arrested her stalker, she'd be leaving. And he couldn't follow. New York was too close to Boston to ever be safe for him.

AFTER TWO FULL days of flaunting her supposed relationship with Tate all over town, Sabrina was exhausted. And Adam—if he still here—hadn't taken the bait.

Still, as she walked beside Tate around the cute set of shops outside downtown, hyperaware of the feel of his hand in hers, she didn't care if Adam took a week to make his move. The outdoor shopping center, a quirky assortment of stores that seemed to have holiday lights on the roofs year-round, was normally one of her favorite spots. But she couldn't focus on them with Tate beside her.

If she squinted a little, she could make their surroundings go blurry and just keep Tate in focus. If only there were a way to do that with her life. Make all the challenges drop away and just be here with him for real.

For the first time in two years, it felt like someone actually *knew* her again. Sharing more and more about herself with him each night seemed right. Even if she'd met him back in New York, surrounded by plenty of friends and family, she would have wanted him in her life.

"What made you decide to become a cop?" The words popped out of her mouth without her even realizing she'd been thinking them. But it was something she'd wondered about since the moment that truck had raced toward Sitka, and again later, when she'd heard Tate had been knocked off his feet chasing Mario McKeever.

He seemed surprised by the question, but then his steps slowed slightly, something she'd come to recognize he did when he got serious.

"I told you my parents divorced when I was young." When she nodded, he continued. "I wouldn't say it was an ugly divorce, not compared to the things I've seen as a cop. But as a seven-year-old, it felt scary. It seemed like all they did was argue, and I was always in the middle. They shared custody, which in the long run, I'm glad about. But at the time, it felt like as soon as I got settled in one house, I was shuttled to the other."

"I'm sorry," Sabrina said when he paused, his lips pursed, his forehead creasing. "My dad took off when I was five. Totally different thing, because he spent most of my childhood chasing after the next new thing—usually his next girlfriend or his next car. He reappears every few years, wanting to reestablish a relationship. Even as an adult, it's disorienting. And honestly, I saw him occasionally, but I'm not that interested. It's not much of a bond when it's all on one person's terms."

He squeezed her hand. "I'm glad you had your mom and brother. And I'm glad you'll get back to them soon."

His words sent a pang through her—a desperate longing to see her family mixed with dread at the thought of leaving him behind.

Maybe he saw how conflicted she suddenly felt, because he cleared his throat and started walking again. She hadn't even realized they'd stopped.

"So, dealing with my parents' divorce made me angry, frustrated." His lips tilted downward as he added, "Lonely. And just adrift. My dad had already moved across town, into a different school district. Then mom couldn't afford our old house by herself. She moved closer to my dad, thinking it would be easier. But it meant I also had to change schools, and I started getting bullied."

Sabrina put her free hand against his arm. "That's a lot to deal with all at once. I'm sorry you went through that."

He gave her a quick smile that seemed to say *Don't worry*. It was so typically Tate that she couldn't help but smile back. The smile faded as he looked forward again, kept talking. How had she gotten to know what all of his smiles meant? How had it happened so quickly?

She'd known him for just over two weeks. They weren't even *actually* dating, and already, she felt more connected to him than she had with Dylan after three months.

The thought made guilt rush through her. She tried to push it back, to just focus on this moment, on this man. Even if it wasn't real, it was the best thing she'd had in her life in years.

"I started getting into fights, too." At the surprised

glance she shot him, he laughed. "I know. It's out of character. It was then, too. My parents didn't know what to do with me. Then one day I was walking home from school, and a group of kids started beating up on me."

Sabrina gasped, and he squeezed her hand again.

"I was ten then, I think. Three years of struggling at school and at home and letting my anger get the best of me. A police officer stopped his car, sirens flashing. All those kids took off *fast*. I wasn't in any shape to go anywhere, so the cop gave me a ride home. He talked to me about channeling anger the right way, about making the right choices even when the people around me are making the wrong ones. It made an impression."

Sabrina tried to imagine a younger Tate, angry and hurting. She pictured him at ten, his light brown skin covered in bruises, his deep brown eyes—always so intuitive and kind—filled with cynicism and frustration. "Did you stay in touch with him?"

"It wasn't *that* big a town. Even if I hadn't wanted to, he would have found me." Tate laughed. "He retired a couple of years ago down to Florida." The fondness in his tone faded to something wishful. "I haven't talked to him in a while."

"Maybe you should call him," Sabrina suggested, wishing the solutions were so simple for the people she missed.

He paused, regret flitting across his face before he smiled down at her. "Yeah, I should."

She stared back at him, wondering if there was any way to turn what they had into something real. If he could stay connected with his friend in Florida, he could do the same for her in New York. Maybe he'd want to visit, let her show him around. Could they build a relationship from that long a distance?

Then again, did it make any sense to let someone like Tate go over something as simple as geography?

Her pulse picked up as he continued to stare at her, as if

he was trying to read her mind. But wondering if he'd ever leave Alaska if they got serious was getting ridiculously ahead of herself. They'd never broached the idea of dating for real. They'd never even *kissed*.

His gaze darted to her lips.

Could he read her mind? A smile trembled on her lips, and each breath came faster as it occurred to her. What better way to see how Tate felt about her? And as an added bonus, maybe it would finally give Adam the incentive he needed to take the bait.

Before she lost her courage, Sabrina fisted her free hand in Tate's T-shirt, pulling him downward and swiveling him toward her all at once. She grinned at the surprise that flashed in his eyes, followed immediately by a dark intensity that told her he wanted to kiss her, too.

Dropping his T-shirt, she pulled her other hand free from his and slid both of her hands slowly up his arms, holding his gaze. His eyelids dropped and his muscles flexed under her fingers, emboldening her. She kept going, leaning up on her tiptoes as she slipped her hands beneath the sleeves of his shirt. She vaguely registered the feel of puckered, uneven skin beneath her left hand, and then his lips were pressed against hers.

They were soft, even fuller than she'd realized. Electricity buzzed over her skin as he brushed his lips against hers, once, twice, before sliding his tongue across the seam of her mouth.

She sank against him, gripping his shoulders as his hands clamped onto her hips and raised her up more. Opening her mouth, she invited him in, flicking her tongue against his as her body flushed at the feel of him against her.

Then, too quickly, he was setting her away from him, his hands on her biceps, the apology in his eyes not hiding the desire. "Maybe we should do this without an audience," he suggested, his voice huskier than usual.

A smile broke free, echoing the hope bursting in her chest. He shared her feelings. She could see it in his gaze, feel it in his touch.

Maybe she wasn't a fool to think about a future with him. Maybe, thanks to him, she could finally *have* a future.

Before she could voice any of the things she was thinking, he frowned and dug into his pocket. Then, he was holding his phone out for her to read a text message from Chief Griffith.

I don't know if Adam left or if he's just not taking the bait with so many people around.

Sabrina glanced around the sparsely populated shops. She could see Officer Nate Dreymond in plainclothes pretending to window-shop down the street, a couple arguing about their weekend coming out of the shop next to them, and a handful of people wandering in and out of stores. It was less busy than the park where Adam had set Talise's truck on Sitka. Then again, maybe he was worried the police were watching. Maybe he suspected it was a trap. She glanced down at the rest of the text.

We have a new plan. Something that will look like an easier mark for Adam. You and Sabrina pretend to go away on a romantic weekend together.

Chapter Seventeen

"His real name is Adam Locklay," Tate announced as Sabrina opened the door to her hotel room.

He paused to hand her the tea and muffin he'd picked up for her in the hotel's restaurant, taking in her hair, which seemed more wavy and untamed than usual. From the sleepy way she blinked at him, she hadn't been awake long. He paused to take in a fresh-from-sleep Sabrina as she seemed to register what he'd said.

"What?" Her voice was barely above a whisper as Sitka pushed past him and sat at Sabrina's feet, wagging her tail.

Sabrina's eyes were wide enough to momentarily distract him with their various shades of green, shifting from emerald to moss. The scent of the tea he'd bought her wafted toward him, along with the faint smell of vanilla. Her shampoo or lotion? Whatever it was, it was as distracting as the rest of her.

Closing the door behind him, he asked, "Does the name mean something to you?"

"No. How did you figure it out?"

"By spending a lot of time on social media. Using that picture I found, we identified other people in the background close to Adam and dug into their social media until we finally got to a picture where he was tagged. With his real name, we could dig up a lot more about him, too."

As Sitka gave a short whine, Sabrina smiled briefly at his dog, absently petting her. "I can't believe I finally have a real name to put to these years of notes and…" She lifted her hand, palm up, as if she couldn't sum up all of the horror of her past two and a half years.

He slid his hand underneath her upturned palm and she flipped it over to entwine their hands. "A name is the first step. We're on *his* tail now. It's a matter of time before we catch up to him."

"I hope so." She glanced down at their linked hands, then up at him, and he could see the questions in her eyes.

Questions about that kiss they'd shared yesterday. About his suggestion that they hit pause until they were alone again.

They were alone *now*.

Nerves tightened his chest, and anticipation quickened his breathing. She'd always seemed shy, so despite the heated looks she'd been giving him, he'd been shocked when she'd grabbed him and kissed him yesterday. And damn, she really could kiss.

His gaze dropped to her lips, and her tongue darted out to wet them, making him sway forward. But he caught himself before he pulled her to him.

He hadn't come here to finish something he never should have let her start. He'd come to talk about the status of their search for Adam and their plan to finally lure him out of hiding and end the threat against Sabrina for good.

Letting go of her hand, he stepped around her and set his take-out coffee on the table, giving himself a chance to refocus. He leaned against the wall, putting a little space between them. "Adam Locklay moved out to New York for college and stuck around. He's got a history of stalking."

Sabrina set her tea and muffin on the table beside her bed, moving toward him.

Sitka stuck close to Sabrina's side, her tail wagging. His

dog stared up at Sabrina happily, the way she did with him at home, when she was relaxed and off duty. She was going to miss Sabrina as much as he was.

"He's done this to other women?"

She sounded furious on their behalf, and it made him like her even more. She'd spent two and a half years afraid for herself, afraid for the people she loved because of Adam, and here she was, mad that he'd dared to make anyone else feel that way.

"Yeah." He tried not to get distracted by her approach, by thoughts of how little time he might have left to spend with her. "But as far as we can tell, never like this. In the past, he stalked women he knew. Two ex-girlfriends and one coworker, who all went to the police. Two of them ended up with restraining orders against him, and one called the police multiple times because of incidents, usually him stopping by unwanted and refusing to leave."

"Any violence?" Sabrina asked, her tone hesitant, like she was afraid to hear who else he'd killed chasing the objects of his obsession.

"None that I could find. He escalated with you."

"Aren't I lucky," she muttered darkly.

The only one who was lucky in any of this was him. If Adam hadn't stalked her, then Tate never would have met her. She would have gone on with her life in New York, gone on dating Dylan Westwood, maybe even married him.

Even the idea of never having the chance to know her put an uncomfortable tightness in Tate's chest that made it hard to take a full breath. But he wished Adam had never set eyes on her, wished Sabrina had never known this terror.

When he didn't immediately answer, she stepped a little closer, sending another waft of vanilla his way, and asked, "Have you been able to track his movements? Has he been behind me this whole time?"

"I don't think so. We don't know how he found you, but

there's evidence he was still in New York five months ago. He works as an independent software developer, and he's able to work from home, so it's possible he's been traveling and returning to New York. But given what you've told me about all the places you've been, I have to think he found you here and then followed."

Her shoulders jerked, and she let out a huff. "Of all the places I've hidden, this one is the most remote. The place I felt most safe. The place that felt most like *home*."

Something pensive crossed her face, some emotion he tried to latch onto but couldn't quite read.

It wasn't fair to her not to keep his distance. But he couldn't seem to stop himself from moving a little closer. "This *is* your home, at least right now. It's your town. And we look out for each other here. We're going to find him. It just…" He frowned, trying to figure out the best way to tell her, then decided straightforward was the best approach. She'd managed the threat alone for two years. She could handle his other news.

"It just might take a little longer than we'd hoped. Which is why I think the plan the chief mentioned yesterday is a good one. If you're okay with it, we're getting things prepped right now. In two days, it will be set up."

Sabrina stared at him a minute, like she wasn't sure which part of that to question first. Finally, she asked, "Why will it take longer?"

"We assumed Adam's stories about living in Alaska were all lies." When shock and compassion crossed Sabrina's face, Tate rushed on. "And they were. He was never married. You don't need to feel sorry for his loss. We suspect he made it up as a way to connect with you, to get you to talk about your own loss."

Grief and fury flashed across Sabrina's face in rapid succession, and Tate felt an answering pang of sympathy.

Adam had killed someone she cared about and then tried to connect with her by pretending a similar loss.

Sabrina clamped a hand against her stomach. "He was hoping I'd talk to him about Dylan's death, never knowing he'd actually caused it? That's even sicker than the notes."

"I know. I'm sorry."

Lines creased Sabrina's forehead as she wrapped her arms around her middle, seeming to sink inward. "I'm glad I never did."

But he could hear it in her words. She'd thought about it, thought Adam was someone who'd understand her loss.

Cursing inwardly, Tate readied himself to give her more bad news. "He never lived here, either. The thing is, he was probably able to convince someone like Lora who *did* grow up here, and in the mountains, no less, because the wilderness isn't foreign to him. He grew up in Michigan's upper peninsula, with parents who were known to have some survivalist mentality."

"He understood how to hide here," Sabrina summarized. "That explains why he was so comfortable trekking through the woods to spy on me."

"Yes," Tate confirmed. He took another step closer, until all he'd need to do was reach out and take her hands in his, pull her to him and hold her until the worry and betrayal left her face. He wanted to, especially when his movement made heat spark in her gaze again.

He wanted to forget all of his good intentions of remaining professional, helping her reclaim her life without making it even harder to say goodbye. He wanted to feel her lips on his again, wanted to run his hands through her hair and walk her to the bed that was way too close. Instead, he fisted his hands at his side.

From the way Sitka's gaze moved from him to Sabrina, he couldn't even fool his dog.

The last of the anger left her face as her lips twitched

with sudden amusement. "So you want to go away with me for the weekend, then." Her tone was teasing, but her gaze was serious as she moved close, slid her hands up his arms. The soft glide of her fingertips and the mix of nerves and desire in her eyes weakened his resolve.

Her fingers stalled on the edges of the scar hidden by the sleeve of his T-shirt. "What happened here?"

"A danger of the job," he answered, a semitruth because he didn't want to outright lie to her. "Gunshot wound." At her gasp, he added, "It was a long time ago. And it just skimmed me."

Summoning his willpower, he took a step back, watching the confusion in her eyes as he said, "I don't want you to worry. You're not going to be in danger. We have two days to set this up right. This is going to be a trap for Adam."

She bit the edge of her lip, then whispered, "I'm not worried. I feel safe with you."

Her words sent a rush through him even before she moved forward again. This time, she was less hesitant, giving him a shaky smile before she pressed her hands against his chest.

His arms twitched at the contact, and her smile grew more confident as she leaned into him, replacing her hands with the length of her body. "I think it will work."

It took him a minute to take his focus off the feel of her pressed against him and understand her words. "I think so, too." Adam was less likely to be able to resist if he and Sabrina were supposedly alone.

"And once he's no longer a threat—" she slid her arms around his waist and leaned back slightly to stare up at him "—I was hoping you and I could try this for real."

His mouth went dry, and for an instant, he couldn't breathe. The desire to nod and press his lips against hers was overwhelming, but how could he make a promise he couldn't keep? Even though there was no indication Kevin or Paul had found him as a result of the news article, he'd planned to leave town as soon as he'd eliminated the threat of her stalker. Even if he decided it was safe enough to stay in Alaska, what would he say when she inevitably wanted him to come see her in New York? What if he got too close to Boston again and the threats against him became a danger to her?

"I can't," he said, his voice a scratchy whisper.

She flushed deep red and backed out of his arms as Sitka whimpered and nudged up against her, eyeing Tate like he'd just become the enemy.

"I'm sorry. I want to. You have no idea…" He took a deep breath, trying to be as honest as he could. "But Desparre is a long way from New York City."

She nodded, ducking her head as she backed farther away.

An ache settled in his gut, for hurting her, for saying no when he so desperately wanted to say yes. But it wasn't right. He'd come to care about her too much to hurt her. In the long run, pursuing a relationship with Sabrina could make her the target of someone new. The threat against him might never end.

"I promised to give you your life back." He stepped closer, tipping her chin up with his hand even as he longed to pull her back into his arms. "I won't stop until I do it. But that means leaving everything in Alaska behind. Including me."

NERVES CHURNED IN Sabrina's stomach as she waited for Tate to come to her hotel room and pick her up for their supposed romantic weekend away together.

Three days ago, when she'd kissed him in the street, their pretending had felt so natural, so *real*. When he'd said he wanted to continue what she'd started in private, she thought he felt all the same things she did. So when he'd shown up the next morning and insisted long-distance would never work, it had been a shock. Embarrassing. And devastating.

Yet, he'd kept coming to see her the next two evenings, bringing dinner and smiling at her like nothing had happened. She'd tried to smile back, act as unaffected as he appeared, but *that* pretending had left her exhausted and depressed.

At least he'd continued to bring Sitka with him. The sweet dog definitely sensed something was wrong, and she'd spent a lot of the visits at Sabrina's feet, her head perched on Sabrina's knees. She would miss Sitka when she left, too.

Despite everything, she still believed their plan could work. Adam had gone after Dylan the day she was meeting his family for the first time. Back then, she'd thought it was a terrible coincidence. But now, knowing how closely he could have been watching her in her cabin? Remembering how he'd managed to slip a note into her purse even after the police had been on high alert trying to find him back in New York? He'd probably known.

She'd been about to take a serious step in a relationship, and he'd stopped it. Given how much she and Tate had been spreading news about their intended getaway to a secluded cabin, she had to believe he'd repeat that pattern.

Her nerves intensified, shifted into fear that made her breathing way too fast. "Relax," she told herself. Tate was a trained police officer. And they wouldn't be alone. Much of the Desparre PD would be hidden nearby, ready to take Adam down.

It would work. It had to work. Because Tate was right. It was time for her to go home.

Acute homesickness swept through her, pricking her eyes with tears. Without conscious thought, she moved toward her phone. She'd never dared to go onto social media, hadn't wanted to sign into an account that might leave some kind of trail. But if Tate had been able to see details about her brother...

Pulling up Conor's social-media account without signing in, she realized he'd made a lot of his posts public. Her stockbroker brother, who lived by numbers and rules and always warned her about keeping her personal information locked up, had purposely left pieces of his life open to the world.

As she scrolled through, so fast the pictures and posts were nothing more than quick glimpses, she realized he'd done it two years ago. A way for her to stay connected with them, no matter how far she ran. And she'd never known, never even thought to check, because she'd been focused on pure survival.

Conor's face blurred, and she swiped at the tears that had welled in her eyes as she scrolled back to the top of his feed. His latest post, dated yesterday, showed him beaming beside Jie, his longtime girlfriend. Jie was grinning, one hand held up to the camera, showing off a sparkling diamond.

They'd gotten engaged. Finally. They'd met in college, dated ever since. In the year or two before Sabrina had run, she could tell Jie was starting to get frustrated. They'd been together a long time. She wanted to get married and have kids. Conor was dragging his feet.

Sabrina got it. Their dad had taken off when she was five and Conor was seven. While she and Conor had watched their mom struggle to make ends meet, to try to fill the void their father had left, their dad had jumped from one woman to the next, carefree. He'd appeared every few months, or sometimes every few years, and dropped off presents, wanted to take them out. It hadn't really put Sabrina off the idea of marriage, but from a young age, Conor had vowed never to wed.

Jie was so good for her brother. Sabrina had been worried he would lose her if he didn't make that commitment. Now the leap of faith had happened. And she'd missed it. Still, a bittersweet smile pulled her lips at the happiness radiating from that picture.

Maybe she'd make it back to New York for the wedding. The idea buoyed her, took away some of the pain of seeing all she'd missed. She scrolled more, seeing birthdays and holidays. More happiness, but she could see it on everyone's faces that they missed her as much as she missed them.

Then she found a picture of Conor and her mom from a few weeks earlier, smiling in Central Park, and a sharp pain clamped back down on her chest. She ran her finger over the side of her mom's face, seeing new lines at the corners of her mouth and across her forehead. She looked like she'd experienced way too much sadness in the past two years. Conor, too, looked older, more weary.

Sabrina had done this to them by leaving. If she had to go back and make the same decision now, she'd do it again. But she was tired of being forced to choose safety over happiness.

There was a familiar knock at the door, a particular beat she recognized as Tate's, followed by Sitka's enthusiastic *woof!*

Closing the browser on her phone, she stood and took a deep breath.

It was long past time she made a stand for herself and reclaimed the life she'd left behind.

Chapter Eighteen

"Hi," Sabrina breathed, feeling a flush creep up her neck and cheeks at the shy, uncertain tone of her voice. Clearing her throat, she opened the hotel door wider.

Sitka rushed inside at the invitation, running around Sabrina in a circle that made her laugh.

Tate smiled, something hesitant in his gaze, but he couldn't seem to help a laugh at his dog's antics. "She's a pro at work, but get her off duty and she's a big goofball."

Woof! Sitka glanced back at him briefly, then returned her attention to Sabrina.

"You know you are," Tate teased his dog as Sabrina leaned down to pet Sitka and hide her face behind a curtain of hair.

This was the Tate she wanted to know better. The Tate who teased his dog, who made her feel safe and excited at the same time. Even knowing that today was all for show, it was too easy to imagine a version of this that was real. The idea of going on an actual romantic weekend away with him made her pulse pick up again.

Her attraction wasn't one-sided, that much she knew for sure. But Tate was too practical and realistic, probably the result of being a police officer—or maybe why he'd become one. She, on the other hand, had always indulged her creative, fanciful impulses. It was how she'd ended up in fashion design and now, finally, jewelry-making. More than once, those impulses had led her to take a chance on the wrong relationship. But until Adam had forced his way into her life, she'd lived without fear.

She hadn't been irresponsible. Her mom had drilled into her from a young age the need to be diligent about safety. But she'd refused to let her dad's leaving color the way she looked at relationships just like she'd refused to let her mom's overprotectiveness and caution send her into a safe, staid career instead of the uncertain field of creative arts that she loved.

After six months of notes and then Dylan's murder, she'd lost too much of that freedom to fear. Tate made her want to toss aside caution, toss aside her own pride and go after what she wanted, no matter the obstacles.

Sitka gave a sudden wet slosh of her tongue over Sabrina's cheek, as if she knew what Sabrina was thinking and was on board. Laughing, Sabrina wiped away the dampness, pet Sitka once more, then stood.

It was still awkward, with Tate standing there, looking way too tempting in black pants and a T-shirt that didn't hide the lean muscles underneath. At least some of her embarrassment had faded, and her face no longer felt like it was on fire.

She'd kissed him. He'd ultimately rejected her. But that didn't mean she had to give up.

The idea brought a slow smile to her face, and he swayed backward slightly, as if he'd felt the sudden force of her determination. Still, he gave her a smile in return, then asked loudly, "You ready to go?"

Then she realized something. Usually, he closed and locked the door as soon as he arrived. Today, it was wide open. She didn't see anyone in the hallway behind him, but that didn't mean Adam wasn't somewhere nearby.

Shoving back a surge of fear, she nodded and grabbed

her duffel bag, packed with enough clothes and toiletries for the weekend. Hopefully, Adam would take the bait early and not make her and Tate play out a whole weekend of this awkward farce with all of Tate's colleagues watching. If he didn't, maybe she should take advantage of it, see if she could change Tate's mind.

The idea gained traction as he reached over and took her bag, slinging it easily over his shoulder. Then he took her hand in his and pulled her toward the door.

She sidled closer to him, the way she'd do if they were really dating, and he shot her a quick glance, full of surprise and heat, before calling, "Come on, Sitka."

The dog raced after them, sticking close to Sabrina as they took the elevator down to the lobby. Even where no one could see them, Tate kept his hold on her hand. But his gaze was focused on the closed door.

She could see his reflection in the shiny metal, the stern set of his jaw, the stiffness of his posture, the seriousness in his gaze. But his fingers slid back and forth over her knuckles, a soothing caress she wasn't sure he was aware he was giving.

As the numbers on the elevator readout counted down, Sabrina tilted her head and rested it against Tate's arm. She breathed in his familiar sandalwood scent and closed her eyes, trying to mentally prepare for the weekend ahead.

The idea of spending any romantic time with Tate—even if it was pretend—made her pulse quicken. But it couldn't eliminate the building fear.

Adam was still out there, still obsessed with her and presumably still willing to kill anyone who got in his way.

Her hand clenched reflexively in Tate's as the elevator dinged and came to a stop.

"You okay?" Tate whispered as the doors slid open.

"Yes." She opened her eyes and took a deep breath, leading him through the lobby. "Let's do this."

"Hang on a second," he said, tugging on her hand just as they stepped outside. With a sudden grin, he pulled a cap from his back pocket, showed her the logo for a police K-9 training facility. "I got us a nice, secluded cabin where you'll be able to see the mountains and water, and even a glacier. But this is still Alaska, not New York City." He settled the cap on her head, then nodded. "Now you fit in."

She gave him a perplexed smile, glancing down at her simple jeans and top. Okay, yes, her jeans were slim and showed off her figure, and her top was a piece she'd found at one of the quirky shops in Desparre, flowy and lacy and the same green as her eyes. She'd swiped on some lipstick and a couple of coats of mascara before he arrived. But she wasn't exactly decked out for a party in the city.

Instead of asking about it, she turned toward his truck, parked out front. She itched to glance around, reassure herself that other police officers were keeping watch, but she resisted. If Adam was nearby, she didn't want to tip him off.

Before she could get more than a step, Tate was tugging on her hand again, pulling her back to him. "I'm glad we're doing this," he told her, his voice dropping to a husky whisper.

His eyes locked on hers as he threaded his free hand through her hair, then cupped the base of her neck. The feel of his fingers made her nerve endings spark to life, sending zings of electricity through her body.

He dipped his head slowly, the intensity in his eyes telling her he wanted to kiss her, even if the location said this was all for show. To prove to Adam it was real, to goad him into making his move.

Looping her free hand around his neck, she rose up on her tiptoes to meet him. Surprise flashed briefly in his eyes, followed by desire, and then his lips settled softly against hers.

He tasted faintly of coffee underneath mint toothpaste.

The scent of sandalwood she'd started to crave when he wasn't around filled her senses as she closed her eyes and gave in to his kiss. Gave in to the intoxicating feel of his body pressed against hers, the way she could rest all of her weight on him and he'd hold steady. Gave in to all of the emotions she'd been trying to deny.

He paused for half a second, and then his hand slipped free of hers to clamp onto her hip, to haul her higher onto her tiptoes against him. His fingers flexed there, kneading into her hip as he nipped at her lips with his mouth and tongue. Then his tongue slid between her lips, sending sparks down to her toes.

She hung on tighter, linking her hands at the back of his neck as she urged him with the slide of her tongue to go faster. She felt frantic, desperate to get closer to him, as all of the dreams she'd started to envision of a future with him swept over her. Maybe those dreams were possible. Or maybe this was her one chance to create a memory with him.

Either way, she wasn't going to waste it. She tried to slow down, to memorize the imprint of his body against hers, the slight rasp of his chin as his mouth claimed hers over and over.

Too soon, he eased back, and she dropped down to her feet, tugging on her shirt where it had ridden up slightly. He stared at her, a mix of surprise and uncertainty in his gaze, until Sitka made them both jump with a sudden *woof!*

"You're right," Tate said, shifting his gaze to the dog and breaking the spell. "We should get going. You don't mind Sitka joining us for our romantic weekend, do you?"

He looked at her again, and even though his gaze was more controlled, his emotions veiled again, he let out a heavy breath that told her he wasn't as composed as he was pretending.

She gave him a knowing smile. "Of course not." Threading her hand through his, she said, loudly enough to be overheard, "I'm ready."

He blinked at her again, his forehead creasing as if he wasn't sure if he should be reading into her words or not.

Letting him wonder, she tugged on his hand as Sitka trotted along beside her toward the truck.

He held open the door for her, then warned, "It's a little tight in the cab for three. I'm sorry about that. I've never needed to fit an extra person in here with us."

He'd only had Sitka a few months. But the way he said it made it sound like he'd never taken another woman on a romantic getaway like this—at least not while he'd had this truck. Maybe she was reading into it, but the idea made her smile.

The dog leaped into the truck, settling into the middle and taking up some of Sabrina's seat, too.

Sabrina stepped up after her, settling her hand on Sitka's back as Tate closed her door and went around to the driver's side.

On top of everything else, he was a gentleman. Of course, maybe that was part of the problem. Part of the reason he was so determined to do what was right and practical by not jumping into anything when they were trying to make it safe for her to leave.

How could she change his mind? The distance from Desparre to New York City was no joke. And this town could easily snow you in through winter. But she didn't care. She wanted to try.

Maybe Adam would wait, give her at least part of the weekend to show Tate that the bond they'd developed was worth the effort, worth the challenges. But when the truck came to a stop ten minutes later, she realized she wasn't sure how.

Glancing around with surprise, she took in the cute house with the big front porch in the woods. It was much closer than she'd expected. Then the garage door in front of them opened, and Sabrina realized they weren't at the vacation spot he'd mentioned at all but his house.

She turned toward him, questions forming, as he turned off the truck and shut the garage door behind him.

Then the door leading to his house opened, and a woman stepped into the garage. She had wavy blond hair and wore a cap identical to the one Tate had slid onto Sabrina's head. She was even wearing the same jeans and green blouse— the outfit she'd shown Tate two days ago when he'd asked what she planned to wear. Until this moment, she'd never really wondered why he'd asked.

Realization about what was happening hit at the same time as the knowledge that she wouldn't get a chance to convince Tate of anything. Because she wasn't going on the romantic getaway with him at all.

TATE WAS DOING the right thing. He knew he was.

Still, as he glanced across the truck at the rookie police officer from nearby Luna—on loan because she looked enough like Sabrina to pass for her—dread clamped down and refused to leave. He gave her a forced smile, trying to reassure her. "There are officers already in place around the cabin. We'll be fine."

"I'm not worried," she said, an echo of the words Sabrina had told him earlier, her face strategically hidden behind an open map.

Unlike Sabrina, Officer Angie Hallen didn't quite sound like she meant them.

He'd been a rookie once, on foot patrol back in Boston, with a veteran officer whose training method was to toss you into the fray and hope you came out in one piece. He remembered the adrenaline and the nerves all too well. Time and experience calmed both, but if you were smart, they never fully dulled, because losing your edge on the job could cost your life.

"I appreciate you agreeing to do this," he told her. Angie didn't know the Desparre officers, and although she'd been briefed on the threat, she didn't have a history with him, didn't know what kind of officer he was.

Then again, he knew all too well that sometimes even people you knew and trusted could become a threat.

Angie nodded stiffly, and Sitka, maybe noticing her nerves, or maybe just missing Sabrina, let out a whine.

"We'll be there soon," he told his dog.

The romantic getaway spot was well-known among Desparre locals and would be easy for Adam to figure out. It was on the far southern border of Desparre, an hour away from downtown. People who weren't used to the area tended to be shocked when they suddenly came out of the woods and upon another, smaller mountain, this one edged with water and a small glacier.

Sabrina would have loved it. The thought popped into his mind and wouldn't leave, along with an image of the look in her eyes when she'd fallen into his arms and taken his kiss to a whole other level. But the look on her face when she realized she wasn't coming with him? That one stung. He'd seen a hint of betrayal, along with regret. The same regret he was feeling now.

Her kisses had held more than simple passion. There had been a promise in them, a glimpse of what he could have if he gave in to what they both wanted.

There was an ache in his chest just thinking about what he was giving up. But he needed to find a way to just be happy they were going to get her life back. Because as he glanced once more at Angie, tensing as their cabin came into view, he felt it in his gut. Adam was going to take the bait.

Even though it meant saying goodbye to Sabrina, Tate

couldn't help feeling a sharp anticipation at the idea of snapping a pair of handcuffs on Adam and throwing him behind bars for good.

He pulled into the drive of the cabin he'd rented, far from the others scattered along the glacier's edge. Officers Riera and Dreymond had already picked up the key for him, letting the owners know to stay away. So now all he had to do was grab his and Sabrina's bags from the back of his truck. Then he tucked Angie into the crook of his arm, her face hidden against his chest, and hustled her into the cabin. With one sharp whistle, Sitka raced in after them.

Shutting and locking the door behind him, Tate did a quick check of the cabin, confirming it was empty and secure and that all the shades were drawn. "We're good," he told Angie as he returned to the main room.

She nodded and tucked her pistol back into the waistband at the back of her jeans. "Good. Let's check in with your backup."

"Our backup," he reminded her, grabbing his cell phone from his bag. He sent a quick text to Lorenzo Riera, and the response came back almost immediately.

We've got you. Stay alert.

"They're in place," Tate told Angie. "Now let's hope Adam makes his move quickly."

He settled onto the couch across from the front door, which gave him good visibility into the bedroom and the window access there. Then, he raised his eyebrow at Angie as she stood by the door, knowing that even though he wanted a fast resolution, this kind of operation was often a waiting game.

"I'm good here," she told him.

An hour later, she pulled a chair next to the couch and sat stiffly in it. An hour after that, she started pacing. Ten hours after that, she was slouched on the other side of the couch. By then, Tate was ready to do the same. But he also knew the darkness was Adam's friend, a time when he might feel safer sneaking up on the woman he'd been stalking and her new police-officer boyfriend.

So, when his cell phone rang, he grabbed it fast. "Talk to me," he told Lorenzo, hoping the veteran officer had already wrestled Adam to the ground and slapped cuffs on him.

"It's… We're—" The sound of gunshots made Angie jerk beside him just as Tate realized it wasn't Lorenzo, hiding in the woods with most of the Desparre officers.

It was Charlie Quinn, who was back at Tate's house, keeping Sabrina safe.

He leaped to his feet as Charlie's garbled voice filled the room again, too high-pitched with pain. "Sabrina… Get her—"

Then, another gunshot fired, and the line went dead.

Chapter Nineteen

Sabrina sat in the living room in Tate's house, with the shades drawn and one lone light on, frustrated and worried and anxious for news.

According to officers Charlie Quinn and Max Becker, she hadn't been given the full details of the plan because they were need-to-know, and it was better if she really planned for a trip in case anyone was watching. Tate had never intended to take her on a weekend away, even a pretend one.

Pushing aside her frustration, Sabrina stood from the couch where she'd been sitting for over an hour, with nothing to entertain her but her thoughts.

Charlie wanted her to keep the television off since the house was supposed to appear empty and he didn't want to take any chances—a decision that had made Max roll his eyes and mutter something about "BS protection detail." But Charlie was the veteran so he'd won.

The two officers had been flipping through magazines in between walking around the small house and checking all the entry points. Sabrina had turned down the offers for their leftover police magazines and just waited.

After the way she and Tate had announced their plans all over town for the past few days, then flaunted that kiss in front of the hotel, she'd expected Adam to strike fast. As the time went by, she worried she might be here for days. And Tate had taken her weekend bag with him.

If she had to be here without him, she wanted to go upstairs and explore the rest of his house, see if it matched the easy comfort of the first floor. Tate had told her a lot about himself in the past few days, but he hadn't invited her into his home. Knowing it was probably the only chance she'd have to see it, she was tempted to explore. Instead, she walked over to the curtained windows.

"Please don't touch those," Charlie said, without looking up from his magazine.

"I was just—"

"If Adam followed you from the hotel to here and *didn't* fall for our ruse, we don't want to confirm anything."

He must have sensed her sudden apprehension, because he looked up and gave her a kind smile. "Don't worry. That's unlikely. But it's why we're here. And it's why we're keeping the shades down and most of the lights off. Just in case. Until we hear from Tate."

"I'm going to check in again," Max said, heading into the other room.

Sabrina strained to hear the conversation, but only the low rumble of Max's voice reached her.

When Max returned, all he said was, "No action."

She got the same update every hour for the rest of the day, until it got dark enough outside that even Charlie had given up on his magazines and was scrolling on his phone, periodically sighing.

"Maybe he's too smart to fall for this," Max suggested from the opposite side of the couch, where he'd settled an hour ago and had looked half-asleep ever since. "Or maybe he's moved on entirely, left Desparre and decided to find himself someone new to stalk."

Charlie scowled at his partner, then suggested to Sabrina, "Why don't you go upstairs? I saw a full bookshelf in Tate's second bedroom. I'm sure he wouldn't mind."

She debated only a few seconds, then hurried up the stairs. Lining the hallway were framed prints that looked like various nature scenes from Alaska. When she stepped closer to one, she saw it was labeled *Sitka, Alaska*. Wondering if he'd ever been there, if he'd loved the place enough to name his dog after it, she continued into the first room on the right.

Tate clearly used the room as his home office. There was a laptop open on a small desk against one wall, a pair of comfortable-looking chairs on another, and a bookshelf in between, overflowing with paperbacks. Smiling, Sabrina stepped closer, studying the titles in the light coming in from the hallway.

Tate had an affinity for historical nonfiction and spy novels. He also had a whole section devoted to K-9 training. Even though he'd stuffed the shelves, he hadn't put anything on top of the bookshelf. She could picture her romance novels lining that space.

A wistful smile twitched, then dropped away, leaving behind an ache in her chest she didn't think would leave anytime soon.

The sudden boom from downstairs made her jump. Was that a gunshot?

For a brief moment, she felt paralyzed. Then she eased to the edge of the room, peering into the hallway. Should she go downstairs, look for Charlie and Max and stick close to them?

Boom! Boom! Boom!

A scream punctuated the final blast, and Sabrina raced into motion, scanning the room for something she could use as a weapon. Her heartbeat thundered in her ears, dimming the noise around her, but she still heard another anguished scream, followed by footsteps pounding up the stairs.

Spinning in a circle, Sabrina desperately looked for anything that might do some damage. But there was nothing except books and a laptop.

Hide! her mind screamed at her. Racing for the closet, Sabrina had just yanked open the door when a hand clamped on her shoulder.

A scream lodged in her throat, choking her, as she spun around, lifting her fists to fight back. But it wasn't Adam. It was Max, with smears of blood across his cheeks and a look of horror in his eyes.

"Charlie?" she managed to ask, but he either didn't hear her or couldn't answer as he hustled her to the doorway, peeked out, then shoved her through it and across the hall into the bathroom.

"Get in. Lock the door." When she hesitated, wondering what he would do, he gave her a push. *"Now!"*

Shutting the door behind her, Sabrina fumbled with the lock, her hands shaking violently on the simple push mechanism. Someone could break through it easily.

Boom!

Sabrina shrieked at the gunshot, louder now, closer, and instinctively dropped to her knees in the dark bathroom.

Then the whole house seemed to fill with gunshots, and the sounds seemed to be all around her. She slapped her hands over her ears, blinking to try and see in the darkened room. Vague shapes took form—the bathtub, the toilet, a vanity—and she launched herself at the medicine cabinet.

She knocked her hand through it, searching for something useful, in the process dumping half the contents out. Then her hands closed around a straight razor. But what good would it do against a gun?

As another blast and then a loud thump sounded from right outside the bathroom, Sabrina dropped the razor and grabbed the lid off the toilet tank. Standing just past the edge of where the door would open, she hefted it, ready to swing, even as she prayed Max would knock and tell her the threat was gone.

Instead, the door smashed inward with a loud thud, making Sabrina jump. It bounced against the wall, and then a hand caught it.

Sabrina lurched forward, raising the porcelain lid with shaky arms, hoping Adam would pause long enough at seeing her to let her get a swing in before he fired.

But it wasn't Adam who entered. It was someone shorter, but much more muscular. Someone decked out in dark fatigues, a ski mask over his face and a pistol in his hand.

In her surprise, she hesitated, and then his fist flew toward her, smashing into her face before she could jerk out of the way. The lid flew out of her hands, shattering as it hit the ground. She fell hard after it, the sight of Max's prone, bloodied form wavering at the edge of her vision before the world went dark.

Chapter Twenty

"What's going on?" Tate barked into the phone, sliding Sitka's vest on as Angie took the roads at dangerous speeds.

She was handling his vehicle like a pro, instead of a rookie who'd probably only done tactical driving at police academy.

"We're heading there now," Chief Griffith replied. "I don't have any updates. You know most of the officers were with you." His voice was dark and filled with self-blame as he said, "I didn't see this move coming."

Neither had Tate. In fact, Tate had thought this was the best way to keep Sabrina far away from any danger.

"Have Charlie or Max checked in?" If they had, the chief already would have told him, but Tate couldn't stop himself from asking the question. "Do we know if Sabrina is okay?"

"I don't know anything right now," the chief told him patiently. "Sam and I are on our way to your place. We closed up the station. I'll update you as soon as I can."

He hung up without another word, and Tate looked at Angie.

She didn't even glance his way, just hit the gas harder as Tate put his arms around Sitka to keep her from sliding around the truck. Then, mostly one-handed, he slid his own vest over his T-shirt, thankful that Angie had had the foresight to put hers on while he was trying to call Charlie back at the cabin.

Two other vehicles kept pace behind them, filled with the rest of the Desparre PD officers who'd been at the cabin to provide backup to him instead of watching Sabrina.

Frustration and anger built inside him until they burst out in a single curse.

"It's not your fault," Angie said, her voice high-pitched enough that he knew her outward calm was a facade. "This guy's a software engineer. Yeah, he's killed before, but I saw the report before I agreed to help. That murder was sloppy. He was going against a civilian, a marketing specialist with no reason to think he was in danger, not a pair of experienced officers."

How the hell had Adam gotten the jump on Charlie and Max?

Off the job, Tate was neutral on both of them. Max was the kind of guy who loved the power of the job, who didn't fraternize much with his fellow officers and wouldn't stick his neck out if you were in trouble with the brass. Charlie was a longtime veteran with strict ideas about who belonged on the force—and that hadn't included Tate's former partner, because Peter was hard of hearing. Still, if you were in danger on the job, both men would be there in an instant. In fact, they'd both risked their lives for him in the past. He respected them as officers.

He'd trusted them to watch over Sabrina without question. Even now, having heard the sheer amount of firepower Adam must have brought to the scene, Tate wasn't sure how Adam had gotten past both men.

Maybe he hadn't. The hope that refused to die was foolish, he knew. But he hung on to it as tightly as he could. Because ultimately, Adam's target wasn't Charlie or Max. It was Sabrina.

Stalkers who got to this level of obsession often killed

their targets and anyone who stood in their way. But sometimes, they'd go a different route—abduction, assault.

Tate closed his eyes, wishing he didn't need to pray for the second choice. But at least she'd still be alive. At least he'd still have a chance to find her.

"We're close," Angie announced, and Tate opened his eyes, realizing he'd had them closed awhile, praying for Sabrina, Charlie and Max.

"All right," Tate said. "Let's—" He frowned as his phone buzzed with a text from the chief at the same time that an ambulance rounded the corner, coming from the direction of his house, sirens blaring.

They'd gotten help fast. The nearest hospital was an hour away, so they'd probably also gotten lucky, with medics happening to be nearby. It meant someone was still able to be saved. But who?

Tate's pulse rocketed as he opened the chief's text, hands shaking. But all it said was Scene is contained.

"Shit," Tate breathed. It was bad if the chief wasn't giving him news over text. The screen on his phone went blurry as tears flooded his vision. He blinked, swiping a hand over his eyes, and told himself it didn't mean Sabrina was dead.

It didn't mean all the impossible dreams he'd had about a real future with her were forever gone. It didn't mean the promises he'd made to her about getting her life back had been lies.

"We're here," Angie announced, slamming his truck to a stop and making Sitka yelp. "You good?"

"Yeah," Tate said, his hoarse voice marking him a liar. But even if the scene was contained, he still had a job to do. Justice to mete out.

Taking a deep breath, he tried to shove his fear and grief as deep as he could. Because being unfocused right now could get someone killed.

He stepped out of the truck, and Sitka leaped out beside him, moving one pace ahead of him as if she was trying to protect him from what he was about to see.

His house looked okay from the outside, except for the trail of blood leading down his front steps. His breath caught at the sight, then lodged painfully in his chest, and Tate faltered.

Before he could get moving again, the chief stepped outside. There was blood on his arms beneath the rolled-up sleeves of his uniform, and exhaustion and grief on his face.

As other vehicles slammed to a stop behind him and his fellow officers crowded around him to hear the news about their own, Tate stared at the chief. The air felt too heavy, too thick to get a solid breath, and his house wavered in front of him.

"Charlie was just rushed to the hospital," the chief said. "Max died at the scene."

A collective gasp behind him registered as the words hit Tate like a punch to the gut. No, he hadn't been personal friends with Max, but the man had put his life on the line for Sabrina. He was only a few years older than Tate, with a wife and two young sons at home.

"Sabrina is missing."

Tate blinked, trying to focus. Sabrina wasn't dead.

"There were at least two gunmen here today," the chief continued. "As Charlie was being loaded into the ambulance, he said they were wearing all black, looked like tactical gear. And black ski masks."

Tate swayed violently on his feet, an image in his mind of two masked men emerging from the trail parallel to him on a run five and a half years ago. Someone's hand— Angie's?—slapped his back and kept him upright as the chief demanded, "Talk to me, Emory. Could Adam have an accomplice?"

"It's not Adam," Tate breathed, a million regrets filling his mind.

He should have left Desparre the moment that news story had gone national, if not before then, when it had first been printed. He should have left Sabrina in the capable care of his fellow officers. Instead, he'd been selfish and stayed. That mistake had probably just cost Sabrina her life.

But not in a quick burst of gunfire like it might have happened if this were Adam. No, the officers who'd tried to kill him back in Boston were out for blood. His blood. And if they couldn't have it, they'd settle for making someone he loved suffer.

Chapter Twenty-One

Sabrina's head throbbed violently, shooting pain through her eyes as she tried to open them. Her mouth was cotton dry, and her hands and feet felt swollen and heavy.

She tried to move, tried to open her eyes. Panic flooded when she couldn't seem to do either, and her heart pounded frantically, almost painfully. Fear sent adrenaline shooting through her system, along with a realization of the last thing she'd seen.

Officer Max Becker lying in a pool of blood outside the bathroom door. A masked man standing over her, wielding a pistol. Then, the world had shifted and disappeared.

Was she still in Tate's house? Had the gunman left her for dead?

Swallowing back the sudden nausea, Sabrina forced her eyes open. The world in front of her swayed as it finally emerged from darkness.

She was lying awkwardly on her side on the floor. She definitely wasn't in Tate's bathroom or hallway but lying on dusty concrete. The world around her was dim, and she didn't think it was just her vision. The light seemed to be coming from certain areas only, the rest of the space in darkness. She could make out the wall across from her. It was concrete, too.

Where the hell was she?

Did Tate's house have a basement? Could she be down there? Or had the man taken her from Tate's house?

As she tried to push herself upright, her hands and feet caught, refusing to separate. The panic intensified, bringing tears to her eyes. She was bound at her wrists and ankles, tight enough that her hands and feet were partially asleep. Movement sent pins and needles pricking her nerve endings.

"She's awake."

The hard, emotionless statement made Sabrina jerk, searching for the source.

Booted feet stepped into view and she twisted, straining to see the face above her.

It wasn't covered by a mask anymore, yet she still didn't recognize him. Somehow, her abductor looked much taller than he had in Tate's bathroom. Lankier, too, with pale skin and reddish-blond hair. As he leaned toward her, she saw light blue eyes that didn't match her memory of hazel eyes behind the mask. He smirked at her and stood straight again as she tried to get her mouth to work.

"Whhhoare you?" she slurred.

"Get the camera," he called, and it took Sabrina a minute to realize he wasn't alone.

Another set of boots moved toward her, and as she twisted to look up at the person wearing them, she saw the hazel eyes from Tate's house. The man who'd knocked her out.

He was shorter than the first one by a solid nine inches, but he made up for it in bulk. His dark hair was sheared short, and his nose looked like it had been broken, probably more than once.

Hired guns Adam had found? It seemed more likely than him having made friends in Alaska who were willing to abduct someone for him.

The muscle-bound guy dragged a tripod across from her and set an old-fashioned video camera on it.

Dread dropped to her stomach as her fear multiplied and tears rushed to her eyes. What were they planning to do to her that they wanted to record?

Instinctively, she fought the bonds at her wrists and ankles, even though it just caused more pain.

The lanky one let out a harsh laugh and muttered, "No need. We'll take these off for you." The tone was so dark, it sent new fear through her.

"Who are you?" she managed, blinking until her vision cleared. "Why are you doing this?" Her voice came out stronger than she'd expected, sounded less afraid.

If Adam had sent them, why? Was he too much of a coward to hurt her himself?

"You picked the wrong man to shack up with," the lanky one said.

His accent registered as Bostonian, and Sabrina frowned, trying to understand. Did they think she'd *wanted* Adam to chase after her?

The bulky one snorted. "She doesn't get it," he told his friend.

His accent was also distinctly Boston. But none of the information Tate had shared about Adam's past mentioned him having lived there.

The lanky guy leaned close to her again, and Sabrina instinctively jerked back, wanting to get away.

"He didn't warn you, did he? He let you think he was some kind of stand-up guy, but the truth is he's a rat who's only loyal to himself." He gave her a crooked smile. "Sorry, honey, but you're going to pay for it."

"I didn't even know who he was until a week ago," she insisted, even though the dread building in her chest told her this wasn't about Adam at all.

The bulky guy shrugged, standing again. "When you found out, you should have run."

"Wouldn't have mattered," the lanky one put in. "He loves her, so it doesn't matter how she feels about him." Then he told his friend, "Get the ropes off. Camera is ready to go."

As his friend reached for her hands, Sabrina tried to wriggle away, but he yanked her arms upward, making her gasp at the sharp pain across her shoulders.

"Stay still." The blade of a knife slid too close to her wrists, and then her arms fell loose.

She wanted to wrench them in front of her, use them to claw at the guy's eyes while he was close to her, but they dropped uselessly, pain pricking like a thousand tiny pins.

How long had she been restrained and unconscious? How far away from Tate's house had they taken her?

The knife sliced again, this time through the bonds at her ankles, and then her feet were free, too. The sharp pains dancing across her feet at the sudden blood flow brought tears to her eyes.

"Get her up," the lanky guy said. "Remember, he'll probably take this to the cops, so no talking."

The bulky guy pulled her to her feet, but they were still asleep and wouldn't hold her. He grabbed her before she hit the ground, rolling his eyes as she tried to get her body to work.

She wiggled her toes and fingers, trying to get the blood flowing properly again, and just as she was starting to feel more stable, the guy let go. She swayed and fell backward against the cold concrete wall.

Glancing up, she saw more concrete above her. Where the hell was she?

The lanky guy stood across from her by the camera, against another wall. On either side of her, the space narrowed into what looked like hallways without doors to block the way. But there was only darkness, so she had no idea where either led.

"Let's do this," the bulky guy said, drawing her attention back to them as they both slid the masks over their faces again.

Panic struck. She knew she wouldn't make it, but she had to try. Shoving herself off the wall, she veered toward the hallway farther from the men, but her feet still weren't working properly, and the run she'd expected was an awkward stumble.

The lanky guy caught her easily and shoved her back into the wall.

She bounced off it, righting herself before she fell again.

"Sorry, honey. You sealed your own fate when you hooked your future to Tate Donnoly."

This was about *Tate*? The nonsensical words ran through her mind as she tried to process the wrong last name they'd used. Had they confused him with someone else?

Then the red light on the camera flashed on, and they both stepped purposely toward her.

Sabrina backed up, then she hit the wall again, and they were still coming. She threw her hands in front of her face, her mind whirling. Tate had grown up in the Midwest. He'd never mentioned Boston. But these men must have seen him picking her up at the hotel, dropping her at his house. They'd seen his face, so presumably they knew him.

"Please don't," she begged as they took another step closer and the lanky one smiled.

Panic overtook her, sending her heart rate into overdrive. "Tate doesn't care about me! It was all a setup. We're not really dating."

The bulky one snorted and then threw a punch that smashed into her cheekbone. It lifted her feet out from under her and made bright flashes of light strobe in front of her eyes.

She hit first the wall and then the ground, slamming into

the hard concrete with a force that stole her breath. The sound seemed to echo in the hard-surfaced room, worsening her already-shaky equilibrium.

The other one swung a boot at her ribs, and she rolled, but not far or fast enough. It connected, sending new pain through her chest, and she curled into a ball, hoping to protect herself.

But one of them yanked her to her feet, only to hit her again, this time a punch to the other side of her face near her lips that made blood splatter across her face and fill her mouth. She flew backward, slamming into the wall.

Her head bounced against it, and her vision went dark, so she didn't see the next hit coming.

It landed under her chin, snapping her head back into the wall yet again. Her legs crumpled, and she threw her hands out to try and catch herself. Then, she hit the ground face-first, and the whole world blessedly disappeared.

"You've got some explaining to do," the chief told him, hands planted flat on Tate's kitchen table as he leaned over it toward Tate. "And I want the whole truth right now. No more lies. I need to know what we're dealing with here. I need to know *who* we're dealing with."

Noise from his fellow officers reached him from a distance. The officers were in the mudroom near his back entrance, dusting around the broken window where the assailants had entered. It was where Charlie had been found, facedown in a pool of blood, his hand still clutching his cracked cell phone.

Others were upstairs, dealing with evidence near where Max had been killed and Sabrina had been taken. Evidence of a struggle both inside and outside the bathroom suggested Max had locked her in there before he'd been killed defending her. The smashed lid from his toilet suggested Sabrina had grabbed the only available weapon and tried to defend herself. The blood on his bathroom floor said she'd paid for it.

"I'm sorry," Tate said, and his voice came out a pained whisper. "I never thought my past would catch up to me like this. If I had—"

The chief put up a hand. "We don't have time for regrets right now. What we need is a plan to move forward. So give me what I need to make an informed decision here, Emory."

Tate flinched at the use of his fake last name, at all of the mistakes he'd made. If it could help save Sabrina, he'd gladly give up all of his secrets, even if it landed him in jail.

"My real name is Tate Donnoly."

The chief leaned back, as if pushed by the force of his surprise, then nodded for Tate to keep going.

"I was a police officer back in Boston before I came here. I was…able to create a fake name and start over in Alaska." He left out mention of his family friend in Witness Protection and the role his former chief had played, but the way Chief Griffith's eyes narrowed, he knew there was more to it.

"Back in Boston I witnessed three fellow officers taking a payoff from a crime lord. I reported it, and the whole situation was under investigation by the FBI when there was an attempt on my life." Tate blew out a heavy breath, remembering how close he'd come to dying that day. Jim Bellows, Kevin Fricker and Paul Martin were trained to take down an opponent fast and efficiently. He'd had the same training, but all Sabrina had was two years of running and trying to stay ahead of the threat against her.

Trying to focus, he told his chief, "The crime boss and one of the officers ultimately went to prison. But I never actually *saw* Kevin Fricker and Paul Martin try to kill me that day, only Jim, who fired the shot that hit me. And the FBI could only find a money trail to Jim. So Kevin and Paul got off. They stayed in the department until the stain got too bad, then went on to other departments. Other officers didn't trust them. They didn't trust me anymore, either. I knew that I'd gotten lucky and that Kevin and Paul might try again. Kevin made a threat on his last day, and I didn't want to risk my life or the people I loved so I took on a new name and started over here. Went through the academy again, came in as a Desparre PD rookie. I kept tabs on them over the years, but it seemed like I was safe here."

The chief nodded slowly, his gaze still assessing, probably seeing a lot more than Tate was saying. "Then that news article went national."

"Yeah," Tate agreed. "And we made a big show of how I fell for Sabrina."

Lines creased the chief's forehead, an understanding that since the Boston officers had gone after Sabrina instead of Tate, it meant they wanted to hurt her to get to him. "So what's their next step? Are we waiting for some kind of ransom note? A request to make a trade? You for Sabrina?"

"I sure hope so," Tate breathed. "But I think that's a best-case scenario. They blame me for all of it. Not just one of their closest friends going to jail and them being ousted from the Boston PD, but I cut off their second source of income—their payoff. Not to mention that I destroyed their reputations. They've hopped from one two-bit department to the next ever since."

"I'm not sure that's on you," Chief Griffith said. "Sounds like they may be doing it to themselves."

"But they blame me," Tate reiterated. "I thought if they ever came after me, it would be a bullet in the head in the middle of the night or maybe out on a remote call somewhere. But this..." He stared hard at the chief. "No matter what happens, Sabrina is the priority. I take responsibility for myself. If they want me, they can have me. Just please get her out." He glanced at Sitka, who whined and shuffled her feet, nudging him hard. His voice broke a little as he added, "And please take care of Sitka."

The chief nodded slowly. "You know civilians are always our priority. And we look after our own. Sitka is one of us."

From the front of the house, Officer Sam Jennings yelled, "We've got a delivery!"

Tate turned to run for the front yard when the chief added, "You're one of us, too, Tate."

He nodded his thanks, knowing how much of a show of faith that was, given how he'd lied and broken the law to get here. Then he hurried to where Sam stood, gingerly holding a manila envelope with gloved hands.

"How did it arrive?" the chief demanded from right behind Tate.

"Someone tossed it out of a van, then took off," Sam said. "Lorenzo and Nate went after him, but we all recognized the van. It's Old Oliver."

"Shit," Tate breathed. Old Oliver was Oliver Yardley, the dad of Young Oliver, who was equally eccentric. Old Oliver lived up in the mountain somewhere and periodically came into town and scared the newer locals with his long, untamed hair and beard and constantly darting eyes. He thought the government was spying on him, that anyone could be working for them, and even though the Desparre PD considered him generally harmless, half the time he didn't make much sense.

"Open it," the chief said.

"I got it," Tate said, grabbing the envelope from Sam. "After Paul left the Boston PD, he got training as a bomb tech at a different department." Ignoring the looks of confusion from his fellow officers, Tate walked far enough away that if it was a bomb, it wouldn't take out anyone else with him. "Stay!" he warned Sitka when she tried to follow.

She plopped onto her butt, but glanced up at his chief as if waiting for him to overrule Tate.

She whined when the chief ignored her, leaning forward as Tate took a deep breath and ripped open the envelope. What fell out wasn't a bomb but a flash drive.

Dread hit like a punch to his chest as he hurried wordlessly back inside and upstairs to his laptop. He tried not to see the huge bloodstain in his hallway, tried not to imagine Max's prone body there, but it didn't work.

He fit the flash drive into his computer, then braced himself as he felt the chief and several of his colleagues crowd behind him.

The audio came on first, Sabrina's terrified voice pleading, "Please don't!" Static covered most of her next words, but he heard his name. Then the video flashed on his screen, two men in all black partially blocking the camera as they stepped toward Sabrina. One of them laughed at her, then smashed a fist into her face.

Tate cringed, clenching his hands as she hit the floor hard and then got kicked in the ribs as she tried to roll away. They yanked her up, hit her twice more, sending blood flying before she crashed into the ground and didn't move.

Then the shorter, bulkier guy walked toward the camera, a self-satisfied smile showing through the mouth hole in his ski mask. Tate knew that smirk. Paul Martin.

Paul's hand reached toward the screen, showcasing bloody knuckles, before the video went dark.

A couple of the cops behind him swore, and the chief's hand clapped on Tate's shoulder as the camera flashed on again, this time facing the wall, where a piece of paper had been taped. Tate had to squint to read the sloppy, angry writing.

You did this to her. You want her pain to end? Go downtown and shoot yourself in the head. Otherwise, we'll get her back to you eventually. In pieces.

"We'll find her," the chief said softly as Tate's mind whirled and his stomach threatened to bring up the coffee he'd sipped at the cabin by the glacier.

"Old Oliver isn't giving us much," Lorenzo announced as he burst into the room. "He got paid to do it, says he doesn't know the guy who asked him to drop it off. We can pick him up again, but he's a dead end."

"Hey, I know that place," Nate said, pointing at the image frozen on the screen, all concrete around the single piece of paper.

Tate grabbed the young officer by his shoulders. Nate had grown up in Desparre, and he often complained that he'd run out of things to do here. "Where?"

Nate jerked slightly at the force of Tate's desperation. "It's an old army fort at the base of the mountain, near Luna. It's deserted and boarded up, but when I was a teenager, you could slip through the boards at the main entrance if you were thin enough. It used to be a place to go drinking."

"Let's go," Tate said, moving toward the door.

The chief stepped in his path. "We need a plan."

Tate stared him directly in the eyes. "I know these men, Chief. They're going to keep making tapes. They know I won't actually shoot myself, because *I know* they wouldn't let her go even if I did. But eventually, she won't be able to take any more." His voice broke, and he paused for a breath. "We need to hurry."

The chief nodded. "Okay. We'll plan on the way. Tate, you're with me. Sam, Lorenzo, Nate, you three follow." He turned to the final two officers present. "You two, continue securing the scene. And call the state PD or the FBI and tell them we need a bomb tech immediately. Don't stop calling until we get someone who will meet us there now."

Then the chief led Tate and Sitka down the stairs to his SUV, and the other officers followed on their tail. During the hour-long drive, the chief put the other officers on speaker, and they went over details.

According to Nate, there was only one entry point. "There is a maze of rooms in that fort," Nate insisted when

Tate pressed him on it, "and I think at one point, there were multiple exits. Windows, too, but those have long since been closed up solid or collapsed. The actual entrances are all blocked off now or buried against the mountain and the forest that grew into it. There's only one way in."

The news made dread churn in Tate's gut. Kevin and Paul weren't the kind of guys to trap themselves anywhere. Did they think the fort was so out of the way, old and unused, that no one would recognize where they were? Or had they banked on Tate and his fellow officers recognizing it? Had they already moved somewhere else and left the single entrance rigged?

He shared his fears with the chief, who got back on the phone and confirmed the FBI bomb tech was already en route via helicopter and would probably beat them there.

They beat her, but only by five minutes. As soon as she arrived, she donned a massive bomb suit and waddled up to the boarded-up entrance of the fort.

"We've got a bomb," she confirmed grimly less than ten minutes later.

The entrance was set against the side of the mountain, hidden off an old, overgrown trail that seemed to lead nowhere now that the fort was defunct. The building was derelict, pieces of it crumbling around the entrance. The structure itself went on seemingly for miles, disappearing into the side of the mountain and within the forest that seemed to have swallowed most of it up.

"How long to defuse it?" the chief asked.

The bomb tech, a tiny Black woman with sharp eyes and sure fingers, shook her head. "Probably a couple hours."

Tate swore. Maybe that was Kevin and Paul's ultimate plan. Let him get here with enough time to save her but spend so long trying to get into the fort that it was too late. Because one thing he knew for sure: in a couple of hours, Sabrina would be dead.

Chapter Twenty-Two

The first thing Sabrina felt was an intense pounding in her head. It radiated down her neck and along her jaw. Even her eyes hurt.

She wanted to groan, but couldn't summon the energy. She cracked her eyes open, and they refused to go any farther. It wasn't exhaustion, she realized, but swelling.

Swallowing the moisture that had gathered in her mouth, she almost choked as she discovered it was blood.

The two men huddled across from her didn't seem to notice. They were arguing, their words echoing too loudly in her ears, intensifying the agony in her head.

Sabrina gently moved her jaw, trying to figure out if it was broken. New pain jolted up to her ears and down her neck, and tears blurred her vision.

Blinking them away, she looked down at herself. There was pain along her spine, and her hands and feet still throbbed. But she was still dressed, and no one had bothered to retie her bonds.

"What if he really *doesn't* care?" the bulky guy snapped.

"Relax, Paul," the lanky one replied. "You saw them at the hotel. He couldn't keep his hands off her. He'll come. And if he doesn't, we send another video." He shrugged. "Or we do what we threatened."

He glanced her way, and Sabrina closed her eyes, her

heart thundering. But no footsteps sounded, at least not any she could hear over her pounding heartbeat and throbbing head. Finally, she eased her eyes open again. They weren't looking at her.

Paul's shoulders twitched, and there was discomfort on his face. "Or we just kill her. Drop her on his doorstep."

"Cops are there, moron," the lanky guy said.

"I didn't mean *literally*," Paul answered. "Geez, Kevin. But *I'm* not cutting her up. You want to do it, that's on you."

A shudder raced through Sabrina, violent and unstoppable, making her legs and arms twitch.

Both men glanced at her but immediately turned back to each other.

Her eyes were so swollen her captors couldn't tell they were open. The knowledge was only mildly comforting in the sea of panic swallowing her.

Her breathing hitched, threatening to make her choke on blood again, and Sabrina tried to tune out the men and focus on staying calm, on formulating some kind of plan. But she wasn't sure she could stand if she tried, and she certainly couldn't outrun them, even if she knew where to go.

Tears flooded again, and this time, she couldn't blink them away.

"You think Tate will recognize this place?" Paul asked, and Sabrina tried to focus again.

"If not, I'm sure one of the locals will. Stop second-guessing this. That local guide said the back entrance has been boarded up for a decade, and everyone knows it's impassable. There's no one out here to notice that we blew through those boards. We're good. They'll go to the main door, and they'll get themselves blown up."

Sabrina jerked at that, and Kevin looked her way, a slow smile on his face that told her he'd realized she was awake. Beyond enjoying her fear, he didn't seem to care, because he turned back to Paul and said, "Just relax. It'll all be over soon, and no one will ever know we were here." Then he pulled out his phone and focused on that.

Paul rolled his eyes, sank to the floor and leaned his head against the wall, staring upward.

Sabrina wiggled her toes in her shoes, bent her fingers. Her toes moved okay after a minute, but her fingers felt stiff and swollen, and she realized she'd thrown her hands up to block at least one blow. She'd probably taken a hit there. Or maybe she'd smashed them when she fell to the ground. She didn't remember falling again, but the ache across her face and chest and the way she was lying on her stomach, with her face twisted to the side, told her she had.

She needed a plan. Even if it was just to find her way to the door and blow it up herself before Tate could get there and trigger it. She didn't want to die like this, at the brutal fists of two men with some agenda she didn't understand. If this was the end, she wanted to go out fighting. Or at least saving the man she'd fallen for.

Trying to shift her body even slightly, maneuver her arms and hands out from underneath her, was surprisingly hard. It made new pain flash through her body and drew a groan she couldn't stifle.

The men barely spared her a glance, which told her she looked as bad as she felt. She kept trying, lifting her head to get a better look at her surroundings. Her neck made a terrible cracking sound, and the throbbing in her head amplified, obscuring her vision until she lowered her cheek down against the cold concrete.

Dizziness overwhelmed her, and she could feel herself being sucked under again. She tried to fight it, but the darkness claimed her.

It had been too long.

Tate shuffled from one foot to the other, watching the bomb tech—Njeri was her name—in her massive bomb suit meticulously working. He and the other officers were waiting at a distance.

The chief was continuously on the phone, digging up intel. He'd connected with Tate's old chief back in Boston, who'd been shocked to learn Tate had returned to Alaska and had expressed more worry than anger over Tate's illegal name change. Chief Griffith had also spoken with multiple police chiefs in Massachusetts who'd worked with Kevin and Paul. And he'd touched base with the officers handling the crime scene at Tate's house.

So far, he'd uncovered that a string of problems like unwarranted aggression and some suspected dirty dealing had followed Paul and Kevin from one department to the next. He'd found a general lack of surprise that they'd come after the man they'd apparently spent a lot of time railing against to their coworkers. But from their current departments, Chief Griffith's questions had been met with only careful statements that both men had taken personal time off. The chief had hung up those calls cursing about people covering their asses.

Tate's colleagues were on their own phones, following up on other connections the chief had dug up on his calls. Only Tate was left out of the work, since it seemed many of the people being contacted would either know him or know of him. Depending on what they'd heard from Kevin and Paul, that might not be good.

When the chief hung up his latest call and ran a hand over his eyes, Tate stepped closer to him. "There has to be another way in."

The chief shook his head. "Nate doesn't know of one, and he knows the mountains of Desparre better than any of us. I called the park service. They say normally this place might have become a tourist attraction, but the remote location and the fact that there are health concerns with it has kept it boarded up and off-limits. The fort originally had at least three entrances. One of those caved in a long time ago. The other was boarded up ages ago, but it might still be accessible. Unfortunately, they don't know where it is because the fort has been defunct since the end of World War II. The forest grew in around it. They're tracking down some local guides and are supposed to get back to me."

"I'm going to see if Sitka can sniff anything out."

At the sound of her name, Sitka jumped to her feet. She ran a tight circle around him, wagging her tail.

The chief glanced from him to Sitka, then back again. He nodded slowly. "Okay. Just keep me in the loop—and I mean every fifteen minutes, Tate. If you weren't Sitka's handler, I'd send someone else with her right now. As it is, I need the rest of my team here, ready to go as soon as the bomb is defused. Njeri is making faster progress than she'd initially thought."

Tate nodded, then walked Sitka up next to Njeri.

She spun to face him and demanded, "What the *hell* are you doing?"

"We just need a quick sniff," he answered as Sitka put her nose to the thick layers of wood nailed across the entrance. Whatever gap had existed when Nate was a teenager had apparently been boarded over, because there was barely enough room for air to pass through now.

The boards looked relatively new, but whether Paul and Kevin had nailed them in place themselves after trapping Sabrina in there and rigging the place or whether someone had done so years ago, Tate wasn't sure. The only thing he knew was that if the crooked cops were still inside, they would have had to go in another way.

Sitka sniffed a line across the boards, then her nose came up. She sniffed the air and started moving around the side of the building. Tate followed, with Njeri's curse trailing after him.

Sitka stuck to the edge of the building as it disappeared

into thicker woods, until Tate could no longer see his fellow officers. Then she veered right, away from the mountain, and started running.

Tate hesitated, then ran after her. She'd been right when they'd searched the woods behind Sabrina's house. He had to believe she could do it this time, too.

Hold on, Sabrina, he willed her, as his hand instinctively rested on his pistol. Besides the Taser and pepper spray, it was his only weapon. He had no doubt that Paul and Kevin had more. Hopefully, he wouldn't come across them too abruptly and be forced into a firefight before he could get backup.

As the forest closed in around him and Sitka, she slowed on a trail big enough to hold a four-wheeler and then veered left. Tate unsnapped the top of his holster. Last fall's dead leaves crunched under his feet, but he couldn't hear his fellow officers anymore even if he strained. All he could hear was Sitka's sure footsteps as she raced forward, leaping over a fallen log.

Tate ran around it, trying to keep up. He almost went down as his feet slid across a pile of smaller sticks on the other side, and then his breath caught. Up ahead was more of the fort, emerging from the mountain and surrounded by debris that looked like pieces of plywood, broken and splintered. Beyond it, possibly…a door?

Sitka turned her head toward him, and before she could bark, Tate put his hand to his lips and whispered, "Sitka, quiet."

She complied, her tail wagging frantically.

His pulse doubled as he crept forward. When he glanced down, he realized he'd pulled his weapon out without conscious thought.

After a few more steps, he was certain. Sitka had found the other entrance.

It was no longer boarded up. Apparently, Kevin and

Paul had blasted their way inside with another bomb. Now it was a clear entrance they'd probably assumed no one would find.

Tears rushed to his eyes as he stepped up next to his dog, petted her head and praised her. "Good girl!"

She thumped her tail, and he urged her over to the side, around the corner from the door, in case Paul or Kevin stepped outside. Then he pulled out his cell phone and sent the chief a quick text about where he was, hoping the chief would be able to follow his directions.

Tucking his phone away, he glanced back the way they'd come. He tried to gauge how long it would take for his fellow officers to get here. His stomach churned at the delay, especially as his mind put Sabrina's beating on replay.

"Stay with me, girl," he told Sitka. "We're going to work."

From somewhere inside the cavernous fort, a voice echoed. "I think it's time to cut our losses and get out before they find us. Let's kill her now."

He recognized that voice. Paul Martin.

Saying a quick prayer, Tate stepped inside. Sitka slipped in next to him.

After the bright sunshine outside, his eyes took a minute to adjust to the long, dark hallway. It smelled dank and stuffy, like no one had used it since World War II.

He tried to will his heartbeat to normalize, to treat this like any other police callout. But this wasn't like any call he'd ever been to. This was Sabrina.

As his eyes started to adjust, Tate slipped his finger alongside the trigger. He raised his weapon and slid along the wall, toward the sound of Paul's voice. Sitka stuck right on his heels.

"Don't wimp out on me now." Kevin's voice reached him. "Don't you want to hear the explosion?"

Paul's response was muttered and sounded like a curse.

Beside him, Tate could feel more than see the fur on Sitka's back rise as there was a thump, and then Sabrina groaned in pain.

His whole body tensed with anger and shared pain, and then he was standing next to an open doorway. Gesturing for Sitka to ease in beside him where she wouldn't be seen, Tate peeked carefully around the corner.

Kevin was leaning against the wall diagonal from him, standing near a tripod as he scrolled on his phone. There was a pistol tucked into the waistband of his black pants and a length of rope near his feet.

Tate heard Paul from the opposite wall, muttering. He was pretty sure Sabrina was over that way, too.

Lowering himself slowly, silently to the floor while Sitka remained motionless beside him, Tate edged millimeter by millimeter until he could see around the corner.

Paul stood next to Sabrina's prone form, his hands fisted and his gun within easy reach at his waist. There was a foldable knife clipped to his waistband, too.

Sabrina was lying on her stomach, her arms tucked underneath her. Her legs were curled slightly inward protectively, her neck twisted so she wasn't facedown. There was dried blood caked to her lips and chin, and her eyes were swollen and bruised.

The sight made nausea and fury mingle in his belly. He might not have thrown the blows, but this was his fault.

Focus, he reminded himself. Forcing his gaze off her, Tate darted one more look toward Kevin, who was still on his phone, seemingly oblivious to Paul's fury. Then he slid carefully backward.

There was no good way in.

Kevin and Paul were too far apart. Even if he sent Sitka after Paul while he shot Kevin, it would be dicey getting through the doorway fast enough. Paul and Kevin might have time to pull their weapons, especially Kevin, who had one of the fastest draws Tate had ever seen.

Was his team close? Risking a glance at his phone, he saw that he had no bars. The text he'd sent the chief was marked Unable to send.

A curse built inside him, along with new fear. Did he turn back? Risk the chance of them hearing his retreat? Risk them deciding to get rid of Sabrina before he could make the trek to his team and back?

His pulse thundered as sweat slicked his hands. There was really no decision. He had one chance to get this right.

But if he and Sitka were even the slightest bit off their marks, Sabrina would be the first to die.

Chapter Twenty-Three

"They're here!"

Paul's shout roused her. It took all of Sabrina's energy to force her eyes open again. This time, she could see even less. Just a sliver of the room, partially obscured by her eyelashes.

It seemed like Paul had just stepped over to the doorway on the left a second ago, but now he was moving toward her again, a nervous grin twitching on his face. "They're trying to defuse the bomb."

Hope blossomed beneath her pain until he added, "It'll happen soon. They'll think they've got the bomb defused and trigger the secondary device."

Fear erupted, overriding her pain, and Sabrina tried to stare down the long hallway, estimate how far it was to the door. But she could only see the first few feet, lit up by a lantern they'd set at the edge of the room. Beyond that was darkness. And she wasn't sure she could stand up, let alone run to the door before they caught her.

If Tate and his teammates were already working on the door, her trying to set off the bomb wouldn't save them, anyway. It would kill everyone.

Frustration tensed her chest, sent a new wave of pain through her body that she ignored. She refused to lie here and wait to die. But what options did she have?

She sucked in a deep breath, trying to clear the haze in her mind as well as give her body strength. The faint scent of dog and sandalwood filled her nose, and she couldn't stop her loud exhale, which sounded like something between laughter and a cry. She must be in bad shape if she was hallucinating Tate and Sitka nearby.

Kevin glanced her way, but she didn't hold his interest long before he was back on his phone, muttering to himself, "Soon, soon." Then he paused and glanced at Paul. "You sure we're safe here?" He looked up at the ceiling, which had crumbled in places and was stained from years of neglect and moisture. "I'm not sure how structurally sound this place is."

Paul grinned, seeming suddenly in his element. "We're fine. This fort has been standing since World War II. Besides, it's a directed charge. It'll blow out, not toward us. While they're cleaning up body parts—assuming anyone was standing far enough back not to get hit—we'll go out the back way."

Kevin nodded as he pushed away from the wall, tucked his phone in his pocket. He looked a lot more alert, anticipatory.

Sabrina took another deep breath, and the imaginary scents were gone. She wedged her hand underneath her chest and shifted slightly, getting a better angle for her neck. Then her breath caught and her eyes widened enough to realize she wasn't hallucinating.

That was Tate's head she'd just seen disappearing around the corner, down low, on the ground like her.

Hope and fear mingled, made her heart race. But as her gaze swept Paul and Kevin, she realized there was no good way into the room, even if Tate had a lot of backup.

She thought back over the almost two weeks she'd spent stuck in that hotel room, the times Tate had stopped by and they'd talked about anything and everything. He'd given her some insight into how police officers worked, the precautions and the dangers.

Something that had stuck out to her then because she'd never considered it was the danger of doorways. It made you exposed, gave a prepared criminal an easy spot to focus their weapons on and just wait. If you had to go in, you moved fast and got out of the doorway immediately.

If that was Tate's plan, who was with him? Only one officer could fit through the doorway at a time, and Kevin and Paul were at opposite sides of the room, Paul having taken up his typical spot near her.

They might not know Tate was here, but since Paul's announcement that officers were working to get past the bomb, they were alert. Kevin's hand had settled on his gun, and he kept licking his lips, like he couldn't wait to use it on someone. Paul was pacing back and forth, and he'd pulled his knife out, kept flicking it. Open, closed, open, closed.

If Tate came through that doorway, even if he had the element of surprise, could he really take out both Paul and Kevin before one of them killed him? Or her?

Fear cramped her stomach and tunneled her vision, and she closed her eyes, tried to think. She needed to help. She needed a way to distract them.

Hoping to clear her mind again, she took a deep breath and gagged on something, maybe even more of her own blood. She tried to breathe through it, but it just got worse, choking her as she erupted in a fit of coughing.

"Get her up," Kevin snapped from what seemed like far away. "We might need her. Don't let her choke."

Paul gave a loud sigh, then tucked his knife back into his waistband. Then he stepped closer, grabbed her arms roughly and flipped her to her back.

It only made the coughing worse, and she tried to lean forward to get some air as he dragged her toward the wall.

Tears obscured her vision and ran down her face as he propped her against the wall, then started to straighten.

This was it. This was her chance.

Fighting through the coughing that wouldn't stop, Sabrina lunged toward him, blinking back tears as she made a grab for the gun at his waistband.

"HEY!" PAUL YELLED, startling Tate as he climbed to his feet.

He peered around the corner and saw Kevin, wide-eyed and pulling his gun from his waistband.

From the other side of the room, he heard a scuffling, then a thump and Sabrina's yelp of pain.

He'd run out of time.

"Sitka, go get!" he commanded. Then he lifted his weapon and lunged into the room, breaking right.

Kevin already had his weapon up toward Sabrina, but at Tate's entrance, he swiveled, redirecting it at Tate.

Tate slid his finger under the trigger guard, his heart thundering, his breathing erratic, his movements desperate. Kevin was one of the best shooters he'd ever seen. He was fast, too fast.

From his peripheral vision, Tate saw a blur of fur and lean muscles as Sitka raced past him, then launched herself into the air, straight at Paul.

Tate fired, and the blast of his bullet leaving the chamber echoed and echoed. Too late he realized it wasn't just his own bullet sounding.

His left arm screamed in agony as he flew backward, landing hard on the concrete floor, then sliding into the wall with a dull thud. *A matching scar for the other side.*

To his left, Sitka slammed into Paul, knocking the muscle-bound man to the floor. His gun, which Tate suddenly realized had been in a tug-of-war between Paul and Sabrina, skidded toward Tate.

Sitka shook her head, biting down hard on Paul's arm as the man screamed and twisted, trying to get away.

Ignoring the blood sliding down his left arm, Tate lifted his gun again. His right hand shook as he redirected at Kevin, who'd taken a bullet, too.

It had slammed the man into the wall, but he was recovering faster than Tate, even though Tate could have sworn his bullet had headed for center mass.

He had a vest on, Tate realized as Kevin swung his gun up again, too, hatred in his eyes.

Wasting precious seconds to lift his arm higher, up from center mass where he'd been trained to shoot, Tate fired again, once, twice.

Kevin's eyes widened as a cloud of blood erupted from his neck. He slid down the wall, his gun hitting the floor first.

From the opposite direction of where Tate had entered, a distant *bang, bang, bang* sounded. The sound of a battering ram. His colleagues were coming, breaking through the boards at the entrance. They must have gotten the bomb defused faster than expected.

Pivoting back toward Paul, Sitka and Sabrina, Tate swore and shoved to his feet.

Paul had yanked the knife off his waistband. As Sabrina launched herself toward Paul's gun, groaning as she slammed into the concrete again, Paul flicked the knife open.

He lifted his hand back to drive it into Sitka.

Sitka kept shaking her head, biting down harder, ignoring the threat and never giving up on her target as the knife arced toward her.

Tate didn't have a shot. Sliding the gun back into his belt, he jumped forward, praying his vest would take the stab if he misjudged his aim.

He landed hard, smacking against Sitka and making her yelp. But she still didn't let go.

His injured arm screamed in protest, sending spikes of pain through his head. He twisted, trying to get a hold of Paul's knife, which had been pushed backward at the force of Tate's landing.

Then the knife was up again, coming for Tate's bad arm. The arm he couldn't move well enough or fast enough to block it.

He gritted his teeth, preparing for the pain even as he fought for a grip on the man's arm. He grabbed hold with both hands just below the elbow, his arms shaking as he tried to keep the knife at bay.

Paul's overly bulky muscle wasn't for show. The man was *strong*. He let out a deep, sustained yell as Sitka kept biting, kept shaking him, but still he forced the knife downward, changing direction so he was aiming for Tate's face.

Then he slammed his forehead into the side of Tate's head, letting out another scream as he made contact.

Tate's head bounced sideways with a crack, and his grip loosened.

The knife surged toward him, nicking a line across his cheek before he regained his hold.

Sitka growled low and deep, and Tate let out his own yell as he forced his injured arm to work harder, pushing the knife away.

From a distance, footsteps pounded toward them, but the knife was moving forward again, and Tate's injured arm started violently shaking.

"Drop it. *Now!*" The voice was weak, but the tone was deadly serious.

Tate's gaze jerked up to where Sabrina stood, swaying on her feet, blood dripping from her face. Paul's gun shook in her hands, but she had it angled well, lined up with Paul's face through the gap behind Tate.

Paul's gaze darted from her to Kevin and back again.

Tate took advantage of his momentary distraction to launch sideways, using his weight on Paul's arm as he grabbed the man's wrist and twisted.

Paul yelped, his muscles engaging too late as the knife clattered to the ground.

Tate kicked it aside and pushed to his feet.

Then his colleagues rushed the room, and Tate told Sitka, "Let go!"

She opened her jaw and dropped Paul's arm, then moved out of the way, letting the other officers do their jobs.

Tate could only stare at Sabrina. She'd dropped her arm to the side, but she still held the weapon. She stared back at him through badly swollen eyes, and a wave of intense relief and residual terror and realization washed over him.

She was alive.

She blinked a few times, then the gun clattered to the floor, and she collapsed.

Rushing forward, Tate caught her before she landed. His arm gave out, and he slid to his knees, trying to take her weight.

"Get an ambulance." The chief's voice rang in Tate's ears as he fumbled to see Sabrina's face, to check her breathing.

Arm shaking, he managed to get a hand on her neck and feel for a pulse. Tears rushed to his eyes when he found one.

Then the chief warned him not to move her. "She probably has internal bleeding. We'll get the medevac."

They were closer to Luna and the hospital than they would have been back in Desparre, but they were deep in the woods, in the bowels of an old fort. A helicopter couldn't land here.

Fear once again gripped him. Had he gotten to her in time, only to lose her anyway?

Chapter Twenty-Four

It had been almost thirty-six hours since Kevin had been declared dead at the scene and Paul had been taken into custody. Not only had the Desparre police defused the bomb he'd built, but apparently the secondary device Njeri had spotted was something Paul had trained on only the month before. They were already building a rock-solid case against him. The chief thought maybe this time they'd dig deep enough to find the money they hadn't located the first time around. Paul was unlikely to ever again step outside a prison.

Tate blinked at his watch, then rubbed sleep from his eyes and leaned over to pet Sitka, who was snoring on the hospital floor. Technically, she wasn't supposed to be here, but she was a police K-9, so they'd made an exception.

His left arm ached at the movement, but it was dulled by the painkillers they'd given him after they'd stitched him up. The bullet had passed through the muscle in his biceps and gone out the other side. He'd need physical therapy, just like last time, but he would recover. And the plastic surgeon who'd closed up the cut on his face had told him he probably wouldn't have a scar.

In the hospital bed, Sabrina twitched and then let out a whimper in her sleep.

He leaned toward her from the chair the hospital staff

had pulled in, along with coffee for him and a bowl of water for Sitka. Once they'd gotten Sabrina into a room, he hadn't left her side.

But she still hadn't woken up. As soon as she'd arrived at the hospital, doctors had rushed her in for CT scans of her brain, facial bones, neck, abdomen and pelvis. She'd been wheeled away from him, looking small and battered and helpless in that hospital bed, a far cry from the determined woman who'd stood, blood-covered and swaying, and saved his life.

At the time, overhearing snippets of the doctors' conversations, phrases like *check for a fractured skull* and *could have an intracranial hemorrhage* had terrified him. They'd gotten him stitched up only by assuring him they'd tell him if there were any changes to or any news on Sabrina's condition.

Hours later, they'd told him either she was very lucky or her assailants had known exactly how to hit to cause a lot of visual damage but not to kill her. They said she had a couple of fractured ribs that luckily hadn't punctured her lungs. But she had a lung contusion that would need pain management. Amazingly, despite the massive swelling and bleeding on her face, she hadn't broken any of the bones there. But she did have a brain contusion. The doctors had called it minor, said the microbleed would require a longer stay in the hospital. It was also what was keeping her unconscious.

She was medicated, needed time to heal, but every moment her eyes stayed closed made him more anxious. Her doctors planned to keep her in the hospital for at least a week but said she would most likely make a full recovery within six months. But *most likely* wasn't good enough.

Somehow, in the time he'd spent with her at her hotel room and pretending to be her boyfriend, he'd fallen for her for real. Or maybe it had happened long before that, when she'd first come to the police station asking for help. Or even before that, when he'd run into her in town and felt an instant connection he wanted to pursue.

"Tate."

The whisper came from the doorway of Sabrina's room. After giving her one more glance to be sure she wasn't waking, Tate forced himself to his feet. His whole body ached as he hobbled toward his chief.

"How's she doing?"

"Nothing new," Tate told him. His fellow officers hadn't left the hospital until a few hours ago, exhausted. Luna police had taken over, stationing an officer at each of the two hospital entrances to protect both him and Sabrina. At this point, they all assumed Adam had left, that finding him would become a longer-term investigation. But they weren't taking any chances.

Tate hadn't realized his chief had stayed.

"I've got an update on Charlie."

Worry clamped down on his chest until the chief said, "The surgery was a success. They stopped the internal bleeding. He's got a lot of healing ahead, but he's going to make it."

Tate let out a relieved breath.

"And so are you."

When Tate shook his head, not understanding, the chief said, "The two of us have a lot of paperwork ahead, getting your personnel file in order. And there's a suspension in your future because I can't just pretend this didn't happen. But obviously, the threat against you was real. So, I'm willing to accept that you did what you had to do."

Relief loosened the tension he hadn't even realized he'd felt underneath his worry for Sabrina. "Thank you."

"You're a good officer, Tate. We want to keep you." He held out his hand as Sitka jerked upright, then ran over.

Tate shook his hand, then the chief bent over and petted Sitka. "You, too. You make one hell of a K-9 unit."

She gave the chief's arm a slobbery kiss, and he smiled, then stood.

He turned to leave, then twisted back toward Tate. "Don't give up," he advised, nodding toward Sabrina.

"Doctors said—"

"I know what the doctors said," the chief interrupted. "I'm talking about you. Don't give up on her. Believe me when I say I know what I'm talking about." Something wistful and sad flashed over his face as he said, "This kind of connection doesn't come around often. When you find it, hang on as long as you can."

"Thanks," Tate replied when he finally found his voice. By then, the chief was already striding away.

He glanced down at Sitka, who looked from him to Sabrina.

Tate's gaze followed, then he jerked in surprise. Her eyes were open, staring at him. She looked groggy, but far more aware than he would have expected after all she'd been through.

Rushing back into the room, with Sitka keeping pace, he carefully took hold of her hand. "How are you feeling?"

"Like a couple of assholes beat me up," she rasped.

Relief made his laughter come out sounding like a half sob. He stroked his thumb over the skin on her hand, mottled purple with bruises. "You're going to be fine."

The words seemed to reassure her, but her eyes closed again. They didn't open again for several long minutes. When they finally did, a nurse came in and listened to her heartbeat, then checked her pupils and helped her sit.

She gave Sabrina some water, then patted her arm, above where Tate still held her hand. "I know you don't feel so great now, but you'll be all right. You press your call button if you need me, okay?"

When Sabrina gave a shaky nod, looking a lot more alert, the nurse smiled at both of them, then left them alone.

Sabrina stared at the open doorway for a long moment. Then her lips pursed, lines forming between her eyes as she turned back to him, her expression one of wariness and distrust. "Who were they? Why were they trying to get back at you?" Her tone turned accusatory as she demanded, "And why did they call you Tate *Donnoly*?"

"I'm sorry." His voice came out barely more than a whisper, so he cleared his throat and tried again. "I'm sorry." He gave her the short version of the attempt on his life and his subsequent name change and return to Alaska.

Her gaze shifted to Sitka. "You didn't grow up in the Midwest." She looked back at him. "You grew up in Sitka, Alaska, didn't you?"

His dog let out a soft woof, then laid her head on the edge of Sabrina's hospital bed.

"Yes."

"You lied to me."

"I had to. I was trying to keep you safe. I was trying to keep *everyone* safe. I swear to you, Sabrina, I thought that article had gone unnoticed. Just in case, I was planning to leave after I helped you find your stalker. If I thought there was an immediate threat, I never would have—"

"You dug into my life without my permission," she cut him off. "And I get it. You did it to help me. But I told you *everything* afterward. I was really honest with you. Not just about what happened but about my *life*. About my family and my friends and who I really am. The whole time you were lying to me."

He clamped his lips shut as she spoke, letting her talk. But then he couldn't keep quiet anymore. "I tried to be honest with you."

She let out a huff. "When?"

"With everything. I told you more about myself than I've

shared with anyone since I left Boston. Yes, I hid some of the small details that I thought were dangerous for you to know—like the fact that I used to be a cop in Boston, that I'd grown up in Alaska. But the rest of it? All the things I shared with you about my family and my dreams for my life? That was all true."

"The things you left out weren't small details," Sabrina said, her voice too calm now, like she was tired of it all. Tired of him. "You hid pretty important pieces of yourself. Including a threat. And I paid for it."

"I know." He slid his hand over hers, and she frowned, pulling her hand free.

Dread built up, the fear that he'd messed up so badly there was no coming back from it. But the chief was right. He had to try.

"I'm so sorry, Sabrina. I can't take that back. If I had suspected what would happen, I would have left."

She flinched a little at that, and it gave him hope.

He leaned closer and stared into her eyes, hoping she could see the truth there. "I love you, Sabrina."

Her lips parted as she stared back at him. Then tears welled up, and she blinked them away. Her voice was a whisper when she said, "I don't think I can forgive you."

SABRINA WOKE WITH a start, her heart thundering in her chest, her head and ribs aching. She blinked, trying to get her bearings.

She was in a dark hospital room. Not a hidden concrete fort, trapped in by crooked cops, thinking her only option was how she might die. By bullet, beating or bomb.

Taking a deep breath, she glanced around. Tate was asleep in a chair across from her bed. When she strained, she spotted Sitka sprawled at his feet, lightly snoring.

She didn't remember drifting off to sleep again, but the stiffness in her body that turned into sharp pain at any movement, told her it might have been a while. She did remember the doctor coming in, giving her a whole lot of medical speak that had made her head spin, then summing up with "You'll be okay. Your brain and your ribs need time to heal, but you'll get there."

Then she'd been alone with Tate again, struggling to figure out what else to say. He'd told her he *loved* her. But it didn't matter how she felt in return, not if she couldn't trust him.

He'd hidden his past from her. Hidden the threats against him. After she'd spent two years running from a stalker, he should have known how much of a difference the right information could make. Instead, he'd left her in the dark, clueless about the additional danger she faced.

Her fists clenched, and the movement tugged on her IV, stinging. But the pain was a welcome distraction from her building anger.

If he'd been totally honest with her, maybe she wouldn't have done anything different. Maybe she would have felt the same way he had about the likelihood of his past coming to get her. But at least then she wouldn't have this sense of betrayal that hurt worse than all of her injuries combined.

She loved him.

The realization hit with the force of one of the punches she'd taken to the head. She huffed out a humorless laugh, and her chest started to ache.

How hadn't she realized it earlier? Of course she'd fallen in love with Tate, no matter his last name. He was sweet and smart and funny, and all the struggles of the past few years had seemed lighter when she was with him.

When Jessamyn had joked that maybe she'd meet her soul mate in that bar two and a half years ago and Sabrina had rolled her eyes, she'd thought about how her married friends liked to tell her that when she met the right one she'd just *know*. Adam had spotted her in that bar, begun his unnatural obsession that had led her to Desparre. That had led her to Tate. And now, suddenly, she *knew*.

But did that matter if she couldn't trust him?

Squeezing her eyes closed, she tried to imagine going home and never seeing him again. The idea was painful, and she didn't want to face it. When she opened her eyes again, a silhouette in the open doorway made her jump.

She almost didn't recognize him, with his hair dyed darker, the glasses, and the hospital scrubs. Obviously the Luna cops watching the entrances hadn't recognized him. But when he stepped inside, there was no doubt.

Fear mingled with a deep sense of betrayal. Adam had spent more than two years destroying her life, then convinced her to see him as a friend.

Adam smiled with a darkness in his eyes as he put a finger to his lips. Then he twisted toward Tate, his expression shifting into a possessive fury. His arm twitched, drawing her attention to what he held. A gun.

Sabrina's gaze went from him to Tate, asleep on the chair.

She didn't think. She just leaped.

The IV ripped out of her hand, and her bruised ribs set off a ferocious, searing pain that nauseated her. Her head jostled, and it felt as if her brain was bouncing inside her skull.

Then everything seemed to happen at once.

She smashed into Adam, propelling him back and pushing the gun sideways. Adam's gaze locked on hers, a mix of jealous rage and sinister intent that sent goose bumps across her neck. Then his hands shifted, ready to shove her back.

Before he could move, Tate jumped out of his seat, awakened by the noise. He knocked over his chair as he pushed his way between them, smashing Adam's gun hand into the wall, and making him drop the weapon.

Then somehow, Sitka was there, pressed up against her when she might have swayed and fallen.

Tate spun Adam face-first into the wall, yanked handcuffs off his belt and slapped them on as nurses and doctors rushed toward them and Tate told them to call for backup.

"She's mine," Adam snarled, trying to twist out of Tate's grip.

Tate pushed him back into the wall as he turned his head to look at her. "You okay?"

She stared back at him, at the intense protectiveness in his eyes, at the love she could see there.

The love she felt in return made her chest ache, made the words want to burst free.

Instead, she managed to nod as tears filled her eyes. She gave him a shaky smile to reassure him she really was okay and that she hadn't reinjured herself badly.

When Sitka whined, Sabrina stroked her fur, still staring at Tate. She didn't take her gaze off him, even when a pair of officers rushed into the room and pulled Adam away.

It was over.

After two long years of running and hiding and thinking she'd never have her life back, they'd caught her stalker. She could go home, return to the life she'd made for herself there.

So, why did her chest suddenly ache so badly over all the things she was giving up in Alaska?

Epilogue

Sabrina pulled back the curtains on her living room window, exposing the glorious view she'd fallen in love with the moment she'd stepped foot in this cabin.

She took a deep breath, smiling when her ribs gave only a slight twinge in protest. She'd spent a full week in the hospital, while doctors gave her medication to help her manage the pain and tests to check her neurological state. Then they'd declared the small bleed in her head healed enough to release her.

For the next three months at least, they'd told her to expect her symptoms to persist. Ringing in her ears maybe or some dizziness or just not feeling quite right. They wanted her to have regular follow-ups with a neurologist back in New York. But they'd cleared her to travel.

Her bags were already packed. She'd left New York two years ago with a trunk full of belongings. She was returning with two duffel bags.

But she was also returning with a feeling of safety. Adam was in custody. He had admitted to killing Dylan. He'd admitted to setting the truck on Sitka. He'd even admitted to giving her a shove in the woods, then grabbing her arm to ostensibly save her.

Apparently, he'd searched for her for over a year and a half without success after she'd left New York. Then she'd started her online jewelry business. She didn't remember it, but years ago, she'd posted something on social media about her dreams of designing jewelry, even shared a drawing of a necklace. A friend had shared that post. Then in Alaska, Sabrina had finally made that necklace. Adam had spent so much time obsessively trying to trace her online that the single post had eventually led him to her, through the PO box she used when she mailed out the jewelry.

She shivered at the deviousness, the obsessiveness he'd demonstrated. But it was over now. She straightened, pushing Adam from her mind as she looked around the place she'd come to call home.

She was going to miss this cabin. She was going to miss this town, miss the people.

A familiar pain clamped down on her chest, and she pressed a hand against her heart. After Adam had been arrested, she'd told Tate to go home, that she needed time. She knew how she felt about him, but she didn't know if she could do anything about it.

She hadn't told him she loved him. She wasn't sure she ever would. But meeting him and Sitka, coming to love him and Sitka, made leaving Alaska painful.

Glancing around the cabin one more time, she reached for her duffel bags. Lifting them sent a searing pain across her ribs and caused her head to swim. She closed her eyes and breathed through the pain until it eased up. Then she moved slowly toward the door.

No matter what she decided, she'd call Tate once she got to New York. She'd debated stopping by his house on her way to the airport, but worried if she did, she'd break down. She wanted time to feel more whole, to have more distance from the attacks in the army fort, before making any big decisions about her future.

She might come back here someday. Might see Tate and Sitka again. But maybe they both needed to return to the lives they'd left behind before they could decide what their futures held.

Pulling the door open, she drew in a hard breath. "Tate."

He stood on her porch, his hands twisted together like he'd been wringing them. He looked serious and determined and exactly what her eyes wanted to see.

Woof!

A smile trembled on her lips as she looked to his side, at the beautiful dog. "Sitka."

"I know you wanted time," he said, his gaze going to the bags she carried. His lips tightened briefly, then his gaze returned to hers. "But I just needed you to know something."

Sabrina nodded slowly as she took a step backward, never taking her gaze off him. Her chest felt like it swelled with all the emotions battling inside her: hope and fear and love.

He stepped inside, into her personal space like he had just under a month ago, when she'd felt like she was taking such a big step letting him into her cabin for the first time. Sitka followed, tail wagging as she pranced next to Sabrina, nudging her leg.

Sabrina couldn't help but smile as she put down her bags and stroked Sitka's fur. She couldn't stop the smile from fading into something more serious as she looked up at Tate, breathed in his familiar sandalwood scent.

"I love you, Sabrina."

Her throat clenched, her own words of love wanting to escape past the barriers she'd put up.

But she'd spent two years being afraid. Two years keeping people at a distance. As much as she wanted it to, that fear didn't just magically disappear simply because the threat of her stalker was gone. The ability to trust again wasn't easy.

Was she keeping Tate at a distance because he'd broken

her trust? Or because she'd become afraid to trust her own gut, trust her own feelings?

"I messed up," Tate continued. "And I will forever regret not being more honest with you."

He reached out, took both of her hands in his, and she felt the contact all the way down to her toes.

She had to be honest with herself. In the week she hadn't seen him, she'd missed this man desperately.

"I know you care about me," he said, his tone as intense as his gaze. "I *know* you do."

She felt herself nodding, saw a brief smile tip the edges of Tate's lips.

Then he was serious again. "We're right together, you and me. If you need more time, I understand and I'll give it to you. But I don't want to wait any longer."

He paused, as if waiting for her to speak, but she couldn't seem to form words before he rushed on.

"I'll do whatever it takes to regain your trust."

She stared up at him, thinking of all the opportunities she'd missed to be with him while she'd lived in Alaska. Thinking of how she'd tried to do what was best for her family, even though it hadn't been what they'd wanted. Of how she'd snuck out in the middle of the night, without a goodbye, so they wouldn't try to follow.

He'd made mistakes, too. But she knew he thought he was protecting her by keeping his past from her. And every time she'd needed him, he'd shown up.

She loved him. She was angry with him, but if she hadn't fallen for him so completely, she wouldn't have been so mad or felt so betrayed.

She couldn't deny what she felt any longer. She didn't want to let her own fear hold her back and lose him. Didn't want to spend the next part of her life missing someone else she loved.

"Whatever you need," Tate repeated, stepping even

closer, so she had to tilt her head back to keep staring into his dark, serious gaze. "I know we both need to reconnect with the lives we had to leave. But I want to do it together. I want to see my family again, *finally*, and not feel like I'm compromising their safety or my own by doing it. I want to introduce you to them."

She jerked at the words, at the implied commitment there, and he spoke even faster. "I know you need to go home to your family in New York. I want to meet them. If you want me to," he added. "Whether it's now or later. I want to be with you, whether it's here or in New York or it's long-distance for a while." He glanced at Sitka and added, "The chief has agreed that whatever you want, if you'll let me be with you, Sitka can come, too."

Woof!

He smiled at his dog, then turned his serious gaze back on her. "You can think about this as long as you need. But I won't give up on us. I love you too much, Sabrina."

He let go of one of her hands to cup her cheek. "If you decide you want me to go and leave you alone, I will. But I'll always be waiting. I'll wait as long as it takes."

She stared up at him, words caught in her throat and fear still lodged in her chest.

She loved him. She didn't want to lose him. But was she ready to make such a big leap of faith?

He nodded, gave her a sad smile as he dropped his hand and backed away.

He'd started to turn for the door when she grabbed his arm, gripping tight, knowing it was time to truly move forward. And she couldn't have the life she wanted without him in it.

He turned back, his gaze filled with surprise and a sudden, fierce hope.

"I love you, too, Tate," she croaked, then suppressed a

laugh at how tearful she sounded, how joyous she felt. "I love you, too."

Woof! Sitka nudged her again, and Sabrina gave in to the laugh ready to burst inside her. "I love you, too, Sitka."

Then Tate stepped closer, lowered his lips to hers and gently kissed her.

His lips only touched hers for a brief moment, careful of the bruising still coloring her jaw. When he lifted his face again and gave her a huge, brilliant smile, she felt better than she had in more than two years. They'd figure out the details, but she knew one thing for sure: she'd gotten two amazing gifts out of her two years on the run—him and Sitka.

And she wasn't going to ever let them go.

* * * * *

CLOSE QUARTERS
WITH THE
BODYGUARD

LISA CHILDS

For cat lovers, including me and my daughters, whose furry babies have stolen our hearts like heroine Jocelyn Gerber's cat has stolen hers!

Chapter One

Landon Myers shook his head. The bodyguard could not have heard his boss correctly—because what Parker Payne had said made no sense at all. Landon leaned closer to Parker's desk and asked, "*Who* do you want me to protect?"

"Jocelyn Gerber," Parker replied.

When he'd resigned from the River City Police Department, Landon had hoped he'd never have to see that particular assistant district attorney again. "Why?"

"She's being threatened, along with everyone else associated with Luther Mills's upcoming trial." The notorious drug dealer had been charged with first-degree murder of a police informant. Mills thought himself so above the law that he'd shot the kid right in front of an eyewitness—the informant's sister.

Anyone else would have accepted a plea deal, knowing they'd be convicted. But Luther had gotten away with murder before, along with countless other crimes.

Landon snorted derisively. "What? Is Gerber's boss threatening to kill her if she loses this one like she has every other case she's tried to bring against him?"

None of those cases had ever made it past the grand

jury, though, for an indictment—despite all the evidence she'd been given. Landon knew because he'd brought her some of that evidence only to have it mysteriously disappear.

"Luther's threatening her," Parker said. "The police chief learned about a plot Mills has in place to take out everyone associated with his trial. And Chief Lynch thinks Luther has help from within the police department and within the district attorney's office."

Landon snorted again. "Yeah, and I can tell you who. Her. Jocelyn Gerber is his help within the district attorney's office." That was the only thing that made sense for why Luther had never been tried before.

"If that's true, why would he be threatening her?" Parker asked him.

Landon leaned back in his chair, his knees bumping into the front of Parker's desk again. He would have pushed it back to accommodate his long legs, but the wooden chair was already against the paneled wall behind him. "So she'll do what he wants—like she has every other time River City PD got close to taking him down for his crimes—and the evidence against him will miraculously disappear." Along with the eyewitness. He probably should have been glad he hadn't been assigned to protect her; whoever was guarding Rosie Mendez had been given a death sentence.

Parker shook his head. "The district attorney wouldn't have assigned the case to Ms. Gerber if she had any doubts about her."

"The district attorney should be trying the damn case herself," Landon said.

"Her doctor has ordered her to bed rest because of

her high-risk pregnancy, and once she delivers, she'll be out for a while for maternity leave," Parker said.

Landon furrowed his brow, surprised his boss knew so much about the district attorney.

As if he'd read Landon's mind, Parker replied, "Amber Talsma-Kozminski is married to my brother Logan's brother-in-law Milek."

The Paynes were related to just about everyone in River City. The former chief of police was Parker's half brother, and the current one, former FBI bureau chief Woodrow Lynch, was now his stepfather.

An only child of only children who'd passed away a few years ago, Landon didn't have any family but for his fellow team members, who were also former vice cops like he was. But while he was the only Myers left in River City, Jocelyn Gerber wasn't the only assistant district attorney. Not in a city the size of theirs. River City, Michigan, was even bigger than Detroit but on the west side of the state near Lake Michigan. "The DA should have picked someone else for Luther's trial, after all the times Jocelyn has failed to bring charges against him despite the evidence we brought her."

"I'm sure that she didn't purposely drop those charges," Parker defended her.

"You left River City PD before I did," Landon reminded him. Parker had left the vice unit when his twin brother, Logan, started the Payne Protection Agency. He'd worked for Logan for a few years before starting his own franchise of the agency, which consisted of all former vice cops, like Landon. "You don't know Jocelyn Gerber."

"And you do?"

Landon felt heat rush to his face. If he didn't distrust her so much, he would have liked to know her better. With her long, silky black hair and long, lithe body, she was gorgeous. But she was just as treacherous as she was sexy—probably more so because she was so damn sexy. He shook his head.

"Well, you're going to get to know her since you'll be protecting her 24/7 from the threat to her life," Parker told him.

Landon groaned. "C'mon. She's not being threatened." She was the threat—to the case and maybe to him, as well, since he would have to spend so much time around her. She was definitely too damn sexy.

THE SOUND OF her heels striking the concrete echoed throughout the dimly lit parking structure. But instead of slowing down, Jocelyn Gerber sped up as she hurried toward her vehicle. She hadn't needed the chief of police phoning to warn her that she was in danger. She'd known the minute she'd taken the case against Luther Mills that she was putting her life at risk.

But neither the chief nor Luther Mills was going to scare her into giving up the trial. This time the charges would stick, and she would win.

She had to…

That win mattered most. No, putting Luther Mills out of commission mattered most.

A chill chased down her spine, and it wasn't just from the crisp autumn wind whipping through the parking structure. Someone was watching her. She was used to that. Since she'd been assigned this case, she knew everyone was watching her—waiting for her to fail again.

But someone was following her now, too. She heard an echo from more than her heels. She heard the echo of louder footsteps—from someone bigger and heavier than she was.

She shivered.

Of course, it didn't mean that someone was following her. Maybe he was just heading to his vehicle like she was hers. But, since all the downtown offices had closed hours ago, there were very few vehicles parked yet in the structure. Most of the spaces were empty. The couple of cars she had passed, it sounded as though those footsteps had gone by them, as well. No lights blinked on, no horn tooted.

She pressed her key fob, but she wasn't close enough to her vehicle for her lights to blink or horn to toot. Where the hell had she parked?

She needed to get to her SUV. But just in case she didn't make it to her vehicle before the man caught up with her, she reached inside her purse, which hung over her shoulder next to her bulky briefcase. As she fumbled inside her leather bag, she turned her head to glance over her shoulder. She could see only a shadow behind her, but that shadow was enormous.

Her heart began to pound even faster and more furiously. The chief had warned that Mills would probably go after the eyewitness first. But what about Jocelyn?

She should have been safe—at least until the trial started. But it was weeks away and that enormous shadow was only feet away from her now. Her fingers finally closed around her weapon. She pulled it from her purse and whirled around to face her stalker, yelling, "Stay away from me!"

"That's going to be damn hard to do when I've been assigned to protect you," a deep voice drawled.

"Who are you?" she demanded to know as the man remained in the shadows. A hood was pulled over his head, and it shadowed his face like the dim light shadowed his entire body—his long, broad-shouldered body.

"Your bodyguard," that deep voice rumbled.

She shivered again and clutched her weapon tighter.

That was the other thing the chief had told her, that he was hiring the Payne Protection Agency to protect everyone involved in Luther Mills's trial. And like she had told him, that was a mistake. One that could prove fatal.

Was it going to prove fatal now—to her?

"Who are you?" she asked again, and she raised her weapon to point directly at his chest.

He chuckled. "You're going to tase me?"

She moved her finger toward the trigger of the weapon. She knew how to fire it to plunge those probes into his chest because, unfortunately, she'd had to use it before. Luther Mills wasn't the only criminal who had tried to hurt her.

"Yes." But before she could fire it, the weapon was snapped out of her grasp and she was spun around so that her back was pressed against his chest, his strong arms wrapped around her.

She screamed.

But he just chuckled again. He knew there was nobody around to hear her. To help her...

She struggled in his grasp, but his arms just tightened around her, stilling her movements. She tried to kick back, with her stilettos, but when her heel struck his leg, the shoe slipped off her foot. And she hadn't even fazed him; he was that strong, that muscular.

If this man really was her bodyguard, it was just as she'd feared. He was as big a threat to her as Luther Mills was—because, if she was right, someone within the Payne Protection Agency could be working for Luther. She had a horrible feeling that she'd just found out who—the man who had already overpowered her.

"WHERE ARE THEY?" Chief Woodrow Lynch wondered aloud as he looked around the nearly empty conference room.

Parker Payne shrugged. "They should all be arriving soon." Right now he was the only other person in the room, sitting at the other end of the long conference table from Woodrow. He seemed confident in his team, though, which should have eased Woodrow's concerns.

Woodrow had called the meeting at the Payne Protection Agency, so he could explain why he'd hired a private security company to protect everyone involved in the trial of a local drug dealer.

Luther Mills was not just any drug dealer. He was the biggest drug dealer in Michigan. Hell, probably in the entire Midwest, and he was so rich and powerful that he could hire or threaten anyone into doing what he wanted. And Woodrow had recently learned that some of those people Luther had either bought or manipulated were within the police department and the district attorney's office.

That was why he had hired the Payne Protection Agency. He was going to make sure that Luther Mills didn't hurt anyone else and that he finally went to trial for his crimes.

But not everyone was going to be happy with having a bodyguard. The assistant district attorney, Jocelyn Gerber, was certainly not happy. She thought he was stupid for trusting the Payne Protection Agency—at least Parker Payne's franchise of the agency—because every member of his team was a former vice cop. She suspected at least one of them could be working for Luther.

Of all his stepsons' franchises, Woodrow had chosen Parker's because of their connection to Luther Mills. He knew Parker and his team had tried for years to bring down Luther Mills, so he knew they would have a vested interest in making sure he was finally brought to justice.

But as Jocelyn had pointed out, they had tried for years with no success. She believed one of those former vice cops hadn't just been working for the River City Police Department but for Luther Mills, as well.

Could she be right?

If she was, instead of protecting everyone associated with the trial, Woodrow had just put one of them in even more danger. Which one?

Her?

Chapter Two

Landon had figured his protecting Jocelyn Gerber was a bad idea. But now he knew for certain he'd been right. She writhed in his arms, jerking around as she kicked at his shins. As her one remaining heel connected, he flinched, and a grunt of pain slipped out of his lips, stirring her black hair. "Stop struggling!"

"Let me go!" she yelled back at him.

But he kept his arms locked around her, holding hers down at her sides as her back pressed against his chest. He didn't trust that she didn't have another weapon on her. "What else you got in that bag of yours?" he asked.

In addition to not wanting to be tased, he didn't want to be pepper sprayed or shot either. And he suspected she might have a concealed-weapons permit to carry a gun as well as that Taser.

"None of your damn business," she told him.

"I'm your bodyguard," he reminded her. "Everything about you is my damn business now."

"You're not protecting me," she said. "You're the one hurting me."

He'd been careful not to hold her too tightly. But he was big and sometimes stronger than he realized. He immediately loosened his grasp, and she broke free and whirled around to face him.

As he'd suspected she would, she pointed another weapon at him, the small pepper-spray canister that was attached to her key ring.

He snorted. "I don't know why the chief and Parker think *you* need a bodyguard." Just as he'd worried, he was the one who needed protecting from her.

But while she had her finger on the trigger of the canister, she didn't press down on it. Yet. "I don't need a bodyguard," she said.

He suspected he knew why: She was working for Luther. She was the leak within the district attorney's office. Maybe he could use this opportunity to prove that to Parker and to the chief.

"But you got one," he said. "So you're going to have to accept that."

Her eyes were such a brilliant shade of blue that they gleamed even in the dim lighting of the parking structure. Then she narrowed them in a glare. "I don't have to accept *you* as my bodyguard," she said.

"Do you even know who I am?" he asked. What could she have against him personally? He'd brought her evidence to indict Luther Mills, and he wasn't the one who'd made that evidence mysteriously disappear.

She narrowed her eyes into slits of suspicion. "You obviously don't want me to know," she said. "Or you wouldn't have your hood up. You wouldn't have been slinking in the shadows."

"Slinking in the shadows…" He chuckled. "That's kind of what bodyguards do." Unobtrusively protecting their clients. But she wasn't his client; Chief Lynch was. She was just his principal, the person he'd been assigned to protect.

"Why?" she asked. "Wouldn't you be more effective if everyone knew you were protecting me?"

He shrugged. "I'm not making that call. That's up to Parker Payne and the chief. They might want Luther to actually make a try for you, to flush out whoever's working with him."

She tightened her grasp on her canister of pepper spray, and he instinctively took a step back. "Is that what you were really trying to do here? Make a try for me?"

He chuckled again. She was crazy. "You actually think I'm going to try to take you out?"

She glanced around the dark garage and shivered. "This would be a good place to try."

"I'm your bodyguard," he repeated, and this time his teeth were gritted when he said it. How damn dense was she? Maybe that was why she'd never gotten a grand jury to indict Luther—because she wasn't very bright.

"I only have your word that's who you are," she said.

He reached up and pushed back his hood. Not that seeing his face clearly would probably make her recognize him. So he added his name, "I'm Landon Myers. I work for the Payne Protection Agency. I have been assigned to protect you."

"You worked vice," she murmured.

She must have recognized him.

"Yes, I did."

His admission just had her tensing more. What was she worried about? Why didn't she trust him?

Did she realize that he was onto her? That he suspected she was Luther's leak in the DA's office?

IF THE MEETING at the Payne Protection Agency had been meant to reassure her, it had done exactly the opposite. Jocelyn was even more on edge than she'd been before it—when Landon Myers had accosted her in the parking garage.

Now he was using her keys to let himself into her house. She wouldn't have turned them over, but he'd insisted on going inside first, on checking to make sure that nobody had broken in while she'd been gone. The minute he turned them and pushed open the door, the alarm began to blare.

"What's the code?" he shouted over it.

She wasn't about to give that to him. But she joined him in the foyer and surreptitiously punched in the numbers. When the alarm stopped blaring, she told him, "That's why I know nobody has broken in here. They can't get past my security system. That's why you don't need to be here."

"You heard the chief," he said. "He wants you and everyone else involved in this trial to have around-the-clock protection until the trial is over."

She'd heard him. And she hadn't had the chance to argue with him since everybody else had been arguing against the need for protection. She hadn't wanted anyone who needed protecting to lose it—like the eyewitness.

She could not lose the eyewitness. And she actually trusted Clint Quarters to protect Rosie Mendez. He was the one who'd turned her late brother into an informant.

He blamed himself for Javier Mendez's murder. Unfortunately, so did Rosie. But because Clint felt guilty, he would do everything in his power to keep her safe. He'd already saved her from an attempt on her life tonight.

She shivered.

Landon must have thought she was cold because he closed the door, shutting them inside the dark foyer. She shivered again.

While she trusted Clint to protect Rosie, she didn't trust Landon. He had no stake in this trial. Clint had walked away from the River City PD because of his guilt over Javier's death. Why had Landon walked away?

Needing to see him clearly, she flipped on a light. The golden hue of the chandelier's bulbs made his thick light brown hair glow like gold, as well. His eyes were brown, too, but a richer milk-chocolate brown. He stared down at her, which was an uncomfortable and unfamiliar sensation for Jocelyn. She was tall and wore heels to make herself even taller, which was usually taller than most of the men she encountered.

Except Landon Myers.

He was tall. But he wasn't just tall. He was big all over—broad shoulders, huge chest and arms, long, thick legs. If he was working for Luther, like she worried he was, then he could have easily taken her out back in the parking garage. He could have snapped her neck with very little effort.

She shivered again—at the thought, and at the way he was staring at her. So intensely...

But he wasn't looking at her with the admiration

most men looked at her with. He didn't seem to find her attractive at all.

"That's some fancy security system," he mused.

She nodded.

"Expensive."

She shrugged. She had no idea. Her parents had insisted on installing it. They were paranoid about protection. They would probably approve of her having a bodyguard following her around, but Jocelyn didn't.

"And not just the security system," Landon remarked as he glanced up at the chandelier and at the artwork on the walls.

Her house had probably been expensive. But like the security system, it was something else her parents had bought for her. She'd been happy with her small apartment downtown, close to the office. Her parents had wanted her to live in a more secure neighborhood.

But she wasn't about to share her private life with Landon Myers. "As you can see, I'm perfectly safe inside my house," she told him. "You don't need to stay."

He was already walking beyond the foyer into the dark living room. And as he walked, his hand moved toward his holster. He couldn't have heard anything, though. There wasn't anyone inside.

Then she heard it, too, the clatter of something falling onto the hardwood floor. Landon pulled his weapon and swung the barrel around, but before he could pull the trigger, she grabbed his arm. Muscles rippled beneath her fingers. "Don't shoot!" she yelled. "It's just my cat."

"Cat?"

As if to confirm it, Lady let out a pitiful meow. Jocelyn flipped the living room switch, but the light was dim from the lamp lying on the floor.

"That little thing knocked over the lamp?" Landon asked skeptically as Lady trotted up to them. The Singapura cat was naturally small-boned and light. But she was also active and athletic, too.

Sometimes a little too active and athletic. "She's naughty," Jocelyn said, but she smiled as she leaned over and petted the cat's smooth beige coat. "You're a naughty girl."

As if insulted, Lady walked away from Jocelyn and wound between Landon's legs.

His brow furrowed as he stared down at the animal. "I didn't figure you for a cat lady."

Her parents had not bought her the cat. They wanted real grandchildren, not furry ones.

"She came with the house." She must have belonged to the previous owner because Jocelyn had found her inside when she'd moved in. The cat had been alone and hungry for food and affection.

Landon turned his attention to her, asking, "And you kept her?"

Jocelyn could have turned her in to a shelter or even sold her once she'd learned how rare the breed was, but removing Lady from the house hadn't seemed right. And Jocelyn appreciated her company. Like she'd told her parents, Lady was as close as they were getting to a grandchild. Jocelyn was not about to wind up like her boss—missing out on a major case because she was having babies.

"Are you allergic to cats?" Jocelyn asked hopefully. And Landon must have heard that hope because he chuckled. He reholstered his weapon and leaned down to pick up the cat. "Not at all," he said.

The small cat looked even smaller in his huge hands. But instead of being frightened, she purred and rubbed against him.

"She likes me," he said.

"She's hungry," Jocelyn corrected him, and she headed toward the kitchen.

He was right with her every step—as if he still suspected an intruder could have gotten inside the house. If anyone had made it past the security system, Lady would have been hiding, not out knocking stuff over. Usually she shied away from strangers. But she kept purring and fawning all over Landon.

"Traitor," Jocelyn murmured.

"What?" Landon asked. But his mouth had curved into a grin, so he'd probably heard her.

The minute Jocelyn rattled the cat's box of food, the fickle feline squirmed from Landon's arms and jumped down to trot over to her bowl that her mistress dutifully filled.

"She is a traitor," Landon agreed.

Was he?

Was he a traitor to the police department and the city he'd once sworn to serve and protect? Jocelyn stared at him, wondering.

Could she trust him?

Not like the chief and Parker Payne did. She tried again. "You don't have to stay. I'm safe here."

"I have my orders," Landon said. "You were there— you heard."

She sighed. She'd heard too much—about that attempt on the witness, about the plan for all the body-guards to act like boyfriends, or in Detective Dubridge's case, Keeli Abbott was to act like his girlfriend. Jocelyn shuddered in revulsion. She didn't want a boyfriend at all, let alone someone like Landon Myers.

Someone she couldn't trust.

"Don't worry," Landon said as he walked out of the kitchen and headed back to the living room. "You won't even know I'm here."

Jocelyn doubted that. She followed him into the living room, where he shrugged off his jacket and undid his holster. After putting the weapon and his coat onto the ottoman next to the couch, he reached for his shirt, tugging it up and over his head, so that he stood before her with that enormous, muscular chest bare but for the golden-brown hair on it.

Jocelyn choked on her own saliva. How the hell long had it been since she'd had a boyfriend?

She couldn't remember the last time she'd seen a man shirtless. It had been too long ago, and it had never been a man with a chest like this guy's.

"You okay?" Landon asked her. And there was a wicked gleam in his brown eyes.

She nodded.

And he teased, "Cat got your tongue?"

Heat rushed to her face. But she refused to let him know he was affecting her, any more than he must have already guessed. She glared at him. "I'm fine," she said.

"Really?" he asked. "You look a little frustrated."

"I am," she agreed. But not how he was implying—if that was what he was implying. She wasn't sexually frustrated. Not at all...

"I'm frustrated that you insist on staying here when I don't need protection," she said.

He shrugged, and muscles rippled in his arms and chest, as well.

She nearly choked again.

"I'm just doing my job," he told her.

Was that all he was doing, though? Or was he working for Luther Mills as well as the Payne Protection Agency?

Fortunately, he'd returned her Taser, so she would have that if he tried anything. It wouldn't kill him, but at least it would give her time to get away from him.

And she needed to get away from him now—before she did something stupid, like continuing to stare at his chest. But before she turned away, she felt socially obligated to tell him, "There is a guest room upstairs."

Actually, there were three of them. The house was entirely too big for just her, but her parents had not yet given up their hope for her to get married and have children.

He shook his head. "I need to stay down here, make sure nobody tries to get in." He narrowed his eyes with suspicion. "Or out…"

Had he guessed that she was thinking about ditching him? Probably. She'd made it a little too clear that she didn't think she needed protection.

She certainly didn't need him to protect her. But maybe she did need protection—from him.

THE PAYNE PROTECTION AGENCY.

Luther had heard of it. A person couldn't live in

River City and not know about it. But he didn't just know the agency. He knew Parker Payne.

He leaned back on his bunk and laughed. Parker Payne had tried for years to take him down. Instead, the former vice cop had nearly been taken down.

Too bad Parker hadn't died when that hit had been put out on him years ago. So many assassins had tried… and failed. Regrettably.

Maybe Luther should put out another hit on Parker Payne and on every damn bodyguard working for him.

Luther knew all of them. Clint. Hart Fisher. Tyce Jackson. Landon Myers and that little hottie, Keeli Abbott. They were all former vice cops who, like Parker and Clint Quarters, had tried for many years to take down Luther and his organization. But eventually, they'd all given up and quit the River City PD.

Luther ran his fingers over the cell phone that was still warm from his last, lengthy conversation. He'd been apprised of the situation.

The chief knew that Luther had gotten to someone in the police department. Obviously, he didn't know who yet, or Luther wouldn't have gotten all the information he just had—that the chief had hired the Payne Protection Agency to guard the witness and everyone else associated with the case against him.

Someday soon, when he was free, he would have to thank Chief Lynch for making it all so easy for him. Now he wouldn't just take out the witness and the other people going after him; he would take out all those former vice cops, as well.

He would take down everyone who had tried to destroy him for so many years. But it wouldn't take him years to accomplish his objective.

Just days…

Or hours…

And all of them would be dead.

Chapter Three

Landon listened to the echo of her heels striking the wooden steps as she went upstairs to her bedroom. He was tempted to follow her, and not so he could use that guest room she'd mentioned. He'd rather share her bed. And for a moment, the way she'd looked at him, he'd thought she might not mind sharing with him.

Sure, she didn't like him. That was obvious. But she hadn't been able to stop staring when he'd taken off his shirt. He grinned again, like he had then. Teasing her had been fun but futile.

She hadn't taken the bait. She'd just ignored his innuendos. Looking the way she did, she had to be used to dealing with unwanted advances.

But he wondered if his advances would have been unwanted. She had been staring at him.

His body tensed and hardened. But he dragged in a deep breath and exhaled it. While he couldn't help being physically attracted to a woman as beautiful as Jocelyn Gerber, he couldn't act on that attraction—because he couldn't trust her.

In the glow of the lamp he'd lifted back onto an end table, he stared up at the coffered ceiling over his head.

The house was a mansion, the security system highly rated and expensive. And he'd recognized some of that artwork on the walls. It had been original, not prints.

He didn't think the salary of an assistant district attorney was enough to cover all her purchases and expenses. So where the hell was she getting her money?

Luther Mills?

It would make sense that he'd been paying her off to lose that evidence. But Landon needed evidence to prove that she was on the take. Luther threatening her, too, had proved her innocence to some, but not to him.

He didn't think she was really in danger.

He suspected he was the one in danger. Maybe he shouldn't have given her back that Taser. But her using that on him was the least of his concerns at the moment.

Clint was protecting the witness. He let a ragged sigh slip through his lips. While he was close to everyone he'd worked with in the vice unit, he was closest to Clint. They even rented a house together, a small one that was nothing like Jocelyn Gerber's.

Clint had nearly died tonight. And in order to protect Rosie Mendez, he still could die. Luther would probably be happy to take out Clint along with the eyewitness. Hell, Luther would be happy to take out any of them or all of them.

They'd all tried really hard to bring him down. Landon wanted to make certain that this time justice was finally served. It wouldn't be, though, if Jocelyn was working for the drug dealer.

He needed to know.

As his thoughts stopped racing, he noticed that the house had fallen silent. There was no creak of floorboards overhead. Jocelyn wasn't moving around anymore. Neither was her damn cat.

So it was time for Landon to move around, to see what he could find in her house. Hopefully, she had some kind of home office or den someplace where she might keep financial records.

With the security system she had to keep everyone out, she might not even lock up her records. He hoped that was the case. And he hoped that home office was downstairs, so he wouldn't have to risk getting tased.

Before leaving the living room, he grabbed his Glock out of the holster. Despite the security system, he didn't want his weapon far from his reach. He knew he might need it, either for protection from Luther's crew or from Jocelyn Gerber.

Along with his shirt, he'd taken off his boots, too, so he moved softly across the hardwood floors, which creaked only slightly with his weight. The house was some kind of Tudor design with dark trim and plaster walls. It was rich and almost untouchable looking—like Jocelyn.

He'd touched her earlier, though, when he'd struggled with her in the parking garage. And he'd wanted to touch her again. He would get the chance if he pretended to be her boyfriend. The chief and Parker had suggested the ruse to fool Luther's leaks. They didn't want the ones within the police department and DA's office to know that the chief was aware of them.

But Landon had a feeling the leak in the DA's office already knew. He just had to prove she was the leak.

Her den was easy to find. Its double doors opened off the opposite end of the living room from the kitchen.

Through the glass panes, he could see her desk. A computer sat on it along with a pile of folders.

The doorknob turned easily. Just as he'd hoped, she hadn't locked up anything. He pushed open one of the double doors and slipped inside the room. Like the living room, it had a coffered ceiling, but in here the beams had been painted white and so had the paneling on the walls. When he flipped on the lamp on the desk, which was also white, the entire room glowed. Unlike what he'd seen of the rest of the house, this space was bright and feminine—like Jocelyn.

Had the rest of the house been decorated by someone else? Had she lived here with someone else? A former husband? Maybe she'd gotten the house in a divorce settlement. He turned his attention to the files and the computer sitting atop the desk. He flipped on the computer to a log-in screen and cursed. He was no hacker, and he didn't know Jocelyn Gerber well enough to guess her log-in or password.

So he pressed the power button, turning it off, and reached for the folders instead. They appeared to be case files. Was it legal for her to remove them from the DA's office? Were they copies of information?

Some of the cases appeared to involve Luther, or at least some of his crew. Landon's former and current coworker Tyce Jackson had taken down quite a few members of that crew when he'd gone undercover within Luther's organization. None of them had turned on Luther, though, but they'd still gone free despite the vice unit's efforts to put them away.

Was that because of Jocelyn?

She hadn't worked every single case, but she'd been assigned quite a few of them. Too many of them…

But would Luther really have threatened her if she was working for him? Unless that threat was just a cover, so no one would suspect she was his mole.

But Landon wasn't the only one. Sure, he hadn't convinced Parker, and the chief obviously didn't suspect her. But his team members did. He'd seen the suspicion on all their faces tonight. They all had their hands full with their own assignments, though. So it fell on Landon to get the proof.

And, despite her top-notch security system, Jocelyn was unlikely to leave that lying out on her desk where a visitor or cleaning lady might see it. So he reached for one of the desk drawers. While he tugged on the handle, the drawer didn't budge. Then he noticed the lock.

So this was where she kept the things she didn't want anyone to see. Too bad the lock was flimsy. He grabbed her letter opener and easily jimmied open the drawer. A gasp slipped through his lips at what he found.

This wasn't evidence of her collusion with Luther Mills. If anything, it might have been proof of her innocence—if he was the one who'd sent the threats.

The first thing he'd seen was a paper with letters pasted to it that spelled out: *You're dead, Bitch!*

There were papers beneath that one, some written in thick black marker, some neatly typed, but all contained similar death threats.

Why hadn't she mentioned them during the meeting?

When they'd arrived, they'd seen a threat the judge had received regarding his daughter. A slashed-up photograph of the beautiful heiress. While none of these had photos of Jocelyn included, it was clear that the threat was meant for her—to end her life.

JOCELYN JERKED AWAKE just as she'd finally closed her eyes. She could not sleep with someone else in her house, especially when that someone was Landon Myers.

He was shirtless…

And ridiculously muscular and sexy and…

Suspicious. She could not trust him. While he was probably in his early thirties, like she was, he had worked vice long enough that he should have been able to bring down Luther Mills. But that hadn't happened until after he'd left the department.

There had to be a reason for that—like he had been working for Luther the years he'd been in the vice unit. Was he working for him now?

Instead of protecting her, did he intend to get rid of her? She reached beneath the pillow next to hers, where she'd stashed her Taser gun. Would the shock be enough to stop him? Or would she even have time to fire it at him?

He had a real gun with bullets. He didn't have to get close to her to kill her. But he was close.

Just below her.

She scooted up against the headboard to listen for any noise. Was he asleep? It wasn't as if she would be able to hear him snoring unless he snored really loudly. She did hear something, though—the metallic creak of hinges. Somebody was opening a door.

She waited for the blare of the alarm but then remembered that she'd shut it off. She hadn't turned it back on before going to bed like she usually did because her damn bodyguard had distracted her.

And if that wasn't her bodyguard moving around downstairs, it could have been someone who'd taken advantage of the security system being off. Someone could have broken inside her house.

She pulled the Taser from beneath her pillow and stepped lightly onto the floor. She moved quietly toward the door. But she had to unlock and open it. And the hinges on her door creaked like the ones she'd heard.

Damn.

Now whomever she had heard might have heard her, as well. It didn't matter if it was the bodyguard or an intruder. She was in danger no matter who was out there. With her Taser in both hands, she moved to the back stairwell, which descended into the kitchen. She drew in a deep breath as she stepped onto the tile floor. The ceramic was cold beneath her bare feet. She shivered, but being cold wasn't the reason.

She heard another creak—from behind her. But she had no time to whirl around, and point her weapon, before strong arms closed around her. A scream tore from her throat as she struggled in the grasp of her attacker.

Through the thin cotton of her nightgown, she could feel the heat of his body and even the bareness of his chest. The bodyguard was the one who'd grabbed her.

Now what did he intend to do with her?

Kill her?

Or…

Her pulse quickened in anticipation as he turned her in his arms, and her breasts pushed against his chest as she panted for breath. "What—what are you doing?"

she asked. But she didn't sound as angry and haughty as she wanted to sound.

"What the hell are you doing?" he asked.

"I—I heard someone moving around and remembered that I hadn't turned the alarm system back on," she said.

He cursed. "How the hell did we forget…?"

Because he'd taken off his shirt and she'd lost all her common sense. Maybe she'd been too focused on work lately. Maybe she needed more of a personal life than she'd been allowing herself.

Of course, she didn't want a husband or children like her parents wanted for her. But maybe a date every once in a while wouldn't interfere too much with her work.

What was Landon's excuse for forgetting, though? Had she distracted him, as well? She nearly snorted. She doubted that. He didn't seem at all attracted to her. But now…

The light from the microwave clock and various other appliances illuminated the kitchen enough that she could see him and the way he was looking at her, his dark eyes gleaming. He stared down at her nightgown. She wore no bra beneath the thin cotton, so her nipples pushed against the fabric, the tips taut as if begging for attention.

A strange tension began to wind inside her, from her breasts to her core. How could she be attracted to this man? She didn't even trust him.

It was purely physical—because he was so damn good-looking. His gaze met hers now, and his eyes looked more black than brown, as if his pupils had dilated. He leaned down until his mouth nearly touched hers.

Maybe it would have…had something not crashed somewhere else inside the house.

"That damn cat…" Landon murmured.

But she shook her head. "You don't know that. Not with the alarm being off."

He released a ragged breath before stepping back and finally letting her go. "You're right. I'll check it out. You go back upstairs."

She shook her head again. If someone had broken into her house, she sure as hell wasn't going to hide. She wanted to see who the intruder was. "I have my Taser," she reminded him as she raised the weapon.

"And that's not going to be effective if Luther sent a crew here like the one he sent to Rosie Mendez's apartment."

She shivered again because she knew he was right. If that many people had broken into her home, they both needed to run. But Landon wasn't running away from danger.

He raised his weapon and turned toward the kitchen doorway. He'd taken only a few steps before he turned his head and looked over his broad shoulder at her. "Stay behind me," he advised her.

As if his body alone could protect her from a barrage of bullets. But it was so big and muscular that maybe it could. She stayed close to his bare back as he headed out of the kitchen and across the living room.

No gunfire rang out—only his curse again.

"That damn cat," he said as he pushed open the door to her office. It creaked; she suspected it was what she'd heard earlier. It must have creaked when he'd closed the door to her office and locked the cat inside.

"What the hell were you doing in my office?" she asked him.

"I— What?" he asked as Lady streaked out between them. She'd knocked the files on Jocelyn's desk onto the floor along with a glass paperweight that had shattered against the wood.

"I didn't let her in there," she said. She was always careful to keep the cat out of her office since the feline was so active. "So you must have. What were you doing?"

Then she saw the drawer that had been forced open. He hadn't even bothered to put the letters back inside it. They lay across the keyboard to her computer.

"What the hell were you doing?" she demanded to know.

He gestured at those letters. "What the hell were you doing?" he asked. "How come you haven't told anyone about those threats?"

"That's none of your damn business," she said. "Nothing in this office is. You had no right to come in here."

"I'm your bodyguard," he said. "Those threats are damn well my business and so is whatever else you're hiding."

She shivered once more—but it was at the coldness of the look on his face. "Just what the hell are you implying?"

"I'm not implying anything," he said. "I'm flat out accusing you of not being truthful." He pointed toward those threats. "And those letters are proof."

She snorted. "Those letters are proof that I'm good at my job."

He snorted now. And her face heated with indignation. He was one of those—one of the officers who blamed her for not being able to get an indictment off sloppy police work. Figured.

"That's what those threats are about," she said.

"You're saying none of them have anything to do with this case—with Luther Mills?"

Because he'd already accused her of not being truthful, she couldn't shake her head—because she honestly didn't know. Did Luther Mills want her dead?

ANYTIME THE PHONE rang in the middle of the night, it wasn't with good news, like Luther Mills had been shanked in jail and nobody was in danger any longer.

Parker reached for the cell phone vibrating next to his bed with the expectation of only bad news, especially with as determined as Luther seemed to be to take out the eyewitness. Suspecting it was Clint calling, he didn't even look at the phone before answering, "Tell me you're alive."

The caller's gasp sounded soft and feminine. "Who do you think could be dead?"

He swallowed a groan as he recognized Jocelyn Gerber's voice. The assistant district attorney already seemed on edge. Woodrow had warned him that she also didn't trust his team. Parker had chosen not to share that information with his team, who he already knew didn't trust her either.

Especially the man protecting her.

"Tell me!" she demanded.

"Nobody's dead," he assured her, although he

couldn't know for certain, not with all the attempts Luther had already made on the eyewitness.

"Then why did you say what you did?" she asked, as if she had him on the witness stand and was going to interrogate him.

"Because usually when the phone rings at this hour, it's not good news," he pointed out. "Why are you calling me now?" If there had been an attempt on her life, Landon would have called him—unless he'd been injured during that attempt. "Is Landon all right?"

"No," she said.

And Parker gasped now. "What's wrong?"

Sharon murmured in her sleep and turned toward him on the bed. So he slipped out of it and moved to the hall to finish the call.

"What happened?" he asked.

"He snooped through my office," she said.

And Parker's brow furrowed with confusion. "What? I thought you two were going to your house after the meeting."

"We did," she said. "He went through my home office, even broke into my desk."

Parker swallowed a curse. Damn it. What the hell had Landon been up to? But he could guess—trying to find evidence that Jocelyn Gerber was Luther's mole in the DA's office.

"I want a different bodyguard," she demanded. "I'd prefer not to have one at all, but the chief insists that everyone involved with the trial has one."

Parker swallowed a groan now. Had she called the chief? Hopefully, she was just going by what he'd said during the meeting when everyone had been arguing against having protection.

"That's not possible," Parker told her. "Everyone else has already been assigned to another principal."

"Principal?"

"Person to protect," he replied.

A frustrated-sounding sigh rattled his cell phone. "What about one of your brothers' agencies? I'd prefer to have someone who hasn't worked in vice anyway."

"And the chief prefers that you do," Parker reminded her. "You and Landon will need to work this out." Before the lawyer could argue with him any more, he clicked off his cell.

Why was she so angry with Landon? Because she felt like he'd invaded her privacy? Or because he'd come close to finding whatever she might be hiding?

Could Landon be right? Could she be working for Luther Mills?

Parker hoped like hell Landon was wrong—because Jocelyn Gerber was too close to everyone else involved in the trial. She could help Luther get to any of them at any time.

And Landon.

She would be able to get to him all the time. Instead of protecting her, he might wind up needing protection from her. Especially now with as furious as she sounded with her bodyguard.

Parker had been worried that the eyewitness might not survive the night. Now he was worried about Landon.

Chapter Four

His friend was in pain, and Landon hated seeing him like this. It wasn't the shoulder Clint had injured jumping out a window to save Rosie Mendez the night before that was hurting Clint—it was the guilt. That had been weighing heavily on him since Javier Mendez had died.

Clint blamed himself for the kid's death, and he was not the only one. Rosie Mendez blamed him, too. She thought Clint had forced the kid to become an informant for him. She thought he'd planted the drugs on her brother that he'd found when he'd busted the kid. But that wasn't the case. Landon knew the kid had wanted to bring down Luther as a way to make amends to his sister. Despite all her efforts to keep him away from the drugs that had ruined their mother's life, Javier had been selling for Luther.

But Landon doubted Clint had told Rosie that. He wouldn't have wanted to add guilt to the pain of her loss. Watching Luther murder her brother had already traumatized her.

But it hadn't scared her like it should have. She was insisting on working her shift as an ER nurse, which was why Clint had called Parker with the request for Jocelyn to talk some sense into her.

So Landon had brought Jocelyn to the safe house where Clint was staying with Rosie. The condo was in a converted warehouse in the nearly abandoned industrial area of River City. With metal-and-brick walls and a security system even better than Jocelyn's, it was safe.

Or it had been, until Landon had brought Jocelyn there. "You sure about this?" he asked as he stepped closer to where Clint leaned against the kitchen counter. The condo was open concept, almost like a loft, except for the bedroom, which was closed off with the door shut. Rosie Mendez must have been in there because Landon hadn't seen her since Clint had let him and Jocelyn in a few moments ago.

Clint cocked his head. His blond hair was mussed as if he'd been running his hands through it, and his green eyes were rimmed with dark circles as if he hadn't slept at all. Landon knew the feeling. He hadn't slept at all the night before either, and nobody had been shooting at him.

"Are you sure?" Clint asked.

And it was clear he was asking about Jocelyn. He shared Landon's suspicions. But those threats Landon had found had gone a long way to assuage his doubts about her. At least some of those had to have been from Luther's crew. And none of his crew did anything without his ordering it. He nodded.

But his finding those threats had made Jocelyn distrust him. She eyed him even more suspiciously than she already had. And he'd overheard her call to Parker.

His lips curved into a grin. Too bad for her that

Parker hadn't replaced him. Then he remembered how close he'd come to nearly kissing her last night. And his grin slipped away. No. It was too bad for him that Parker hadn't replaced him.

It wasn't easy being so close to Jocelyn Gerber—not with as gorgeous as she was. She wore another of her suits with the tight skirt that molded to her curves. Her black hair hung like a silk curtain around her shoulders. She looked more like a model than a lawyer. Maybe she modeled on the side and that was how she afforded her house and furnishings.

A door creaked open and Rosie Mendez stepped out of the bedroom. The young woman wore scrubs with her hospital badge pinned to one of the pockets. That was why Clint had wanted Jocelyn to talk to her. But Rosie didn't know because she asked, "Why are you here?"

"You need to stay here," Jocelyn told her.

Rosie's brown eyes narrowed in a glare directed at Clint before she turned back to the ADA. "What about you? Are you staying in a safe house?"

Jocelyn shook her head. "It's not necessary for me," she replied. "You're the only witness. If *you* die, the case is over. If I die, someone else will just take over the case. So it makes no sense for Mills to kill me."

"Unless the DA on his payroll takes over the case," Landon said. Maybe that was why she'd been sent all those threats, so she would give up the case to whoever really was working for Luther. Jocelyn glared at him now. Despite the chief's meeting, she still refused to accept that anyone within her office could be working for Luther. Landon had thought that was because she was the leak and didn't want her department investigated.

But now he wondered if she was just naive.

"We're not talking about me," Jocelyn said. "We're talking about the key witness for the prosecution."

"We're talking about *me*," Rosie Mendez interjected. "I'm a person—with a life."

"A life you're going to lose if you don't stay safe," Jocelyn said. She looked around the condo. "And you're safe here. Far safer than you were staying in your own place, where Luther knew where to find you whenever he was ready to get rid of you."

Rosie snorted. "You better get to know Luther better if you intend to prosecute him. He can find me anywhere. He has people in the police department and in your office. You don't think that he already knows where I am? Where you are?"

Jocelyn shivered. She was probably thinking about all those death threats Landon had found locked in her desk drawer.

"She's right." Clint surprisingly came to Rosie's defense. "Luther probably has eyes on this place already." But then he added, "That's why you can't leave, Rosie."

"No, you can't," Jocelyn agreed.

Thinking about all those threats he'd found, Landon felt compelled to agree with Rosie. "So you should stay here, too, Ms. Gerber."

She glared at him again. "You said that the guards outside haven't seen anyone watching the place. You said no one followed us," Jocelyn fired back at Landon. Then her face flushed as she must have realized she'd just contradicted what Clint had said. She turned toward Rosie now. "That doesn't mean that Officer Quarters—

that Clint—isn't right. You said so yourself that Luther probably already knows where you are."

Rosie nodded. "So there's no more reason for me to stay here than there is for you."

"You have to testify," Jocelyn said, and only now did she sound frightened. She wasn't worried about losing her life. She was worried about losing her case.

"I will testify," Rosie assured her.

"Not if you're dead," Jocelyn told her. "If you leave this place where you are safe, you're risking your life, but most of all, you're risking justice for your brother. Do you want his killer to go free?"

Seeing her in action like this, arguing her case, Landon was surprised that she'd ever lost, let alone as many times as she had. And those niggling doubts grew again.

But maybe she'd pushed too hard, because tears pooled in Rosie's eyes just before she ran back into the master bedroom.

"Damn it!" Clint cursed.

"I'm sorry," Jocelyn said, but she sounded unapologetic. "She needed to hear it, though."

"It's too much," Clint said.

"Parker told us that you wanted Jocelyn to come here and talk some sense into the witness." Landon reminded him of the reason for their visit. After those threats, he would have preferred to bring her to a safe house to stay, not just visit.

"I wanted ADA Gerber to talk some sense into her," Clint said, "not manipulate her and make her feel guilty."

"It will be her fault if Luther Mills gets away with her brother's murder," Jocelyn said.

Thinking he might need to protect his principal from his best friend now, Landon stepped between them. But then he realized what she was doing—taking no responsibility, just as she had when she'd failed to get those other indictments against Luther or some of his crew. She'd blamed sloppy police work then.

He snorted his disgust. "You're already setting up someone else to blame if you lose this case, too."

She bristled with righteous indignation. "I don't do that," she protested. "I just want my witness to make it to the stand." She turned toward Clint now. "And if she doesn't, then that's your fault."

Landon opened his mouth on the curse word he was tempted to call her, but Clint cut him off. "She's right," he said. "It's my job to protect Rosie Mendez."

"Make sure you do your job," Jocelyn told him as she headed toward the door. "Because with her testimony, I won't lose."

"This time," Landon muttered as he trailed her toward the door. He reached around her and pressed the security code into the panel to open the big steel door. Jocelyn had turned back to glare at him, so he didn't think she saw the code he inputted. But as he walked out the door, he could see his friend was concerned that he'd made a mistake.

Clint had obviously wanted Jocelyn to convince the young woman to take no chances with her safety. But after having Jocelyn come to the safe house, Clint was clearly worried that he might have put Rosie in danger himself.

But Landon was the one who'd brought the ADA. If something happened to Rosie, Landon would take the blame for it. His friend already carried too much guilt.

DESPITE THE COOL breeze swirling around the sidewalk as they stepped outside the condo, Jocelyn's face stayed hot. She wasn't embarrassed, though. She was angry. How could Landon think she was to blame for failing to get indictments or losing cases?

It was clear that he'd thought it was her fault, and he wasn't the only one. Clint Quarters had seemed to share Landon's low opinion of her.

Did they think she was incompetent? Or worse?

Landon wouldn't even look at her as he held open the door of the black Payne Protection Agency SUV for her. His attention was on the bodyguards protecting the perimeter of the condo. "Be extra careful," he advised them before he closed her door and walked around to his side.

"You're worried," she said after he slid beneath the steering wheel. He was such a big man that despite the size of the vehicle, his shoulder nearly touched hers over the console between them. She was worried, too, but even more so after realizing he was, as well.

Despite what she'd told Rosie, she didn't think she would lose the trial if she lost Rosie's testimony. There was evidence, too, that would impact a jury even more than eyewitness testimony that the high-priced defense lawyer would tear apart on cross-examination. But she didn't want anything to happen to Rosie Mendez—anything else. She'd already been through enough with losing her brother.

Jocelyn knew what it felt like to lose loved ones to violence. All these years later, her heart still ached with loss.

"We shouldn't have come here," Landon said.

Jocelyn shook her head. "No. Rosie needs to know how much danger she's in."

"You don't think she knows?" Landon asked. "She saw her brother gunned down in front of her. She knows better than anyone else what an animal Luther Mills is."

She shivered. While violence had affected her and still did because of the career she'd chosen, she hadn't personally witnessed it happen. She'd only seen the aftermath. "He is an animal," she agreed.

"And anyone who works with or for him is an animal, too," Landon said, and his deep voice rumbled with emotion.

Had she been wrong to suspect him? She had no doubt that someone in the police department had helped Luther over the years, though. According to the chief, someone was still helping him now. She could believe that. But to think someone within her department…

She knew everyone too well. Nobody worked in the district attorney's office for the money. Maybe some did for politics—to move up. But most, like her, did it because they wanted to take criminals off the street.

That was why people became police officers, too. "Why did you leave River City PD?" she asked.

He shrugged, and his broad shoulder bumped against hers. "Parker offered me the job. Clint was leaving, too. And Tyce and Hart and Keeli…"

She winced as she thought of all the bodyguards. Luther's mole in the vice unit could have been any of them. And now each of them was protecting one of the people he'd threatened. Which one was the mole?

She was beginning to believe it wasn't Landon. He seemed to want Luther off the street as badly as she did.

"You're that close to them?" she asked. "That you would leave a job you loved…just because they did?"

He snorted. "I wouldn't say that I loved it."

"You didn't enjoy working in the vice unit?"

He glanced across at her, and his brown eyes were hard. "I didn't enjoy watching perps I arrested walking away with no charges."

She narrowed her eyes. "Are you blaming me for that?"

He cursed, but it wasn't at her. His focus was on the rearview mirror.

"What?" she asked.

"We're being followed."

She whirled around in her seat, but there were so many vehicles behind them, as they headed downtown to her office, that she couldn't tell which one he was talking about. "Where? What one?"

But instead of answering her, he pulled out his cell phone and punched in a number. A deep voice emanated from the speaker. "This is Parker."

"Landon," her bodyguard identified himself.

"Everything all right?" his boss asked, and his voice sounded as tense as it had when she'd called him late last night. "What?" he asked anxiously. "What is it?"

"I—" Landon kept glancing into the rearview "—think we're being followed."

"You have backup," Parker reminded him. "I'll have them intervene."

"I can lose whoever this is tailing us," Landon said. But he hadn't sped up. He hadn't switched lanes. It was almost as if he wanted the vehicle to follow them.

She shivered again.

"Good," Parker said. "So what's the problem?"

"I'm not sure where I picked up the tail," Landon admitted, and a muscle twitched along his tightly clenched jaw. "They're good."

"So what are you saying?" Parker wondered. "That the people following you probably aren't some of Luther's flunky drug dealers?"

A ragged sigh slipped out of Landon's lips. "I hadn't thought of that, but it's true."

"They could be cops." Jocelyn uttered her first thought aloud.

Landon glared at her. Even though he didn't work for River City PD anymore, he apparently wasn't any more willing to consider that one of them could be Luther's mole than she was to suspect one of her coworkers.

"I don't know who the hell they are," Landon said.

"If you don't need backup to intervene, why did you call?"

Landon sighed again before slowly admitting, "I might not have noticed them earlier."

"Okay…"

"We just left the safe house," Landon said. "We just left Clint and the witness."

"You think you might have led them there?" Parker asked.

"I don't know if I led them there," Landon said, his voice gruff with guilt, "or if they were already there."

Even though she was still mad at him for his comments and over his snooping the night before, she automatically defended him. "Rosie and Quarters said that Luther Mills probably already knew where they were."

The thought made her sick with concern and fear for their safety. She wasn't the only one afraid.

Parker Payne said, "I'll send more bodyguards to the safe house—make sure none of Luther's crew tries anything."

"Good," Landon said, and now he uttered a shaky sigh of relief.

"You focus on protecting Ms. Gerber," Parker added.

He glanced across at her. "That would be easier to do if she took her own advice and stayed in a safe house instead of insisting on going into her office."

"Parker has more important things to do than listen to us argue." She reached over and pressed her finger on the disconnect button on his cell phone. Payne needed to get more protection on the witness.

"I don't need to go into a safe house," she said. "Luther is not going to have me killed because, like I told Rosie, it doesn't matter if anything happens to me. The trial will still go on."

"But will the new prosecutor get the conviction you seem pretty confident you'll be able to get?" he asked.

She had been confident—until she'd learned about Luther's plan to take out everyone associated with the trial. Sure, that included her, but he wasn't going to start with her. He would use all his resources to get rid of Rosie first.

"You are so sure someone in my office is a traitor," she said. "It seems like you'd be happy to go to work with me and try to figure out which one it is."

He glanced across at her, and his gaze was speculative. "That's exactly what I plan on doing."

Was that why he'd searched her office the night before? She intended to ask him, but he suddenly jerked the wheel, sending the SUV into another lane but barely missing the vehicles already in it. Horns blared, and she cursed.

"Hang on," he advised her. "I'm going to get rid of our tail."

The vehicle he thought he'd noticed following them? Or their backup?

She didn't entirely trust him yet. He could still be working for Luther and just very good at hiding it.

LUTHER CLICKED ON his vibrating cell phone to a curse. "What the hell's going on?" he asked.

"I'm following the lady DA like you said," his caller replied. "But her bodyguard is trying to lose me."

Blaring horns emanated from the cell phone.

"Aren't you trained for this kind of driving?" Didn't the police academy have some kind of a class for it? Like how not to lose a suspect?

"Yeah, but he was trained for it, too."

He? Who was protecting Jocelyn Gerber? And how the hell would he be able to focus with her around? She was too damn good-looking to be a lawyer.

"Don't worry about the lady DA," Luther advised him. "Focus on Rosie Mendez. You already lost her once." Last night—when she was supposed to have died. Instead, Clint Quarters had literally leaped to her rescue. *Damn him.*

"What about Gerber, though?"

"I can have Jocelyn Gerber taken out anytime I want," Luther said, and a self-satisfied smirk crossed his face. He didn't just have help in the police department; he had help within the district attorney's office, too.

And that person could easily get to Jocelyn. She, and whoever her bodyguard was, would never see the threat until it was too late.

Until they were both dead.

That was going to happen. Luther wanted them all gone: everyone associated with the trial and every damn bodyguard of Parker Payne's agency, including Parker Payne. Luther needed to send a message—a very loud message—that nobody better ever try to take him down again.

Or they would wind up dead...

Chapter Five

Landon lost the tail—almost too easily—as if the person had suddenly given up. Of course, they had probably already known where he and the ADA were headed. Anyone who knew Jocelyn Gerber knew where she spent most of her time: divided between her office and the courthouse. The two buildings were close, so close that the parking garage that stood between them serviced them both. After pulling into a space designated for the staff at the district attorney's office, Landon glanced around the garage.

It was early, so not all the spaces were full.

Jocelyn reached for her door handle, but Landon reached across and covered her hand with his. "Wait for me to make sure it's safe," he told her.

Her willowy body bristled, but she stayed inside until he walked around the SUV and opened her door. "You don't have to pretend to be my boyfriend," she said.

"I didn't open your door because I think we're on a date," he assured her. "I just want to keep you safe."

And to find out the truth about her.

"I'm safe," she told him as she headed toward the side of the parking structure where doors opened into the district attorney's office. She gestured at the guard who sat near the metal detectors at the entrance.

Landon opened his jacket to show his holster to the middle-aged guard. "I have a permit and the chief of police's permission to carry inside this building," he told him.

The man nodded. "I know, Myers."

And Landon grinned as he recognized the former police sergeant. "Good to see you."

"You, too," his former boss said with a grin. But when he turned toward Ms. Gerber, his grin slid away. "Ms. Gerber."

She nodded at the man as she proceeded through the metal detectors. She didn't wait for Landon, just kept going.

The guard shook his head as Landon rushed off to keep up with her. He was obviously not a fan of the assistant district attorney.

Landon suspected not many of her coworkers were. The ones they passed did the same thing the guard had; if they were smiling or talking with someone else, they tensed and stopped—talking and smiling. Jocelyn didn't seem to notice or care, but Landon took note.

Her keys jangled as she pulled them from her purse and unlocked her door. Like her desk at home, this one was piled high with folders. They also covered the credenza behind her and the top of a filing cabinet. He pointed at it. "Too busy to use that?" he asked.

She glanced at it. "It's too full to hold any more."

And there was no space in her small office for another filing cabinet. A chair barely fit behind her desk and another in front of it. "Why do you have so much work?"

She tensed again. "Because I want it."

A chuckle followed her pronouncement, and Landon glanced at the man standing in the doorway. "Jocelyn wants every case—every trial," the gray-haired man remarked. "And if she doesn't get it, she goes behind our backs to the DA and steals it."

Jocelyn chuckled, as well, but like her coworker, it held no amusement. "Still stings that she gave me Luther Mills's trial, huh?"

"Gave?" The man snorted. "You stole that, and you know it."

Why had she wanted it so badly? Because Luther was paying her to lose it?

"Amber thought I was the best attorney for the trial."

The guy shook his head. "Was that it—or was it because you're the only female ADA?"

Jocelyn chuckled again. "Are you claiming the DA is guilty of reverse sexism in the workplace?" she asked.

"I'm not saying anything I wouldn't want her to hear," he replied, "because we all know you're her eyes and ears in the office while she's off having her baby."

Jocelyn bristled again. But she didn't deny being the tattletale her coworker had basically accused her of being. If everyone else suspected the same thing he did, it explained why they'd all stopped talking when she'd arrived.

Landon held out his hand and introduced himself since Jocelyn didn't seem so inclined. "Landon Myers." He didn't bother explaining what he was.

"Mike Forbes," the man replied, as his gray brows lowered over narrowed eyes. "Myers? You a cop still?"

Landon shook his head.

Before the guy could ask anything else, another man joined him in the doorway. This one was younger and thinner—his body and his blond hair. He had the lean build of a runner. "Hey, Forbes, quit giving Jocelyn a hard time. She just wants what we all want—Luther Mills behind bars."

As she looked at this man, her smile lit up her already beautiful face and stole Landon's breath. She'd never looked at him like that. "Thank you, Dale."

The blond guy smiled back at her. Maybe he was the one person in the DA's office who didn't care what she told the boss. Or he wanted to be more than a coworker.

Something about the way he looked at her had Landon's stomach muscles tightening and his hands squeezing into fists.

But then the guy reached out a hand to him. "Dale Grohms," he introduced himself.

"This is Landon Myers," she said before he could. Then she added, "He's my boyfriend."

And now the guy's smile slid away. He definitely wanted to be more than her coworker.

Landon waited until both men left and she closed the door behind them before saying, "I thought you didn't want me pretending to be your boyfriend."

"I don't want you *acting* like my boyfriend," she said.

And he frowned. "I don't understand."

"I can tell people that you are," she said. "But I don't want you…touching me…or…"

That feeling in his gut, that he'd had watching her smile at Dale Grohms, intensified now. He wasn't sure what the hell it was, but he didn't like it. He didn't like her much either, but that didn't stop him from being attracted to her. And he knew, after the night before, that it wasn't just one-sided. Not with the way she'd looked at him.

Before she could move behind her desk, he stepped closer to her—blocking her path. Her body came up against his, and she sucked in a breath and stared up at him. "What—what are you doing?"

"Calling you out," he told her. And he wanted to do that—about so many things—but this one was suddenly most important to him.

"Calling me out?" she repeated, her brow furrowing slightly.

Her skin was so creamy and flawless, her features so perfect. She was that kind of beauty that seemed as untouchable as she claimed she wanted to be. But he didn't believe her.

"You're a liar," he said.

"What?" She was also full of self-righteous indignation again as her blue eyes widened with shock.

"You wanted me to touch you last night," he said, "when I held you in the kitchen."

"You grabbed me," she said.

"You didn't fight me off," he said. Not like she had in the parking garage earlier that evening. "You didn't pull back when I started leaning down…" And he began to lean down again. "You didn't push me away…"

She didn't this time either, even as her body tensed. It was as if she waited for it—wanted it—just like he wanted to kiss her. Even if there'd been another crash, he wouldn't have denied them this time. He brushed his mouth across hers, lightly at first, but then her lips parted on a soft sigh and he deepened the kiss.

Her lips were as silky as her hair looked. Needing to know, he slid his hands into the long, smooth locks as he held her head to his. He slid his mouth over and over hers before tracing her fuller bottom lip with the tip of his tongue. Then he slid his tongue inside her mouth and tasted her.

And he was shocked by the hotness and the sweetness when she always acted so bitter and cold. Her fingers slipped into his hair, too, and she kissed him back. Passion burned through him, heating his body, making his pulse pound.

He couldn't remember ever being so damn attracted to anyone else. Why her?

Finally, as if remembering what he'd said, she moved her hands from his hair to his chest, and she pushed him back. But her lips stayed open as she panted for breath. Her skin was flushed. She was attracted to him, too.

She didn't try denying it now. She just moved around her desk and murmured, "I—I need to get to court soon."

Landon wasn't sure if she actually had a trial to go to, or if she just didn't want to stay alone with him in her office. With the door closed and the attraction between them heating up the place, the room felt even smaller than it was.

And Landon felt like he was suffocating. He was tempted to open up the door for some air, but when he glanced at it, he noticed, through the window in the wood, that the two men who'd left her office hadn't gone far. They stood just out in the hall, looking toward her office. Neither could have missed that kiss.

Had they bought it? Did they believe he was her

boyfriend? Or did they suspect he was really her body-guard? He hadn't kissed her to convince them, though. He'd kissed her because he'd wanted to.

And, damn it, he wanted to do it again.

But he couldn't let her distract him from protecting her or from finding out if she or one of her coworkers was also working for Luther.

DESPITE ALL THE hours that had passed since that kiss, Jocelyn's lips still tingled from it—from the heat of it, the passion.

She couldn't remember a kiss ever affecting her like that, a man ever affecting her like that. She'd had to force herself to push him away. She'd had to force her-self to focus on the job that had previously always con-sumed her.

All she cared about was getting justice, just like Dale Grohms had said. Forbes didn't believe it. He thought she was lobbying for the same job he was—their boss's.

Jocelyn didn't have to be in charge. In fact, she didn't think she'd like it because she wouldn't be able to try as many cases as she did now. Forbes had been right when he'd said she wanted them all.

She did—to make sure they weren't lost. But de-spite how hard she worked, she didn't win every case. In fact, she'd had a string of losses that haunted her. A string that had seemed to end when some of the vice unit had quit River City PD to go to work for the Payne Protection Agency.

Could she really trust Landon?

He hadn't respected her order for him to not act like her boyfriend. But as he'd pointed out, she hadn't pushed him away when she'd had the chance. Sure, she could have used the excuse that she knew her coworkers were watching them, and she hadn't wanted to draw any more attention than his following her around already had. But she hadn't realized Mike and Dale were outside her office yet until she'd settled, with shaky knees, into the chair behind her desk.

Despite the cool night air blowing through the parking structure, her face was burning. And it wasn't just with embarrassment over her coworkers witnessing that kiss. She was hot because that kiss had been damn hot.

Landon Myers was damn hot. His body, his mouth… his hands slipping through her hair as he'd held her head to his. She stifled the moan that rose in her throat as desire rushed over her again. She had to remind herself that kiss had just been part of his cover; it hadn't been real. He didn't even seem to like her.

But he did seem determined to protect her. He walked so close to her that his body brushed against hers with every step they took. He wasn't trying to turn her on, though. He wasn't even looking at her. Instead, he peered around the dimly lit structure, as if looking for killers lurking in the shadows. And he was ready for those killers, with his gun drawn and held at his side.

Even though he wasn't trying to affect her, his closeness did. Jocelyn's pulse quickened, and her breath burned in her lungs, as if stuck there. It didn't matter how close he was to her, though. In the courtroom, he'd been forced to sit in the gallery a few seats behind the prosecutor's table. But she'd been aware of him the entire time, had known he was watching her, and her skin had tingled with that awareness—with that attraction.

Her body had flushed with heat and desire, like it was now. But then a sudden chill raced down her spine, and she shivered.

"Somebody's watching us," Landon murmured.

So he'd felt it, too.

She glanced around now, staring into the shadows at the few cars left in the parking lot. "Where?"

He shrugged even as he covered her hand with his. She'd thought he was reassuring her, and she leaned closer to him. But instead, he clicked the key fob she held in her hand. The beep of her horn and the flash of her lights startled her so much that she stumbled. She might have fallen had he not caught her and steadied her with his arm around her.

He held her for just a moment—as if waiting for her to regain her balance. But when he touched her, she lost her balance, lost her focus. She could see only him, feel only this damn attraction to him.

His gaze held hers and he leaned slightly toward her, as if he intended to kiss her again. But before his mouth touched hers, he jerked back. Then he quickly guided her toward the passenger's side of the black SUV and opened the door for her.

She didn't know if he was in a hurry to get some distance between them or if he was really worried about whoever was watching them. "Didn't Parker say that he had backup bodyguards following us?"

"Not anymore," Landon said. "They were needed to help guard Rosie Mendez."

Jocelyn nodded. "That's good. She's the one in danger."

Landon gently nudged her into the seat, and before closing the door, he reminded her, "She's not the only one."

He could have been talking about the evidence tech or the judge's daughter who'd been threatened, too, or the detective who'd investigated the murder and arrested Luther.

But she knew he was talking about her. She wished he hadn't seen all those threats. She watched as he rounded the front of the SUV to the driver's side, and a twinge of panic struck her heart.

If she was in danger, then so was he.

Because, with how determined Landon was to protect her, if anyone truly wanted to hurt her, they would have to hurt him first.

HAD JOCELYN AND that giant with her seen him? He held his breath with concern that they might have. But then he expelled that breath on a ragged sigh. It didn't matter if they had. This was the parking garage where he parked, too—since he worked at the same place Jocelyn worked.

But they must not have noticed him behind the tinted windows of his car since they walked past him to a black SUV that must have been *his*.

Who the hell was he?

Boyfriend?

He shook his head. He wasn't buying that story. Jocelyn Gerber was too damn ambitious to let anything get in the way of her aspirations. She wanted the district attorney's job. Hell, she probably wanted even more than that, and she had the resources to go after whatever she wanted.

And she didn't care who else wanted or deserved it more.

No. The only way to stop her was to get rid of her.

Luther Mills was supposed to do that. But for some reason he wanted to wait. He thought he needed to kill the others first.

But *he* wasn't going to wait. He had to get rid of Jocelyn—and whatever the big guy was to her—*now*.

Chapter Six

She went straight from working at the office to working at home. Landon stared through the leaded-glass
doors of her home office, watching her as she studied
the papers strewn across her desk.

Was she working on the case that she'd started today,
with a preliminary hearing in court, or was she working on Luther's case? Or worse yet, had she received
another threat she hadn't shared with him?

He just knew that someone had been watching them
a short while ago in the parking garage. Even though he
hadn't seen them, he'd felt their presence and the intensity of their stare. He reached for his cell and punched
in the contact for Parker. While he was confident he
could protect Jocelyn while they were in her house, he
needed to make sure she was safe everywhere else—
especially the parking garage.

He needed backup at least there.

Hell, he probably needed backup everywhere since
she was so damn distracting to him. What the hell had
he been thinking to kiss her?

Because all he wanted was to repeat it.

It was a good thing she'd locked herself away in her

office. She was out of his reach. And out of the reach of whoever had been watching them.

He'd been especially vigilant on the drive back to her house, making sure nobody had followed them. He hadn't seen anyone, but that didn't mean they hadn't been there, still watching.

Waiting for the chance to make good on all those threats she'd received.

Parker's voice emanated from his phone, but it was his outgoing message. Landon's brow furrowed as he tried to remember if his boss had ever not answered a call. He couldn't remember.

He punched in the number again, murmuring, "What the hell's going on…?"

The call connected this time, but it wasn't Parker's voice he heard. The sound of sirens and a disjointed conversation emanated from his cell now. He only caught bits and pieces of it—only enough to scare the hell out of him.

"Parker!" he shouted. Had his boss been wounded? Why the hell wasn't he speaking into the phone?

Then he heard his voice in that disjointed conversation, just a word here and there as Parker conversed with a few other people.

And finally that conversation must have ended, for, at last, he spoke directly into his cell. "Have you heard from him?"

"Who?" Landon asked.

"Clint," Parker replied.

And Landon knew—all those sirens and the urgency of that conversation…

"He's been hurt," he said.

"Shot—we think," Parker replied. "There was an ambush at the safe house."

"Did—did they get the witness?" Landon asked.

"We don't know," Parker replied. "Clint got her away from the scene, but we don't know if she'd been hit, too."

Landon groaned. "It's my fault," he murmured. "I knew I shouldn't have brought her there."

"What?" Jocelyn asked. She stood in front of him in the open doorway of her home office. "What's going on?"

He ignored her, as anger gripped him. It had to have been her. She had to be working with Luther.

"Let me know when you hear from him," Landon told his boss.

"The same," Parker replied.

But Landon doubted Clint would call him for help. After the ambush, there was no way he would trust Landon again, not as long as he had Jocelyn with him.

He clicked off his cell and slid it back into his pocket with a slightly shaking hand.

Jocelyn stepped closer and gripped his arm. "What's wrong? What happened?"

He looked at her then, and anger coursed through him. But he was angrier with himself than he was with her. How had he kissed her? How had he been attracted to a woman like her?

"You tell me," he said as he pushed past her into the office. He glanced around even though he'd already searched in here for the answers he sought. "When did you tip Luther off to where Rosie Mendez was?"

She gasped. "Wh-what happened to her? Is she dead?"

Landon shrugged.

And she tugged on his arm, as if she was trying to shake him or maybe pull him out of her room. "Tell me!"

"I don't know," he said. "Clint got her away from the ambush. But he was shot—" His voice cracked with emotion. Where the hell was his friend? Was he okay?

"Call him," Jocelyn urged him.

Like Clint would answer his call.

After what had happened, Clint was probably struggling to trust anyone right now. Especially him.

"Why?" Landon asked. "You need to find out where he is now, so you can update Luther?"

"What the hell are you talking about?" she asked, her brow furrowing. "I have not and would never tell Luther where Rosie Mendez is."

Landon snorted. "Yeah, right."

She bristled, her willowy body tense with that self-righteous indignation.

But Landon didn't think she had any right to it. Any right to anything but a long prison sentence along with her real boss: Luther Mills.

"What are you accusing me of?" she asked.

"We all suspected it for a while," he said. "Nobody could be as bad a lawyer as you seemed to be."

She gasped again. "How dare you—"

"How dare you," he interrupted. "How dare you destroy that evidence and let a guilty man go free to threaten and kill innocent people."

"What are you talking about? I never destroyed any evidence."

"Then how the hell did you fail to get indictments?"

he asked. "My unit worked damn hard to get Luther Mills off the streets. We built cases for you. Gave you what you needed—"

"Bullshit." She interrupted him now. "I didn't get enough for indictments because of sloppy police work. It had nothing to do with my abilities as a lawyer."

"Of course not," he said. "You would never take any responsibility for what you've done." She'd always been quick to blame the cops instead of herself.

Something like a growl emanated from her throat. "I haven't done anything but my job," she insisted.

He snorted again.

"What the hell do you think I've done?"

"I think you are the leak within the district attorney's office," he admitted. "I think you're the one working for Luther, that you've been working for him for years."

She pulled her arm back and began to swing her hand toward his face. He was ready for her—ready to catch her wrist and stop her from hitting him.

But she stopped herself. Then she stumbled back a step against her desk and began to laugh. Maybe it was a relief for her for the truth to finally come out.

JOCELYN FELT TEARS streak from her eyes as her stomach ached from laughter. How the hell could *anyone* accuse her of working for Luther Mills?

At first she'd been insulted, so insulted that she'd been tempted to lash out. But then it had struck her how hilarious the ridiculous accusation was. So hilarious that she could barely stop laughing.

But she forced herself to draw in deep breaths and calm herself. "You're insane," she told him.

Landon arched his light brown brows. "*I'm* insane?"

His inference sobered her up, and she drew in one more deep breath before replying, "Yes, you are, if you actually believe I could be working for Luther Mills."

"I'm not the only one who thinks you are," Landon told her.

And now her stomach ached with nausea. Was it possible? Could other people believe she'd work for a killer? That she would help an animal like Luther Mills evade justice?

She shook her head. "Anyone who thinks that is insane," she said. Or complicit.

Was casting doubt on her a way to remove it from himself?

"Explain to me how you failed to get all those indictments?" he asked.

"I've told you before," she said. "Sloppy police work. I never received the evidence that the arresting officer claimed we had."

Landon narrowed his dark eyes and stared at her with suspicion. "That's a lie. You lost it."

"That's not true," she said. "I'm very careful to never lose the chain of custody with evidence. I double-and triple-check."

"So it just disappeared?"

"Or it was never collected in the first place," she said. She'd always thought that was the case, but now she was beginning to wonder...about a lot of things.

"You're blaming the police," he said. "Why the hell would we claim we had evidence that we didn't? We wanted to take Luther off the streets even more than you do."

She snorted now. "I doubt that."

"What? You have a personal beef with him?" he asked. But again he sounded doubtful, like he thought her path would have only crossed with Luther because she was working for him.

"I have a personal beef with all criminals," she said. "I want to take them all off the streets."

"That's why you try to take all the cases at work?" he asked. "For justice?" He sounded skeptical again.

She nodded. "That's right."

"Not for your career?" he asked.

Mike Forbes had gotten to him. "Despite what my coworkers think, I am not after my boss's job."

"Just justice," he murmured again. Then he opened his arms, gesturing at the room. "How the hell do you afford this place?" He pointed toward the office walls. "The artwork? Your vehicle? Hell, that alarm system even."

"I didn't buy it," she admitted.

"No," he said. "Luther did."

She lifted her arm again, but before she could even begin to swing her hand at his infuriatingly handsome face, he caught her wrist and jerked her up against his body. "Let me go!" she said through gritted teeth, and she tried to pull free of his grasp.

But his arms tightened around her. "So you can hit me? Or go get your Taser?" He shook his head. "Not going to happen. I'm not letting you go until you tell me the truth."

"I'll tell you the truth," she agreed. She would tell him everything—things she hadn't talked about in years. But only on one condition. "If you tell me the truth."

He didn't release her, but he drew back slightly and stared down at her, his brow furrowed. "About what?"

"About who within the vice unit was working with Luther," she replied.

He laughed now—not uproariously like she had, just a gruff chuckle. "You really are insane."

"Think about it," she urged him. "That evidence you and your coworkers supposedly collected never made it to the DA's office. It was gone before it got to us. Where did it go?"

He tensed now, and his brow furrowed. Then he shook his head. "No…no way in hell was anyone I worked with working with Luther. We all wanted to nail him. We all still want to nail him."

Even Parker. That was why he'd accepted the assignment from his stepfather, the chief. He wanted to make sure Luther was finally brought to justice.

She arched a brow now with skepticism. "Really?"

"Of course."

"Then why did you quit?" she asked. "Why did you give up?"

He flinched as if she had struck him. "I tried," he said. "For years…but with no results, with no accountability for what he'd done. He kept getting away with it—no matter what evidence we found against him."

She pursed her lips now. "Evidence you claim you found."

"We did," he said. "I had it. A gun. A recording…" He shuddered as if abhorred by whatever had been on that tape. "But they disappeared."

She felt a twinge now. So they had been working toward the same goal all those years. And someone else had been undermining them.

"You know I'm not the one who told Luther about the safe house," she said.

"I do?"

"You were with me all day," she said. "How would I have talked to anyone without you knowing about it?"

He stared down at her, but he didn't look quite as suspicious anymore.

"You can check my phone," she told him. "You can see every contact I've had. None were with Luther or any of his crew."

He released a shaky sigh. "So Luther just knew, the way he knows stuff…"

"Through his sources," she said.

"Within the police department and your office," he said.

She snorted. "I still don't believe anyone within my department would work with him."

"You have a lot higher of an opinion of your coworkers than they seem to have of you," he said.

She flinched now. She told herself repeatedly that it didn't matter. She wasn't looking to make friends at work; she was looking for justice. And to ensure that justice was served, she sometimes had to step on some toes.

"You think highly of the people you work with," she pointed out.

"I'm not claiming Luther doesn't have a leak within the police department," he said. "I fully believe that he does. In fact, it makes a lot of sense."

About how that evidence had disappeared. Anyone

could have gained access to the evidence locker and destroyed it. So maybe it wasn't someone who he'd personally worked with in the vice unit. But it made more sense that it was.

"I'm talking about the people you work with now," she said, "at the Payne Protection Agency."

He tensed again. "What?"

"They all know where that safe house is," she pointed out. "One of them must have told Luther where the witness was."

He gasped—like she had. While his mouth was open, he didn't spew any denials. He didn't argue with her. He just looked, once again, like she'd slapped him. Then, finally, he shook his head again. "No."

"You'd rather believe I did it?" she asked. Maybe he thought she'd sneaked in a call while she'd used the ladies' room. It was the only time she'd been out of his sight that day.

He nodded. "Yes, I would. It makes more sense." He glanced around her office.

And her face heated with embarrassment. She'd promised him the truth. "I didn't buy this house, and neither did Luther Mills," she said before he could hurl that accusation again. "My parents bought it and the artwork and the security system. They're paranoid about my not being safe enough."

"Having seen those threats, I understand why," Landon interjected.

"They have not seen those threats," she said. She couldn't imagine how scared they'd be if they had. "They're paranoid about safety because my grandparents were murdered."

He sucked in a breath. "I'm sorry."

"It happened years ago," she told him.

"I'm still sorry," he said. "That kind of pain doesn't lessen."

"Sounds like you speak from experience," she mused.

He nodded. "My parents are gone. My grandparents, too. None of them were murdered, though. Just health issues. Cancer. Heart attacks. I must not have good genes."

He looked healthy to her. He looked strong and vital. He felt that way, too, as he continued to hold her. His hand around her wrist, his other arm around her back.

"How were your grandparents murdered?" he asked.

She closed her eyes as she remembered what she'd seen—all the blood. "They were killed during the course of a home invasion robbery. Tortured..." She shuddered, and now his arms tightened around her. He pulled her close to his chest. "The thieves must not have believed they didn't have much money or jewelry in the house. As rich as they were, they were smart, too. They kept their valuables in safety-deposit boxes in banks."

"Were you there?" he asked.

She shook her head. "No. But I found them."

"Oh, my God. How old were you?"

"Sixteen," she said. "I just got my license and drove my new car over to show them. They'd bought it for me." She shuddered again. "The door was open. I shouldn't have gone in."

Because she'd never gotten those images out of her head. He hugged her closer, and his hand stroked her hair. "I'm so sorry..."

Her breath escaped in a shaky sigh. But she pulled back. "It was a long time ago," she reminded him.

"But you don't ever forget something like that," he said. "I still remember my first crime scene." He shuddered. "And I didn't even know the victims. I couldn't sleep until we arrested their killers. Were your grandparents' killers ever arrested?" He wasn't a cop anymore, but he still thought like one.

She nodded. "It took a few years for them to be found. And a few more years for the trial. But they were convicted and sentenced. They killed four more people before they were put away, though."

More families had been devastated like hers had been. Like Rosie Mendez was by her brother's murder.

"That's why I do what I do," she said. "I have no need for money or for a job title. My only need is for justice."

"I'm sorry," Landon said again. And she knew he wasn't offering condolences now, especially when he cupped her face in his palms and tipped it up to his. "I'm sorry," he said again, "for ever doubting you."

"I doubted you, too," she said.

His lips curved slightly into a weak grin. "You don't anymore?"

"No."

"Why not?" he asked. "I don't have a story like yours. I didn't go through the kind of tragic loss because of violence like you did."

But he'd endured loss all the same. It didn't matter how his family was gone—just that they were gone. All of them. At least she had her parents still, no matter how crazy their overprotectiveness sometimes drove her.

"Do you have any siblings?" she asked him, hating the thought of him being all alone.

He shook his head. "Nope. I'm the only child of only children."

She winced, feeling for him. "So you have no family. You're on your own now."

He chuckled. "Not at all. I have family."

She gasped as a horrible thought occurred to her. "Are you married?"

He didn't wear a wedding band, but then, plenty of married men did not, especially when one of the requirements of their job was to occasionally pose as someone else's boyfriend.

Laughter rumbled in his chest, pushing it against her breasts. "Hell, no!"

Maybe he shared her views on marriage, as an unnecessary distraction.

"My family is my coworkers," he said. "They're my friends."

She felt a pang now. She had family—her parents, who loved her so much. But she had no real friends. She admired and tried to emulate her boss, but Amber Talsma-Kozminski was not a friend. She wasn't like the girls who'd worried about Jocelyn after her grandparents had been murdered. They'd been concerned about how much she'd changed. Then they'd begun to complain about how she wasn't fun anymore and eventually they'd stopped trying to talk to her.

When she'd lost her grandparents, she'd lost her innocence—that part of herself that had believed that all people were inherently good. She knew better now.

She knew there were monsters like Luther Mills in the world who had no conscience, who felt no empathy when they took the lives of others. And sometimes those monsters were not that easy to spot.

Like the people who'd murdered her grandparents. One of them had been a teenager who'd mowed their lawn. Her grandmother had fed him cookies, and Jocelyn had had a crush on him. But then, she'd just been a kid herself, so she couldn't feel too bad about missing his true nature. She'd learned to be more careful now about whom she trusted. Maybe that was why she had no friends and rarely dated.

"Are you sure you can trust your friends?" she asked him.

"Yes, I'm sure," he said, "with my life."

"What about the witness's life?" she asked.

"Clint would gladly give up his life for Rosie Mendez's," Landon said with pride in the man who was obviously the closest of his friends.

"What about the others?" she asked. "Would they die to protect the person they've been assigned to?"

His mouth curved into a slight grin, and he chuckled. "I'm not sure about Keeli and Detective Dubridge. She might kill him herself."

During the meeting, Jocelyn had heard how the detective had talked to her—how he'd called the petite blonde Bodyguard Barbie. She wasn't entirely sure she would blame Keeli if she did kill him. But Jocelyn needed his testimony to corroborate what Rosie had told him at the scene of her brother's murder.

"Keeli aside, everyone else feels the same way I do

about our assignments. We would willingly risk our lives to protect our principal."

She tilted her head and studied his handsome face. "You would?"

He nodded. Then his gaze slipped down to her mouth and he murmured, "I hope that's all I give up for you, though."

"What else is there?" she asked.

But she knew. His heart. She felt a twinge in hers now, too. That had to be fear, though—just fear. Then her heart began to pound—fast and furiously—as he lowered his head to hers.

His mouth had just brushed across hers once when gunfire rang out, so loud that the windows rattled. Then the glass shattered as bullets broke through the windows.

Landon pushed her to the office floor and covered her body with his. And she had her answer. Yes, he would give up his life for hers.

As the gunfire continued to ring out, she only hoped that he wasn't about to die now. But with so many bullets striking the house, sending shards of glass raining onto them and the floor, she doubted he could avoid getting hit.

CHIEF WOODROW LYNCH was not happy. He had still not found the leak within his department or within the district attorney's office. Hell, he couldn't even get a handle on the guards at the jail. Some of them had to be helping Luther. The drug lord had to be communicating with his crew somehow because they kept coming after the people associated with the trial.

The witness had barely survived all the attempts on her life. There'd been some issues with the evidence technician, as well. More threatening photos sent to the judge and even a break-in at his daughter's apartment.

And now the prosecutor.

But Woodrow wanted to keep that quiet. He hadn't even told his wife. Yet. Of course, he hadn't seen her yet. The minute he got out of his vehicle and stepped into the house, she would know that something else had happened.

Hell, she probably already knew. Penny Payne-Lynch had an eerie sixth sense in which she just knew things were going to happen before they actually did. Well, she knew when bad things were going to happen.

So she probably knew.

He drew in a deep breath, bracing himself to push open the door and step onto the driveway. But his cell vibrated before he could reach for the door handle. "Chief Lynch," he said as he accepted the call.

It could have been his wife calling him from inside the house, wondering what was taking him so long to get inside, but it wasn't her number on his screen. He knew he'd seen it before, but he hadn't added a contact in his phone for the person. "Hello?"

"Chief," a female voice said. "This is Amber Kozminski." She sounded breathless. Maybe she'd gone into labor. Even though she was the district attorney, she wasn't trying Luther's case because she'd been ordered to bed rest weeks ago.

"Is everything all right?" he anxiously asked her.

"You tell me," she implored him.

"About...?" he asked. His wife had warned him not to upset the heavily pregnant woman. Penny had emotionally adopted the woman's husband and brother and sister-in-law even though their father had been accused of killing her first husband years ago. She pretty much adopted everybody she met but was especially protective of the Kozminskis. Amber wasn't supposed to know about the threats to everyone involved with the trial. She wasn't supposed to worry at all.

But she sounded very worried. "Chief! I need to know if Jocelyn is all right."

So she had heard. How?

He'd been trying to keep it so quiet. And even if Penny had, with her uncanny ability, figured it out, she wouldn't have told Amber.

"How did you hear about what happened?" he asked, because it was clear that she'd heard.

"What does that matter?" she asked.

"It matters," he insisted. "A lot..."

Because he was trying to contain that damn leak. The dispatcher had passed the report of shots fired at the ADA's home on to him directly—because he'd had Jocelyn Gerber's address flagged. And he'd sent out his most trusted detective to investigate those claims.

So who had called Amber? Which one of them?

"Somebody in my office called me," she said. "They told me there was a shooting at Jocelyn's house. I need to know if she's okay."

She wasn't the only one who needed to know that.

He hadn't heard back from his detective yet. Or from Landon Myers…

Had he and the assistant district attorney survived that shooting?

Chapter Seven

What the hell had happened? Landon still didn't know. One minute he'd been kissing Jocelyn and the next…

That had been his first mistake. Kissing her. That wasn't part of his assignment—at least, not when there was no one to witness his acting like her boyfriend. The only person he'd been fooling with that kiss was himself.

He was her bodyguard—nothing else. And he wasn't doing a very damn good job. Sure, he'd knocked her to the floor. But he should have noticed the person outside before they had even started shooting. Hell, he should have heard the vehicle drive up.

But he'd only heard it drive off, and after that he'd helped her up from the floor, anxiously asking, *Are you all right?*

She'd silently nodded at him, her blue eyes wide and bright with fear. *Are you?* she'd asked.

He'd nodded back at her. *But we need to get out of here.*

I—I have to find Lady, she'd said as she looked around her home office, her eyes wide with terror.

She's not in here. She didn't get hit, he'd assured her.

She's hiding. And we don't have time to look for her. We need to leave. Now.

No. We have to stay for the police.

The sirens had already wailed in the distance. *That's why we have to leave*, he'd pointed out. *We don't know who—if anyone—we can trust in the police department.*

She'd gasped. But she'd stopping arguing with him. She'd just shoved some things in her briefcase and closed the office door before hurrying out with him.

"Where are we?" she asked as she looked around the house he'd brought her to, which was nothing like hers. The entire place could probably fit inside her living room. It was just two bedrooms, one off the living room and one off the kitchen, with a bathroom in between them.

"This is where I live," he said.

She pointed toward the gun in his hand. "Then why do you need that?"

"Because other people might know that I live here," he said.

"Nobody's trying to kill you," she said.

It hadn't felt like that earlier when all those bullets had been flying into her house. It had probably just been one clip, though—from one gun—not like the onslaught Clint and Rosie had faced down at the safe house.

"I'm not the only one who lives here," Landon said.

She glanced around again. "I thought when you laughed at the thought of being married…"

"That I didn't have a serious relationship?" he asked. "My roommate is Clint. He's probably the most serious relationship I've had—friendship."

The women he'd dated hadn't understood the long

hours of being a vice cop. They hadn't appreciated his being late or missing dates altogether, so those relationships had never gone beyond dating. Not much had changed since he'd become a bodyguard, though. Protecting someone around the clock left even less time for dating.

Maybe that was why he'd kissed Jocelyn.

No. He'd kissed Jocelyn because he'd wondered for years what it would be like. If his lips would stick to hers like the kid's tongue did to the flagpole in that Christmas movie he and Clint watched every year.

"Clint!" he called out as he moved through the few rooms, checking to see if his friend had come home.

"You thought he might have brought Rosie here?" she asked, and she peered around now, too—looking inside the bedrooms and bathroom.

"He's too smart to have done that," Landon said. Smarter than he was. He should not have brought Jocelyn here. He needed to get her somewhere safe. But what she'd said…about the people who knew about the safe house…

No. She had to be wrong. Nobody he'd worked with could be colluding with Luther. They'd all wanted to bring him down just as much or even more than he had. Landon pushed a slightly shaking hand through his hair. A shard of glass nicked his skin before falling onto the floor with a few other pieces.

"You're bleeding," Jocelyn said, and she grabbed his hand to inspect the wound.

Her skin was so silky. And as he knew, she wasn't at all as cold as he'd thought she was. She was warm. Hell, she was hot. So damn hot…

He wanted to kiss her again. Last time he'd done that, though, they could have been killed. The shots fired into the house had gone wild, hitting everything in her office but them. He couldn't believe the shooter had been one of Luther's crew. Even the young ones were more familiar with firearms than their shooter had seemed to be.

So it could have been someone else—someone who'd sent one of those other threats she'd received.

"I need to call Parker and the chief," Landon remarked.

"You need to get a bandage on this," she said as she continued to hold his hand. "It won't stop bleeding."

The blood was just oozing, though—not flowing. "It's nothing."

His friend was out there somewhere, according to Parker, bleeding, as well. Landon should have immediately gone out to look for him. But then Jocelyn would have been alone and unprotected in her home when the shooting happened...in her office with all the windows.

He'd thought her house was safe with its high-tech security system. But now he wondered if anyplace was safe. "We need to get out of here," he said.

But he wasn't sure where they should go. Dare he trust the others? He knew for certain it hadn't been any of them outside her place shooting at them. Any one of them would have hit them. They were that good of shots.

And even better people.

No way. He wasn't going to let her distrust of his team affect him. They were his family. The only family he had.

"I need to call Parker," he said, "and find out where I should bring you."

"Home," she said. Then she glanced around. "My home."

"This place not nice enough for you?" he teased. He knew it wasn't much. But he and Clint worked so much that they didn't need much.

She tensed again, as if she thought he was insulting her. "I wouldn't have the house I do if my parents hadn't bought it for me," she said. "I was happier in my apartment downtown, and that was much smaller than this."

He believed her. She would have gone for the convenience of having a place close to work over the grandness of her big house. But she'd moved to make her parents happy.

He had seriously misjudged her. And he felt so bad about it that he couldn't argue with her. But he wasn't going to bring her back to her house either. "Your place isn't as safe as your parents thought it would be," he pointed out. "We need to put you in a safe house."

"Because that worked out so well for Rosie Mendez?"

He flinched.

"C'mon," she said, and she tugged him—not toward the outside door, though, but toward the bathroom. "We'll put a Band-Aid on this and then you can call Parker."

And he remembered why her coworkers found her threatening and annoying. She was bossy and controlling. Now he knew the reason why she was...because of how she'd lost her beloved grandparents.

So he let her tug him along with her, and something

tugged at his heart, making it ache in his chest. It had to just be sympathy.

Nothing else.

He would never fall for anyone like her—whatever her reasons for being bossy and controlling.

JOCELYN STARED DOWN at her hand, which was smeared red with his blood. An image flashed through her mind of the last time she'd had blood on her hands. And her knees weakened and wobbled. She swayed slightly and might have fallen into the sink if strong hands hadn't closed over her shoulders and steadied her.

"Are you okay?" Landon asked.

She looked up at him. He was so big. So strong...

So heavy. She could remember the weight of his body lying atop hers, pressing her down to the floor, protecting her. He could have been killed.

His blood was on her hands because it was her fault he'd been hurt. "Thank you," she murmured.

She couldn't remember if she'd done that yet.

His brow furrowed. "For what?"

"For saving me," she said. "You reacted so quickly."

He grimaced. "I shouldn't have had to react," he admonished himself. "I should have noticed him getting close to the house before the shooting ever started."

But he'd been kissing her.

And she hadn't wanted him to stop—even when the shooting started. She was losing her mind. Maybe she had been working too hard—like everyone always told her she was.

But with so many criminals on the streets, she felt as if she still wasn't working hard enough. That she wasn't doing enough. That wobbly feeling in her knees began to spread, making her tremble. Landon's arms wound around her, pulling her against his chest.

"You're not okay," he said.

She couldn't stop shaking. "I don't know what's wrong," she murmured. She hated this weak and helpless feeling.

"You're in shock," he said. "I should take you to the hospital."

"I'm fine," she insisted, even though she didn't feel that way. She felt so strange—so unlike herself. So out of control…

"You're not fine," he said. He drew back and stared down at her, into her eyes.

And she shivered at the intensity of his stare. It was as if he was peering right inside her, as if he could see something no one else could.

"You're scared," he said.

She tensed as she realized that she was.

"That's good," he said. "You should be. You should have been after receiving those threats. And knowing that Luther's determined to take out everyone involved in his trial, you should be very afraid. I was worried when you weren't."

"Is that why you thought I was working for him?" she asked. "Because I didn't seem scared?"

"That and all those times you failed to get indictments," he said.

Frustration gripped her. But she wouldn't defend herself again. That only made him think she was unwilling to accept the responsibility for her losses. She shrugged it off. "I don't know… Maybe I could have done more."

"Not without the evidence," he said.

"We need to look into that," she said. "Find out where it went. But first we need to find Rosie." She could not lose her eyewitness to the murder Luther had committed. He often didn't carry out his dirty work himself.

Even when he wasn't in jail, he usually sent out his crew instead…as if he didn't want any blood on his hands. But it was still there, no matter what he did.

Landon released her. But the bathroom was so small that his body still touched hers as he reached around her and turned on the water in the sink. First he put his hand, that was still bleeding, under the faucet, and then he put hers under it, washing away his blood.

A little sigh of relief slipped through her lips. That was always the hardest for her—to see the blood in the crime-scene photos.

Landon looked at her again, like he was looking through her. "It's good to be scared," he told her.

She snorted. "Yeah, right…"

"I was worried when you weren't because it's hard to protect someone who doesn't realize they're in danger," he said. "Or they know, and they don't care."

She flinched. She'd fallen into that second category. "It doesn't make sense," she said.

"That Luther would try to kill you? I know it's difficult for you to accept, but someone in your office is working for him," he said.

She released a ragged sigh. She couldn't deny that it might be true. With Luther, really anything was possible. "But why try for me now?" she asked. "Why not wait until closer to the start of the trial?"

He shrugged. "I don't know. Maybe he doesn't want to risk a postponement that would leave him in jail longer."

That was true. If she was killed now, there was time for another assistant DA to get up to speed on their case.

"I don't know…"

"I don't know if it was Luther behind the shooting either," Landon admitted.

And she was relieved that he shared her doubts.

"You have all those other threats," he said. "It could have been any of them."

She'd thought those threats were empty. That was why she hadn't reported them to the chief. But now she realized that had been stupid. She'd been stupid. Like Landon had pointed out, it was smarter to be afraid. Then she would be careful.

She wasn't just afraid for her life anymore, though. She was afraid for her heart, too.

That was fear Landon must have seen when he'd looked so deeply into her eyes. She was afraid she was starting to fall for him.

But then he tensed and drew out his weapon. "Shhh…" he said, even though she hadn't been about to say a word.

She listened, though, to the sound of their breathing and the creak of a door opening. Someone was here.

She doubted it was Clint Quarters. He wouldn't have risked bringing Rosie here, where other people would know to look for them. No. This was someone either looking for Rosie and Clint or for her and Landon, to finish what they'd started—to finish them off.

WHERE THE HELL had everyone gone?

Were Rosie and Clint dead? A dead man couldn't

drive, and Luther had learned that Clint had driven away from the ambush. But that hadn't been the only ambush that evening...

Someone had shot up the assistant district attorney's house. He punched in the number for the person he figured had done that.

"Hello?" the caller greeted him curiously. He wouldn't have recognized the number. Luther kept having to change cell phones—kept having to destroy the ones that might have been traced back to him.

"What the hell did you do?" he asked.

"Do?" the person innocently asked. Too innocently.

"I heard about the ADA getting shot at," Luther told him. "I did not give the order for that."

What the hell was happening? Why was no one listening to him? At least his source at the police department was keeping him informed—had let him know about the call of shots fired at the ADA's house and about the break-in at the judge's daughter's apartment.

He just wanted eyes on Jocelyn Gerber and the judge's daughter, Bella Holmes. He didn't want either of them dead. Yet.

"I didn't—"

"Don't lie to me!" he shouted, drawing the attention of a guard passing his cell. But the guard only glanced back at him once before turning around and acting as if he hadn't seen a thing.

Nobody saw what he was doing. So how had the damn chief of police gotten wind of his plan to take out everyone associated with his trial?

"I didn't hit her," the man finished. "She and the guy she calls her boyfriend are fine."

"Boyfriend?" Luther snorted. That bitch was too uptight to have a lover.

"Big guy—light brown hair, brown eyes."

"Landon Myers." Had to be Landon.

"Yeah, I think that's his name," the guy replied.

Luther chuckled. The former vice cop could be pretty damn uptight, too. "He's her bodyguard."

"He's going to fail," the guy replied.

Luther opened his mouth to reiterate his order to keep Jocelyn alive for now. But then he thought about it.

He needed the judge's daughter alive. He couldn't use threats against her to influence the judge to rule in his favor if she was dead.

But it didn't really matter to him when Jocelyn Gerber died.

He uttered a ragged sigh. "When you get the chance, do it," he agreed.

The guy chortled. "I'll get the chance soon. Very soon."

As Luther clicked off the cell, he felt a moment's regret. Jocelyn Gerber was so gorgeous, it really was a shame that he wouldn't be able to look at her much longer.

But then he shrugged off that regret. It would be good to have at least one person dead that he wanted gone.

Chapter Eight

Landon pushed Jocelyn behind him. "Get in the bathtub," he whispered. "Stay down." She would be safe in the old steel claw-foot tub if the shooting started—as long as the shooter didn't take him out. Then Jocelyn would have no protection at all.

There wasn't even a window in the bathroom through which she could escape. But she did as he'd ordered.

And again, he was glad that she was finally afraid. It would make protecting her a hell of a lot easier. As long as he wasn't outnumbered too much. How many people had come after them this time?

The door creaked as it opened all the way before softly snapping shut again. And then the floorboards creaked with the weight of the intruders. There had to be at least two, as he heard two distinctly different sounds of footsteps. He'd partially closed the bathroom door, so he could only peer out through the crack between it and the jamb. He heard the front bedroom door open. He didn't have much time. They would open this one next. So he slipped out—with his gun drawn and his finger twitching against the trigger.

"Don't shoot," a female voice yelled. And a blonde stepped between him and another man holding a gun.

"Keeli!" Landon exclaimed. He jerked his barrel up to point at the ceiling.

Spencer Dubridge did the same and expelled a shaky breath. "Stop doing that!" he growled, but the comment was directed at Keeli.

"It's my job to protect you," she reminded him as she stepped back.

"It's okay," Landon called out to Jocelyn. "It's Detective Dubridge and Keeli."

The ADA must have already discerned that because she stood in the open doorway to the bathroom. But she arched a black brow and asked, "Are you sure it's safe?" as the two continued to bicker.

He grinned. Who knew Jocelyn Gerber could be funny?

He was actually beginning to like her as well as understand her. The grin slid away from his mouth. That wasn't good, though. She was already too much of a distraction. He forced himself to turn away from her and focus again on the detective and his diminutive but fierce bodyguard.

"Clint's not here," he told them.

"I'm not looking for Quarters," Dubridge said. "I found who I'm looking for."

Landon furrowed his brow with confusion. "Me?"

"Both of you," Dubridge replied as he turned toward Jocelyn. "The chief sent me out to investigate the shooting at Ms. Gerber's house. But by the time I—"

"We," Keeli interrupted him.

Dubridge sighed. "Whatever. You guys were gone.

What the hell happened?" he asked. "Who shot up the place?"

"I don't know," Landon admitted.

"You didn't see anyone?" Keeli asked the question and narrowed her eyes to study him.

Heat rushed to his face. It was as if she knew what he'd been doing—that he'd been distracted. "It all happened so quickly."

"There were no spent shells inside the house," Dubridge remarked.

"The shooter didn't get inside," Landon replied.

"Were you inside or outside?" Dubridge asked.

"Inside."

"You didn't return fire?" he asked, and now he exchanged a glance with Keeli.

Landon's face burned now with embarrassment. He knew he'd been a piss-poor bodyguard, but now they knew it, too.

"There was no time," Jocelyn said.

He was surprised she would defend him.

"He saved my life," she added.

And Keeli and Dubridge exchanged another look. They knew he could have done more, that he could have caught the person who shot at her if he'd been more alert.

Less distracted…

Or maybe that was less attracted—to the person he was supposed to be protecting.

He'd saved her life this time. But there would be more attempts. Landon just wasn't sure who was coming after her—some of Luther's crew or one of the people who'd sent her those other threats.

JOCELYN LOOKED AROUND her house and shuddered. She hadn't wanted to move here. She hadn't wanted the house her parents had insisted on buying for her. But she hated seeing it as it looked now, with the windows of her home office shot out, pictures knocked to the floor and holes torn through the paneling she'd painted white.

At least Lady had finally come out of wherever she'd been hiding. She'd run right to Landon the minute they'd opened Jocelyn's front door. He'd carried her into the kitchen to feed her.

"I already called the company we recommend for crime-scene cleanup," Spencer Dubridge assured her. "They'll secure the place tonight and then can start on repairs once you or your insurance agency okay their estimate."

She nodded. She wouldn't have thought of all of that—of what her parents must have had to do to clean up and repair her grandparents' home. Of course, once those repairs had been made, they'd sold the house right afterward. Nobody had ever wanted to go back there again—least of all her.

She wasn't sure she wanted to be back here now, but Spencer had insisted. And she knew she and Landon shouldn't have left the scene until police had arrived. But he hadn't trusted the police.

Or so he'd claimed.

She studied the dark-haired detective. Should she trust Detective Dubridge? He was ambitious. But then, everyone thought she was, too, because she worked so hard. Maybe he worked hard for the same reason she did, though—to get criminals off the streets.

"What about the crime-scene lab?" she asked him.

"Has anyone been here yet?" The techs usually took a long time to process a scene, but she'd caught no sight of the van. She hadn't even seen any police tape cordoning off the area.

Spencer shook his head. "No. The chief sent me out because he wants to keep this quiet. I'm supposed to be the only one to investigate." He glanced at Keeli Abbott, who moved around the home office, inspecting the damage. "I took pictures and bagged the spent shells I found on the street outside. Whoever shot at the house shot from the open window of their vehicle."

"A drive-by, then…" That should have scared her, but she actually breathed a sigh of relief. "That has to be Luther's people."

Spencer shook his head. "Luther doesn't send just one shooter to a scene. I don't think he had anything to do with this."

"Then who?" she asked.

Spencer held up a plastic evidence bag. It didn't contain the spent shells he'd picked up. It contained the letters from her desk. "Any one of these people…"

She shivered.

"Why didn't you report these?" he asked.

She shrugged. "I didn't consider them any more credible threats than when people tell me in court that they're going to get back at me." That happened so often, a perp swearing vengeance as bailiffs dragged them out of court. It was only every once in a while that she was accosted outside court; that was why she carried the Taser—to protect herself during those rare occasions.

Dubridge pointed toward the shattered front windows of the office. "Looks pretty credible to me. You should have reported the threats."

"I really didn't think I was in any danger," she said. "At least, not here. My address is not a matter of public record."

"Anyone can do a deed search," the investigative detective said.

"But my name isn't on the deed," she said. "It's in the name of my maternal grandparents' trust, with no way to trace it back to me." Her parents had wanted to be doubly careful to protect her.

"Then someone must have followed him," Dubridge murmured.

Landon had just stepped out of the kitchen, where he must have left Lady. But he was deep in conversation with Keeli on the other side of the large living room. While they both glanced over at the people they were supposed to be protecting, they did not appear to be eavesdropping on them.

Keeli wasn't just petite and protective. She was appealing. Was Landon attracted to her? Had they ever been involved? Something cold chased over Jocelyn, like she'd been doused with ice water.

"Don't you trust him?" she asked.

"Myers?" Dubridge asked, and his dark eyes widened with the question.

"All of them," she said. "The Payne Protection bodyguards who used to work vice. Do you trust them?"

He glanced over at Landon and Keeli now himself, and his voice deep with conviction, he replied, "With my life."

"You do?"

"I used to work with all of them," he reminded her. "They're good people, hardworking, honest people. I trust them. It's our current coworkers you and I need to worry about."

She shivered again. "You believe the chief, then—that there are leaks in our departments?"

He nodded. "In fact, I would sooner believe that a coworker of yours knows where you live than that someone followed Landon Myers here. He would have noticed the tail right away."

He'd noticed the one that had followed them from the safe house after her meeting with the eyewitness. And as soon as he'd noticed him, he'd lost him.

She drew in a shaky breath, bracing herself to accept the truth. Someone she worked with might have tried to kill her. Someone she worked with was also informing for the enemy.

Dubridge, who was usually all business, slid his arm around her shoulders and squeezed her reassuringly. "We'll find out who," he promised. "We'll keep you safe."

"I'm not worried about myself," she said. At least, not just herself...

She was worried about Luther Mills getting away with not just one murder but quite a few more.

Like the witness and the evidence tech and the judge's daughter and...

Hers.

HE FELT LIKE he was on the damn witness stand right now, and he didn't like it one bit. At least his boss wasn't interrogating him in person—just over the cell phone pressed to his ear.

"How did you know about the shooting at Jocelyn's house?" Amber Talsma-Kozminski asked him.

He shouldn't have called her. But he'd wanted to know himself if any of those bullets had struck Jocelyn. He'd also wanted to be the first one to talk to his boss about the shooting that would be attributed to Mills, so that he would get the case before she assigned it to anyone else.

He still couldn't believe she'd assigned it to Jocelyn. Not when he had more experience than the young female lawyer. He was the better man for the job.

He was also the better man for Amber Talsma-Kozminski's job as the district attorney. And he would have that job, too. Someday…

As long as he didn't get caught.

He figured that Kozminski wasn't just being curious about how he'd heard about the shooting. She sounded suspicious. Had someone realized that there was a leak in the district attorney's office? That he was the leak?

He had to be careful—so damn careful—right now. He couldn't claim that Jocelyn had called him; unless she was dead, she'd call him a liar. He could cast doubt on someone else in the office. He considered it, but no name but Jocelyn's came to his mind at the moment.

"Are you there?" Amber prodded him, and the suspicion in her voice was even more evident, along with the impatience. "I asked you—"

"I heard about the shooting from a friend at the police department," he said.

Someone in the police department had called him—

Luther's someone in the police department. So he wasn't lying.

And because he wasn't lying, Amber must have heard the truthfulness. "I need to know who," she said.

He uttered a rueful sigh. "I'm sorry, boss. I promised this person I wouldn't say anything. They know the chief was trying to keep the shooting quiet, and they're worried they'll get in trouble."

That was all true, as well.

"This is important," Amber persisted. "Jocelyn could have been killed."

Could have been.

So she hadn't been.

That damn bitch had survived despite his emptying his entire clip of bullets into that house. How the hell had she done that?

Then he remembered the size of the guy who'd been hanging around her. Like Luther had said, he had to be a bodyguard. And he'd guarded her successfully.

This time.

Next time he would make certain that he took them both out. And he needed to do it soon—before anyone discovered that he was Luther's leak.

Chapter Nine

Where the hell had they gone? Nobody had heard from Clint and Rosie since the shooting. Parker had gathered several people in the conference room because he wasn't the only one worried about what had happened to the missing eyewitness and her bodyguard. At least he knew where Jocelyn and Landon were now, and that they were okay since they sat around that table, too.

"You're sure he was hurt?" Parker asked his sister Nikki about Clint.

"There was blood on the sidewalk where he'd pulled the SUV," Nikki said. "And I swear I saw him get hit at least once."

A twinge of pain struck Parker's heart. But he wasn't the only one bothered by the news. Landon Myers looked sick. He and Clint were close—so close that they shared a house in the city.

Clint hadn't gone there. Landon had already checked. Jocelyn Gerber sat next to Landon. She looked sick, too.

But she wasn't worried about Clint. She was worried about the witness. "What about Ms. Mendez?" she asked Nikki. "Had she been injured?"

Nikki shrugged. "Like I just told my brother, the SUV came under heavy fire. She could have been."

Jocelyn gasped. "That is unacceptable. The Payne Protection Agency's main responsibility was to make sure that nothing happened to the witness—"

Usually Landon was pretty patient, but now he lost his temper. "Do your damn job," he told Jocelyn, "and you won't need Rosie's testimony."

"What do you mean?" she asked, and her blue eyes looked bright, almost as if she was about to cry. Despite how tough she always acted, Landon had hurt her feelings. "Of course I've done my job."

"Offer those shooters a plea deal to turn on Luther. There are plenty of them in custody, thanks to the Payne Protection Agency," Landon said with pride. "Even you should be able to get through to one of them."

Jocelyn glared at him. "Then I need to go down to the jail," she said as she rose from her chair around the conference table. "We're obviously wasting our time here."

Landon grimaced, and Parker mouthed *I'm sorry* at him. He'd had no idea that Jocelyn Gerber would be so difficult for his friend to handle. Landon got up to follow her out, but he paused at the door and turned back. "Let me know when you find Clint."

"Do you have any ideas?" Parker asked. "He's not answering his phone."

"And I can't even pick up a signal for it," Nikki added.

Landon shook his head and turned back toward the door. But then he stopped and swiveled around. "What about his cabin? Did you check there?"

"What cabin?" Parker had never figured Clint for the outdoors type. All he ever remembered him doing was working—first as a vice cop and now as a bodyguard.

"He just bought the place a little while ago," Landon said.

"He didn't mention it."

Landon grimaced again. "Yeah, he probably wouldn't have said anything about it to you…"

Parker felt a pang. And now he knew what his brother Cooper had gone through when he'd become the boss to his friends. It wasn't always as easy to maintain that friend relationship when you were suddenly the one in charge. "Why not to me?"

"It's the cabin Cooper owned."

"My brother?" As far as Parker knew, Cooper had never owned a cabin, unless he'd been keeping things from him, too.

"Officer Cooper," Landon said.

The man who'd killed Parker's father. He shuddered. He'd never intended to go back there. Ever.

"He bought it really cheap from the guy's estate, which just recently got settled," Landon said. "It had been in probate for years…"

"Does anyone else know about it?" Parker asked.

Landon shrugged. "I think everybody in vice knew he'd bought it. He'd been trying to buy it off the estate before it even got settled."

So everybody but Parker knew about it. Of course, Parker had left vice long before these guys had.

"Do you remember where it is?" Landon asked.

Parker nodded. He would never forget. Now he had

to go back. He only hoped that when he did, it wouldn't end as it had the last time—in another death.

SINCE THE SHOOTING at Jocelyn's house, a heavy pressure had settled on Landon's chest. It was a mixture of guilt and anxiety—over her shooting and over the shooting at the safe house. That guilt and anxiety had caused him to lash out at her during the meeting moments ago.

And that had only intensified his guilt. He shouldn't have snapped at her to do her job, but her concern seemed to be just for her case and not for the people who could be out there—hurt, dying even. Then she'd disparaged the Payne Protection Agency's ability to keep the witness and everyone else safe, infuriating him even more.

She seemed furious, as well, bristling with anger. "Let's get to the jail, then," she said as she stomped on her stiletto heels down the hall ahead of him.

He groaned and uttered an apology. "I'm sorry."

And she whirled around on the tip of one heel to face him. A black brow arched over one of her bright blue eyes. "What?"

"I'm sorry," he repeated.

"For what?" she asked.

"For making that crack about you not doing your job," he clarified. "I know that you work your ass off." Actually, her ass was perfect and perfectly displayed in all those tight little pencil skirts she wore with her suits. She definitely needed to change before they headed over to the jail, or she might cause a riot.

Hell, she was causing a riot in his chest right now, as

his heart began to pound even harder than it had been since the shooting hours ago.

She sighed. "I'm sorry, too," she said. "I know you're worried about your friend."

Tension gripped him, tightening his jaw as he gritted his teeth. He could only nod.

"If you want to go look for him while I go to the jail…"

He shook his head now. "You're sure as hell not going to the jail without protection."

She snorted. "Like what could happen at jail? There are guards."

"Guards who must be smuggling phones in to Luther," Landon reminded her. "Or helping him get messages to his crew other ways. You can't trust them."

She tilted her head and narrowed her eyes, as if wondering if she could trust him. Hadn't he proved himself yet? Hadn't he shown her that he wasn't working for Luther any more than she was?

"I know you would rather be going with Parker to that cabin to look for Clint," she said, "than going to the jail with me."

He couldn't deny that he was worried about his friend. But Clint wasn't the only one he was concerned about. After the shooting at her house, he was stressed about her, too, and worried about how he had nearly failed to protect her.

That weight on his chest pressed down even more, stealing away his breath. And he shook his head. "My job is to protect you."

But she was more than just an assignment to him.

He wanted to keep her safe because he was beginning to care about her.

Before, he'd thought they'd had nothing in common—because he'd suspected she worked for Luther—but now he realized they had too much in common. All either of them cared about was work, protecting people from criminals. Since he hadn't been nearly as effective as he'd wanted as a vice cop, he'd switched to being a bodyguard. But he was worried that he might not be any more effective as a bodyguard—if he let her distract him again.

It was better that they keep infuriating each other than caring about each other.

SYMPATHY TUGGED AT Jocelyn's heart. She knew how it felt to lose someone you loved, and Landon clearly loved his roommate. They were more than just coworkers; they were obviously very good friends.

She was already anxious for Parker to find Clint and Rosie alive and well. But now she didn't just worry about that because of the case. She worried about him because of Landon, because she didn't want him to lose someone else he loved.

He'd already suffered enough loss and no longer had any family left in his life. Still standing in the corridor outside the conference room, they had to step aside as the others walked past them.

"I'll find them," Parker told Landon. "I'm also bringing in Logan's team to help with backup, so everybody will have extra protection."

"We're fine," Landon said. "Even Dubridge didn't

think the shooting at her house had anything to do with Luther or his crew."

Parker narrowed his eyes as he looked speculatively at Jocelyn. "You have someone else after you?"

"Yes," she replied, and she felt her defenses rising again. They really thought so little of her. "Despite what Landon thinks, I win more than I lose, so I've sent a lot of people to prison. They're usually not very happy about that."

But she knew none of those people would have been able to find her very easily or at all since she and her parents had been so careful to hide her home address. No. It probably had been someone from her office— the real someone who was working for Luther Mills. But her pride was already stinging too much for her to admit that they were all probably right about there being a leak in her office.

Parker nodded. "Doesn't matter who's after you. You need extra protection."

Landon sighed. "You're right."

"I thought you'd already left for the jail," Parker said. "So Logan's guards were going to catch up with you on the way there."

"We're heading there now," Jocelyn assured him as she walked with him down the hall. "I will talk to those shooters and get one of them to turn on Luther."

Following behind them, Landon snorted. And her sympathy for him ebbed.

"You really don't think that I can do my job," she murmured as she stopped at the outside door and turned back toward him.

"I think it's going to be hard to turn anyone against

Luther," he said. "Especially after he killed Javier Mendez for becoming an informant."

"It was your idea for us to go there," she reminded him.

Parker uttered a ragged sigh and shook his head. "Why the hell can't any of you get along?" he wondered aloud.

They could. It was just safer—for both of them—if they didn't. But she doubted Landon was about to admit that any more readily than she was.

"I can't stay to mediate this squabble," he said. "You two are going to need to work this out on your own."

"Go," Landon urged him. "Find Clint and Rosie."

Parker nodded and headed out the back door to the parking lot. Landon caught the door and looked around outside before letting her exit with him. All of the black Payne Protection Agency SUVs looked alike, and there were several of them since some of the other bodyguards had stayed behind in the conference room.

Landon must have noticed it, too, because he murmured, "Parker shouldn't be heading there alone," as one of those black SUVs drove out of the parking lot.

"Maybe some of his brother Logan's team is meeting him at the cabin," she suggested. Since Parker seemed adamant about everyone else having backup, she doubted he would go anywhere without some of his own.

Landon released a shaky breath and nodded. "You're right. I'm sure they are."

"And I'm sure Clint is okay," Jocelyn said. "He probably just doesn't know who to trust."

She knew the feeling. Could someone in her office

really have fired those shots into her house? Have tried to kill her?

She shivered, and not just because of the cool night air blowing around them, tangling her hair across her face.

"He knows he can trust me," Landon said. Then he reached up and pushed her hair back from her face. "And you can trust me, too."

She drew in a shaky breath. She wanted to be able to trust him—to believe, like Detective Dubridge did, that no one working at the Payne Protection Agency was also working for Luther. But she was scared to trust the wrong person.

Maybe it was safer just to trust no one at all. That was probably what Clint Quarters had decided, why no one had heard from him. Or the alternative was that he was dead—and Rosie didn't dare to trust anyone.

Jocelyn could understand that, but she didn't want Landon to have lost his friend. Even though she struggled to bring herself to trust him completely, she did care about him. Maybe too much...

He must have cared, too, because he began to lower his head to hers. But he was moving too slowly, so she rose up on tiptoe and pressed her mouth to his. Then she moved her fingers to his nape to hold his head down to hers as she kissed him deeply.

He groaned, and his hands moved to her back, clutching her close—but then within seconds, he was pushing her away and shoving her down. And just as her body hit the asphalt, she heard the shots ringing out.

Someone was shooting at them. But Landon hadn't

hit the asphalt with her. Instead, he'd drawn his weapon and was returning fire.

"Get down!" she screamed at him, afraid that he would be hit. She had just uttered the words when he dropped to the ground. And she knew that she'd probably warned him too late.

He must have already been hit.

Chapter Ten

Landon grimaced at the sight of the jail. "We should be going to the hospital," he said. "Not here."

"You said you weren't hurt!" she exclaimed as she turned in the passenger's seat of the SUV and studied him over the console.

"I'm not," he said. "But you are." He stared at the torn sleeve of her suit jacket. The skin visible through the tear was scratched and swollen and oozing blood. "You're bleeding," he said. "You might need stitches."

She shook her head. "I'm fine. Thanks to you."

He was the one who'd hurt her. The shots had missed them both wildly. The vehicle from which they'd been fired had moved fast—too fast for the driver to take any real aim at them. That was why Landon hadn't been hit.

She probably would have been less injured had he not pushed her down. But when he'd heard the vehicle pulling into the lot Parker had left, he'd instinctively known there was going to be trouble. Fortunately, he'd heard the motor and opened his eyes.

Or he might have just gone on kissing her…until they were both dead. Because if he hadn't reacted, the shooter might have just stopped the car and shot at them.

Then he wouldn't have missed. But he'd been driving fast, so fast that Landon hadn't gotten a good look at the driver or the vehicle.

He shook his head. "You could have been killed."

"We don't know that he was shooting at us," she said. "He could have been expecting someone else to be coming out of the Payne Protection Agency."

"He could have been." But Landon suspected he had been shooting at them. At her.

So had the other bodyguards when they'd rushed out to the lot at the first sound of gunfire. Nikki Payne-Ecklund hadn't wanted them to leave the agency, but Jocelyn had insisted on being brought here, to the jail.

She really thought she might turn some of Luther's crew against him. She'd never been successful at that before Luther had murdered Javier Mendez. He doubted she would succeed now. But because he had suggested it during the meeting, he had to support her.

So he'd driven her here. He hated the thought of her being inside the jail, though. And he hated it even more when he wasn't allowed into the small visiting room reserved for meetings with lawyers.

"We're right here," one of the guards said.

That was the problem. The guard was probably working for Luther just like his young crew member had been when he'd ambushed Clint and Rosie at the safe house.

"Nothing will happen to her," the older man assured Landon.

He was not reassured.

"What the hell's going on here?" he asked.

The guard shrugged. "I don't know what you're talking about."

"You don't think the chief of police and the district attorney's office have figured out that someone on the inside is helping Luther?"

"On the inside?" the guard asked, as if he didn't understand.

Landon figured he didn't just understand but that he probably knew exactly who was helping Luther Mills. Like probably himself.

Landon was not going to budge from outside the door. But that door was steel and the walls solid concrete. If Jocelyn was screaming inside the room, he wouldn't be able to hear her. He would never know—until it was too late—that she had needed his help.

JOCELYN GLANCED AROUND the hotel suite where Landon had brought her after the jail. She'd wanted to go home, to her own house, to her cat.

He'd assured her that he'd shut the feline into the laundry room, where her litter box was, and that he'd given her plenty of food and water.

Besides her cat, what Jocelyn wanted most was her bathroom. She needed a shower, and not just because Landon had knocked her down in the parking lot. She needed a shower to wash away all the comments the perps had made when she'd tried to talk to them.

The things they'd called her...

The suggestions they'd made to her.

She shuddered.

"That bad?" Landon asked.

She tensed with defensiveness. Her parents were always trying to get her to quit her job. They didn't understand that she just didn't want to be a prosecutor; she *needed* to be a prosecutor. "Don't," she said.

"Don't what?" he asked.

"Don't tell me that I shouldn't be doing this job," she said. "That I'm not equipped for it."

He stared down at her, his brow furrowed with confusion. "Why the hell would I say that?"

"My parents do all the time," she said.

"Then I guess they don't know you very well," he replied.

A tightness she hadn't even realized she had in her chest eased now.

"You're tough," he said. "You can handle anything."

That tightness turned to a warmth that spread throughout her chest. "I'm glad you realize that."

"You're tough," he said. "But you're not invincible. That's why we came here instead of back to your house."

He'd rented a hotel suite, not just a room. So there were two bedrooms—with two separate beds—and a big bathroom between them. She wondered if he could afford it, or if the Payne Protection Agency had picked up the tab. Ultimately the police department would— since the chief had hired them because he didn't trust his own officers to protect those associated with the case.

The sky was already getting lighter outside, dawn making the blinds glow at the windows. She glanced at the window and shivered.

"We're safe here," Landon said. "The backup Parker promised is outside, guarding the perimeter."

And he was inside with her.

"I wish I'd been allowed in that room at the jail," he said. "I hated thinking of you alone in there through all those hours of interviews."

"Unfortunately, I wasn't alone," she remarked.

"Do you think you got through to any of them?"

She shrugged and flinched as the torn jacket rubbed against her scraped shoulder. "I think you were right. That they're all too afraid of Luther to risk testifying against them."

After the attempts on her life, was Rosie too afraid now? Jocelyn wouldn't blame her if she was. She had not enjoyed getting shot at either.

"I don't know," Landon said as he continued to stare down at her. "You're pretty damn scary yourself. I'm sure you threatened the hell out of them and got them thinking."

People commented on her appearance all the time, but those compliments never affected her. His comment—about her being scary—might not have even been a compliment, but given her profession, she took it as such and smiled.

He chuckled. "You're happy about being scary."

She nodded. "Yes." But then she looked up at his handsome face grinning down at her, and she was the one afraid—very afraid—of how he made her feel.

Of how much she wanted him.

His mouth curved down as the grin slid away, and his brown eyes darkened. "You are so damn scary," he murmured with a shaky breath.

"You're afraid of me?" she asked. If he would have admitted that earlier, she might have thought he had something to hide—like his association with Luther Mills. But she didn't believe that anymore.

If he was working for Luther, he wouldn't have risked his life for hers. He would have just let her get shot, killed. But instead, he'd saved her life.

"I'm terrified," he said.

The thought that he could be afraid of her had a laugh bubbling up from her throat. "Yeah, right."

He touched her with just his fingertips sliding along her jaw. "You do," he insisted. "You scare me because of how damn much I want you."

Then his mouth lowered to hers, covering it, as he kissed her. There was such heat, such passion, in the kiss.

Her heart pounded, her skin heated…and that fear she'd felt intensified. But now she was afraid that he would stop, that something would make him stop like it had the other times he'd kissed her.

He was tense, too, as if he was braced for the same thing. But no gunfire rang out. There was no sound but their pants for breath as the kiss went on and on.

Not wanting him to pull away, she slid her hands around his nape, holding his head down to hers. His thick hair was soft against her skin. She wanted to feel it against more than her fingers.

But he pulled back and broke the kiss. Maybe he just needed air because he panted for breath—like she did.

She wanted him. So she reached for him again, tugged at his shirt. She dragged it from his jeans and over his abdomen. His stomach rippled with sculpted muscles. The man was so damn perfect.

But the shirt caught on his holster and went no farther up. A protest slipped through her lips.

And he grinned. But he didn't pull off his holster. Instead, he undid the buttons on her suit jacket. He was careful of the scrape on her shoulder when he eased it down her arms. It dropped to the floor. Then he lowered his lips to her shoulder and gently kissed the wound. "I'm sorry," he said.

"You saved me," she said as she reached for the button of his jeans.

"Is that what this is about?" he asked. "Gratitude?"

She snorted. "This is about greed. I want to feel something besides fear and frustration. I want to feel passion." And with him, she felt that more intensely than she ever had before.

He grinned again. "What about pleasure?"

"Can you give me that?" she asked, knowing she'd issued a challenge.

One he obviously accepted as he swung her up in his arms. He carried her into the bedroom where he'd brought her overnight bag. They weren't spending the night, though, since it was already almost morning. Light filtered through the blinds on the window.

He laid her on the bed. But before following her down, he removed his gun and holster, setting them on the table next to the bed. Then he pulled his shirt up and over his head. Next he reached for the button of his jeans. He undid it and lowered the zipper.

And Jocelyn's breath rasped out along with the sound of the zipper lowering. He was so damn sexy…

Just looking at him brought her pleasure, had heat

coursing through her body. Had certain spots tingling and throbbing with desire.

He kicked off his jeans but left on his knit boxers. His erection strained against them, though, begging to be released. She reached for him, but he didn't join her on the bed. Instead, he knelt beside it, and he started undressing her now. He moved his hands down the front of the sleeveless blouse she'd worn beneath her jacket. He carefully and slowly released every button.

Why were there so many buttons?

Her breath caught each time his fingertips brushed across the skin he exposed. Her heart pounded fast and furiously. She wanted his hands on her, wanted him touching her.

A moan of frustration slipped through her lips.

And he chuckled.

Then her blouse parted. She arched up and jerked it off her shoulders, uncaring of the scrape on her skin. That pain was nothing compared to the tension winding so tightly inside her. She felt as if she might snap.

Before he could torture her any more, she unclasped her skirt and lowered the zipper. Then she wriggled out of it until she lay on the bed clad only in her blue silk underwear.

A groan emanated from him now, and it sounded as if he was being tortured. He stared down at her, his face flushed and his nostrils flaring. "You are beautiful…"

When he said it, the praise affected her because she suspected he wasn't one to throw around empty compliments. From the look on his face, he was obviously sincere.

Her skin heated even more just from his look. Then

he touched…running his fingertips along her every curve, from her neck to the arch of her foot. Despite the heat, she shivered as sensations raced through her.

Then he unclasped the front closure of her bra and pushed it away from her breasts. And he touched them…cupping them in his hands as he stroked his thumbs across the peaks of them.

She arched up from the bed as that tension wound painfully tight. "Landon…"

She needed him like she couldn't remember ever needing anyone else. She needed him to ease the tension, to give her the pleasure he'd promised.

Then he moved his hands from her breasts to her waist. He pushed her panties down, his hands skimming over her ass and along her thighs as he discarded the scrap of silk. He continued to stroke her legs and hips as he leaned across her. And as his hands moved over her, his mouth closed around a nipple. He nipped lightly at it, and she cried out.

He pulled back. "Did I hurt you?"

She shook her head in denial. But she was hurting—so bad. She'd never felt as out of control, a feeling she usually hated. But for some reason with Landon it felt liberating.

She reached for him, running her hands over all his hard muscles. But he didn't let her pull him down onto the bed with her. Instead, he stayed beside it, just leaning over her body. His mouth moved from her breast, over her abdomen to her core.

She arched up again and cried out at just the heat of his breath touching her there. Then his fingers slid inside her, as his tongue flicked over her most sensitive part. And she cried out as the tension eased a little.

"Wow," he murmured. "You're responsive."

She was desperate and needy. And what he'd just done wasn't enough. She clutched at his shoulders, trying to pull him onto the bed with her—onto her.

But he held back. She heard something tear. Then she glanced down and saw him rolling a condom on the length of his erection. He was big everywhere. So damn big…

Finally he joined her on the bed, but he held his weight off her. Lowering only his mouth to hers, he kissed her deeply—over and over again. His lips nipped at hers; his tongue teased hers.

"Landon." She murmured his name again—in an unspoken plea.

And finally he lowered his body to hers.

She lifted her legs and locked them around his waist, as he eased his erection inside her. He was so big that she had to shift and arch and move to take him deeper. And still she could not take all of him.

He moved his hips with gentle thrusts. But instead of easing the tension, he just built it more.

She was going out of her mind. She raked her nails down his back to his butt, clasping him against her. Then she nipped her teeth into his shoulder and rubbed her breasts against his chest.

He shuddered. "You're driving me crazy."

"Good!" She didn't want to be the only one slipping into madness. She arched her hips more, trying to take him deeper, trying to move him faster.

He chuckled, but the sound was gruff, like his pants

for breath. His chest moved with his harsh breathing, the soft hair brushing over her nipples.

She bit her lip. And he brushed his tongue across it. Then he arched back and moved his head lower until his tongue brushed across a nipple. Pleasure moved from that point to where she throbbed in her core. She needed more, though.

And then his thumb was there, brushing over her as he slid deeper inside her. He moved her legs higher and thrust deeper yet.

And finally that tension broke as an orgasm moved through her. The intensity of it had her crying out as her body shuddered. He kept thrusting, pushing her to another one before the first had even finished.

The second was even more intense, and she shouted his name now. Then he tensed, and a low groan tore from his throat as his big body shuddered against hers for a long while.

He flopped onto his back next to her as he panted even louder for breath. "You are so damn scary, Jocelyn Gerber."

But she was the one who was scared now—to her core. She'd never experienced anything as intense or as pleasurable as what they'd just done, as what he'd just given her. She was afraid that it—and he—might begin to matter to her—too much. She'd vowed long ago to focus only on her job. She'd wanted no distractions.

But she'd never met anyone who distracted her as much as Landon Myers did. He was the far bigger threat to her than Luther Mills ever was.

LUTHER LAY BACK on his uncomfortable bunk and closed his eyes. But he couldn't close his ears to all the chatter around him. He knew Jocelyn Gerber had survived another shooting attempt. He knew because she'd been in his house. The jail had become his house because of her—because she'd managed to outwit his high-priced lawyer and make sure bail had been denied him.

He owed the bitch for that. Hell, he owed her for a lot. She'd spent last night trying to turn members of his crew against him, trying to get them to finger him for giving the order to kill Rosie Mendez and Clint Quarters, and then she'd promised them lighter sentences.

He blew out a breath and even managed a chuckle. That was her problem. She couldn't entirely forgo justice. If she'd offered to drop the charges in exchange for their testimony, she might have found someone willing to talk. But his men knew that if they were in here—in his house with him—they wouldn't survive betraying him. He would kill every last one of them, just like he intended to kill every last person associated with his trial.

Maybe he'd made a mistake in starting with the witness, though. Maybe he should have started with Jocelyn Gerber.

But it didn't matter when she died. His men wouldn't talk to her. Nobody dared to turn on him—not since his killing Javier Mendez. He just had to make sure the only thing that came of his killing Javi was a lesson to everybody not to betray him. He could not get a murder conviction and life sentence out of this.

That was Jocelyn Gerber's intention—to send him to prison for the rest of his life. So, yeah, hers had to end soon before she could make good on her intention.

Chapter Eleven

What the hell had he done?

Landon hadn't just crossed the line with Jocelyn Gerber; he'd trampled all over it. He couldn't believe how stupid he'd been. His assignment was to protect, not to fall for her. Not that he was falling.

He had no time for love. No time for a relationship. And he couldn't afford any distractions right now, not with Luther Mills trying to get away with murder.

Landon had spent too many years trying to bring Luther to justice to help him escape it now. If something happened to Jocelyn, there was a damn good chance that Luther would not be convicted.

Like Spencer Dubridge, Landon believed the person who'd shot up her house was someone she worked with, someone who knew where she lived.

They were at her office at the district attorney's now. While she sat behind her desk, speaking on the phone, Landon stared out the window in her door, watching people watch them. He recognized the two guys he'd met, but they weren't the only ones taking an unnatural interest in him and Jocelyn.

"I'm going to get some coffee," Landon told Jocelyn,

but he said it more for those standing outside her office than for her benefit. When he jerked open the door, he startled a young man who jumped and lost a folder he was carrying.

Landon bent down to help him pick it up and noticed the guy was shaking. "I'm sorry," he told him, then narrowed his eyes and asked, "Are you okay?"

The young man nodded. "Yes. I just—I just had to bring them to Ms. Gerber. I'm a paralegal."

Landon took the folder from his hand and promised, "I'll make sure she gets it."

A sigh slipped through the young man's lips and he murmured a grateful "Thanks" before rushing away.

Just as he'd told her, Jocelyn was scary as hell. Even scarier to Landon now that he'd had sex with her. He'd never felt anything as intense as what they'd shared. Hell, he wasn't even sure what it had been, and before he'd been able to figure it out, her cell had blared out an alarm.

It must have been her wake-up call for work—since she'd scrambled to get ready to come into the office. But it had been Landon's wake-up call to remind him that keeping her safe was his job—not seducing her.

But he wasn't exactly sure who had seduced whom. She'd seemed to want him as badly as he'd wanted her. As he still wanted her...

His hand shook, and the folder nearly slipped from his grasp. He glanced down at it and noticed it was a dossier on her coworkers. Despite her arguing that nobody in her office could be Luther's mole, she must have had her doubts, or she wouldn't have asked the young paralegal to compile the information for her.

No wonder the kid had been so nervous. He hadn't wanted any of his coworkers to know that he'd helped her investigate them. He shouldn't have been the one doing it. Landon was the one who needed to help her, not just to keep her safe but because he personally wanted to deal with whoever the hell kept shooting at them.

So, after making sure his backup bodyguards were within sight of Jocelyn, Landon continued down the hall toward the employee break room. He wasn't much of a coffee drinker, but he approached the pot a few other people loitered around. Mike Forbes and Dale Grohms glanced up at him with feigned surprise. They'd been close enough to her office to overhear him telling Jocelyn where he was going.

He smiled as he reached for a cup and the pot. "Good morning, gentlemen."

"Morning?" Dale asked. "It's a little later than that now."

"That's because Jocelyn was late this morning," Mike Forbes said. "What's up with that lately? Your fault?"

Landon chuckled. "What makes you think I have anything to do with it?"

"You've become her shadow lately," Forbes said. "And I'm not buying the boyfriend act. Who are you really?"

"You don't know?" the young paralegal asked from where he stood behind the men. "He's a bodyguard with the Payne Protection Agency."

Had Jocelyn had the kid investigate him as well as her coworkers? How did he know who Landon was? Landon studied the kid now, wondering if he'd been more nervous over running into him than he'd been over having that folder on him. Had he met the kid before, back when he'd been working vice?

Could he be one of Luther's crew or at least an indebted customer? He narrowed his eyes and studied the kid—even while he felt everyone else studying him.

"Is it true?" Grohms asked. "Are you her bodyguard?"

"I'm a bodyguard," Landon admitted. There was no point in denying what they could easily find out on their own.

"Why does Jocelyn need a bodyguard?" Dale asked.

"Didn't you hear about the shooting at her house last night?" the kid asked. And now the other men were studying him as intently as Landon was.

They were surprised that he knew, but they didn't look surprised about the shooting. They'd already known about it. How? Because one of them had been the shooter? Or was it now just common knowledge around the office?

"I don't envy you," Dale Grohms said.

Which surprised Landon because he'd thought the guy had a crush on Jocelyn. But of course, now he knew that Landon was just her bodyguard—not her boyfriend. Except after last night—or this morning, actually—Landon wasn't just her bodyguard.

He wasn't her boyfriend either. He wasn't sure what the hell he was but in trouble. Deep trouble…

"Why's that?" Landon asked.

"You have a very dangerous job," Grohms said.

"Jocelyn Gerber has a lot of enemies," Mike Forbes added.

A chill chased down Landon's back as he realized

the other man spoke the truth. Jocelyn did have a lot of enemies. So keeping her safe was going to require all his concentration. He had to redraw that line and make damn sure he didn't cross it again.

Both their lives depended on him staying focused. He had to protect her. And he had to protect himself, as well.

JOCELYN STARED DOWN in confusion at the folder Landon slid onto her desk. "Where did this come from?"

He lifted his broad shoulders in a faint shrug. "Male paralegal. I didn't catch his name."

"I didn't ask him for this," Jocelyn said. She knew who her coworkers were; she didn't need a list of names with their addresses, marital statuses and criminal history. Fortunately, not many of them had a criminal history beyond some speeding tickets, and one had a driving-while-impaired charge on his record.

"You should have," Landon said. "You need to find out which of them is working for Luther."

She sighed. "I'm not sure it is one of them."

"You're not naive, Jocelyn," he said. "You know it has to be one of them. I would have noticed someone following us to your house. The shooter had to know where you live."

She shivered. "That doesn't mean they work with me. Someone in the police department could have found out."

He tensed, then begrudgingly nodded in agreement. "Maybe…"

"You said yourself it's possible that someone within the police department got rid of the evidence you and your unit brought me to bring to a grand jury," she reminded him.

"Not someone within my unit, though," he said defensively. "We were all determined to get Luther off the streets."

She hoped he was right. Or the chief had put the wrong franchise of the Payne Protection Agency in charge of protecting the people associated with Luther's trial. But another department had aroused her suspicions. Not like Landon aroused her, though.

Just looking at him chased away the chill of fear from her as passion rushed through her. He was so damn good-looking. And now she knew how magnificent his muscular body looked with no clothes.

How it felt.

How he'd made her feel.

She barely resisted the urge to wave the folder in front of her face to cool herself off. But she closed her eyes to shut out the temptation that he'd become.

"I think it could be a CSI," she admitted.

"Wendy Thompson?" he asked with a gasp.

She opened her eyes again. "Not Wendy. She didn't handle the evidence for those other cases—just this one." And that was why she'd been able to get a grand jury to indict—because the evidence hadn't mysteriously disappeared before she'd been able to present it to them.

He nodded. "That makes sense," he agreed. "But CSIs aren't the only ones with access to the evidence."

With the evidence locker in the police department, pretty much every officer had access. And when the evidence was sent to the district attorney's office…

"I know," she said. "But let's start with the CSIs. Let's talk to the chief." She could have just called Chief Lynch, but since she didn't have court today, she needed an excuse to get out of the office. The space was too small to share with Landon for too long.

His scent already filled her head. It was a combination of soap from the quick shower he'd taken mixed with male muskiness. She wanted to bury her face in his neck and breathe in it, breathe in *him*. And her body tingled with awareness and desire. She wanted him closer, wanted him touching her like she wanted to touch him.

No. They could not stay any longer in her small office. She jumped up from her desk. "Let's go."

"Don't you want to see if he's available first?" Landon asked.

She shook her head. "If he's not, we'll talk to Wendy Thompson and see if she has any suspicions. We should check on her anyway. With the witness missing, Luther will probably focus all his attention on taking out Wendy."

If anything happened to that evidence or the evidence tech, Jocelyn's case against Luther would be in serious trouble. Landon held the door for her, and when she passed him, her body reacted to his closeness—her pulse quickening, her skin tingling—and she knew she was already in serious trouble.

With him…

For years, there had been speculation that someone in the district attorney's office was working for Luther. Some people even suspected it was Jocelyn. The real spy grinned at his reflection in the rearview mirror.

That was perfect. He would have to figure out how to frame her for it. But first he had to get rid of her—because he worried that she would figure it out first.

She was too damn smart.

And she worked too hard.

Or she had until this bodyguard had started protecting her. Of course, she'd been a little busy trying to stay alive to worry about work. That was why he couldn't stop trying to take her life—it kept her from tearing his apart.

And if she was dead, she could never discover the truth. He watched as they opened the door from the district attorney's offices and stepped into the parking garage. When he'd seen the bodyguard standing at her door, he'd figured they might be leaving, so he'd rushed to the parking garage and started the vehicle he'd rented a few days ago.

He hadn't wanted to risk anyone seeing his. He pulled his hood tighter around his face and adjusted his dark glasses. He didn't want to risk anyone seeing him either. But he had to take the risk of trying to kill her again.

The longer Jocelyn lived, the more likely she was to discover his connection to Luther Mills. He had to kill her and her bodyguard, too.

He couldn't wait until they got into the SUV. He'd tried to follow the bodyguard before, but he drove too damn fast. They would get away from him if they got into their vehicle.

Fortunately, he'd had his rental running beforehand. He'd already pulled out of his spot and gotten into position. So the minute they stepped away from the door to the building and headed across the parking area, he gunned his engine and bore down on them.

There was no way they could outrun him. No way they could escape him.

The man was definitely a bodyguard—with the quick reflexes and protective instincts. He shoved Jocelyn between two parked cars and jumped just as the rental's bumper neared him. Instead of striking the bodyguard or Jocelyn, the car struck those other cars. Metal crunched and screeched.

He pressed harder on the accelerator, cramming into that small space between those cars. Either they would crush Jocelyn and her bodyguard or his rental car would.

But the bodyguard surged up from the ground to which he'd fallen with Jocelyn. His arm was outstretched, the barrel of his gun pointed at the windshield, and he began to fire.

He ducked as the windshield shattered, but he kept his foot on the gas. He needed to take them out, needed for them to die. The shooting stopped, and he glanced up, peering through that broken windshield.

And finally his front bumper struck the concrete half wall of the parking structure. Either they were beneath his car or the ones he'd crumpled, or they'd gone over the wall.

He grinned. Either way, they were dead.

And he needed to get the hell out of there before he was caught. He shifted into Reverse and tried backing up. Those other crumpled cars caught on his, metal catching and twisting, rubber burning.

But it wasn't just the other vehicles he had to worry

about escaping. People had rushed up behind him, a security guard and a couple of burly men he'd noticed inside the building. More bodyguards?

They began to fire at his vehicle as they advanced on him. But finally his car jerked free of the wreckage. The back bumper struck one of the men, sending him flying back into another one—knocking them both to the ground.

He shifted into Drive now and accelerated, careening around corners as he headed all those stories down to the exit to the street. He sped up as he neared the garage exit and crashed through the gate at the end. It wasn't as if he could have used his parking pass. That would have been traced back to him.

He had to make sure that nothing could be traced because now he wouldn't just be facing conspiracy or aiding-and-abetting charges. He would be facing murder charges.

Jocelyn Gerber had to be dead. There was no way she or her bodyguard could have survived a fall from the fifth story of the concrete parking structure.

He waited for a flash of guilt or regret or something…but he felt nothing but triumph. Of course, if he'd had a conscience, he wouldn't have started working for Luther Mills in the first place.

Chapter Twelve

The parking structure had been designed in such a way
that every other level had an area of uncovered parking. So when the car had kept coming at them despite
Landon shooting at it, he'd had no choice. He'd grabbed
Jocelyn up from the asphalt and he'd leaped over the
half wall to the level below them.

It had just been a one-story jump down to the uncovered parking area. But the fall, and subsequent crash
onto the roof of a vehicle, had knocked all the air from
Landon's lungs. They burned as he struggled to breathe.

There was such a weight lying on them—on him.
He moved his arms and reached up and found Jocelyn pressed tightly against him. He'd held her as he'd
jumped, turning so that he took the brunt of the fall.

It was what Clint had done when he'd leaped out
of the witness's apartment to avoid getting killed. But
they'd fallen three stories into a dumpster. Landon had
just struck the roof of an SUV. And Jocelyn was light.
She hadn't hurt him.

But she wasn't moving.

He stroked his hand down her back and then up to her

neck. He needed to check for a pulse. But before his fingers brushed her skin, she shivered and finally moved.

And he sucked in a breath as his ribs, which must have been bruised, ached in protest along with a twinge in his lower back.

"Are you okay?" she asked.

He should have been asking her that. But before he could, someone leaned over the half wall above them and called down, "Are you all right?"

He tried to reach for his holster, but it and his weapon were trapped beneath her body. He had no way to defend them—to protect her—if that person started firing.

But then he recognized the voice, and he focused on the face of the man leaning over the half wall. Unlike Cooper Payne's team, who were all former Marines who wore their hair in military brush cuts, this guy's hair was long and dark blond.

"You all right?" Garek Kozminski asked again. "An ambulance is on its way."

Maybe Jocelyn had recognized him, too, because she moved against him, struggling to sit up. Not wanting her to fall off the car, Landon caught and held her. He was finally able to draw in a deep breath again, so he sat up. Then he helped her down to the ground again.

Her legs nearly buckled beneath her. But he'd jumped down from the car and caught her before she fell. "You're not okay," he said.

"I'm scared," she said. "But I'm not hurt. What about you?" Her gaze moved over his body, reminding him of how she'd looked at him and touched him the night before.

Heat rushed through his body. If he could feel attraction and desire, he wasn't in too much pain. He shook his head. "No. I'm fine." He glanced back up at Garek. "We don't need an ambulance."

"The security guard does," Garek replied as he glanced over his shoulder. "He got hit when the guy backed up."

"Did you get a look at him?" Landon asked.

Garek shook his head. "No. You?"

Landon cursed. "No. He had a hood drawn tight around his face and dark glasses."

"I'm surprised you saw that much with the tinted windows," Garek remarked.

Landon wouldn't have seen that much had he not broken the windshield. He must not have hit the guy, though, not if he'd been able to escape. "So he got away?" he asked for confirmation, a sick feeling roiling through his stomach.

Garek sighed and nodded. "Sorry…"

It wasn't his backup bodyguard's fault. It was Landon's. He should have made damn certain the man had not escaped. Hell, because of that disguise, he didn't even know if it had been a man trying to run them down.

He was no closer to finding out who was after Jocelyn than he'd been after the shooting. He only knew that the person was getting more and more bold, which meant he or she was getting more and more desperate.

That was not good. Desperate people were unpredictable. There was no way to know when they would try to take out Jocelyn again.

The only thing Landon knew for certain was that

they would try again and would keep trying until they were either caught or succeeded in killing her.

JOCELYN COULD NOT deny that someone wanted her dead. She wanted to deny it. She wanted to go on believing all those threats she'd received were empty. But they weren't. Somebody was determined to make good on those threats.

Somebody was determined to end her life.

"Will the security guard be okay?" she asked Landon as the ambulance headed out of the parking structure with the middle-aged guard strapped to a stretcher in the back.

"Looks like it's just a broken leg," Landon said.

How did her bodyguard not have any broken bones? He'd taken the brunt of the fall when he'd propelled them off the half wall onto the level below and the roof of an SUV.

"Are *you* really okay?" she asked him.

"No," he admitted.

And she glanced at the ambulance, willing it back even as it raced out of the garage. "You should have said—"

"I'm pissed as hell," he said. "This idiot shouldn't keep escaping. We should be able to catch him. *I* should be able to catch him."

Whoever was after her wasn't one of Luther's young, careless crew members. It was somebody wiser and far more careful. Maybe it was someone within her department. She shivered as she considered it.

Some of them stood around now, watching her from the other side of the crime-scene tape Spencer Dubridge had had an officer string around the wreckage. They'd already told the detective what they knew—which had been damn little. And so much time had passed between the attempt on her and Landon's lives and the detective's arrival that their assailant could have ditched the vehicle and circled back to the garage to stand with her other curious coworkers. She knew they were just curious and not concerned about her. None of them was going to help her.

And neither she nor Landon could help the detective. They hadn't gotten a good look at the driver or at the car. They'd been too busy trying to stay alive. No. Landon had been too busy trying to keep her alive.

Once again, he'd willingly put his life at risk for hers. But he was just doing his job. She had to remember that, so she didn't get all sappy and fall for him.

Because for the first time in years, she felt sappy and overemotional. She blinked furiously against the tears stinging her eyes. And finally she dashed them away, hopefully before anyone had seen them. She didn't want to show any weaknesses to her coworkers or to the police officers present or especially to Landon.

He might suggest that she ask to be removed from the case. She probably wouldn't have to ask, though. She'd recognized the blond-haired bodyguard. At first she'd thought he was her boss's husband; then she'd realized he was her boss's brother-in-law. Either way, Amber was going to learn about this latest attempt on her life.

Detective Dubridge walked back from where he'd just peered over the half wall. Keeli Abbott stood near him, but not as close as Landon stood to her.

"Damn, Myers, I thought you and the others were

taking the easy way out when you quit the vice unit to become bodyguards," he said. "Now I see how damn dangerous your job is." He glanced at Keeli now, and there was a furrow between his brows.

Landon shook his head. "It's dangerous for the same reason that vice was—Luther Mills."

"You think Luther was behind this?" Dubridge skeptically asked.

"Ultimately," Landon said.

And it was probably true—if someone from her office had tried to run them down—that person was working for Luther. That was why Jocelyn could not be taken off his case. She had to make sure that Luther was finally brought to justice.

She had to make sure that he couldn't hurt anyone else anymore.

PARKER HAD JUST had a close call—too damn close. If not for Clint, he would have died. And he had too much to lose: his beautiful wife, his children...his agency. His friends.

He didn't want to lose any of them. So he'd made a call, warning them all that Luther was extra dangerous.

He might have put out a hit on all of them—not just the people associated with his trial, but on the people trying to protect them.

He might have put out a hit on the entire Payne Protection Agency. Unfortunately, few of them had seemed surprised by the news.

"What happened?" he asked Landon.

"Another attempt..."

"Are you all right?" he asked. "Is Jocelyn Gerber?"

"Yes and yes," Landon replied. But he didn't sound all right. He sounded angry as hell. But he'd survived and so had Jocelyn unharmed, so he'd done his job.

That wasn't enough for Landon, though. He was too much of a cop yet. He didn't just want to protect his principal. He wanted to catch the person after her. And he wanted to stop him permanently.

Parker had a feeling that wasn't just because of Landon's police background, though. This assignment had gotten personal for him.

Something was going on between him and Jocelyn Gerber, just like Parker suspected something was going on between Clint and Rosie Mendez.

Had he made a mistake when handing out assignments?

He'd known nobody would protect Rosie Mendez better than Clint would. Clint felt guilty over her brother's death and would do anything to make sure she was not harmed.

Nobody had felt guilty about Jocelyn Gerber. They'd all just been suspicious of her—no one more than Landon. So he'd assigned Landon to protect her because he'd known the former vice cop would find out the truth about her.

He hadn't realized that truth might have Landon falling for her. And it certainly sounded like he had—at least literally—when he'd fallen off the parking structure to save her.

Was he falling for her emotionally, as well?

"I'm sorry," Parker said. "I shouldn't have assigned you to protect her."

"What?" Landon asked, and he sounded befuddled.

Was he really okay?

"I know you didn't want this assignment," Parker reminded him. "So I'll take you off now. I'll have one of Logan's team protect her." That would be for the best—for all of them.

Parker couldn't risk losing one of his team. And he was already worried that Clint might not survive his assignment. He couldn't lose Landon, too.

Chapter Thirteen

Landon silently cursed himself for putting Parker's call on speaker. Sitting in the passenger's seat next to him, she'd heard every word his boss had said. And she'd tensed more and more. It had been a while since he'd ended the call, but she had yet to say anything.

Making sure that the security guard was okay and giving Dubridge the report at the scene had taken so long that they'd decided to talk to the chief another day. Jocelyn had asked that he bring her home instead—to check on the cat and make sure she still had enough food and water in the laundry room.

Whoever Spencer Dubridge had recommended to repair the house must have had an opening because the windows had been replaced.

Jocelyn breathed a sigh of relief. "We can stay here now."

She obviously didn't want to go back to that hotel with him. Did she regret what had happened between them? He wished he did, but he couldn't regret what had probably been the most powerful sexual experience of his life.

The way she'd fit him…the way she'd felt…and the pleasure she'd brought him.

He'd never known feelings like that before. But it didn't matter. He'd crossed a line with a client—a line that he never should have even gotten close to.

"Why didn't you let Parker remove you from this assignment?" she asked. "It's obviously what you want."

"It's true that I didn't want this assignment in the beginning," he said. "I wasn't a fan of yours."

"You thought I was working for Luther."

"I was wrong," he said. "About that, about you…" So very wrong. It might have been easier had he been right—then he wouldn't have succumbed to his attraction to her. He would have been able to resist her beauty, her sexiness.

But knowing her reasons for working so hard, for wanting justice so badly, had made her even more attractive to him—so attractive that she had become irresistible. He wanted her now.

He sighed. "Yeah, I should have had Parker reassign me."

"Dubridge would probably prefer you protecting him than Keeli Abbott."

"Keeli would prefer that more," he said. If anyone deserved to be reassigned, it was the blonde bodyguard. Her principal gave her nothing but disrespect and grief.

But Keeli was the strongest woman he knew; she could take it. Well, she was the strongest woman he'd known until he'd gotten to know Jocelyn Gerber. She seemed more upset about the conversation she'd overheard than having to jump off a parking structure earlier or getting shot at.

"Would she want to protect me?" Jocelyn asked. "Or, like everyone else, does she think I purposely failed to get those previous indictments against Luther?"

He flinched as he remembered previous conversations with Keeli about this particular assistant district attorney.

"So she's not a fan of mine either," Jocelyn murmured, and she hurried into the kitchen, as if trying to get away from him. But then she continued to the laundry room, opening the door to a mewling cat. Behind her, the water bowl and food dish were full. He remembered that, shortly after they'd left her house the night of the shooting, Jocelyn had called someone to check on her pet. Had it been a neighbor or that office intern?

Lady wound around her legs, purring rumbling from her furry body. Jocelyn bent over and wrapped her arms around the feline. "I'm staying here," she said. "The house is secure—especially with my alarm. And the glass I had them install is bulletproof. It's safer than the hotel."

She was right. It was.

"So you don't need to stay," she told him.

She really wanted to get rid of him. Because of what had happened between them? Or because of the conversation she'd overheard?

"I'm staying," he said. "I am your bodyguard." He crouched down, like she was, beside the cat, and he slid his fingers under Jocelyn's chin, tipping her face up so she had to meet his gaze. "And I am a fan now."

Her face flushed with color, and her eyes brightened. But then she blinked away the moisture in them. "Why?"

"Because you're tough," he said.

Her breath shuddered out. "I'm not sure about that…" she said. "Maybe I'm just hard to kill."

He hoped like hell that that was the case because he didn't want her to die.

"Or maybe you're just a really good bodyguard."

He chuckled. "I'd go with your being hard to kill." Because he hadn't been doing his job—at least, not as well as he usually did. And he was about to fail again and give in to the temptation to kiss her.

But then her phone rang, making the purse dangling over her shoulder vibrate. She pulled out the cell and accepted the call. But she didn't put it on speaker.

Landon had no idea who'd called her and why all the color suddenly drained from her face. "What's wrong?" he asked, fear gripping him because he could see fear on her face, as well. "What's happened?"

She shook her head, as if unable to speak. As if whatever she'd heard was too terrible to repeat. Finally she murmured, "The witness. It was about the witness…"

Had something happened to her? To them?

Now Landon wasn't sure he wanted to know what that call had been about—because he was worried that he might have just lost his best friend.

EVEN AS UPSET as Jocelyn was, she was still aware of Landon, still attracted to him. She even felt bad that she'd worried him. But she didn't want to talk about that call she'd taken—not yet. She needed confirmation before she could believe it.

But she felt a sick churning in her stomach that it was true. So she didn't even notice the trip from River City to the Payne Protection Agency safe house near the shoreline of Lake Michigan. Landon didn't press her for information during the drive. He'd seemed more focused on the rearview mirror, and making sure they weren't followed, than on her—except for a few worried glances he'd cast across the console at her.

She'd wanted to reassure him. He was probably thinking the worst. And for him, this wasn't the worst. For her, though…

Landon made one last turn off the street, through the opening door of a garage on the main level of a townhouse condo. Once the door closed behind them, he opened his and hurried around to her side of the SUV. But she'd already opened her door before he could. She doubted she was in any danger in the garage.

No. The danger was upstairs, where Landon led her to meet with the witness. He released an audible breath, obviously relieved that his friend and Rosie Mendez appeared unharmed. But something was going on between them.

The minute Rosie saw Jocelyn, she turned toward Clint and implored him, "Please, can you give us a minute alone?"

Clint glanced over at Jocelyn, and his green eyes were narrowed with suspicion.

And that sick feeling roiled in her stomach. Apparently everybody had suspected that she worked for Luther. The thought made her physically ill.

Clint shook his head. "That's not possible."

"I'm not leaving either," Landon said.

Jocelyn grimaced. She would have preferred to speak privately with Rosie; she figured it might be her only way to get through to the frightened young woman.

"Bodyguards don't understand that sometimes we need to be alone," she said with a pointed look at Landon, hoping he'd take the hint.

She probably should have told him about the call. But she'd been too focused on the argument she needed to present to Rosie to talk at all. She focused on the woman now, and Rosie shivered. She knew that Jocelyn knew. So she dropped all pretenses.

"What the hell were you thinking?" Jocelyn asked. But she directed the question at Clint Quarters. "Why would you bring her to the jail?" She didn't wait for his response, though, before she turned on Rosie. "And what the hell were you thinking? You might have jeopardized the whole case!"

"What?" Landon asked, his dark eyes wide with shock.

She should have clued him in after she'd taken the call. But she did so now. "She went to see Luther Mills." She pointed a shaking finger at Clint. "And he brought her!"

Landon turned to Clint, his brow furrowed with confusion. "What was the deal? Did you have her wear a wire?"

"Like Luther Mills would have said anything incriminating!" Jocelyn exclaimed. But then she turned back to Rosie and asked, "Did he?"

Rosie shook her head.

Jocelyn felt the case slipping away from her, felt Luther slipping away from justice once again. "His lawyer could have a field day with this—with you—when he cross-examines you on the witness stand."

"He won't," Rosie told her.

"The man is a shark," Jocelyn said. "Of course he will. He's going to tear you apart."

And Clint tensed, his hands curling into fists. Now he chose to act protectively? What the hell had he been thinking to let the witness anywhere near Luther Mills?

"No, he won't," Rosie said, "because I have no intention of testifying."

"What!" Clint beat Jocelyn to the exclamation.

And that was why Jocelyn hadn't spoken during the trip to the safe house; that was the fear she'd had. "That's why you shouldn't have brought her there. He intimidated her into changing her mind."

Landon, predictably, came to the defense of his best friend, turning on Jocelyn to ask, "You don't think all the attempts on her life were intimidation enough?"

Clint ignored his friend, though, and spoke only to Rosie, his voice soft. "I promised I would keep you safe."

"There's no need," she told him. "I'm safe now."

Jocelyn narrowed her eyes and studied the two of them, how intensely they were looking at each other. Had Rosie gone to see Luther for her sake or for Clint's?

Clint snorted. "You really believe that Luther Mills will keep his word to you? That he won't have you killed the minute you walk out of here with no protection?"

"Quarters is right," Jocelyn said. "There is no way that Luther Mills will let you stay alive—not when you are the greatest threat to his freedom. You have to testify."

"You should be glad that I changed my mind," Rosie said.

Confusion furrowed Jocelyn's brow and she incredulously asked, "Why the hell would I be happy?"

"Because now you're safe, too," Rosie told her, as if she'd done her a favor. "He won't have any reason to threaten you or the others if there's not enough evidence to bring him to trial."

Horrified, Jocelyn could only gasp. "There's still enough evidence." And now the person who'd collected it was in even more danger than she'd previously been. She glanced at Landon. "The CSI tech—Wendy."

"Wendy Thompson," Landon said. "Hart Fisher is protecting her."

"She hasn't changed her mind about testifying, has she?" Had Luther gotten to her like he must have gotten to Rosie? Had she been nearly killed?

Jocelyn silently cursed the incident in the parking garage. If they hadn't been nearly run over, they would have talked to Wendy, and Jocelyn would know how badly her case against Luther was falling apart.

Landon shrugged.

"We need to talk to her," Jocelyn said, and she turned toward the stairs they'd come up from the garage. "We need to make sure Mills hasn't gotten to her like he has this witness." She suspected now that it was disgust churning in her stomach. She couldn't believe how many people would help a monster like Luther elude justice. She turned back toward Rosie Mendez and asked, "What did he give you? Money? What did it take for you to sell out? To sell the justice your brother deserves?"

Rosie flinched. "You don't know my brother," she said. "Don't act like you know what he deserves or wanted."

She'd known other victims. She could have told

Rosie about them—about her grandparents. But she was more worried about Wendy Thompson right now, so she turned on her heel and headed toward the stairs leading down to the garage.

Before following her down, Landon turned back toward his friend and murmured, "What the hell...?"

Jocelyn was glad he sounded as disgusted as she was. But when he joined her in the SUV, he defended his friend. "I don't think Clint knew that she'd changed her—"

"He shouldn't have brought her to the jail," Jocelyn said.

"I brought you there," Landon said.

"I am not the witness," she said. "And I didn't see Luther. She shouldn't have either. What the hell was he thinking? Is he working for him?"

Landon's hands tightened around the steering wheel until his knuckles turned white. "Absolutely not. Clint wants justice for Javier as much as you do."

"And apparently we both want that more than his own sister does."

"I think Rosie wants justice," Landon said. "I think she's just scared. She's nearly been killed so many times."

"So has Clint," Jocelyn murmured. So he probably wasn't working for Luther.

"That's his job," Landon said. "My job. That's what bodyguards do—risk our lives to protect our clients."

Jocelyn remembered the look that had passed between Clint and Rosie—an intimate look. They were more than bodyguard and client. Rosie hadn't seemed worried about her own safety before. And maybe she wasn't worried about herself now either.

Maybe she was worried about Clint instead.

Remembering the fall from that parking-garage half wall, remembering how hard Landon's body had struck the roof of that SUV… Jocelyn shuddered.

And she wished that Landon would have let his boss remove him from this assignment. She wished that he wasn't going to keep risking his life for hers. And she suspected that, just like Rosie Mendez, she was getting too attached to her bodyguard.

But unlike Clint Quarters, Landon wasn't in love with her. He was just doing his job. Jocelyn had to remind herself of that—so that she didn't fall for him like Rosie had clearly fallen for Clint.

DESPITE ALL THE muscle he'd built up weight lifting in the jailhouse gym, Luther felt a hundred pounds lighter. He'd struck a deal with Rosie Mendez—a deal he had no intention of keeping. But that didn't matter.

She wasn't testifying against him either way. And now that he could focus on that annoying little evidence tech, he wouldn't have to worry about her much longer either.

He snickered, then pulled his cell phone from his pocket. He punched in the number that had dialed him last. The guy thought he'd taken out Jocelyn Gerber. But he'd learned that those damn Payne Protection bodyguards were good at their jobs—too damn good.

"Hello?" the man tentatively answered.

"Hey," Luther said. "I am no longer concerned about

that little problem you've been trying to take care of for me."

"You're not?" the man asked with obvious surprise.

Luther chuckled again. "No. I have no worries anymore. And I really want to see Jocelyn Gerber's gorgeous face when she loses. Again…"

Maybe he would offer to take her out for drinks afterward—to console her on yet another loss to him. After all the weeks he'd spent in jail with only ugly mugs around him, he'd enjoy looking at her.

Hell, he would enjoy doing a lot more than just looking.

"It's in my best interest to continue with the original plan," the man cryptically replied.

"Then you're the one with another loss on your record," Luther pointed out.

"I'd rather have the loss than a personal conviction."

Oh. He thought Jocelyn was onto him. And maybe she was. She was pretty smart.

He sighed. "Then do what you have to do…" But he felt a flash of disappointment as he clicked off the cell. It was too bad—really. She was so hot.

But soon she would be so dead.

Chapter Fourteen

"I want you to fire the Payne Protection Agency!" Jocelyn Gerber demanded, her heels clicking against the
tile floor as she paced the chief's office.

Woodrow's head pounded more with each click, but
she seemed too wound up to slow down now. On the
other side of the windows, Landon Myers watched her
from the detectives' bullpen. He was probably getting
dizzy from following her pace.

"I looked into your concerns that one of them could
be working for Luther Mills," Woodrow told her. "And
I can assure you that's not the case." Even though he
trusted his stepson Parker's judgment, he'd wanted to
make sure he hadn't made the mistake the ADA had
claimed he had in hiring Parker's franchise of the Payne
Protection Agency.

She stopped to cast him a speculative glance. Obviously she didn't believe he'd done a thorough investigation, for she just shrugged. "I'm less concerned about
one of them working for Luther," she begrudgingly admitted, "than I am that none of them is working for me."

He glanced through those windows at Landon again.

The man had not taken his attention from her for a second even though Spencer Dubridge was talking at him.

"I think you're wrong about that, Ms. Gerber," he said. "Myers is obviously taking his job very seriously. I've heard he's saved your life a few times now."

Her pale skin flushed, and she glanced down. "I'm not talking about Landon."

It was clear that she didn't want to. Woodrow narrowed his eyes and studied her. Did she want the Payne Protection Agency fired for another—more personal—reason? Was she falling for her bodyguard?

"I'm talking about Clint Quarters," she said.

He groaned. He'd been informed about the jailhouse visit and the witness changing her mind about testifying. "I understand."

"You know?"

He nodded.

"What are you going to do about it?"

He'd had an idea how to keep the young woman safe. But, like Jocelyn, Rosie Mendez wanted nothing to do with the Payne Protection Agency anymore. And Woodrow didn't trust any of his officers to keep her safe.

He wasn't sure who he could trust within his own damn department. And that was infuriating.

"Don't worry about the witness," he said. "She could still change her mind." If she wasn't already dead. "And you have all the evidence the CSI collected."

She drew in a deep breath before shakily releasing it. "I hope I do."

"Of course you do," he assured her.

"I thought I had evidence for prior cases, but when I tried to present it to a grand jury, it was gone."

"That wasn't the case this time," he reminded her. "Wendy Thompson provided you with the evidence then and will again for the trial."

"Wendy will," Jocelyn agreed. "But what about the CSIs in those other cases? Why didn't they produce the evidence I was told we had?"

He gasped. "I'll look into that."

"I need Wendy," Jocelyn said. "You need to make sure she stays safe."

"That's why I can't fire the Payne Protection Agency," he told her. "I need them."

She glanced through that glass at her bodyguard and her usually icy blue eyes seemed to thaw a bit. And he wondered if she'd had another reason for wanting him to fire the bodyguards. If maybe she'd begun to care about Landon Myers.

"I GET WHY you're mad," Landon told Jocelyn. They'd returned to her office after her meeting with the chief.

She glanced up from her desk and studied him through narrowed eyes.

And he added, "I just don't get why you're mad at me."

She sighed, but it sounded ragged with frustration.

"I agree with you," he reminded her. "Clint shouldn't have brought Rosie Mendez anywhere near Luther Mills."

"Are you sure he's trustworthy?" Jocelyn asked.

"I live with the man," Landon said. "I'd know if he was on the take."

And now he understood why she was studying him

so intently. He groaned. "You're not back to thinking I'm working for Luther, too, are you?"

She closed her eyes, as if she couldn't even bear to look at him anymore.

"What the hell is wrong with us?" Landon murmured. "Why can't we trust each other?"

Jocelyn opened her eyes and stared at him. But this time there was no suspicion, just confusion. "I don't know," she murmured. "Maybe we've both seen too much."

He moved away from the door to come around her desk and lean against the front of it. His thigh brushed across her arm, and they both tensed. "Maybe we're both worried about getting hurt."

"We have been hurt," she said. "You hurled us onto the roof of a car the level below us in the parking garage."

He stretched and flinched at the tense muscles in his lower back. "Yeah…but we both know that's not what I'm talking about…"

She jumped up from her chair then, as if trying to get away from him. But before she could move away, he caught her arm and held on to her.

"Let me go," she told him.

But he shook his head. He didn't want to let her go. He wanted to hold on to her. So he closed his arms around her and brought her tense body against his.

She felt so good. Smelled so good, too…like something cool and sharp. Just like she was—cool and sharp.

"Landon…" she murmured, and her gaze moved to his mouth. She stared it at as intently as she'd studied him moments ago. But there was no suspicion now—

just a longing that he shared, that had his guts twisting into knots. He wanted her so damn badly.

"Let's go back to your house," he said.

She shook her head. "We can't."

"The workday's over," he said. "Pretty much everybody has left already…" So maybe he could take her here—on her desk. He needed her so intensely. He slid his hand down her back to her waist, then the curve of her hips, which were pressed against his.

Did she feel how she affected him?

She must have because her eyes dilated, the pupils swallowing all but a pale blue circle of her irises. "This is a bad idea," she said even as she leaned into him, arching her hips against his erection.

He groaned and nodded. "A very, very bad idea." But even as he said it, he lowered his mouth to hers.

While she smelled cool and sharp, she tasted so sweet. And she was hot, her body burning his everywhere they touched. He wanted to touch her all over, wanted nothing between them but their skin.

She pulled back, and he reached for the button of her suit jacket. But she caught his fingers in her hand. Panting for breath, she shook her head. "We can't…"

He glanced around and noticed a few shadows outside the office. Probably the backup bodyguards. But he needed to be certain. "Let's go back to your place, then," he said. "You've done all you can for the day."

But she shook her head again. "We really can't do this," she said, but she sounded conflicted and looked it, too, as her pulse pounded and she leaned against him yet. "We can't get distracted from what's important."

At the moment, he couldn't remember what was important. He couldn't think beyond the insistent throbbing in his groin. He wanted her so much.

"Like Clint and Rosie got distracted," she said. "They forgot how dangerous Luther is, how important it is to get him off the streets for good."

Landon released a shaky breath of resignation. "You're right…" He suspected the same thing with his friend and the eyewitness. They'd gotten personally involved. And those kinds of emotional attachments just caused problems.

In their business, it was better to stay single—easier to stay focused. But Jocelyn didn't step back, didn't move away from him.

He groaned again.

She rose up on tiptoe and pressed her mouth against his again. He kissed her back with all the passion burning inside him. But when he heard the door creak open behind him, with his back to it, he realized how damn right he'd been. How dangerous it was to get distracted.

How they might both wind up dead because he'd forgotten what mattered most was keeping Jocelyn safe.

HEAT RUSHED TO Jocelyn's face, and not just from passion. She was embarrassed to look up and find Dale Grohms standing in her doorway, though she could barely see him around Landon's broad shoulder. When that door had opened, he'd made certain that he stood entirely between her and whoever was coming into the office.

She wanted to take his protection personally, to believe that he really cared about her, but she knew he was just doing his job. Which was what she should have been doing.

"Sorry," her coworker said, although he sounded anything but. "Didn't mean to interrupt."

Jocelyn doubted that and opened her mouth to tell him as much.

But he continued, "Just figured you'd want to know about the latest attempt on the life of your witness."

She gasped. Rosie Mendez should have known better than to trust Luther Mills. If she'd told him during her jailhouse visit with him that she didn't intend to testify, he either hadn't believed her or had decided to take no chances that she might change her mind.

"Is she all right?" she and Landon asked together.

Grohms looked at Landon instead of her, and he grinned. "Figured you would have heard this before I did. You're the one who works for the Payne Protection Agency. Don't you guys talk to each other?"

Landon glared at him, and his hands clenched into fists. Jocelyn grabbed his arm and held him back in case he intended to leap over the desk and attack Dale. She kind of felt like throttling him herself, though.

"Is she all right?" Jocelyn asked.

He nodded. "Yeah, yeah. Her bodyguard saved her."

"Is he all right?" Landon asked, his deep voice gruff. It clearly galled him to have to ask Grohms.

Dale shrugged. "I don't know. The guy who tried killing her is dead, though. Some rookie cop who had originally been assigned to protect her before the chief learned about the threats. Guess the chief was smart for hiring the Payne Protection Agency." He turned to head back out the door.

"Wait!" She called him back. "How do you know all of this, Dale?"

"What?" he asked. "About the shooting at the cemetery? That's all over the news."

"About the Payne Protection Agency, too," she prodded. "How do you know the chief hired them?"

"Word gets around," Dale said. "We've all heard that someone within the police department is working for Luther. Guess we know who that is now. Only thing yet to learn is who within our office is working for Luther." He stared at her now, his brows arched as if he waited for her to confess.

And that sick feeling churned in her stomach again. All of Landon's coworkers seemed to suspect her. Now, apparently, so did all of her own.

Before she could say anything in her own defense, he shrugged, turned and walked back out of her office.

Landon cursed, then murmured, "I really hope he's the leak."

She smiled. "I wish, but I doubt it." She'd read the contents of the folder the DA had had the intern bring to her. Nothing incriminating had been found out about Dale Grohms. Mike Forbes was the one with the gambling debts. And the person with the driving-under-the-influence charge was a young ADA named Eddie Garza.

"And I doubt some rookie is the leak within the police department," Landon said. "It has to be someone higher up than that." His brow furrowed. "A detective…"

Did he suspect Spencer Dubridge?

"Or a CSI," she reminded him.

He drew his cell phone from his pocket and punched in a number. Within seconds, Parker's voice emanated from the speaker. "You okay?" he anxiously asked Landon.

"We're fine," Landon replied. "How about Clint and Rosie?"

"You know about the attempt on Rosie Mendez at the cemetery?" Parker asked.

She must have been at her brother's grave site. Maybe Jocelyn had gotten through to her during their meeting at the safe house.

"Clint saved her," Parker said. "She's fine."

"And Clint?" Landon asked, his voice gruff with what was obviously fear for his friend.

"He's fine, too," Parker assured him.

"Where are they?" Jocelyn asked. She needed to talk to Rosie now—while the attempt was fresh in her mind, while she had to know that the only way to be safe from Luther was to put him away for life.

Parker paused for a long moment.

And Jocelyn groaned. "You don't know, do you?"

"No," Parker said.

"Damn it!" she cursed. How the hell was she supposed to try this case without the eyewitness?

"It's good I don't know where she is," Parker assured her. "The fewer people who know, the safer she'll be. But she will come back for the trial, though. She is determined to testify."

Jocelyn's breath escaped her lungs in a ragged sigh. "Oh, thank God."

"Don't be so happy," Parker cautioned her.

And she felt a flash of guilt. She shouldn't have been

happy that the young woman must have been scared into testifying.

"Why not?" Landon asked the question.

"Mills will be even more dangerous now," Parker said. "Since he won't be able to get to the witness, he'll try extra hard to take out everyone else associated with his trial."

"Did you warn Hart and Tyce?" Landon asked.

"Yeah," Parker said. "But you two need to be careful, too. There is still a leak within the district attorney's office that we need to find ASAP."

Landon picked up that folder from her desk. "We're working on it," he assured his boss.

Working…

That was what they should have been doing. Not kissing.

Landon clicked off his cell and opened his mouth to say something. But Jocelyn pressed her fingers to his lips. "I know," she assured him.

What had happened between them could not happen again. Their lives depended on it. They needed to stay focused to stay alive.

Chapter Fifteen

Being with her 24/7 and not touching her, not kissing her…

Now Landon knew what torture felt like. He wanted Jocelyn badly. But he wanted to keep her safe even more. There was no doubt that the danger had been heightened since Rosie and Clint had disappeared. More attempts had been made on the life of the evidence tech. Hart had saved Wendy from bombs and shooting attempts. Tyce had had his hands full with the judge's daughter, too.

Only Dubridge and Keeli knew what the hell was going on between the two of them. Landon didn't want to know. His only concern was keeping Jocelyn safe.

He wanted Jocelyn to disappear, too. But she insisted on working her other cases while following up on those leads on her coworkers. Mike Forbes currently occupied the chair in front of her desk while Landon stood behind her desk, next to her chair, to protect her—and drive himself out of his mind with her closeness.

He didn't really expect anyone to try anything in her office. But with the way Jocelyn interrogated suspects, she might push them too far, might push them into snapping.

"Mike, I know about your gambling problem," she said.

The older man cursed her. "That's none of your damn business, Jocelyn!"

"Our boss made it my business," she said. "She gave me a folder of information she compiled on all of us."

"Why?" he asked, his blue eyes narrowed.

"Because she wants me to find out who the leak in our office is."

He snorted. "She's not going to find the real leak that way."

Jocelyn flinched. "It's not me."

He snorted again. "You're the one with the fancy house and car. Not me."

"No," she agreed. "You lost your house to your gambling debts."

"Do you think that would have happened if I was working for Luther?" he asked. "Don't you think he would have paid those off for me?" He jumped up from the chair.

And Landon stepped forward, making certain he didn't reach across Jocelyn's desk.

Mike glanced at him. "You were a cop," he said. "You must know she's the best suspect to be working for Mills."

"I thought she was," Landon admitted. "But she's not."

"I couldn't afford her place on the same damn salary she makes."

"Actually, Mike, you make more than I do," she informed him. "Seniority and all."

He glared at her. "If seniority mattered at all around here, I would have that case—not you!"

"Luther can't tempt me with money," she said. "My family has more than he does."

Instead of mollifying Mike, her words seemed to enrage her coworker. He stalked out of her office and slammed the door behind himself.

She flinched again and uttered a shaky sigh. "Well, this is fun."

"You should tell your boss you don't want to do this," Landon said.

"She's busy having a baby," Jocelyn reminded him. And she glanced down at her phone. Amber Talsma-Kozminski was at the hospital right now, and Jocelyn was obviously concerned about her.

"We can go see her," Landon suggested because he saw that concern.

She nodded. "We have one more meeting, though."

Her door rattled with a soft knock.

"Come in," she called out to a young man. "This is Eddie Garza," she murmured to Landon as the dark-haired man entered the office. He didn't look much older than the paralegal who'd brought her that folder. How was he already a lawyer? Already an ADA?

"You wanted to see me?" he asked. And he looked nervous. Way too nervous.

Of course, maybe he'd seen Mike Forbes leave. And he didn't want to leave that same way—embarrassed and furious. This man was younger and bigger than

Mike Forbes. So Landon stepped even closer to Jocelyn's chair. He had to keep her safe.

He had to keep his sanity, too, though, and standing this close, spending this much time with her, was sorely testing it.

"I'm sure you heard all the rumors going around the office," she began.

And the man glanced at Landon.

What were the rumors about him? That he was her bodyguard? Or that he was more than that? He wished he was more than that, but it was as if that one encounter had never happened, as if he'd just dreamed that he'd made love with her. It must have been a dream because surely nothing could have been as powerful as he'd imagined that was.

"Someone within our office is working for Luther Mills," she clarified.

The young man gasped. "You really believe that?"

"I don't want to," she said. "I hope that the rumor is wrong. But the DA wants me to look into it."

The young man tensed. "So you're looking into me?"

She nodded.

"You know about the under-the-influence charge?"

She nodded again.

His face flushed with embarrassment. "It wasn't alcohol or drugs—at least, not street drugs." He shuddered. "I would *never*." His voice shook like his body.

And Jocelyn tilted her head. "Why not?"

Eddie glanced at him again. "I had a brother who got hooked on them."

Had...

Jocelyn must have picked up on the past tense because she murmured, "I'm sorry."

He jerked his head in a nod. "That's why I would never work for Luther. I blame him and…"

"Who?" Jocelyn asked when he trailed off.

He glanced at Landon again, and he looked even more nervous than he'd been when he walked in. "Uh, I don't want to say."

"In front of me?" Landon asked. He'd never seen the kid before.

Jocelyn glanced up at him now. "Would you mind stepping outside for a moment?"

"Yes," Landon replied. "I'm not leaving you alone—"

"You'll be right outside the door," she said.

But it wasn't close enough—if Eddie Garza had a weapon. Hell, he was big enough that he wouldn't need a weapon. He could kill her with his bare hands.

"Please," she implored him.

Now he knew how Rosie had gotten Clint to take her to the jail. She'd asked. And Clint hadn't been able to say no even when he should have. Like Clint, Landon couldn't say no, so he walked toward the door.

But he stopped next to Garza's chair and warned him, "Don't try anything."

The guy nodded. Landon wasn't satisfied, but he stepped into the hall and pulled the door closed.

"When's my turn?" Dale Grohms asked with a grin, pointing toward Jocelyn's office.

"Your turn?"

"For the hot lights," he said with a chuckle. "For the interrogation."

"You sound almost eager," he said.

The guy shrugged. "I've got nothing to hide." And because that appeared to be the case, he wasn't on the list. But Landon was worried that something had been missed. He looked through the window in Jocelyn's door and shook his head. "Too bad Eddie can't say the same."

"What do you mean?" Landon asked.

Dale sighed. "I'm not sure why the boss hired that kid. He was in trouble—big trouble."

"The under-the-influence charge?" Landon asked. It couldn't have been too severe because he'd only been given community service.

Dale shook his head. "Guess it was on his juvie record. Must have been sealed."

Landon swallowed a curse. They hadn't thought to look for sealed records. "Sounds like we need to dig a little deeper," he agreed. But he was looking at Dale—not Garza.

Grohms just laughed as he walked away.

Jocelyn's door opened, and Garza stepped out. He didn't look at Landon as he passed him. And Jocelyn didn't look at him when he stepped back into her office.

"What?" he asked. "What did he say?"

She shook her head. "He explained that it was Adderall. Not his prescription, though. He was taking it, so he could stay up all night studying. He graduated high school and college early. Taking it at all, but especially driving under the influence of it, was dangerous and stupid, and he knows it."

So did he really have a juvie record?

Landon didn't know what to believe. But he suspected Jocelyn was holding something back. What?

She stood up and reached for her briefcase. "I would like to see Amber now."

He wasn't sure if that was because she wanted to make sure her boss was all right or if she wanted to talk to her about whatever she'd learned. Clearly she didn't want to talk to him about it.

JOCELYN COULDN'T TELL Landon what Garza had told her. She didn't want to know if he'd already known and kept it from her. She didn't want to know if he'd betrayed her. But she had to tell someone.

But once she stepped into her boss's hospital room, she knew Amber was not the person she needed to talk to about that. Her boss looked exhausted. She was so pale with machines hooked to her.

"Are you okay?" she asked, concern gripping her.

"Yes," Amber replied, but her voice was faint with exhaustion.

Since hearing Amber had gone into labor, Jocelyn had been worried. Her boss had had so many difficulties with this pregnancy.

And now...

Jocelyn shuddered. Why would anyone put themselves through this? Through childbirth? She was glad that she'd decided long ago children and marriage were not for her. She didn't want any emotional complications—like Landon.

He stood so close to her that she could feel the heat of his body. He always stood so close to her that her heart pounded and her skin tingled. Sure, it was his job to protect. But she wondered if he was just trying to drive her out of her mind.

He was succeeding.

"Hey, there," a deep voice said as another man walked into the room. He carried something in a blanket. "Look who I found."

With his long dark blond hair and green eyes, the man looked like the one who'd been in the parking garage that day. But he wasn't. He chuckled when he saw Landon, though, and asked, "Any more falls?" So he must have heard about it from his brother. He settled onto the bed next to his wife.

She reached for the blanket with a trembling hand. "She's sleeping."

Milek Kozminski leaned down and kissed his wife's pale cheek. "You should be sleeping, too." He cast a pointed glance at Jocelyn.

"I'm sorry," she murmured. "I shouldn't have visited."

"No," he said. "She wouldn't have slept until she saw our little princess again anyways."

Amber smiled. "You know me so well."

Milek settled his head against hers. "Yes, I do."

And Jocelyn felt a twinge in her heart, one of longing for that kind of love. But of course, she didn't really want that.

Amber stared down at the bundle in the blanket, and the expression on her face caused another twinge in Jocelyn's heart. She'd never seen such a look.

"I want to hold her," Amber said. "But I'm so weak."

Milek shook his head. "No. No, you're not." But he helped as she held her baby, wrapping his arms around them both.

"We—we should go," Jocelyn stammered, feeling

like a fool for having intruded on such a private moment. She backed toward the door and stumbled against Landon.

"Don't you want to hold her?" Amber asked.

This was another reason Jocelyn was glad that her old friendships had faded away. Everybody she'd grown up with was married with children now. That was probably why her parents kept putting so much pressure on her to do the same. They didn't understand and neither had her old friends. When she occasionally ran into them, they tried to hand off their babies or kids to her—like she was dying to hold a child.

She would really rather not. But this was her boss. And she didn't want to seem uninterested in what clearly mattered so much to her mentor. So she stepped forward.

"Sit down," Milek told her, pointing toward the chair next to the bed.

Jocelyn sat.

Milek laughed. "You don't have to look so terrified. She won't bite. She doesn't have any teeth yet."

"I—I don't want to drop her, though," she said, then forced a smile and added, "Congratulations on your daughter."

"Yeah, you can order the pink balloons for the office," Amber said. "But wait a few months. I don't intend to rush right back."

That was good—because she appeared to need a while to recuperate.

"Hold your arms like I have mine," Milek directed her.

When she imitated him, he settled the infant against

her. The baby shifted, and Jocelyn tensed and closed her eyes. The child would probably start screaming now. But she emitted a tiny sigh and settled against Jocelyn.

And another twinge struck her heart. She was just happy for her boss, though, happy that Amber had figured out a way to have it all—the husband, the career, the kids.

Jocelyn didn't want to try to juggle as many things as her boss did.

"What are you naming her?" Landon asked the question. Once again, he was too close to Jocelyn, but he seemed more focused on the baby than he was on her. "Another Penny?"

"Another Penny?" Jocelyn repeated.

"Everybody likes to name their girl babies after Penny Payne," Milek explained.

"The chief's wife?" Jocelyn asked.

"You haven't met her," Landon said with certainty. "You would understand if you'd met her."

Jocelyn shrugged, and the baby shifted again, opened one eye and peered up at her. She braced herself, waiting for the scream. But the infant only stared at her. "She can't see yet, right?" she asked.

She didn't know much about babies. And she didn't really care to learn.

"She's not blind," Milek said. "But she can't see very far away yet. She can see you, though."

"Then why isn't she crying?" Jocelyn asked.

And the men laughed at her.

Amber smiled, though. "She recognizes her namesake."

"What?" She couldn't have heard correctly.

"Jocelyn Gerber, meet Jocelyn Talsma-Kozminski."

She stared at her boss. "I—I don't understand…" They weren't friends. She only worked for her, but since they both worked hard, they had spent a lot of time together. Amber knew things about her, about her past, that few other people besides her parents and Landon knew.

"She's tough and determined," Amber said. "So she reminded me of you."

Jocelyn stared down at the baby now, but she couldn't see for the tears suddenly blurring her vision. "I—I don't know what to say…"

She couldn't remember the last time she'd been so overwhelmed. Then she glanced at Landon, and she remembered—with him, in his arms.

And she felt another twinge in her heart. But it was fear. After learning what she had from Garza, she was afraid that she'd made a mistake—that she shouldn't have begun to trust Landon Myers.

And she definitely shouldn't have started falling for him. But she was afraid that she had.

SHE WAS TOO close to learning the truth. He had to get rid of her. Now.

The hospital parking garage was set up like the one between the courthouse and the district attorney's office building. If he tried running them over, they could escape over one of those half walls. And since they'd parked only one level up, they wouldn't be hurt any worse than they'd been from their previous fall.

So he wasn't going to try to run them down. He was going to shoot them. He pulled his gun from the pocket of his trench coat. It was the same one he'd used to shoot up her house—the same one he'd taken from evidence a while ago. He'd saved Luther from an indictment then.

He would have saved him this time—if everyone hadn't been so damn careful about this case. His boss and Jocelyn and the evidence tech.

They'd made it impossible for him to get to the evidence. And Landon Myers was trying to make it impossible for him to get to Jocelyn now. He was always around, and now he had that backup team.

Or he thought he did.

They drank coffee. So he'd made sure to spike the pot at the office. While they'd followed Landon and Jocelyn to the hospital, they had since fallen asleep—their heads against the side windows of their Payne Protection Agency SUV. He snickered. But he wasn't sure how long he had before they awakened.

Landon and Jocelyn had to hurry.

What were they doing? What was Jocelyn telling their boss? Had she already begun to suspect him?

Nobody could, or he wouldn't be given the case once she died. And she would die this time along with her damn bodyguard.

Through the open window of his rental vehicle, he heard the click of her heels against the concrete. It could have been another woman wearing stilettos, but he doubted it. There was something distinctive about Jocelyn's walk—a sharpness that reflected her cold personality.

He stared through the new tinted windshield. Luther had referred him to a company that had replaced the glass—one that wouldn't talk to the Payne Protection bodyguards who'd asked if anyone had had to redo a shot-out windshield. They hadn't tracked him down yet.

And they wouldn't.

For soon they would be dead. He waited until they got closer—until Landon noticed his fellow bodyguards slumped in their vehicle. Then he raised his weapon and started firing at him and Jocelyn.

They dropped to the ground, but this time he was certain he hadn't missed. He saw the blood spattered across the concrete. He also saw the doors of the SUV open as the other bodyguards woke up.

And he tore out of the lot before they could catch him.

They would be too groggy to follow him. And too concerned about the wounded. Or the dead…

Chapter Sixteen

Woodrow had already been on the way to the hospital when he got the call that there had been a shooting in the visitors' parking garage. His hand shook as he punched in the contact for his wife. He'd been on his way to meet her there, but a situation in the police lab had prevented him from leaving when he should have.

What if she'd been in the garage at the time? What if she was one of the wounded?

And there were wounded…

He'd seen the blood as he'd passed through the crime scene on his way to the hospital. With his cell pressed to his ear, he headed toward the ER. His stomach flipped when her voice answered, but he realized it was only her voice mail. She hadn't picked up. But his phone buzzed and he glanced down at the text flashing on the screen.

Where are you, darling? I am already cuddling this gorgeous new grandbaby.

He grinned with relief. The child technically wasn't their grandbaby, but that didn't matter to Penny. She'd long ago emotionally adopted the Kozminski children even though everyone had believed their father had killed her husband. Even if he had, Penny wouldn't have cared. She was so forgiving and loving.

She would forgive him for being late because she would understand why. If she'd known about the shooting, she would have been heading where he was, to the ER, to check on the wounded, especially if she knew what he did, that one of those wounded was a Payne Protection bodyguard.

She treated every bodyguard like they were her children. Of course, quite a few of them were. Panic struck Woodrow's heart, making it pound even faster than it had already been. It couldn't be one of his stepsons or stepdaughter, could it? Parker had had a narrow escape from death earlier in the week. And he'd brought in his brothers' teams for backup because of how damn dangerous Luther Mills had become, even more dangerous than they'd thought.

If he'd known how risky this assignment was, Woodrow might not have hired Parker for the job. But then, he hadn't had many options—not with being unable to trust his own damn officers. And now even the lab.

He hurried as he neared the front desk for the ER. He flashed his shield at the security guard who rushed up to meet him. "I'm the chief of police," he said.

It had been odd to say that in the beginning—after so many years of being special agent in charge of a field office of the FBI. But now it felt right.

This was where he belonged. In River City with his wife and his ever-expanding family. And now one of those family members might have been injured, so he had no problem about cutting to the front of the line waiting in the ER. "The people who were wounded in the parking garage," he said. "Where are they?"

"Over here," the security guard said as he pushed open a door marked Employees Only. He led the way down a wide corridor. "A detective's already gone back to take the woman's statement."

So a woman had been attacked but survived. The man could have been referring to Jocelyn Gerber or to Nikki Payne-Ecklund. Nikki might have been working as backup for Landon. If anything had happened to Penny's daughter...

He shuddered and refused to consider it. For one, Nikki was damn tough and had already survived so many close calls that she had to be invincible. When the security guard pulled aside the curtain, he was relieved to see Jocelyn Gerber, with Nikki standing next to her.

They were both all right except for the blood oozing from cuts on Jocelyn's knees. She also had a scrape on her cheek.

"Are you all right?" he asked because she looked so very pale and fragile sitting on the gurney. He'd had his issues with Jocelyn Gerber, but now he felt a deep pull of sympathy and concern for her. While she could be brash and bossy, she was also a damn hard worker and a strong woman. Woodrow had so much respect and appreciation for strong women.

She nodded, and her black hair swung around her face, only slightly tangled from her ordeal. "Yes, but Landon's in surgery," she said, her voice shaking with concern.

"What happened?" He'd heard about the shooting—that it involved the assistant district attorney and her bodyguard—but he didn't know entirely what had happened.

"Landon and I were walking to the SUV when we noticed the backup bodyguards." Her voice caught. "They were slumped against the windows of their SUV. We thought they were dead."

Instinctively, Woodrow reached for Nikki, pulling her into a hug. "Are you all right? What happened?"

Nikki squeezed him before pulling back. Her face was flushed with embarrassment. "Lars and I must have been drugged," she said. "We fell asleep…only waking up when we heard the gunshots."

"Somebody was shooting at us," Jocelyn said.

"Did you see who?" Woodrow asked.

She shook her head. "Landon pushed me down so fast that I didn't even see where the shots were coming from."

Spencer Dubridge stepped behind the curtain with Keeli Abbott at his side. "Landon's out of surgery—"

"How is he?" Jocelyn asked, her blue eyes full of concern.

"The doctor said he'd be fine. The bullet just nicked an artery in his neck—that's why there was so much blood. But they've repaired it. Because he lost so much blood, though, he's not awake yet." Dubridge said the last with recrimination, as if he was angry that Landon was unconscious.

"Give him a minute or two to recover before you hassle him for his statement," Keeli remarked.

He glared at her before realizing everyone was staring at him with the same condemnation she was. "We need to find out who the hell this perp is," he said. "It's gotta be someone in the DA's office."

Nikki nodded. "He's right. It has to be. That's where Lars and I drank the coffee that must have been drugged."

Jocelyn looked even paler than she had moments ago. "You were right," she murmured to the chief.

"I'm sorry," he said. "It doesn't feel good to know you've been working with a traitor."

Now there was a sudden rush of color to her face. She looked around and asked the others, "Can you give me a few minutes alone with the chief?"

Nikki shook her head. "I promised Landon that I wouldn't leave your side," she said. "That's the only way he agreed to be treated."

"I know," Jocelyn said. "But this is private."

Woodrow swallowed a groan. Did she still suspect Landon was working for Luther—even after all the times he'd saved her life?

But he had things he needed to share with her, as well. "It's okay," he told the others. "I have some experience with law enforcement. I think I can protect her for a few minutes."

Dubridge chuckled. "Yeah, well, if you get into any trouble, let us know."

"So you're a smart-ass even to the chief," Keeli muttered as she followed him out of the area.

Nikki hesitated a moment longer. "Are you sure?"

Woodrow nodded. "Yes. Where's your husband? Is he okay?" She was married to Lars Ecklund, the fellow bodyguard she'd mentioned who had also been drugged.

She nodded. "He's in the parking garage, looking for anything Detective Dubridge might have missed."

So nobody trusted his department anymore. But with a rookie cop nearly killing the eyewitness, Woodrow could hardly blame them—especially after what had happened today. Once Nikki left, he turned back to Jocelyn and told her, "You were right."

She tensed. "You know?"

He nodded. "About the CSI, yeah. You were right that it had to be one of them getting rid of evidence."

She gasped. "Not Wendy Thompson."

"No. Terrance Gibbs."

"I thought he was retired," she said.

"Just a short time ago," he said. "But he came back recently to *help* out." He hadn't been trying to help the River City PD, though. He'd been trying to help Luther Mills to get rid of the evidence against him.

Her brow puckered as if she was searching her memory. Then she nodded. "I think he collected some of the evidence that went missing..."

"Well, he won't be a problem anymore," Woodrow assured her. The former CSI had died while he'd been trying to kill Wendy.

"That's good," she said. "Because we have another one."

And this was what she'd wanted privacy to tell him. Dread settled heavily into the pit of his stomach. "What is it?"

"I told you I had concerns about Parker Payne's team of bodyguards..."

He released his groan this time. "How can you—after how many times Landon's risked his life for you?"

"I don't know if he even knows this," she said. "That's why I wanted to tell you first. But then the judge has to hear it, too. He needs to be warned."

"Warned about what?"

"Luther Mills's brother works for the Payne Protection Agency."

Just as Woodrow hadn't been the chief for very long, he hadn't been a resident of River City for long either. He didn't know the history everyone else seemed to know. "I wasn't aware that he had a brother."

"Neither was I," she admitted. "I just learned today."

"Who is it?"

"Tyce Jackson. The man protecting the judge's daughter."

Woodrow sucked in a breath, shocked. He shook his head. "Are you sure that's true? Where did you learn that?"

"From someone within my office," she said.

"Can you trust that person?"

She shook her head. "I can't trust anyone." She looked speculatively at him, as if she was wondering if she could even trust him.

"Then you don't know that's true," he pointed out.

"I doubt this person—another assistant district attorney—would have told me something that could be easily disproved," she said. "It would only make him look guiltier."

Maybe that was all the man had been trying to do—cast guilt onto someone else. But she was right. Woodrow needed to look into it—to hopefully disprove it. Like the other bodyguards, Tyce Jackson had risked his life several times to save the judge's daughter, so Woodrow couldn't believe he was any threat to her.

"I'll find out," he promised, and he pulled back the curtain. He didn't see Nikki or the others. But he doubted Jocelyn, with her scraped knees, was going anywhere. And as she'd said, she didn't trust anyone right now.

So he wasn't worried about her. He was worried about the judge's daughter and just how far reaching Luther Mills's influence was.

Jocelyn had had her doubts about his hiring Parker's team. He hoped she was wrong, though. Or he had put everybody in greater danger—just as she'd feared.

PAIN SHOT THROUGH Landon's neck, blood spurting from the wound. Instinctively, he reached for Jocelyn, pushing her to the ground. But had he been too late? Had she been shot, too?

He reached out, but something tugged on his arm. And he jerked awake. Then he flinched and squinted against the bright lights. "Jocelyn!"

"She's fine," a deep voice assured him. And he turned to find Spencer Dubridge sitting next to his bed. That was not who he'd wanted to see.

As if he'd guessed as much, Dubridge chuckled. "She's talking to the chief in the ER. That's why she's not here."

"In the ER," Landon said. "So she is hurt!"

Spencer shook his head. "Just a little bruised and scraped from you shoving her down."

He flinched again with regret that he'd hurt her.

"You saved her life," Dubridge said. "Did you see who it was? Who was shooting at you?"

He shook his head. "It looked like the car—same make and model—that tried hitting us the other day. But the tinted windshield had been replaced."

Dubridge cursed. "I checked all the glass replacement companies in the area."

Landon shrugged. There were a lot of places that didn't like giving information to cops, even if served with a warrant. He cared less about finding the car than finding the driver. He had a feeling the guy was smart enough to make sure the car couldn't be traced to him anyway.

"What're Jocelyn and the chief talking about?" he asked. And why hadn't she come to see him yet?

"She didn't want us to know," Keeli said, speaking up from where she stood at the door—as if protecting both the detective and him.

Dubridge nodded. "Yeah, she wanted to talk to him in private."

Landon tensed. He didn't like the sound of that. Was she trying again to get the chief to fire the Payne Protection Agency?

Ever since she'd spoken to Garza alone, she'd been acting strangely. He needed to see her—needed to make sure she was all right. He gripped the railings on his bed and sat up.

"What are you doing?" Keeli asked as she stepped toward his bed.

He pushed down one of the railings and tried to swing his legs over the side. But his body felt so damn heavy that he could barely move them.

"You have to take it easy," Keeli said. "You lost a lot of blood."

He lifted his fingers to his neck and felt the bandage covering the wound. "It was nothing…"

"If you hadn't kept your hand on it…" Keeli shuddered. "You were lucky."

He had a feeling that luck was about to change as a strange chill chased down his spine. "You need to check on Jocelyn," he said.

"I need to take your statement," Dubridge told him.

"I gave you my statement," he said, frustration tightening the muscles of his already aching stomach. "I saw nothing more than I did the last time. I don't know who the hell is after Jocelyn."

"Someone in her office," Dubridge said. "That's where Nikki thinks she and Lars were drugged. They were lucky they made it to the parking garage without crashing."

"Lars was driving, and he's a big guy," Keeli said. "So the sleeping aid didn't work as quickly on him as it did on Nikki."

"Another reason petite women should not be bodyguards," Spencer murmured.

Ignoring their bickering, Landon managed to get to his feet. The room tilted for a moment, and spots danced before his eyes. But he powered through—because, like Lars, he was a big guy. Yet it wasn't just his strength driving him. It was his concern for Jocelyn.

And once he got dressed, with Dubridge's help, and made it down to the ER, he found his concern was warranted. She was gone.

JOCELYN KNEW SHE shouldn't have slipped out of the ER without telling anyone. That she shouldn't have gone off alone. But she thought she might be safer alone than with anyone else right now. She did not know whom to trust.

Sure, Landon kept saving her life, but had he known the whole time who was putting her in danger? Was he aware that one of his team members—one of his friends—was Luther Mills's brother? And he hadn't told her?

She wanted to trust him. Most of all, she wanted to make sure he was all right. But Dubridge had assured her that he would be. Still, she felt a sickening lurch in her stomach as she stepped out of the cab onto the sidewalk outside the front entry of the district attorney's office building.

While she wanted to trust Landon, she could not bring herself to trust the others. She didn't know what they knew about Tyce Jackson's relationship to Luther—if they were keeping him apprised of everyone else's whereabouts. So she hadn't told them hers.

It was bad enough that Tyce was protecting the judge's daughter. So she'd warned him.

Judge Holmes had been shocked, the way she had been.

She had to make sure she had no more surprises. She needed to find out who in her office could be working with Luther. She could no longer deny that someone was, not after the backup bodyguards were drugged.

Dubridge had probably already sent a crime-scene tech to retrieve the coffeepot. Since she worked in an office of caffeine junkies, she suspected everybody's prints would be on it. And the break room didn't have a security camera that might have caught the culprit in the act. They didn't have enough cause to *legally* search everybody's office.

She swiped her ID badge through the reader outside, and the exterior doors opened for her. She hurried through the lobby to the elevators. Despite it being way after hours, the elevator worked. The cleaning staff was in the building.

Jocelyn searched until she found one of the unmanned carts and lifted the ring of keys from it. Even if whatever she found wouldn't be admissible, she intended to search everybody's offices; she needed to know who was working for Luther.

But the first office she unlocked was her own. She intended to put her briefcase inside while she searched the others, so she left the door open behind her. But when she opened the bottom drawer of her filing cabinet to slide her briefcase inside it, she found a couple of things.

Things that she had not put there.

An orange prescription bottle with the label torn off, as well as a cell phone. So someone else had already lifted the office keys from the cleaning person's cart. And they'd used those keys to plant evidence in Jocelyn's office.

But it made no sense. Why would she drug the bodyguards who were protecting her? She'd nearly been killed—too many times. And she clearly wasn't the one firing those shots or running herself down.

She stared down at the bottle. She needed a plastic bag or something to put it in so that it could be checked for prints. Whereas the coffeepot would have a lot, she doubted the bottle would have any. The same with the cell phone. She would bet it had been wiped down and was an untraceable burner phone—a phone that no doubt had a record of calls to Luther Mills or to his lawyer.

Whoever had put the prescription bottle and phone in her filing cabinet was desperate not to be caught. Maybe that was why the things had been placed in her office, just to get them out of the one in which they had really belonged. Hopefully, even with the label torn off, there was a way to trace the pills—some pharmacy serial number or something.

She leaned over to peer closer at the bottle without touching it when she felt a sudden presence. Before she could straighten up and turn around, something slipped over her head and wound tightly around her throat.

She gasped for breath as she clawed at it, trying to scream for help.

No. She shouldn't have gone off without her bodyguards because now there was no one to save her from her attacker.

Chapter Seventeen

Landon had been torn between heading to Jocelyn's house or to her office. He'd chosen the building for the district attorney because he figured she had left the hospital determined to find out who in her office was working for Luther Mills.

He'd had to wait for a security guard to let him into the building, though. The guard confirmed that her key card had opened the doors just a short time ago. So he wasn't far behind her.

But even a few minutes was too long for her to be alone—with someone very determined to kill her. Her attacker would take any opportunity she gave him, and by going off alone, she'd given him a big one.

Landon rushed over to the elevator and stabbed the button for her floor. If he was feeling stronger, he would have used the stairs. But it would take too long for him to make it up the five flights.

Finally the elevator dinged, and the doors slid open. He jumped into the car and pressed the button for five. And he willed it to hurry as a sudden urgency gripped him. She would have been safer had she gone home to her cat and her high-tech security system.

Here the distracted security guard was her only protection. And there was no way he could hear her screaming from the lobby. The elevator lurched to a stop, the movement adding to the dizziness Landon was already fighting from all his blood loss. He pressed his fingers to his head and tried to clear it.

Maybe he should have waited for Keeli and Dubridge. But he'd rushed off without them as backup—without any backup. He regretted that now as he worried that he might not be strong enough to save Jocelyn if she needed saving.

And he was afraid that she did the moment he looked through the window in her office door and noticed two dark shadows. One leaned over the other. He shoved open the door and rushed into the room.

The taller shadow charged him, knocking Landon over as he ran into the hallway. The other shadow dropped to the floor. The lamp on Jocelyn's desk cast a glow onto her pale face. She lay across the open bottom drawer of her filing cabinet. Her skin was so ashen but for the angry red mark across her throat.

Whoever had been inside the office with her had been strangling her.

"Jocelyn!" Landon shouted her name.

But her long black lashes lay against her cheeks. Her lids didn't so much as flicker. She had to be unconscious.

He refused to consider the alternative. That he'd been too late.

That he'd lost her.

"Jocelyn…" He murmured her name as he crouched over her. Then, with shaking fingers, he reached out and checked her damaged throat for a pulse. Panic pressed on him when he felt nothing but the coolness of her silky skin.

His chest ached, and his lungs burned. "Jocelyn!"

He leaned down and pressed his lips to hers, breathing through her lips as he began compressions. He was trained in CPR and regularly recertified, and he was never more grateful than now for that training.

He couldn't lose her.

She had to come back to him.

JOCELYN CHOKED AND SPUTTERED, her throat and lungs burning as she struggled to breathe. She reached up to tear that rope or whatever it had been away from her neck—but it was gone. Her hand bumped against a shoulder, though, and she opened her eyes to see a dark shadow leaning over her. She tried to scream, but she could make no sound but a rasp.

"Shhh…" a deep voice murmured, his voice sounding nearly as raspy as hers. "You're safe. It's me. It's me."

Landon! She sat up and threw her arms around him, clinging to him. She'd known she shouldn't have left the hospital without checking on him. But she hadn't wanted to put him in danger, too. She grasped his arms and pulled back. "We…" Her voice cracked, and she struggled to clear it. "We need to get out of here."

"He's gone," Landon said. "Whoever it was took off when I came in." He reached for the phone on her desk. "I need to call down to Security—see if they saw him leaving."

"Did…did you see who it was?" she asked.

He shook his head. "He ran out fast—so fast that he has to be long gone. I couldn't get a good look at him, but he was big enough to knock me over."

She saw the blood seeping through the bandage on his neck and touched it. "Did he reopen your wound?"

Using his free hand, he covered her fingers with his. "No. I'm fine. We need an ambulance, though. We need to get you to the hospital."

She grabbed the phone from his hand. "No. I'm fine."

"You weren't breathing when I found you," he said, and his voice was raspy again with emotion. "You need to be treated."

"I'm breathing fine now." And while her throat hurt, she could speak even though it sounded hoarse. "I'm fine."

"You could have died," he said. "You shouldn't have left the ER without protection."

She shook her head. "I shouldn't have left without checking on you." He'd saved her life over and over again, putting himself in danger every time. And she hadn't even seen him after he'd been shot.

"Why did you?" he asked, and his eyes darkened with pain.

A twinge of regret struck her heart. She felt bad about hurting him. "I didn't know what to do."

"Or you didn't care…"

She gripped his arms again. "No. I do care." And maybe that was why she hadn't wanted to see him—because when he'd been shot, she'd cared too much. Seeing that blood—*his blood*—spurt from the wound in his neck had nearly paralyzed her, she'd been so afraid. For him…

If he hadn't shoved her to the ground, she would have been shot, too. He'd saved her then, even when he'd nearly been mortally wounded. And not fully recovered from that wound, he'd saved her again.

She slid her hands up his arms to his shoulders. "I care."

He chuckled. "But you don't want to."

"No," she agreed. "I don't."

"Because you don't trust me," he said. "Even now…"

She closed her eyes and sighed. "I—I…"

"You're keeping something from me," he said. "Something you told the chief in private."

Dubridge must have told him that or maybe Keeli had. Because if he'd talked to the chief, he would probably know what she'd told him. She doubted Chief Lynch was going to keep it secret, so it was going to come out soon anyway.

She opened her eyes and studied Landon's face, needing to see his reaction when she told him.

"Luther Mills has a brother," she said.

He shrugged. "He probably has a few half siblings. His parents were never married."

"He has one who works for the Payne Protection Agency, and before that, he worked for the vice unit."

Landon's brow furrowed with confusion. "What are you saying? That one of my friends is Luther's brother?"

"Tyce Jackson."

He laughed, but then the laughter stopped, and the grin slid away from his face as he must have realized it was a strong possibility. "It doesn't matter if they are."

"Of course it does," she said.

He shook his head and flinched as his neck moved.

"No. Tyce was even more determined to bring down Luther than the rest of us in vice ever were—even Clint. And Clint blames Luther for the death of his cousin."

She sighed. So Clint Quarters had had a personal reason for wanting justice—an even more personal reason than hers.

Landon continued, "If Tyce and Luther are related, it's by blood only. They weren't raised together, and they are nothing alike."

Even while she admired his fierce loyalty, she wondered if he was just fooling himself. "Isn't the saying that blood is thicker than water?" Then she grimaced as she remembered how the bullet had sprayed Landon's blood around the parking garage. It had seemed like water then.

How was he alive?

How had he saved her life once again?

"I'm sorry," she said. "I shouldn't have told you."

"You should have told me sooner," he said. "Before you told the chief."

"And that's why I didn't tell you," she said. "Because I knew you'd try to protect him." Like his fierce loyalty, being protective was second nature to Landon. He had made the right choice to leave the River City Police Department to become a bodyguard.

She only hoped that his new career choice didn't get him killed—that protecting her didn't get him killed.

"I'm not protecting him," he said. "I'm defending him. As a lawyer, you should realize the difference. And you should know that everybody's innocent until proven guilty."

"Everybody?" she asked. "Even Luther Mills?"

"Luther's never been innocent," he said. "If the rumors are true, he was just a kid when he killed for the first time."

"I heard that rumor, too," she said. "I heard the person he killed was his father. Maybe Tyce Jackson's father, too."

"So if anything, Tyce might want revenge against Luther," Landon said, "not to aid and abet him."

She sighed. "Maybe you should have been a lawyer. You're mounting a strong defense for your friend."

"Tyce is my friend," he said. "But he's my friend because he's a good man. I know he's not working for Luther. Not when he worked vice and not now. He's working against him. Just like you are. Just like I am. That's why we need to find who the hell's working for him in your office. We need to find out who the hell just tried to kill you."

She wasn't about to argue with him about that. "You're right," she said. "Let's talk to the security guard."

Landon helped her up from the floor. Maybe she'd stood too quickly, for she swayed on her heels and nearly fell. But he caught her, sliding his arms around her to pull her close to his chest.

His heart pounded so hard that she could feel its frantic beat. "Are you all right?" she asked him.

He shook his head.

"You left the hospital too soon." Because of her. Because he'd been worried about her.

"We need to go back," she said. He'd just had surgery to repair the gunshot wound. She doubted doctors had released him yet.

"Yes," he agreed. "We need to go back for you to be treated."

And of course he would be more worried about her than he was about himself. Just as he supported his friend who'd obviously lied to him. And just as he protected her—with no concern for his own life or health.

She felt that panic again that she'd felt when he'd gotten struck in the garage. That feeling that she was falling...but it wasn't over a half wall to the pavement below. She was in far more than physical danger.

She was in danger of falling in love with her bodyguard.

HE WAS SHAKING. He couldn't stop shaking. He'd come so close to getting caught.

How the hell was that damn bodyguard even alive?

He'd seen the blood spurting out of him. He should have died. But like some avenging angel, he'd rushed to her rescue. He hoped Myers had been too late, though—too late to save her.

She'd stopped fighting him. She'd stopped breathing. She had to have died.

But if Landon Myers had come back from the dead, she might have, as well. So he waited on the street outside the building—deep in the shadows where hopefully no one would see him. He tilted his head, listening for the sound of an ambulance or a police car.

If the bodyguard had been real and not a ghost, wouldn't he have called for help by now? Wouldn't he have tried to save her? And even if he hadn't, the police should have been called...

What the hell was going on?

Then, after several long minutes of waiting, he saw them—standing in the lobby. Both of them. They were alive.

Why the hell couldn't he kill these people no matter how damn many times he'd tried?

He reached for his gun—desperate enough to risk shooting at them again. They might have seen him— might have recognized him. He had to kill them.

But before he could pull out the gun, his phone began to vibrate. Not his real phone but the disposal cell that only one person used to contact him.

Luther Mills.

Damn it. He couldn't talk now. He could barely think for the fear coursing through him. What if they'd seen him?

He'd pulled that hood up around his face again. He wore gloves. They shouldn't have...

But it wasn't a chance he was willing to take. Neither was missing Luther's call, though.

He stepped deeper in the shadows, into an alley between two buildings across the street from the district attorney's offices. "Yes?" he asked in a low whisper.

"It's time," Luther told him.

He'd already been trying, but he didn't want to admit that to Luther—not after the man had told him to back off from Jocelyn Gerber. Did every man she meet fall for the black-haired bitch?

He shook his head. "So you want me to do it now?" He reached for his gun again. Maybe he'd give Luther the satisfaction of hearing the shots ring out...

"Not that," Luther said. "We have bigger concerns."

His stomach lurched with dread. Someone must have figured it out.

Luther continued, "A couple of *things* have gone missing, but not the way I wanted them to. I'm pretty damn certain that they're going to turn up at the worst possible time."

Like his trial.

He knew that the eyewitness had already disappeared to some safe house nobody had been able to find. But now Luther was making it sound like the evidence tech had disappeared, as well. With the evidence?

"So we need that little insurance policy we talked about," Luther said.

"What does that have to do with me?" he asked.

"I need someone I can count on to carry this out," Luther said.

He didn't feel any pride that Luther thought he could count on him. In fact, he just felt sicker, like the walls were closing in on him. Or maybe the bars.

He did not want to wind up in a cell next to Luther Mills. But if he didn't help him, Luther had enough on him to make damn sure he went down with the drug dealer.

He sighed. "What do you want me to do?"

"Pick up that little insurance policy for me," Luther said. "Make sure it's known we have it."

Even though Luther couldn't see it—or maybe because he couldn't—he shook his head. "That's too risky."

"It's necessary," Luther said. "Our insurance policy will be of no use if nobody knows we have it."

But Luther wouldn't have it. He would. It was his freedom he was risking now. Luther had already lost his.

But he was willing to pay dearly to get it back. And he needed money. Badly.

Especially now. The longer Jocelyn Gerber lived, the closer she would get to discovering that he was the one helping Luther. Then he would need that money to escape before he was the one she was prosecuting next.

"Okay…" He murmured his agreement.

And Luther chuckled. "As if you had a choice."

He had one—but it involved giving up his freedom. Jocelyn Gerber didn't offer immunity in exchange for evidence. That was why she couldn't get any of Luther's crew to turn against him.

No. The only way he would get immunity was to kill her and get away before anyone figured out what he'd done.

But Lucien wouldn't have it. He would. It was his
freedom he was risking now. Lucien had already lost his
but he was willing to pay dearly to get it back. And
he needed money. Badly.

Especially now. The longer Jocelyn Gerber lived,
the closer she would get to discovering that he was the
one helping Luther. He would need that money to
escape before anybody caught on to him.

"Okay..." He murmured his agreement.

And Luther chuckled. "As if you had a choice."

Chapter Eighteen

Landon swiped the key card through the hotel room
door and pushed it open. He pressed his back against it
to hold it until Jocelyn walked past him. Then he closed
and locked it.

"We're safe here," he assured her as he flipped on
the lights. "I made sure nobody followed us. Not even
the backup..."

They hadn't caught up with him, though. He suspected they'd gone to her house instead to look for her
there. Or maybe they were busy protecting the judge's
daughter since Tyce had probably been removed from
that assignment.

He didn't give a damn who the hell his friend was
related to; he knew Tyce Jackson was a good man, one
who could be trusted with anyone's life. But Jocelyn
didn't trust Tyce or anyone else at the Payne Protection
Agency right now but him. That was why he'd agreed to
her request that nobody know where they were.

"Thank you," she murmured, her voice still raspy.

The line around her neck was still a deep red and
even more swollen than when he'd found her not
breathing. He shook his head. "Don't thank me," he

said. "I should have brought you to the hospital instead of a hotel."

Her lips curved into a smile. "You're the one they would have kept. I'm sure you left against doctor's orders."

He hadn't even bothered to wait to receive doctor's orders, much less follow them. "I'm fine," he insisted.

"So am I," she said.

"I don't know how long you were gone…" His voice cracked as he thought of that moment when he'd felt no pulse.

He touched her neck now, just above the swelling. And he felt her pulse leap beneath his fingertips. He uttered a sigh of relief.

"So you haven't just saved my life," she said as she stepped closer to him. "You brought me back to life." She rose on her tiptoes and pressed her lips to his. "Thank you," she murmured against his mouth.

That kiss jolted him to his core, sending a rush of desire and some other—even stronger—emotion coursing through him. The gunshot wound to his neck and the subsequent blood loss had made him feel so weak—even lifeless. But she…

He lifted his head and murmured, "Now you're the one who's brought me back to life."

Tears rushed to her eyes, making the blue glisten with moisture. She blinked furiously, but a few drops spilled over and trailed down her cheeks.

He lifted his hands to her face and wiped the tears away with his thumbs. "What's wrong?" he asked. "Why are you crying?" She had every right to cry, but she'd been so brave—so strong.

"I don't want to cost you your life," she said. "I don't want you to die because of me."

He leaned his forehead against hers and sighed. "It won't be because of you. It'll be because of Luther and whoever's working for Luther."

"You really don't believe Tyce Jackson could be...?" she asked.

A slight grin tugged at his lips. "You just can't stop yourself."

"What?" she asked.

"From cross-examining a suspect," he said.

"You're not a suspect," she replied.

He arched a brow. "Really?" he asked. "When you found out one of my best friends could be Luther Mills's brother, you didn't wonder about my allegiance? You didn't worry that I had been recruited to work for Luther, too?"

Her silky skin finally flushed with color. "I was shocked," she admitted. "I didn't know what to think or feel at that point."

He flinched. But he wasn't surprised that she'd doubted him. And he really couldn't blame her. He struggled with trust, too. As a cop, he'd seen too damn much—had been lied to too damn many times—to easily trust anyone.

"I'm sorry," she said again. "I shouldn't have doubted you."

He sighed. "I want you to trust me," he said. "I want you to trust the other bodyguards, so you don't run off by yourself again." He forced himself to step back—to move away from her. "But I can understand why you can't. Hell, maybe you're right to trust no one."

Because he had failed her. His attraction to her had caused him to lose focus. He'd saved her life, but she never should have had the close calls that she had. That was his fault.

He had to fight this attraction—he had to stay focused—for both their sakes.

For both their lives...

HIS REJECTION STUNG. But Jocelyn could understand why he was upset with her. She'd nearly gotten him and herself killed too many times.

Because she couldn't trust...

He'd done nothing to make her doubt him. It was clear he'd had no idea that his friend might be related to Luther Mills. Her pride and her heart stinging with that rejection, she'd retreated to the bathroom. She'd needed to shower and clean up. But she had nothing but the robe over the back of the door to wear. They hadn't gone back to her house. She had no bag—no essentials. Not even any makeup or a comb.

Her face looked so pale and washed out. The dark circles beneath her eyes were the only color on her skin, except for the angry red mark around her throat.

What had the man used? A tie? A rope? She peered closer into the mirror and saw no fibers. It must have been a tie. But it had been too dark for her to see it, to identify who might have been wearing it earlier that day.

The door rattled beneath the tapping of a big fist. "Are you okay in there?" he called out.

No. She wasn't. Like at the hospital, she was hesitant to see him again—because she was so damn worried about how much he was beginning to mean to her.

Too much.

And all she was to him was an assignment, one he was worried that he was going to fail. But her getting hurt, nearly killed, was her fault. She should not have gone off alone like she had.

"Jocelyn?" he called out again, his deep voice sharp with concern. "Are you all right?"

She forced herself to open the door. The steam from her shower rolled out like fog, encasing them in a dreamy, warm cocoon. "I'm fine..." she said.

"I ordered some tea and food from room service," he told her. "You must be sore and starved."

Her stomach pitched at the thought of eating. She didn't want food. She wanted him.

She needed him.

But he'd stepped back from her earlier.

Dare she risk another rejection?

She reached for the sash of the robe and tugged it loose. And the soft terry cloth parted, revealing her naked body.

A low groan tore from his throat. "Jocelyn, you're killing me..."

She tensed, worried that she might. She wouldn't be the one pulling the trigger, but it would still be her fault if something happened to him. "I'm sorry..." And she reached for the sash.

But he tugged it from her fingers. Then he tugged the robe from her body, leaving her completely naked but for the flush spreading over her skin. And that angry red mark around her throat.

She lifted her fingers to her neck to cover it. But he wasn't staring at her wound. He was staring into her eyes—deeply, as if he was looking into her soul rather than at her body.

His breath shuddered out in a ragged sigh. "You are so damn beautiful…"

She shivered. But she wasn't cold; her skin flushed as heat raced through her. He stepped closer to her, leaned down and brushed his mouth across hers. Slowly—just their lips meeting and clinging and moving.

He might have meant the kiss to be tender, gentle, but Jocelyn was too hungry, too overwhelmed with passion. She linked her arms around his neck and held his head to hers. Then she kissed him deeply, passionately.

He groaned and lifted and carried her to the bed. After he laid her down, he stared down at her again, with so much heat and hunger in his gaze. He stripped off his clothes until he was as naked as she was—physically.

Then she saw the hunger and need in his dark gaze, and she knew he was just as naked as she was—as vulnerable. He needed her as badly as she needed him.

But yet he took his time with her, moving his hands and lips slowly, seductively, over every inch of her skin. She touched him, too, sliding her fingertips and her lips over muscles that rippled beneath her touch.

"You're the beautiful one," she told him. She'd never seen a man as perfectly built as he was.

His body slid over hers, skin sliding over skin. She shivered and clutched at him. She wanted him—so badly.

Then he was there, making love to her with his mouth, making her cry out as she came. But it still wasn't enough. She felt an ache inside her that only he could fill.

He moved off the bed just long enough to sheathe his erection in a condom. Then he returned, but he flipped on his back and pulled her on top of him. She straddled his hips, then guided his erection inside, and finally that emptiness was filled.

She moved and rocked and rose up and down, driving them both out of their minds. He gripped her hips to hold her steady for a moment.

"You're driving me crazy," he said, his eyes bright with passion.

She was burning up—physically and emotionally—as tension wound tightly inside her. She needed a release. So she ground her hips against him, fighting toward that release.

He slid his hands from her hips up her sides until he cupped her breasts. He stroked his thumbs across her tight nipples and she felt the pull from them to her core.

And finally the release hit her, a powerful orgasm moving through her. Her toes curled as she cried out his name.

His hands moved to her hips again, but this time he didn't hold her still; he propelled her to move faster. And she came again, nearly sobbing as pleasure overwhelmed her.

Then his big body tensed beneath her. He groaned and shouted her name.

She collapsed onto his chest. But he didn't let her rest. Instead, he picked her up and carried her into the bathroom with him.

"What are you doing?"

"Taking a shower," he said as he turned on the faucet.

"I already had one," she reminded him.

"Not with me." And he pulled her under the spray with him. They made love there, too—in the shower, water pouring over them.

Her legs wrapped around his waist, he held her against the tile wall as he thrust into her. She touched the damp bandage on his neck. "Landon, you shouldn't have gotten this wet."

He shrugged, and muscles rippled in his arms and chest. "I'm fine."

He was better than fine. He was perfect.

And Jocelyn was scared…that she was falling in love with her bodyguard.

PARKER CURSED AS Landon's cell phone once again went immediately to voice mail. What the hell had happened to him? Was he all right?

He'd left the hospital against doctor's orders Friday night, and he'd lost his backup bodyguards. Of course Parker had had to pull them for another assignment.

He cursed as he thought about how abysmally they'd failed. He hoped that Landon hadn't, too. He hoped that he and Jocelyn Gerber were all right.

When the voice mail beeped, he said, "Call me back ASAP. Ms. Gerber is going to want to know what Luther's done now. It's going to affect her case."

She'd gone missing, too. Of course, it had only been for the weekend. But this assistant district attorney was known for working weekends. Hell, for working every waking moment.

Was she all right? He'd tried her cell, too, and had

left her a similar message. She must have finally played hers because his cell began to vibrate in his hand.

He moved farther into the foyer of Judge Holmes's house. He didn't want to disturb the judge or the others who were crowded in his den.

"What's going to affect my case?" Jocelyn Gerber asked without preamble.

"First off," Parker said, "are you all right?" She had sounded all right when he'd picked up, but now she hesitated. So long that he asked, "Is Landon all right?"

He shouldn't have left the hospital.

"He's fine," she said. "We're fine."

But she didn't sound fine; she sounded unsettled, on edge. But maybe his messages had caused that. Jocelyn Gerber's first concern had always been her case.

"What's going on?" she asked again.

"Bella Holmes has been kidnapped."

She cursed. "I told the judge to take Tyce Jackson off her protection duty. He's Luther's bro—"

"I know," Parker interrupted. "And the judge did remove him, which is probably how she was taken. Tyce would have made damn sure nothing happened to her." He suspected the bodyguard had fallen for the beautiful heiress.

"We have to get her back," Jocelyn said. "Or the judge will need to be recused. And I don't trust anyone else."

"You think Luther could have a judge on his payroll?"

"If he has police officers, evidence techs and someone in the district attorney's office, why wouldn't he have a judge?" Jocelyn asked.

And Parker groaned. If that was the case, then Luther would want Judge Holmes to recuse himself so someone else could preside over his trial. That meant he had no reason to keep Bella Holmes alive.

"We've got to find her," Parker said.

"Yes, we do," Jocelyn agreed. "We'll come to the judge's house."

"He doesn't want you here," Parker said. He hadn't even wanted him to call her. But Parker had been worried about her and Landon anyway. And he'd thought she had a right to know.

"Of course," she said. "He doesn't want any hint of impropriety."

Impropriety was the least of the judge's concerns at the moment. He was probably upset that he'd removed Tyce as his daughter's bodyguard because of what Jocelyn had told him. And it didn't matter to whom Tyce was related. He loved Bella Holmes.

"We have to get her back," Parker murmured aloud.

"I'll talk to Luther," Jocelyn said.

And a deep voice murmured in the background of the call—probably in protest.

Landon wouldn't want Jocelyn anywhere near Luther Mills. Not when he was threatening her, too. And legally Landon couldn't sit in on that meeting to protect her.

Jocelyn Gerber would be alone with the ruthless killer and his corrupt lawyer. No wonder Parker could hear Landon protesting in the background. But was he just worried about protecting her?

Or had he fallen for the beautiful ADA?

Chapter Nineteen

For two days there had been no attempts on her life. Nobody shooting at them or trying to run them down. The only danger had been that Landon was falling harder and harder for the beautiful assistant district attorney.

But Parker's call had reminded him why a relationship between them would never work. Jocelyn cared only about her career—even more than she cared about her life.

"It's too dangerous," he told her even as he drove the Payne Protection Agency SUV toward the jail. "You should not meet with him."

"I won't be alone with him," she said. "His lawyer will be there, and a guard will be right outside the door."

"His lawyer is a sleazebag," Landon said. He didn't know who was representing Luther, but that anyone who did was as immoral as he was. "You can't trust him."

"The guards—"

"Can't be trusted either," he reminded her. "Especially now. They have to know that they're being investigated. They may blame you for that."

"The chief and I are working together on that investigation," she admitted. "But they don't have anything to worry about—"

"Unless they're working for him," he said. And that concerned him. Luther had gotten to too many people. He'd bought or manipulated them into doing what he wanted. And what he wanted was for Jocelyn Gerber to die, probably so that his mole in the DA's office could take over his case. "You can't do this," Landon said even as he pulled up to take a ticket from the parking meter for the jail visiting lot. "It's not safe."

"I'm a hell of a lot safer than the judge's daughter is right now," Jocelyn said. "I don't even want to think about what might be happening to her…" She shuddered, so it was apparent that she was thinking about it.

Landon sucked in a breath. From his years of working vice, he knew, too.

"We have to do what we can to find her," Jocelyn persisted.

He nodded and pulled the SUV into a parking spot.

She flipped down the visor and looked into the mirror to adjust the scarf she'd looped around her neck. After spending two days in that hotel room barely wearing anything, they'd had to stop at her house to pick up clothes and to make sure the neighbor had been taking care of the cat like she'd promised. Jocelyn had grabbed a couple of scarves to hide the angry bruise around her neck.

"Are you sure you're up for this?" Landon asked her.

She nodded. "I have to be."

"Jocelyn—"

"I am," she assured him. "I feel fine. I just don't like how it looks. And I don't want Luther to see it."

"And know how close he came to succeeding in having you killed?"

"We're not sure that he was behind the attack."

He sighed. "You'd still rather believe it was someone else."

"I don't know what to believe," she said. And she turned toward him, her blue eyes soft with regret. "I was wrong about your friend. Parker made it clear that if Tyce hadn't been removed as Bella's bodyguard, she probably wouldn't have been abducted."

"He can't know that," Landon said. Jocelyn had nearly died several times with him protecting her. "Tyce might have been killed trying to protect her."

"I think that's what he meant," Jocelyn said. "That Tyce would have died before letting anyone take her."

"So you saved Tyce's life," he assured her. "And we'll save Bella's." If she was still alive…

He wasn't sure exactly what Luther wanted with her. Did he really think he'd manipulate the judge into ruling in his favor and that Jocelyn would let that happen? He had to know she'd make the judge recuse himself.

And maybe that was what he wanted. He could have a judge in his pocket just like he had an ADA and who the hell knew how many cops.

"Okay," he said. And he opened his door and walked around the hood, careful to check the parking lot for any sign of that car with the tinted windows. But he'd made certain nobody had followed him here.

The shooter could have been waiting for them, though, because Jocelyn had had to call that sleazy lawyer to set up this meeting. It wouldn't have been legal if she hadn't.

He walked around and opened her door. Jocelyn swung her legs out. And an image flashed through his mind of those long, toned legs wrapped around his waist, wound over his shoulders, bent over…

Desire rushed over him, heating his blood. They'd made love so many times, but he still ached for her.

Jocelyn drew in a deep breath, as if bracing herself, before she stepped out onto the asphalt.

Landon knew she didn't like visiting the jail any more than he liked her visiting it. But it was part of her job, and Jocelyn didn't shy away from any part of her job—no matter how tough or how dangerous.

A GUARD AT her side, Jocelyn walked up to the door of the little conference room where she would meet with Luther and his lawyer. Her heels clicked against the concrete floor, sounding like small-caliber gunshots echoing off the concrete walls and ceiling, too. Instinctively, she felt the urge to duck and take cover.

"His lawyer is already inside," the guard told her as he reached for the door. "But we're bringing Luther down from his cell right now."

Luther. Not the inmate. Not even Mills…

Landon was right. She couldn't trust the guards—at least, not one who was on a first-name basis with a dangerous murderer. She glanced behind the burly guard, wishing she would see Landon. But the guards searching him must not have been done yet. She'd been searched and had headed back alone.

She'd hated to leave him—especially after the two days they'd had together. Two days that had seemed like a dream. They couldn't have been real; she couldn't have experienced as much pleasure as he'd given her.

But she had.

The guard opened the door and held it for her. "Ms. Gerber, have you changed your mind?"

She shook her head and stepped inside. The lawyer sat already at the table in the conference room. Even though it was late at night, he looked perfectly coiffed, his black hair slicked back. His suit was perfect, too.

Jocelyn lifted her fingers to her throat, checking that the scarf hadn't slipped. She wore it for protection, to hide the bruises, but now she realized it could be used as a weapon like her attacker must have used his tie. Maybe she shouldn't have worn it.

But it was too late now. The door on the other side of the room opened and Luther Mills stepped in, a grin curving his lips when he saw her.

"It's like my dream come to life," Luther murmured as he took the seat across from her. "The things you and I were just doing, Jocelyn…" His dark-eyed gaze slipped from her face down over her body, and he wriggled his brows at her.

She resisted the urge to shudder with revulsion. That was what he wanted—to affect her, to scare her. So she stared down her nose at him. "I am not here to discuss your dreams, Mr. Mills."

"That's a damn shame," he said. "I think you might like what I was doing to you."

Her disgust churned in her stomach, but she only glared at him, acting as unmoved as possible. Luther Mills was a predator looking for the weakest victim, so she could show no weakness to him.

"Mr. Mills," his lawyer intervened, sweat beginning to bead on his high forehead. "Ms. Gerber called this meeting with concerns that you're behind the abduction of Judge Holmes's daughter." And it was clear that he shared her concerns but wanted no part of this one of Luther's crimes.

Luther widened his eyes with obviously feigned innocence. "The judge has a daughter?" he asked. "I didn't even know that."

Jocelyn glared at him again. "Everyone knows how much the judge's daughter means to him."

"More than justice?" Luther scoffed. "I find that hard to believe."

Luther had apparently never loved anyone more than himself or his money. He didn't understand how far a person might go to protect someone they loved.

She thought of Landon, of that bullet striking his neck. She could have lost him so easily. But then, he really wasn't hers to lose—despite their idyllic weekend. He was still just her bodyguard.

And the reason she needed a bodyguard was because of this man. Sure, other people had threatened her, but it was too much of a coincidence for them to act on those threats now—when Luther was trying to take out everyone associated with his trial. Even the judge's innocent daughter.

"Your plan is not going to work," she told Luther.

He leaned forward, so that his face neared hers.

She forced herself not to pull back as he studied her very intently and unsettlingly.

"What do you think my plan is?" he asked her.

"You're going to use his daughter to make the judge rule in your favor," Jocelyn said.

"You think he would do something like that? That he would compromise the system like that?" He sounded as if he really wanted her to answer.

And that worried her. She had to be honest, though. "No. Your plan won't work," she answered him. "Judge Holmes will recuse himself, and another judge will get assigned to your trial."

He grinned, probably unable to not gloat over what he considered another victory over justice.

She gasped as she realized that was what his plan really was. "That's what you want. Another judge—one who works for you."

"Everybody thinks you work for me, Jocelyn," Luther taunted her.

Heat rushed to her face. It was so damn embarrassing that everyone thought that. She shook her head in denial.

But he continued, "Because you've conveniently lost every case against me."

"Nothing about that was convenient," she said.

"Hurt your career a bit, huh?" He snickered. "We both know you wouldn't be trying this case if your boss wasn't on maternity leave."

"In all those other cases against you, I didn't have Judge Holmes."

"Of course, I don't know what you're talking about, but you won't have him now either. If something happens to his daughter…"

"It won't," she said, and she was forced to bluff. She hoped like hell that her bluff proved to be the truth.

She could not lose Judge Holmes. "Tyce Jackson has found her."

He leaned closer and narrowed his eyes, studying her even more intently. "Really?" Luther asked. "He found her?"

She nodded.

"Alive?" he asked with surprise.

Jocelyn heard the surprise in his voice, and her heart slammed against her ribs. That poor girl.

It sounded as if Luther was certain she was dead. And there was only one way he would be certain—because he'd ordered her killed.

She gasped.

He wasn't entirely certain, though, because he kept staring at her. "You were lying, right, Ms. Gerber?" he prodded her. "Tyce didn't find her, did he?"

He sounded worried about the man she now knew was his brother. He didn't claim him as much, though, so he probably hadn't ordered anyone to spare his life. Did he think Tyce had been killed trying to rescue her?

It was a distinct possibility. And she felt sick as she thought of Landon losing his friend, of a man losing his life. She hoped like hell if Tyce had found her that he and the judge's daughter had made it out alive.

She stood up and headed toward the door. Just as Landon had warned her, this had been a waste of time. For her...

She had a horrible feeling that Luther had gotten more information out of her than she had him. She had no proof that he'd ordered the judge's daughter abducted or worse.

She had nothing to use against him to coerce him to

turn over the girl. She could only hope that Tyce Jackson was as good at his job as Landon was at his, and that he would save Bella just like Landon had saved her.

Over and over again...

LUTHER WHISTLED AS the ADA turned and walked out into the hall. He hadn't been lying about dreaming about her. It would almost be fun to face her in court. And it definitely sounded as if that was where they were heading. He hadn't been able to get the charges thrown out before the trial.

So he had to win the trial.

And he needed Judge Holmes to either be on his side or off the bench for that to happen.

"What the hell did you do?" his lawyer asked him. But then he held up a hand, with a lot of rings on it, and shook his head. "No. Don't tell me. I don't want to know."

Luther sighed. "Deniable culpability...whatever the hell you go on about."

"I don't want to talk about this," the man said as he began to rise from the chair.

"You're not going anywhere," Luther told him. And he held out his hand now—for the lawyer's phone. He'd hidden his untraceable cell in his jail cell—just in case Jocelyn had ordered him searched when he came into the room. He wouldn't have put it past her.

She was so damn smart.

And careful...

That had to be the only reason she was still alive, that and her damn bodyguard, Landon Myers. Landon had always been a pain in the ass with that protective streak of his. No wonder he made such a good bodyguard.

Was Luther's half brother as good a bodyguard?

Had Tyce found Bella Holmes?

Luther punched in some numbers on his lawyer's cell phone and pressed it to his ear. "Tell me you still have her."

The lawyer closed his eyes and pressed his hand over them. If he was trying to be one of those little caricature monkeys, he should have covered his ears, so he would hear no evil. Closing his eyes just meant he couldn't see it.

"I'm not with her," the ADA on Luther's payroll replied.

"Why the hell not?"

But Luther knew—he was afraid to get caught.

"She's not going to get away. Your crew members are protecting her."

Not enough of them, just some young, dumb kids. Luther needed to send in more mature and more dangerous backup. But thanks to the damn Payne Protection Agency, he kept losing crew members.

Like Tyce. He'd once been a member of his crew. But he'd just been undercover, trying to get evidence to bring down Luther. If he died trying to save the judge's daughter, then so be it.

He probably wasn't the only half sibling Luther had anyway. "You didn't notice anyone watching the place?" he asked.

"No. You think someone found her?" the guy asked, his voice rising with a hint of panic.

Tyce could. He knew the area. He knew a lot of Luther's crew. He felt a flash of panic, too. "I better get more guys out there just in case."

Just in case little Ms. Gerber hadn't been bluffing.

Before he could disconnect to make another call, the ADA said, "I shouldn't have been involved in this. I've met the judge's daughter. She might have recognized my voice."

"Then I guess you should have made sure she was dead before you left the warehouse," Luther said.

And his lawyer groaned.

"But then, I don't think you have the stomach for killing," Luther told the guy. "Or Ms. Gerber wouldn't have just paid me a visit."

"She was there? At the jail?"

"Yup. Alive and well."

The ADA snorted. "Not that well. She's been missing since I strangled her the other night."

That was why she'd worn that scarf around her neck. "Tried," Luther said. "You didn't succeed. Just like I said, you don't have the stomach for it."

"You told me to back off," the ADA reminded him. "So I was just going to slip some evidence into her filing cabinet."

"Evidence? Against me?"

"Against her," the man replied. "The drop phone I used to talk to you."

"Are you framing her or me?" Luther asked. Maybe he needed to take out this ADA instead of Jocelyn Gerber.

"It wouldn't hold up in court, but it makes her look guilty," the man replied. "I saw her coming in as I was about to leave."

"So you decided to strangle her even though I told you to back off."

"I'd put her bodyguard in the hospital, so she was finally alone," the man explained. "I had to take advantage of the opportunity."

"Landon Myers is in the hospital?"

"Was—but just for a little while. He got out in time to save her again."

That was what those damn bodyguards did—swooped to the rescue. He had to get more of his crew over to the warehouse to make sure nobody got the judge's daughter out alive. But before he clicked off, he told the guy, "You better not fail next time you try to kill her."

"When's that?"

"Now." The guy had been able to get close to her because no one had suspected him yet. But if the judge's daughter lived and was able to identify him, he would never get close to Jocelyn Gerber again. And if the guy died trying to kill his coworker, like the rookie cop had died trying to kill Rosie, it was just one more loose end Luther wouldn't have to clean up.

Chapter Twenty

Landon closed his eyes and tried to shut out the sound of water running in the bathroom. As soon as they had returned to her house from the jail, Jocelyn had headed to the shower—needing to wash off her visit with Luther Mills.

Landon wanted to join her in the shower, but guilt was already weighing heavily on him. While his assignment was to protect Jocelyn, he was also part of a team—a team he hadn't been supporting as much as he should have been. He was worried about his friends.

Fortunately, Clint and Hart were safe now—since the people they were protecting had agreed to go into safe houses far from Luther's reach. But since they were safe, Keeli and Tyce were in even more danger. Especially Tyce.

He had to be trying to find the judge's daughter. Landon didn't want to bother him, but he had to know if he was all right.

Even though he expected the call to go straight to voice mail, he punched Tyce's contact on his cell screen. When a male voice answered, he nearly dropped it—especially when he realized it wasn't Tyce who'd picked up the call.

"Parker?"

"Yeah…" His boss uttered a ragged-sounding sigh that rattled the phone.

"What's wrong?" Landon anxiously asked. "Why are you answering Tyce's phone?"

"He was shot. He's in surgery."

Landon's stomach flipped as it filled with dread. "What happened?"

"He rescued the judge's daughter."

"Is she all right?" Landon asked. Or had Bella Holmes been shot, too?

"She's fine," Parker said. "Tyce found her and saved her—all on his own. But he got shot in the process. I'm not sure if it happened before or after we arrived as backup. We got there just as Luther's backup arrived. It was…" His voice cracked. "It got crazy…"

"Is anyone else hurt?" Landon asked.

"I don't think any of Luther's crew survived."

"What about the Payne Protection bodyguards?" Landon asked. "Are they all okay?"

"Everyone is except for Tyce."

"How bad is it?" he asked, fear making his voice gruff.

"He carried her out of the warehouse, got her to safety, made sure she was treated before he collapsed," Parker said.

But that was because Tyce was a beast. He was big and strong and determined.

"How bad is he hurt?" Landon asked again.

"I don't know," Parker said. "He's been in surgery for a while."

Which meant that there was considerable damage. "Damn it…" he said.

"It was weird how Luther's crew showed up," Parker said. "It was as if they'd been tipped off that Tyce had found her. What the hell did Ms. Gerber say to him at the jail? That was where you brought her, right?"

"Yeah…" he conceded. "But I wasn't in on the meeting."

"So you don't know what she told him."

"She wouldn't have said Tyce found her," Landon said. "Until now, I didn't know Tyce had any idea where to find her." But he should have known that he would figure it out. Tyce had been undercover for a long time as part of Luther's crew. So he might have had some idea where she was being held.

Parker sighed. "I don't know."

"What?" Landon asked.

"I don't know if we should trust Jocelyn," he replied. "You might have been right about her this whole time."

"No, I wasn't," Landon said. "And you know it. All the attempts on her life prove she's not working for Luther."

"But you're the one who's gotten hurt all those times," Parker said. "Not her…"

"That's not…" And he remembered he hadn't told Parker about the attempt in her office—when she'd nearly been strangled. So he did it now.

Parker cursed him.

"That's why we disappeared for a while," Landon said.

"Because you didn't trust anyone?" Parker asked.

"Because you believed her about Tyce being in collusion with Luther? I don't know what happened in her office, but I think you were smart not to trust her. And I don't think you should now, not after what happened to Tyce."

Landon knew his boss was upset, so he wasn't going to argue with him—even though he wanted to hotly defend Jocelyn. "Let me know when Tyce is out of surgery," he said.

"Don't bring her near the hospital," Parker warned him. "Nobody wants her around here."

That wasn't true. Landon wanted her. Badly...

Understanding that Parker was rightfully worried about Tyce, Landon just disconnected the call. He was sliding his cell into his pocket when he heard the ding of another cell phone receiving a text. It wasn't his, or he would have felt it.

And he could have sworn Jocelyn had brought her cell upstairs with her when she'd gone to take her shower. The sound dinged again, and he realized it came from the briefcase she'd left on the coffee table. Curious as to why she would have two phones, he walked over to it. She must have shoved something in it as they'd come inside because the briefcase wasn't fully closed. Usually it was shut and locked.

He took the opportunity to flip it open, and his stomach pitched when he looked inside. Lying on top of a pile of folders was the phone and a prescription bottle with the label torn off. What the hell had been in the bottle?

The sleeping pills that had drugged their backup bodyguards? Why would she have drugged them, though?

He stared down at the phone. The text highlighted

on the screen said, Thanks for the heads-up that Tyce had found our insurance policy.

He sucked in a breath, feeling like he'd been sucker punched. He'd wanted to go into that room with her and Luther to protect her. But he'd needed to be inside to protect his friend and himself.

Because not only his stomach hurt; his heart ached, too, feeling as if it was breaking.

He'd been such a fool to change his mind about her. An even bigger fool for trusting her. And the biggest fool for beginning to fall for her.

JOCELYN HAD BEEN hoping that Landon would join her in the shower. Once she'd washed off the revulsion she'd felt from her visit with Luther Mills and his sleazy lawyer, she'd still felt chilled. Scared that Luther might just get away with murder again.

And she'd needed Landon's arms around her, holding her, comforting her, keeping her safe.

She'd needed the heat of their passion to chase away all her fears and concerns again, like it had this weekend. But the weekend hadn't lasted forever, no matter how much she'd wished it had. And because she'd wished they could go back—to the weekend and that safe hotel suite—she'd gone downstairs, in only her towel, to find him.

She found him leaning over her briefcase, and she gasped in shock. "You're still snooping through my stuff?" she asked. And despite the towel wrapped around her, she felt completely naked and vulnerable and incredibly hurt. "You can't still think I'm working for Luther?"

"I can't?" he asked, as he turned toward her. His handsome face was flushed with anger, his jaw rigid with it. "When he sends you a text thanking you for the tip about Tyce knowing where Bella Holmes was being held?"

"What?" she asked. "My phone's upstairs." Out of habit, she'd brought it with her into the bathroom. She never knew when her boss might call her. She'd also wanted it close in case someone called her about the situation with the judge's daughter.

"Not that phone," he said. "This phone." And he pointed to the cell phone lying atop the folders in her briefcase. "The one you use to communicate with Luther Mills."

She shook her head. "That's not my phone."

"The bottle isn't yours either?" he asked.

"No," she said, and now anger gripped her, that he could actually suspect even for a moment that those things were hers. "I found the phone and bottle in my filing cabinet in the office…" Her voice cracked with that anger now as it overwhelmed her. "…right before someone tried to strangle me to death."

Before they'd left her office, she'd shoved them into her briefcase with the intent of turning them over to the chief when she felt safe, when she'd been confident that she could trust anyone besides Landon.

Clearly now he didn't trust her. He closed his eyes as if he couldn't bear the sight of her.

"Do you honestly think I did that to myself?" she asked. "After everything you know about me now, how can you think I would ever work for Luther Mills?"

He sighed and opened his eyes, which were full of regret. "I'm sorry. I just talked to Parker—"

"Have they found the judge's daughter?" she asked.

He nodded.

"Is she okay?"

"She is," he confirmed, but there was fear yet in his voice.

And she knew. "Tyce isn't…"

"He was shot rescuing her," Landon said. "Parker said it was as if someone tipped off Luther and he sent in reinforcements." He held up the cell phone. "Then Luther sent this text to this phone."

She looked at the screen now, reading the thank-you message. She shuddered in revulsion and felt as if she needed to shower again. "That's not my phone," she repeated. "And, unfortunately, there's probably no way to prove that message came from Luther."

But why had he sent it? Did he know she had it now? Was he just messing with her?

Tears stung her eyes, and she blinked furiously to fight them from falling. "But it is my fault," she murmured as guilt pressed on her lungs. "I was trying to scare him into giving up information that might lead to where Bella was being held, so I bluffed that Tyce had already found her." She shook her head at her stupidity. "I should have known that Luther was too smart to fall for it."

"You weren't bluffing," Landon said. "Tyce had figured out where she was being held."

"Is he going to be okay?" she asked, her heart pounding hard with dread and fast with fear.

Landon's broad shoulders lifted in a weak shrug. "He's in surgery."

That didn't sound good.

"But Tyce is tough. He got her out and got her to the hospital to be checked out before anybody even realized he'd been shot."

What kind of people were the Payne Protection bodyguards? Shot in the neck, blood gushing from his wound, Landon had still managed to save her.

She pointed toward the pill bottle. "That must have been what was used to drug the backup bodyguards," she said. "Why would I do that? Why would I help Luther Mills? You know I don't need money. All I need is justice."

And him—she needed him. But he couldn't trust her. So they had no future. Hell, even if he could trust her, they had no future. She had to focus on her job, on making sure criminals like Luther Mills were brought to justice.

Landon stepped closer and cupped her bare shoulders in his big hands. "I'm sorry," he said. "I shouldn't have doubted you."

"I understand why you did," she admitted. "I can't believe Luther sent that text."

"Who else—"

"No," she said. "I know it's him." Even if they would never be able to prove it. "But I don't know why he would have."

"To mess with you," Landon said. "To make you feel guilty, to knock you off your game—because he knows he's going to court now."

She sucked in a breath as she realized he was right.

She would soon have to face Luther Mills again—in court. And she could not lose or he would be free and even more dangerous than he was behind bars.

"That's not all he's going to do, though," Landon said. "He's going to step up his efforts to try to take you out, so that whoever is working for him in the DA's office can take over his case."

She shivered, very cold despite his touch on her bare skin. But she was not about to back down—from Luther Mills or from Landon.

She wanted him. But she was afraid that wasn't all. She needed him. Hell, she might even love him. She lifted her arms to link them behind his neck, and she pulled his head down to hers.

"Jocelyn…" he murmured, his brown eyes even darker with desire and something else. Fear. For her or for him?

It was clear he wanted to say more—about Luther, about the case, about her prosecuting the case—but she didn't want to hear it. She didn't want to think about it.

She only wanted to feel that passion only he had ever made her feel. She rose up on tiptoe and pressed her mouth to his, kissing him deeply.

A groan emanated from his throat as he kissed her back with the same intensity and hunger she felt for him. He pulled away and murmured her name again. But then he lifted and carried her toward the stairs. He rushed up to her bedroom, where he set her on her feet again.

The towel had loosened and dropped from her body, leaving her naked before him. But she wasn't just physically naked. She felt emotionally stripped, too.

Hurt that he'd doubted her. Vulnerable that she'd cared so much that he had.

Did she already love him?

She was more afraid that she might than she was even afraid of Luther Mills. She didn't want to be in love.

But Landon was her hero in so many ways. She reached for the buttons on his shirt, needing him as bare as she was, needing to feel his heart beating against hers. As she attacked the buttons, he slipped off his holster and placed it on the table next to the bed. Then he shrugged off the shirt and unbuttoned his jeans, dropping them and his boxers to the floor.

He obviously wanted her as badly as she wanted him. His erection jutted toward her. But when she reached for him, he pulled back. Then he leaned down and fumbled in his pocket for a condom.

Before he could roll it on, she reached out and closed her fingers around him. Then she leaned over and made love to him with her mouth.

He groaned and tangled his fingers in her hair, gently pulling her back. "I need to be inside you," he said, his voice gruff with desire. "I need to be part of you."

That was how it felt when they made love—like they were no longer separate, like they became one being. She lay back on the bed and held her arms out for him.

His hand shook as he rolled on the condom. Then he joined her on the bed. She parted her legs and he knelt between them, easing gently inside her. She arched up and wrapped her limbs around him, holding him tight as she took him deeper.

A low moan tore from her throat as the first orgasm

moved through her. The tension had been wound so tightly inside her, that was all it took. But he built the tension again with slow, deep strokes, as he lowered his head and kissed her.

First he brushed his lips over hers. Then he moved them down her throat. She gasped as his tongue stroked across her bruised skin.

"I'm sorry…" he said.

The strangling wasn't his fault, and he knew that. She was the one who'd gone out with no protection. So she suspected he was apologizing for earlier—for those brief moments he'd doubted her.

Warmth flooded her, but it wasn't just desire this time. She felt so much more for Landon, things she'd never wanted to feel for anyone or anything but her job.

He slid his arm under her back and lifted her up as he eased back on his haunches. She straddled his thighs, then locked her legs around his waist. In this position, her body was aligned with his, so that her breasts were nearly on the level with his face.

He took advantage of that fact, and he closed his lips around a taut nipple. He gently tugged on it, and she moaned, the tension winding so tightly inside her again.

He thrust up, sliding even deeper inside her. Desperate for release, she moved and rocked against him as she clutched at his broad shoulders. Then she lowered her head and nipped at his shoulder.

He chuckled, then groaned as she swiped her tongue across it. Then she shifted her lips to his throat and then his mouth, kissing him deeply. They moved as one, their rhythm completely in sync, and that was how they found their pleasure, crying out as it overwhelmed them.

Shaken and spent from the powerful orgasm, Jocelyn felt boneless and limply sank into the mattress when he released her. Within seconds, after cleaning up, he was back with her, pulling her into his arms. His chest rose and fell with pants for breath and the powerful beat of his heart.

Hers beat with the same intensity. Even though she'd found release, she'd also found more fear—because she knew without a doubt that she loved him.

HE HAD HIS emergency bag packed, complete with a forged passport and a substantial amount of cash. He would get more—so much more money—if he stayed and made sure that Luther Mills got away with murder again. But if he stayed, he risked getting caught and losing his freedom.

And despite the money he'd made working for Luther, he didn't have enough to get away with his crimes like Luther did. And once it was known what he'd done, he would have no allies—only enemies.

A phone vibrated on the table near his bed. Two of them sat on it, the one on which Luther called him and his real cell phone. He stared at them, wondering which it was.

Luther calling…wondering if he'd killed Jocelyn Gerber yet. Or Jocelyn calling…wondering why the hell he wasn't at the office yet.

He stepped away from the suitcase he was packing on the bed and stared down at the phone. Judge Holmes…

Was it a trick? Was the man calling to put him on speaker for his daughter to identify his voice? He'd been careful to disguise it when he'd spoken to the judge during her abduction. He'd even used a special device to digitally alter the sound of his voice. But because he hadn't thought Bella Holmes would make it out of captivity alive, he hadn't bothered disguising it around her.

Of course, he'd met her only a couple of times in the judge's chambers. And being the social butterfly she was, she met new people all the time. He doubted that she would be able to place him.

So he punched in the accept button.

"This is Judge Holmes." The older man needlessly identified himself. "I am trying to get a hold of ADA Gerber. Do you have any idea where she might be?"

Before he answered, he coughed and sputtered, so that the judge would think he had a cold. "No, Your Honor. I'm sorry. I don't know where she could be."

"She's not at the office."

"I'm not at the office either," he replied. "I've been battling a flu bug for a couple of weeks now." An illness would explain his disappearances and absences over the past couple of weeks—if anyone had noticed.

"I'm sorry to hear that," the judge replied. "I thought you might be Ms. Gerber's second chair for Luther Mills's trial."

He should have been first. "I think Jocelyn has determined she can handle the prosecution on her own. And isn't that trial a couple of weeks off yet?"

"An opening came up in the docket, and we're able to start sooner than expected," he replied, "as long as the lawyers have no objections."

Luther would have objections and more demands on *him*. Jocelyn had to die now before the trial could start.

Of course the judge was eager to begin the trial, because he wouldn't be able to bring his daughter home from wherever he'd hidden her until it was all over.

"I will be heading into the office soon, Your Honor," he said. "If I see Jocelyn, I will tell her to contact you."

"Thank you." The judge clicked off the cell.

He tossed his phone down and uttered a low growl of frustration. He had no choice now. He could not fail again. This time—when he tried—he had to make damn certain he killed Jocelyn Gerber.

Chapter Twenty-One

Jocelyn trembled against him, a cry slipping through her lips. Landon had already been lying awake, unable to sleep, because he was so damn worried about her. She must have been worried, too, because even in her sleep, she could not rest. He tightened his arm around her and rubbed her bare back with his other hand.

"Shhh," he murmured. "It's all right. I have you."

She jerked awake and stared up at him, her blue eyes wide with fear. She reached out a shaking hand and touched his face. "You're okay…"

So her nightmare hadn't been about something happening to her, but to him.

He shook his head. "I'm not okay," he said.

"No." Her fingers skimmed over the healing wound on his neck. "You're going to have a scar."

A scar was the least of his concerns. He was more worried about having a broken heart. And he would if anything happened to her. "I'm not okay," he said, "because I'm worried about you. I want you to give up the case."

She tensed and stared up at him, the fear turning to

confusion then anger in her blue eyes. "What? How can you ask me to do that?"

"Because it's too dangerous."

She shook her head. "What's too dangerous would be letting Luther Mills back on the streets. He can't keep getting away with his crimes. He needs to go to prison."

"You don't have to be the one to send him there," Landon pointed out. "Someone else can do it."

"You're the one who's been adamant that someone within the DA's office is working for him. If I give up the case, that person might get it, and then Luther would once again escape justice." She shook her head. "I can't risk that. I can't be the one who lets him go free."

"If you try this, you might be," he goaded her. "You don't know that he'll get convicted even with you prosecuting him."

Her already pale skin grew paler, and her breath escaped in a shaky sigh. "You still don't think I'm good at my job."

"I don't trust Luther Mills," he said. "And neither should you."

"Of course I don't!"

"You don't know what he might pull next," Landon said. "It's too dangerous for you to take him on."

"It's too late," she said. "I already have."

And she had the marks for her trouble—the scrape on her shoulder, the dark bruise around her neck. She could have already been killed. He didn't like her chances for surviving the trial.

"And I'm not backing down," she said.

Fear filled Landon's heart—fear for her and for himself. But he had to say it. He cared too much not to lay it all out there, not to lay himself bare.

"Not even for me?" he asked.

Her brow furrowed. "I can't believe you would ask me to do this… You've wanted to get Luther Mills probably as long as I have."

"I still do," he said. "But I don't want to lose you in the process. I care too much, Jocelyn." He loved her, but before he could open his mouth to say those words, she put her fingers over his lips.

"Don't…"

Before he could say or do anything else, she tugged free of his arms and rushed out of the bed into the adjacent bathroom. Then he heard it, too, the ringing of her cell phone.

She'd rather take a call than hear his declaration of love. Was that because she didn't feel the same way?

"THAT WAS A quick trip back," Luther remarked as he walked into the small conference room to meet with his lawyer. He watched the other door, but it didn't open. "Just you and me?" he asked as he took a seat at the table.

His lawyer nodded, but not a slicked-back hair on his head moved.

Luther rubbed his hands together, feeling that fortunes were at last turning back in his favor. That ADA must have finally successfully gotten rid of Jocelyn Gerber.

"What's up?" he asked.

"Your trial," the lawyer replied.

He nodded. "Yeah, in a couple weeks," he said.

The lawyer shook his head now. "No. A couple of days. Judge Holmes cleared his docket and got it moved up."

Was that the judge's way of getting back at him for messing with his daughter? Not that he could prove Luther had anything to do with that.

Nobody could. The only person alive who could testify to his involvement was too smart to risk it. Not only would it implicate himself, but it would end his life.

Luther's heart began to race, and not with the good kind of excitement. "No. That's too soon. We haven't found the witness or gotten rid of the evidence yet."

The lawyer shrugged.

"Why the hell did you let that happen?" Luther demanded to know. "I pay you the big bucks to help me." But he'd done damn little of that so far.

"I had no argument to use against the judge moving up the date," the lawyer replied. "I thought you'd be eager to get out of here."

"To go to court?" Luther asked. He shook his head. "I want to get out of here for good." Not just to be brought back at the end of each day of the trial.

Another plan was already taking shape in his mind, though. He wasn't giving up yet. And if Jocelyn Gerber was to suddenly turn up dead, the trial would have to be postponed while another assistant district attorney was brought up to speed on the case. That would give him a little more time to perfect his new plan, so it wouldn't fail as badly as his previous one—to take out everyone associated with his trial—had failed.

That would have been ideal, would have gotten the

charges against him dropped. But since that wouldn't work, he would have to adapt.

The lawyer looked at him uneasily. He probably knew that Luther was coming up with something. But he didn't ask what it was, because of that plausible deniability thing he kept talking about. He was going to have to forget about that, though, and finally earn all the money Luther was paying him.

Because this new plan could not fail. Luther was not going to prison for the rest of his life. Hell, once he got out of jail, he intended to never return. Luther Mills was not going down for the crimes he'd already committed or for the ones he was about to commit.

JOCELYN LOVED LANDON so damn much. That was why she'd stopped him from saying whatever he'd been about to say. If he'd been about to declare his feelings for her, she hadn't wanted to hear them. If he felt the same way about her...

Then she might not be able to follow through with what she needed to do. She needed to prosecute Luther Mills. And she would be doing that sooner than expected per the call she'd just taken from Judge Holmes.

She couldn't give that her full attention if she knew that Landon was in danger because of her. And if he continued to be her bodyguard during the trial, he would be in danger.

She wouldn't be able to get him removed from the assignment, though. After she'd been so wrong about Tyce Jackson, she doubted that Parker Payne would listen to her. Like the rest of his team, he didn't even like her. Those people were Landon's friends. Even if she survived the trial, she knew that she and Landon could never have a relationship.

The people who mattered most to him couldn't stand her. They would never support their being together. So it wasn't as if she had the hope of a future with Landon anyway. But she wanted him to have a future.

So she had to get him to quit his job. She had to make him mad enough to no longer want to protect her. She wasn't sure what that might take since being protective was such a part of his nature.

She reached for the bathroom door and drew in a deep breath, bracing herself for what she had to do. She'd pulled on the robe she'd left hanging on the back of the door and had tied it tightly around herself, as if it might hold her together when she felt like falling apart.

She didn't want to lose Landon. But it was better to lose him as a lover than for him to lose his life. Just as she'd struggled after her grandparents' murders, she would struggle after Landon's—struggle with living in a world without him. He might hate her, but she wouldn't care as long as he was safe.

She pulled open the door and stepped out.

"Who was that?" Landon asked. He'd pulled on his jeans but left them unbuttoned and riding low on his lean hips. He was so damn good-looking it wasn't fair—not to Jocelyn's furiously pounding heart.

She wanted him again. But she loved him too much to keep putting him in danger. She replied, "Judge Holmes."

"Is Tyce okay?" he asked.

She nodded. "Yes. He and Bella are going out of the

country, so nobody can get to her during the trial. The judge has also managed to move up the trial date."

Landon gasped. "Why would he do that?"

She suspected that it was for the same reason she was happy that he had. "So all this will be over soon."

"It's too dangerous," Landon said, as he had just a short time ago.

She agreed, but instead, she shook her head. "It's smart. We need to get Luther convicted and sentenced to a high-security prison with guards who will hopefully do him no special favors."

She hadn't figured out yet which ones were helping him, but she and the chief would. Woodrow Lynch was as determined to stop Luther as she was.

"You don't need to have any part in this," Landon said. "You can let someone else do this."

"The only person I would trust to try Luther besides me is off on maternity leave," she reminded him. "I have to do this."

He drew in a deep breath. "Okay, then I'll do everything in my power to keep you safe."

That was her greatest fear. She shook her head. "I don't think that's a good idea," she said.

His brow furrowed. "What?"

"Your protecting me," she said.

"Why not?"

She gestured at the bed with the sheets tangled from their lovemaking. "We crossed a line, Landon."

"We did more than that," he said, and he moved closer, his arms outstretched for her.

But she stepped back. He could not touch her. If he

did, she might not stick with her plan. "No." She shook her head. "We didn't."

"What are you saying?"

"That being with you was a good distraction from worrying about the case," she said. "But that's all it was. And now I can't afford any distractions."

He snorted. "Just a distraction…"

Maybe he knew her better than she'd realized now. Maybe he already knew how she felt about him, that she loved him.

She turned away from him, so he wouldn't see the longing on her face. And hopefully he would think she was dismissing him and what they'd shared. She opened her closet door and peered inside, but she couldn't see any of the clothes hanging from the rods because tears were blurring her vision.

She kept her voice clear and sharp, though, when she replied, "Yes. You must know you and I have no future together." And they wouldn't, if he died. But she forced herself to sound haughty and snobbish and added, "My parents would never approve of my involvement with a *bodyguard*."

She silently apologized for misrepresenting the people who'd raised her. They were not snobs. They didn't care what anyone did for a living as long as they were a good person. And they didn't come any better than Landon.

Her parents would love him…just like she loved him.

He sucked in a breath, though. "I didn't realize I wasn't good enough for you."

He was too good; that was why she had to let him go. She forced herself to turn back to him and look down her nose at him. "Come on, Landon. You see where I live." She gestured at the massive master bedroom. "You see how hard I work. I have big aspirations."

For law and order—nothing else.

"I don't have room in my life for someone like you," she continued coldly.

A muscle twitched in his cheek just above his rigidly clenched jaw. "No," he agreed. "You don't."

That was what she'd wanted—to make him angry, to hurt him, so that he would give up his assignment. But she felt a twinge of pain for causing him pain.

She loved him so much…that she hated hurting him. But it was better than getting him killed.

"Good," she said. "Then you agree that I need to have another bodyguard for the duration of the trial."

He nodded. "We agree," he said. "You don't need me." He walked out of the bedroom with a finality that had panic flashing through her.

Would she see him again? Was he leaving now? Without even really saying goodbye…

But then, she'd already said it all—cruelly. And she knew that he would probably never forgive her.

Chapter Twenty-Two

She was never going to forgive him. But she'd left Landon no choice. He needed to save her life, and since she didn't want him as her bodyguard, that left him only one option: to make sure she was not able to prosecute Luther Mills.

If she wasn't threatening his freedom, then Luther would have no reason to want her dead. She would be safe.

Safe but furious.

Did it matter, though? If he believed what she'd just told him, then he had no chance of a future with her anyway. But he wasn't entirely sure that he believed what she'd told him…or if she'd only been trying to make him mad enough to quit his assignment.

Something she almost confirmed when she descended the stairs and remarked, "I'm surprised you're still here."

She'd expected him to run off in anger. Maybe she'd been counting on it.

"I wouldn't leave you unprotected," he said. He was too well aware of what had happened the last time she'd taken off alone. Even though she'd looped a scarf around her neck, he could still see a bit of the bruise from her nearly being strangled to death.

How had she not learned how vulnerable she was from that experience?

She moved her hand to the bright-patterned scarf, pulling it up enough that it covered the bruise. "Is Parker sending over someone else?" she asked, and she sounded impatient, as if she couldn't wait for him to be gone.

Before he could answer, the doorbell rang. And she breathed a sigh of relief, probably thinking his replacement had arrived. She would not be happy when she saw whom he'd called and figured out why.

But he would do anything to protect her, even if she hated him for the rest of their lives over what he'd done.

"It's Dubridge," a deep voice called through the door as Landon walked toward it.

"Are you and Keeli switching assignments?" Jocelyn asked almost hopefully.

Keeli was a damn good bodyguard, but Landon didn't trust her to protect Jocelyn any more than he trusted himself right now. Luther was entirely too dangerous. The only way the bodyguards had been able to protect their principals from harm had been to take them away where Luther would not be able to find them.

But Jocelyn refused to leave River City. She refused to give up the case. So Luther would know right where to find her: the courthouse.

Or her office as she prepared for the trial. He had no doubt that was where she was heading now. But she wouldn't get there. He unlocked and opened the door, stepping back to let Dubridge and Keeli walk past him.

They both looked at him as they passed. Dubridge appeared skeptical. Keeli looked triumphant and sympathetic at the same time. She reached out and squeezed Landon's hand as she passed him. And both Jocelyn and Dubridge noticed and narrowed their eyes as if jealous.

Which was funny since Jocelyn had said she cared only about her career and all Dubridge had done was give Keeli grief since she'd been assigned the job of his bodyguard.

"You have to be wrong," Detective Dubridge told Landon.

"No, he's right," Jocelyn said. "I want a different bodyguard. It's for the best."

"Why?" Keeli asked. "Because he figured out what you've been up to?"

Jocelyn's brow furrowed with confusion. "What?"

Landon quickly glanced away from her, though. He couldn't look at her when he did this. So he focused on the detective. "The evidence is in the briefcase," he said. Fortunately, she hadn't had time to close it yet, so the phone and pill bottle were easily visible.

"You called him about that?" Jocelyn asked. "I was going to bring it to him."

Landon shook his head. "No. You weren't." But he was talking to Dubridge instead of her. "If I hadn't heard the text Luther sent her, I wouldn't have found it."

Keeli sucked in a breath. "Luther sent her a text?"

Landon nodded. "Thanking her for tipping him off about Tyce finding the judge's daughter."

Dubridge cursed.

But Keeli cursed louder and lunged toward Jocelyn.

Landon stepped between them. He was trying to protect Jocelyn—not put her in more physical danger.

"How could you!" Keeli shouted. "He could have died."

"I didn't purposely tip him off," Jocelyn defended herself.

But it was too late. Dubridge was inspecting the phone and the pill bottle. "She drugged the backup bodyguards," he murmured. "But why…?"

"To get rid of Landon," Keeli replied. "Just like she tried getting rid of Tyce. She's trying to get us all killed—it's part of her and Luther's plan."

Jocelyn gasped in outrage. "I am not working with Luther Mills."

But Dubridge just shook his head and pulled his handcuffs off the clip on his belt. "I have to bring you in, Jocelyn."

"This is ridiculous," she insisted. "I can explain the phone and the pill bottle. Someone planted them in my filing cabinet in my office."

"A locked office," Landon said, and he shook his head as if he didn't believe her. "And she only claimed that after I found the items in her briefcase."

"You don't believe her?" Dubridge asked, and he focused his dark gaze on Landon now.

He didn't want to lie. But he had to—to keep her safe and alive. He shook his head. "No. I don't."

A cry slipped through her lips, as if he'd slapped her. And maybe he had—emotionally instead of physically. "I can't believe you're doing this," she said. "I don't understand."

"I couldn't let you get away with it," he said.

She cursed him. "How could you! You know I hate Luther as much as you do. That I want to bring him to justice!"

Dubridge linked her arms behind her back and snapped the cuffs around her wrists.

And both she and Landon flinched. He didn't want her hurt. He hadn't thought Dubridge would actually lead her away in handcuffs. But that was the kind of cop he was: by the book. The kind of cop Landon had been.

Shame flashed through him that he'd caused her arrest when he knew the truth. But finding those items in her briefcase looked bad for her.

"What are you doing?" she asked. "You're going to screw up the whole case against Luther. You're going to delay the trial and get another ADA assigned to it." Then the color drained from her face, leaving her eyes wide and bright. "You're the one working for him. You must be. You're trying to get me taken off the case."

He wasn't working for Luther. He was working for her—to keep her safe. But just like he'd had his doubts about her when he'd first found those things in her briefcase, she clearly still had doubts about him.

No matter how much he cared about her—even loved her—he realized she was right. They could never have a relationship, and not just because she claimed he wasn't good enough for her, but because they couldn't completely trust each other.

And now, after what he'd done, he realized he'd destroyed that trust even more as well as what—if any—chance he'd had for a future with her.

But at least she would have a future—if she was

taken off the case. Luther Mills would have no reason to kill her now.

Now Landon was the one in danger, though, because as Detective Dubridge led her away in handcuffs, Jocelyn looked as though she wanted to kill Landon.

SHE'S A LAWYER, Landon had warned Dubridge before he closed the door and locked Jocelyn into the back of his department-issued sedan. *She's good at presenting arguments, so don't let her get to you.*

She'd glared at him then—like she glared at him now as he sat in on the meeting she'd convinced Dubridge to call with the chief and the district attorney and Parker Payne. Fortunately for her, the detective had listened.

"You let her get to you," Landon remarked to Dubridge.

The detective shook his head. "I think you're the one she got to."

No. Landon had gotten to her, had gotten her to trust him. Then he'd betrayed her. He could have destroyed her had she not convinced the detective to take off the cuffs and hold off on booking her until he spoke to the others.

With the cuffs off, she was able to pull down her scarf. "If I'm working for Luther, why would he have tried so many times to have me killed?" she asked. She pointed to the bruise on her throat. "This happened just as I found that stuff—" she gestured toward where the bottle and phone sat on the chief's desk "—in my filing cabinet. Someone had planted it there, and then they nearly killed me."

If not for Landon, she would have died. How could he

save her one moment and then betray her the next? Her heart ached with pain so intense she wanted to double over and wrap her arms around herself. But she would not let him affect her. So she lifted her chin with pride and met the gaze of everyone in the room but him.

She couldn't look at him, not without her heart breaking over his betrayal.

Amber Talsma-Kozminski rose slowly from her chair and walked over to Jocelyn. She pulled her into a hug. "I'm so glad you're all right."

"Why didn't you tell anyone about that attack?" the chief asked. But he was addressing Landon—not her.

She answered, though. "I didn't know who to trust then. I'd just found out that Tyce Jackson is Luther's brother."

"You were wrong about him," Keeli remarked.

"He is Luther's brother," Parker said.

"But I was wrong that Tyce was working with him," Jocelyn admitted. "And you're all wrong if you think I'm working with him." She glanced at Landon then. But he was looking away from her. And she knew that, while he'd initially had doubts about her when he'd found that phone in her briefcase, he didn't still believe she was working with Luther Mills.

So why had he tried to convince the detective that she was?

Amber squeezed her shoulders and assured her, "I don't think that. You're trying this case because you're the one I trust the most. I know nothing and nobody will prevent you from doing your best."

Nothing and nobody would. Not Luther Mills and not Landon Myers.

"Thank you," Jocelyn said, "for believing in me."

Amber turned toward the chief. "I do believe in her," she said. "And I will not bring any charges against her."

"She didn't report her assault. She held on to evidence," Detective Dubridge interjected.

The chief looked at him and then at Keeli. "Have both of you reported everything that's been happening?"

Keeli's face flushed a bright red. And Dubridge looked down.

What the hell had been going on with them?

The chief turned back to Jocelyn. He was beginning to show his age with a few more lines in his face and dark circles beneath his eyes. "I know you're not the leak in your office," he assured Jocelyn. "I know you're the best ADA to prosecute Luther Mills."

She released the breath she hadn't realized she'd been holding. She hadn't wanted to admit to herself how scared she'd been that someone might think her guilty of conspiring with a monster like Luther Mills.

But she knew now that she had been sleeping with the enemy. Landon had proved to be her enemy.

"Then I better get back to work," she told him, "so I can do my job." She turned toward the door and faced Landon. She saw no regret or remorse on his face. He wasn't sorry for having made her look guilty to the others.

And all that love she'd thought she'd felt for him turned to loathing. "I hate you," she whispered as she passed him on her way to the door. But before she could escape that room, the chief called her back.

"Please, stay a few more moments," he implored her.

Did he actually believe her? Or did he only want to interrogate her alone? Because he dismissed everybody else—politely—one by one until only he, she and Parker Payne remained in the chief's office.

She braced herself for an inquisition. But what she got instead had her furiously blinking back tears.

PARKER KNEW AN apology was not enough. So he wasn't surprised that Jocelyn Gerber didn't accept it. She just turned away from him, as if unable to look at him. He understood. He had to force himself to look at the chief as he apologized to him, as well.

"I'm sorry," he said. "I thought my team could be professional."

"I hired you and your team because I knew it was personal," the chief replied. "And that because it was personal, you'd all do your best."

Guilt weighed heavily on Parker's shoulders, though, compounded when he noticed Jocelyn's shoulders shaking slightly. She hadn't turned away out of disgust; she'd turned away to hide her tears.

This strong, independent woman had been reduced to tears, and he felt horrible over that. "I'm sorry," he murmured again—to her.

"Everybody is alive," the chief pointed out. "That's the important thing."

"Keeping them alive is the important thing," Parker said. "I'll protect you myself, Ms. Gerber." Because he knew she would never let Landon close to her again. He'd been close enough to hear what she'd whispered to her bodyguard.

She shook her head. Then she turned around, and her

eyes were dry and cold. Maybe he'd only imagined that she'd been crying. "No. You and your team think I'm conspiring with Luther. Nobody's going to protect me."

"I can give you an officer for protection," the chief offered.

She shook her head again. "One that could be working for Luther, too?"

The chief flinched.

"No, thanks," she said. "I think I'll be safer on my own than trusting anyone else ever again." She turned for the door again.

But Parker called out, "You know why he did it, right?"

She gripped the knob so tightly that her fingers turned white. "I don't care."

"It was because he cares," Parker said. "He wants you off the case, so Luther stops trying to kill you."

"If he cared," she said, and her voice cracked slightly, "he would know that I have to do this. I have to make sure Luther is finally brought to justice."

"He cares more about you than about justice for Luther," Parker said. "And that's a hell of a lot."

Jocelyn didn't argue with him, just pulled open the door and walked off—alone and unprotected. And Parker flinched. Landon's efforts to protect her had put her in even more danger.

Chapter Twenty-Three

She hated him. He could still hear her whisper ringing in his ears even hours later. She hated him.

Landon had lost her. And not just her trust.

He'd lost her respect and whatever feelings she might have had for him. He'd been such a fool. He knew that, but Parker had called him into his office at the Payne Protection Agency, probably to make damn certain he knew how badly he'd screwed up and maybe even to fire him.

Landon didn't care about his job, though. All he cared about was making sure she was safe. "Who do you have on her?" he asked the moment he stepped into Parker's office.

His boss's black hair was tousled like he'd been running his hands through it. A muscle twitched in his cheek just above his rigidly clenched jaw. He was furious with Landon.

"I'm not going to apologize," he warned Parker.

"You deliberately misled Dubridge," Parker said.

"To protect her," Landon said.

"You could have done that without trying to destroy her career," Parker said.

And Landon flinched. He knew how much her career meant to her. He had no intention of ruining that for her. He'd only wanted to cast enough doubt on her to get her removed from the Mills case. "She can't try Luther or she's going to die."

Parker sighed and ran his hand through his hair again. "She might now," he admitted. "Because she refuses to have anyone protect her."

Landon gasped.

"She doesn't trust anyone anymore—thanks to you."

A stabbing pain struck Landon's heart, and he sucked in a breath. "She can't be alone. She nearly died the last time she was."

If he hadn't found her when he had, she would have died for certain. How long had she already been alone? Since that meeting in the chief's office?

He glanced at his watch. It was after hours in her office now—with only that one security guard in the lobby paying no attention to what went on in the offices floors above him. His heart began to pound fast and furiously now.

He'd screwed up. He'd already known that before Parker had pointed it out to him. He just hadn't realized how badly he'd screwed up. He only hoped it hadn't cost Jocelyn her life already.

THE WORDS ON the notebook blurred before Jocelyn's eyes. She'd been working on her opening statement for weeks. Hell, ever since she'd learned she was the one who was going to be prosecuting Luther Mills. But now she couldn't see or remember the clever words she'd written. She could see only Landon's handsome face.

How had he made love with her so passionately to betray her so coldly such a short time later?

Was it because he cared, as his boss claimed? He'd wanted her off the case—just like Luther Mills. Or why had Luther tried so many times to have her killed?

She touched her throat. The skin was still tender where it was bruised. That was why she'd pulled off the scarf. Even having the thin silk rub against it bothered her, but maybe she was overly sensitive because of what had happened. She closed her eyes. It wasn't as if she could read the notebook anyway. And she thought back to that night.

She'd been so shocked over what she'd found in her filing cabinet—over what Landon had used against her—that she hadn't heard her door open. But then she hadn't shut it because she'd intended to search the other offices. She hadn't had a chance to do that before something had looped around her neck. It had been silk— like the scarf—but narrower and thicker. It had to have been a tie.

A silk tie...

Mike Forbes didn't wear ties unless he was headed to court, and then he clipped on bow ties. Unfortunately, he'd taught Eddie Garza the same bad habit of clipping on a tie for court. And like Forbes, Eddie preferred bow ties.

The only man who always wore a tie—and a very expensive silk one—was...

She opened her eyes on a gasp and found him standing in her doorway. Dale Grohms.

The guy was tall, like Landon, but not nearly as broad. He had more of a runner's build. His features were more refined, too, but he wasn't nearly as good-looking as he thought he was. He leaned against the jamb as he fumbled with his already loosened tie.

Her heart slammed against her ribs. And she reached down for her purse and the Taser she kept inside it. But the purse wasn't there. She'd shut it in the bottom drawer of her filing cabinet—along with her briefcase.

She glanced at it, remembering what had happened nights ago when she'd put the briefcase in there, what she'd found and how she had nearly died. Now she knew who had tried to kill her, but she couldn't let him see that knowledge or that fear.

"Hi, Dale. You're working late, too?" she asked.

"You sound surprised," he remarked, and that little grin that always played around his mouth slipped away.

She'd never given Dale much thought beyond thinking he was a pompous ass. That was why she'd figured he always looked so smug, but now she knew the truth. He felt smug because he'd been fooling everyone.

Including her.

"I knew Eddie and Mike were still around," she lied, "but I thought you'd left."

"I saw Eddie and Mike leave a while ago," he said, and the smug grin was back.

"Just for dinner," she said. "They're coming back."

"Not once they get drinking," Dale said. He glanced around. "So it looks like it's just us. Unless your body-guards are hanging around somewhere."

She nodded and managed a short laugh. "Of course they are. They never let me out of their sight."

"Seems like they did some nights ago."

Now she knew beyond a doubt. He was the one who'd tried to strangle her earlier. That meant he was probably also the one who'd shot at her and Landon and who'd tried running them down in the parking garage.

So he had a gun as well as the tie he pulled free of his collar. She had to get to her Taser.

"But Landon showed up," she said, forcing a smile. "He always shows up."

Dale shrugged, as if he didn't care. Or maybe he knew about what had happened today, how angry she was with Landon.

She'd told him she hated him. She'd thought she never wanted to see him again. But now she longed to see him, and not just so he could save her life again. If she died, she didn't want Dale's face to be the last one she saw.

She wanted to see Landon's. She wanted Landon...

But she couldn't count on him anymore. She could count only on herself. She uncrossed her legs from beneath her desk and planted her feet on the floor. She would have to act quickly if she had any hope of getting to the filing cabinet and her Taser. But when she jumped up, Dale moved quickly, stepping in front of her filing cabinet.

He grinned as he leaned back against it. "Have your purse and briefcase locked up in here again, huh?"

She reached for the phone on her desk, but he made a tsking noise. And she knew what he was going to say even before he said it.

"By the time Security gets up here, you'll already be dead, Jocelyn. And then whoever rushes to your rescue is going to die, too."

"Why?" she asked. And she wasn't just trying to stall him now. She really wanted to know. "Why would you do this?"

"Kill you or work for Luther Mills?" he asked, as if both were a matter of fact.

He was convinced that this time she would die. So he didn't care that she saw him, that she knew...

She shivered. But the Taser wasn't the only weapon she had. A letter opener sat atop her desk. Its blade wasn't sharp enough to do much damage, but maybe it would buy her some time.

Some time for what, though?

For Security to check on her? Or for Landon to do that? If he really cared, like Parker claimed he did, why had he left her unprotected?

DALE FELT A rush of power at the look of fear and revulsion on her beautiful face. She didn't look so haughty and superior now.

He grinned. "Why would I kill you, Jocelyn?" He repeated the first part of her question and acted as if he was truly pondering it. "Because you're a pain in the ass of everybody in this office."

She shivered again.

"It's true," he insisted. "We all hate you. You're such a sanctimonious bitch."

"I've never had a problem with you," she said.

"Or a compliment," he reminded her. "Or any interest at all. Hell, you didn't even interrogate me like you did the others to see if they worked for Luther."

"You weren't on the DA's list."

He chuckled. So he'd fooled her, too.

"You have family money, so it's not hard for you to live on an assistant district attorney's salary," she said. "You're not on drugs or addicted to gambling." She shook her head. "So why?"

"I've got to be poor or on drugs to want to kill you?" he teased with a smirk. This was fun.

So much more fun than shooting at her or trying to run her down...

Or strangling her from behind.

This was fun to play with her beforehand, to stoke her fear before he would watch her die. And this time she would die for certain.

"To work for Luther," she persisted. "I don't understand why you would help him."

He felt a sudden chill, as if a door or window had opened somewhere. But the windows weren't able to open. And the only door was to the stairwell. So the chill was all in his head even as it raced over his skin.

He shouldn't talk about Luther. He knew that. But it wasn't as if she was going to live anyway.

Still, he hesitated.

"Why, Dale?" she persisted.

He shrugged. "Your family money and mine are a little bit different," he said. "You have a lot more."

And what he'd passed off as coming from his grandmother had mostly come from Luther Mills. He'd just put it in his grandmother's trust first.

Jocelyn nodded as if she'd been privy to his thoughts.

No doubt she had figured it out; she'd obviously investigated him even though he hadn't been on their boss's list.

That was why she needed to die—even more so than Luther ordering it. She had to die because she was a pain in the ass.

"I do have a lot more money," she said. "And if that's all you want, I can give it to you."

He moved away from the filing cabinet to lean over her desk. "I wanted something else from you, Jocelyn," he admitted. "But you turned me down."

"We work together," she reminded him.

"You worked with the bodyguard, too," he said. "But that didn't stop you."

Her face flushed, confirming what had only been suspicions. She had been romantically involved with Landon Myers. So where was he? That chill intensified, and he realized it was nerves now. Where the hell was Landon Myers?

Dale hadn't shot him again. Or tried to run him down...

Where was he?

He glanced toward the open door and into the hall. But nothing moved—not even the shadows.

"That was a mistake," she said, drawing his attention back to her.

Had she moved? She appeared to be sitting on the edge of her chair now. Did she intend to try to fight him?

As tall as she was, she was thin and delicately boned, too. And he was strong. Far stronger than she knew.

"And this is a mistake, Dale," she said. "You haven't

killed anyone yet. So you can survive this. You can make a deal."

He snorted. "I know about your deals, Jocelyn. They always include jail time. And I'm not going to jail."

She shook her head. "No, no, of course not. You'll be a hero, Dale. You'll be the one who brings down Luther Mills."

He shook his head and sighed. "You're pathetic, Jocelyn. And condescending and superior as hell. Do you really think I'm going to fall for your bullshit?"

Her blue eyes widened with feigned innocence.

"I know you too well," he said. And maybe that was why he should have been prepared when she lunged at him.

But the letter opener struck him, stabbing the corner of his eye. He blinked at the sting of pain and blood that trailed from the wound. Then he grabbed her wrist, squeezing hard until the letter opener dropped to her desk.

"You bitch!" he said. And he swung his other hand at her beautiful face, striking her hard.

Then he reached for her throat. He wasn't even going to use his tie this time. No. This time he wanted to squeeze the life from her body with his own damn hands.

But she wasn't done fighting. She clawed at his hands and tried kicking out—struggling so much that she knocked her chair over and fell to the ground.

He leaped over the desk and jumped on top of her. Her breath whooshed out as his weight hit her lungs and stomach. He grinned as he stared down at her.

She was so scared.

So beautiful…

Maybe he'd take a little more time before he killed her. Maybe he would take what she'd denied him…but had freely given to her damn bodyguard.

Chapter Twenty-Four

Fear pounded in Landon's heart as he rushed up the stairwell. He'd had to argue his way past the security guard in the lobby, who'd informed him that Jocelyn wasn't alone on the district attorney's floor. Dale Grohms hadn't left yet either, which had surprised the guard, who'd remarked how much the male ADA was in and out of the office.

Landon's heart had sunk then as he'd realized Grohms had to be the one working for Luther, the one who'd tried to kill her. But would he try again when the security guard knew he was present yet in the building? On the very same floor with Jocelyn?

Not wanting to alert Grohms to his presence, Landon had taken the elevator up only as far as the floor below the district attorney's. Then he'd switched to the stairwell, running up the last flight of steps. As he pushed open the door at the top of the stairs, he'd heard her scream.

And his already madly pounding heart had slammed against his ribs. He'd never heard her like that, despite all the dangerous situations they'd found themselves in. He'd never heard her sound so terrified.

He drew his weapon and ran toward her office. Grohms must have been the one trying to kill them, so he had a gun, too. One he drew and fired as Landon neared the doorway. A bullet whizzed past Landon's head and broke the window on the door across from Jocelyn's.

He heard another cry, but it didn't sound like Jocelyn's, and something clattered to the floor. Barrel raised, Landon darted into the room. Dale didn't fire at him, but he charged, knocking him aside as he headed toward the hall.

Instead of running after him, he checked on Jocelyn to make sure she was breathing. "Are you okay?" he asked.

She nodded, but her cheek was already swelling from a blow. And her hair was tangled around her face. She clutched a letter opener in her hand, blood dripping from the blade onto her desk.

Instead of him saving her, she had probably saved Landon, for Dale's gun lay on the floor. She must have stabbed him to make him drop it. He wanted to reach for her, to pull her into his arms—not to comfort her, but to comfort himself. He had to make sure she was really all right.

She gestured with her letter opener at the doorway. "Get him, please." Then she stumbled back and, trembling, dropped onto the edge of her desk.

"Jocelyn…"

"We need him to testify against Luther," she said.

And he nodded. If they got Dale to turn, there might not even have to be a trial. Luther might realize he needed to plead guilty.

Landon rushed off in the direction Dale had run, toward the elevators. But he hadn't waited for one of them. The door to the stairwell clicked as it closed, drawing Landon's attention there. He shoved it open to the echoing of footsteps striking against the steps.

He ran down those stairs, trying to catch up with Dale. The man was bleeding from the wound Jocelyn had inflicted. A couple of times Landon slipped on droplets of blood and nearly fell. "Dale, stop!" he yelled after the man. "You need help."

And he would probably need more if Landon caught him. He wanted to kill him for what he'd put Jocelyn through—for all the times he'd tried to kill her.

But despite his injury, Dale didn't stop running. Another door clicked as it swung open. Landon caught up to him just as Dale darted out into the parking garage. "Stop!" he yelled again.

And Dale suddenly stopped, his body going stiff before he dropped to the ground. Gunshots reverberated off the concrete walls.

Landon cursed as he raised his weapon. Someone else was out there, in the shadows of the garage. "Come out!" he yelled. "Show yourself!"

But the only thing he heard was the sound of footsteps running away. He dropped to his knees next to Dale's bullet-hole-ridden body.

"Hang in there," he said as he pressed his hand over the wound in the other man's chest. Blood pumped from it as his heart pumped its last. Landon reached for his cell with his other hand and punched in 911.

But he knew help would not arrive in time to save

Dale Grohms. He heard more footsteps coming from the building and turned with his gun.

Jocelyn ran toward him. "What happened? Did you shoot him?"

He shook his head. "Somebody was waiting out here," he said.

But he wasn't sure if that person had been waiting for Dale or for him and Jocelyn in case Dale had been unsuccessful. He kept his gun clutched in one hand now, the barrel swinging toward the shadows.

"They shot him and ran off," he said. And he peered around, trying to see how far they'd run.

She dropped to her knees beside them. "Tell me, Dale. Tell me that it was Luther. Tell me you have proof that it was," she urged him.

But the man stared up at her with a blank gaze. He was beyond help—for Jocelyn or for himself.

He was already gone.

THE CHIEF DID not like this. They'd caught the leak in the district attorney's office. Hell, they'd caught two, since the security guard was apparently the one who'd shot ADA Grohms. He claimed it was because he'd thought Grohms was armed. But the man had dropped his weapon in Jocelyn's office—when he'd tried to kill her.

After Landon had headed up to the DA's floor, the guard was seen on the security footage placing a call on his cell phone. To Luther Mills?

At least Luther had given him the order to kill Grohms instead of Landon and Ms. Gerber. Or maybe he had wanted them dead, but the guard had worried about being blamed for their murders. Now that Detective Dubridge had busted him, with the help of the man's own security footage, the guard was trying to act the hero—even though he couldn't explain why he'd run away from Landon.

The chief sighed with frustration as he paced his office at the River City PD. A knock rattled his door moments before it opened to the beautiful face of his bride.

Penny walked across the office and right into his arms, as if knowing how much he'd needed her warmth and love. He held her tightly against his madly pounding heart.

She leaned back and stared up at him, her brown eyes wide with worry. "Are you okay?"

He nodded. "Just worried."

"About?" she prodded him, tilting her head to the side and tousling her auburn curls. She was so incredibly lovely and loving.

"Everything," he said. He was worried about everything. "We almost lost Ms. Gerber tonight."

"Oh, no, is she all right?"

He nodded. "Thanks to Landon Myers. He saved her." But had that been enough to earn her forgiveness? Would she let him remain as her bodyguard?

She had to know that she needed one. Even with Dale Grohms dead, she was still in danger. Hell, they all were.

With the trial being moved up on him, Luther Mills had to be getting desperate. There was no way he could escape justice this time—not with the eyewitness and the evidence against him.

And Jocelyn Gerber prosecuting the case.

Penny ran her fingertips along his cheek. "There's something else bothering you."

Woodrow groaned. "I think I've got one of those feelings you get."

Penny Payne-Lynch was infamous for her premonitions of danger. "You feel like something bad is going to happen."

"I don't just feel it." Although the sensation seemed all consuming. "I *know* it…"

His sweet wife didn't try to assure him nothing bad would happen—probably because she had never lied to him. She just hugged him closer, offering him comfort.

JOCELYN COULDN'T STOP SHAKING, and not just over how close she had come to dying. Dale had been determined to kill her and had probably intended to assault her first. He'd reached for the buttons on her blouse just as Landon had pushed open the door to the stairwell. Then her coworker had pulled the gun she hadn't even realized he'd had tucked into the waistband of his dress pants. And he had fired that gun at Landon.

She'd grabbed the letter opener from the desk and swung it into his biceps. She hadn't wanted him dead; she'd just wanted him to drop the gun—which he had. But then he'd run off to his death.

"Do you really think the security guard was acting on Luther's orders?" she asked Landon, who was checking all the doors and windows in her house despite having activated the high-tech alarm. If he was trying to make her feel safe, he wasn't succeeding. She felt more vulnerable now than she ever had.

But that had nothing to do with Luther Mills and everything to do with him.

He turned away from the windows and walked over to the couch where she sat, petting a purring Lady. He nodded. "Yes, I do."

She shivered, and the movement made Lady jump up off the couch and head toward the kitchen.

"Unfortunately, I think a lot of other people could be working for him, too," Landon said. "We don't know who to trust."

She groaned and closed her eyes and murmured, "I can't trust you." Not after what he'd done, after he had tried to have her arrested.

But then when she'd needed him, he'd been there for her. He had saved her life. Again.

"I'm sorry, Jocelyn," he said. "I'm so sorry."

She felt him settle onto the couch next to her. He didn't touch her, but she still felt the heat of his closeness. As always, his nearness made her pulse quicken, her skin tingle, but he also gave her a feeling of comfort she hadn't felt since she'd realized Dale Grohms was the one trying to kill her.

"I was an idiot," Landon berated himself. "An idiot in love."

She opened her eyes now and stared at him. His handsome face was twisted with a grimace.

"That's why I did it," he said. "I couldn't stand the thought of you being in danger any longer. I wanted to make sure you would be safe."

She loved him, too—so much—but she had no hope for a future with him. "You've seen all those other threats," she reminded him. "You know that I'm always in danger."

He flinched.

"And you need to know and accept that I'm not going to stop doing what I love because of those threats or even because of the attempts on my life."

He drew in a deep breath and said, "Then I guess it's good you're going to have a bodyguard around all the time."

"I am?" she asked.

He nodded. "Even after this trial is over, I don't want to leave you. Ever..." He reached out then and covered her hand with his. "Please, Jocelyn, forgive me for being an idiot. Don't make me leave."

Her heart ached, then swelled and filled with warmth. But while she loved him, trusting him was going to be harder for her. "You're not going to keep pressuring me to give up this case or my job?"

He shook his head. "I promise. I know that your job means everything to you."

But she shook her head now. It didn't mean everything. Not anymore. He did.

He continued, "And it's a part of you, makes you who you are—and that's the woman I love. If you lost that part of you, that job, that quest for justice, I wouldn't love you like I do."

She pulled her hand from beneath his, and he lowered his head, as if defeated. "Landon..." She reached up and cupped his face in her hands, tipping it up again. He was so handsome, but he looked so miserable, too. "I love you, too."

He released a shaky sigh. "I thought I wasn't good enough for you."

She shook her head in denial and regret of the cruel things she'd said to him. "I didn't mean that. I was just trying to get you to quit—to protect you." Which was really no different from what he'd done. She'd hurt him in order to try to protect him. Smiling at the irony, she said, "We're both idiots."

"Yes, we are," he agreed. "We're idiots in love."

She smiled bigger, her heart overflowing with love for him. "I do love you…so much…"

He leaned closer and brushed his mouth over hers. The kiss was so tender that tears sprang to her eyes. His love was in that kiss and in the look he gave her, his eyes so warm and adoring.

She linked her arms around his neck and clung to him as he lifted her from the couch. Then he carried her up the stairs to the bedroom. They undressed each other, tearing at buttons and zippers in their haste to be naked, to have nothing separating skin from skin—soul from soul.

Once her bra and panties dropped to the floor, Landon staggered back a step as if she'd struck him. But she wanted him closer, not farther away, and she held out her arms for him.

He shook his head. "I just want to look at how gorgeous you are…" But his gaze met hers and held. Then finally he stepped forward and pressed his muscular body against hers.

His erection swelled between them, prodding at her. She needed him inside her, needed him joined with her again. But he was focused on her, on kissing her lips, then her neck and her shoulders.

Her legs began to tremble, threatening to fold beneath her. So she fell back on the bed. And he followed her down. But he held his body off hers, as he moved his mouth over every inch of her skin.

She squirmed and writhed from his attention, needing release from the pressure he built so tightly inside her. His lips closed around a taut nipple, and she arched off the bed, crying out at the pleasure.

She clutched at his shoulders, his back, trying to pull him down with her. But he moved down her body instead, making love to her with his mouth.

The tension broke, making her cry out again with pleasure. But it wasn't enough. She wanted more. She wanted him.

But he rose from the bed before she could pull him down onto her. He was only gone a second, though, to roll on a condom, before he joined her again literally, easing inside her. She wrapped herself around him, clinging to him, as they found the rhythm that was theirs alone. They moved together, perfectly, in their own dance.

The tension wound through her again, building and building, until it let go, and she screamed Landon's name. And her love. "I love you! I love you!"

He tensed and then yelled as he found his release, too. For a moment, he rested his forehead against hers. Staring deeply into her eyes, he said, "I love you."

Then he pulled away, disappearing for just a few moments to clean up, before coming back into bed. He slid his arm around her as he untangled the covers and pulled them up, over them both.

But she wasn't shivering and trembling anymore. She felt safe and warm…with him.

He stroked his hand down her back, but his fingers trembled slightly. Was he worried about the trial?

"Are you okay?" she asked him.

"Yes…"

But she heard the concern in his voice. She settled her head against his shoulder and murmured, "We need to trust each other. I need to trust that you'll stay safe protecting me and you need to trust that you'll be able to protect me."

He tensed for a moment, but then his body relaxed beneath hers. "We will," he said. "We have. We've survived everything Luther has thrown at us."

Jocelyn knew, though, that Luther wasn't done trying. He wasn't going to give up. He had probably already begun to formulate another plan to get away with murder while committing more.

Landon knew it, too, because his arm tightened protectively around her. But he just squeezed her in assurance as he said, "Together—with our love—we are too strong for even Luther Mills to hurt."

He was right.

Together they were much too strong for Luther to hurt. But she had no doubt that he would try.

Epilogue

The trial...

Court had gone even better than Landon had expected. But then Jocelyn—when she had all the evidence and an unshakable eyewitness—was damn good at her job. If she'd had the evidence and witnesses she'd needed for any of Luther's many previous crimes, Javier Mendez would not have died.

Nor would have so many members of Luther's crew that he'd sent after the Payne Protection Agency and the people they had been hired to protect.

Landon still felt horrible over all those times he'd doubted her and had thought she might have purposely failed to get indictments against the drug dealer. Jocelyn Gerber was too honorable for anyone to bribe and too zealous about justice for anyone to threaten and manipulate.

Even Luther Mills.

He kept trying, though, with the way he stared at her in court. Every time Luther looked across from the defendant's table to Jocelyn's, Landon clenched his hands into fists. He wanted to take the guy down just for the way he looked at her. As if he was undressing her...

But then he'd glance back at where Landon sat in the gallery behind the prosecutor's table, and he would chuckle. And Landon realized he was purposely goading them. Hell, he'd been purposely goading them all. He was smug—too damn smug—like he had no worries about going to jail.

Why?

The judge was ruling against every cheap trick and ploy Luther's sleazy lawyer tried, while every bit of evidence and testimony Jocelyn presented was accepted. Her case wasn't just circumstantial—it was insurmountable for Luther's defense. He was going to prison.

He had to know it.

So why did he look so damn smug? What the hell did he have planned now? Because Landon had no doubt, Luther had something up his sleeve, something dangerous and wicked and certain to result in more deaths.

Landon peered around the courtroom. After testifying, the witnesses and their bodyguards had left it, going back into protective custody until after the sentencing. The judge's daughter and Tyce were still out of the country somewhere well away from the reach of Luther Mills.

The only people who sat near Landon were Parker Payne, a few bodyguards from his brothers' branches of the security agency and the chief of police. The side behind Luther had surprisingly filled up, though.

With so many crew members dead or in jail and denied bail, how did the drug dealer still have so many supporters? And they were supporters, not just spectators. It was obvious from the way they grinned at Luther, who turned back to look at them, and from the way they glared at the judge.

And that uneasy feeling churned harder in Landon's guts. Something was going on. And he saw the moment that Luther put his plan in motion—the moment he and the judge's bailiff exchanged a significant glance.

All Landon had time to do was leap toward the prosecutor's table and Jocelyn as he shouted, "Get down!"

Then the shooting began.

JOCELYN FELL TO the floor of the courtroom, not because of the bullet that whizzed past her head but because of the muscular body that knocked her down. Landon moved quickly, turning the table on its side to use the solid and thick wood top as a shield as the gunshots continued to ring out.

Jocelyn had already been ducking when he'd called out—because she'd noticed the same look between Luther and the bailiff that Landon must have. The judge probably had, too, because he'd dropped down behind the bench. Hopefully before he'd been hit.

Landon had been allowed his weapon in court, so he returned fire. The other bodyguards and the chief hopefully had been allowed theirs, as well.

Shots rang out all around them…until finally either everyone had run out of ammunition like Landon, who'd replaced his clip twice—or they were dead. The sudden silence was nearly as deafening as all the gunfire had been, or maybe her ears were damaged from the noise and close shots.

"Are you okay?" she whispered. Or at least she

thought she was whispering; her words reverberated inside her skull, though, as if she'd shouted.

"Yes," Landon whispered back, his mouth close to her ear as he continued to crouch protectively over her—just as he'd promised he would. They had kept their vow to each other that they would survive the trial.

So far they had anyway. But the trial really wasn't over yet.

"Is it safe?" she wondered aloud.

"Luther is gone," Landon replied as he peered over the edge of the thick table.

She gasped. "He's dead?"

"No. He's gone," Landon regretfully replied. "He made it out of the courtroom with a shield of shooters surrounding him."

And she heard it now, the shots ringing out elsewhere in the courthouse. Hopefully he would not get out of the building, though.

"How about everybody else?" she anxiously asked. "Are they all right?"

Landon moved to stand up, but she pulled him back down, worried that it wasn't safe yet. "Wait, wait!" she advised him. Some of Luther's shooters could have stayed behind; maybe they weren't out of ammunition yet.

He leaned forward and kissed her. "It's okay," he assured her. "All of Luther's crew are either with him or dead." He stood up then and helped her to her feet.

And she saw that the bailiff was dead. He must have been working for Luther. He had to be the one who'd smuggled all those guns into the courtroom for Luther and his crew in the gallery. The guns must have been taped beneath the seats and the defendant's table.

"Judge Holmes!" she called out.

The gray-haired judge rose shakily from behind the bench and gazed around his courtroom. He shuddered at the destruction and carnage.

And Jocelyn looked around, seeing what he saw. The holes in the walls and furniture and the blood everywhere.

She cried out, then pressed a hand over her mouth to hold back a louder scream. So many of those young men who'd been sitting on Luther's side of the courtroom were dead. Even his lawyer lay cowering on the ground, his briefcase held over his head as if he was afraid that someone might blow it off his shoulders.

She was afraid to look at the other side, at where Landon had been sitting with his boss and some of the Payne Protection Agency bodyguards.

Landon shouted, "Is everyone okay?"

Parker and those other bodyguards were checking on Luther's fallen crew members and collecting their weapons. The only one sitting behind the prosecutor's side of the courtroom was the chief. He was slumped on the bench seat, his hand pressed to his shoulder. He had been hit.

"Chief Lynch!" Jocelyn rushed over to him.

Parker rushed to the chief's side, too, but the bodyguard's stepfather waved them off. "Go after him! Don't let him get away!"

All the bodyguards hastened to follow his orders, rushing out of the courtroom. Except for Landon...

He stayed beside her with his gun in one hand and his cell in the other. He dialed 911.

"Help's on the way," she assured the chief of police.

"I'm fine," he told her even as he flinched. "The bullet went right through my shoulder."

From the amount of blood oozing from the wound, she suspected it had done some damage on its way out, though. She pulled her scarf from her neck and wadded it up against his wound.

The chief's face was pale, but his grasp was strong when he covered her hand with his, which was bloodied from his wound. "Luther..." he murmured urgently at her. "They've got to get Luther..."

Unlike the chief, who was injured, and all those other people who lay dead on the floor, she doubted the drug dealer even had a scratch on him. But he could not be as invincible as he thought he was.

"He just got out of the room," she told the chief. "He won't get out of the courthouse." There were guards at all of the exits, and the bodyguards had gone after him.

He would not get away.

But Jocelyn and Landon exchanged an uneasy glance. Even if Luther did manage to escape, though, the two of them would be fine. They, strengthened from the love they shared, would keep each other safe—just as they had during the shoot-out, and like they would for the rest of their lives together.

Forever...

* * * * *

COMING SOON!

We really hope you enjoyed reading this book.
If you're looking for more romance, be sure to
head to the shops when new books are
available on

Thursday 8th
July

To see which titles are coming soon, please visit

millsandboon.co.uk/nextmonth

MILLS & BOON

LET'S TALK

Romance

For exclusive extracts, competitions
and special offers, find us online:

 facebook.com/millsandboon

@MillsandBoon

@MillsandBoonUK

Get in touch on 01413 063232

For all the latest titles coming soon, visit
millsandboon.co.uk/nextmonth